PRAISE

COLD STREETS

"Features a wonderful cast of characters and a great deal of suspense leavened with touches of humor. Recommended."
—*Library Journal*

"Filled with snappy action and sharp dialogue, and featuring a likable . . . hero, Elrod's latest is certain to be a hit with the fang-loving crowd." —*Booklist*

"An exciting supernatural detective tale."
—*Midwest Book Review*

"Elrod crafts . . . some of the snappiest mysteries around that just happen to feature one of the most well-realized vampire characters in current fiction. The pacing never flags, and the plotting never disappoints." —*Crescent Blues Book Views*

LADY CRYMSYN

"Mix ruthless gangsters and tough broads with long-standing secrets at stake and things get dangerous even for a vampire. Several sordid pasts, numerous plot twists, and even a ghostly presence combine for an only slightly supernatural, but altogether entrancing who-done-it." —*Publishers Weekly*

"A delightful mix of mystery and horror . . . P. N. Elrod has written another great novel containing a well-designed who-done-it." —*Midwest Book Review*

"A good mystery wrapped in a fantastic premise."—*Chronicle*

"Elrod's Vampire Files series . . . may be unique in both mystery and fantasy annals for its consistently high quality and her steadfast refusal to repeat a plot or take the easy way out." —*Crescent Blues Book Views*

continued . . .

THE DARK SLEEP

"Tricky plot twists, lots of humor, and plenty of tense action make this good fun, as well as especially revealing for fans of the series." *—Locus*

"Mixing genres is always a difficult task, but it is one P. N. Elrod has mastered in her Jack Fleming novels. She tells an exciting story with all the elements of a classic mystery and blends in the proper amount of vampiric fantasy, resulting in a good story that will keep readers going till the end."
—Tulsa World

"Winning characterizations and enough period detail for flavor enhance a clever and fast-paced detective story."
—Publishers Weekly

"Action-packed . . . mob politics, detective work, and suspense make this one a page-turner with just enough human interest in the right places." *—The Vampire's Crypt*

"An entertaining, nicely paced mystery with lots of period atmosphere." *—Library Journal*

A CHILL IN THE BLOOD

"An entertaining exercise in supernatural noir."
—Publishers Weekly

"Clever and refreshing." *—Booklist*

"Filled with humor and mystery—fans will clamor for more." *—KLIATT*

"Snappy vampire-with-a-conscience yarn, laced with blackish humor." *—Kirkus Reviews*

Also available
BLOOD ON THE WATER
FIRE IN THE BLOOD
ART IN THE BLOOD
BLOODCIRCLE
LIFEBLOOD
BLOODLIST

→ The Vampire Files ←

COLD STREETS

P. N. ELROD

ACE BOOKS, NEW YORK

With thanks to
Teresa Patterson & Roxanne Longstreet Conrad

This is a work of fiction. Names, characters, places, and incidents either are the product of the author's imagination or are used fictitiously, and any resemblance to actual persons, living or dead, business establishments, events, or locales is entirely coincidental.

COLD STREETS

An Ace Book / published by arrangement with the author

PRINTING HISTORY
Ace hardcover edition / January 2003
Ace mass-market edition / January 2004

Copyright © 2003 by P. N. Elrod.
Cover art by Steve Stone.
Cover design by Rita Frangie.

For information address: The Berkley Publishing Group,
a division of Penguin Group (USA) Inc.,
375 Hudson Street, New York, New York 10014.

ISBN: 0-441-01103-9

ACE®
Ace Books are published by The Berkley Publishing Group,
a division of Penguin Group (USA) Inc.,
375 Hudson Street, New York, New York 10014.
ACE and the "A" design
are trademarks belonging to Penguin Group (USA) Inc.

PRINTED IN THE UNITED STATES OF AMERICA

10   9   8   7   6   5   4   3   2   1

1

Chicago, January 1938

I REMAINED invisible during the ride to the ransom drop, with no idea where we were beyond the few verbal cues passed to my partner, who was playing chauffeur. Our cue-giver and client, Mrs. Vivian Gladwell, didn't know I was floating next to her in the rear seat of her Cadillac. Her daughter had been kidnapped two weeks ago, and the poor woman had enough on her mind without having to deal with a supernatural gumshoe.

"He said to stop on that bridge just ahead," she told Escott, using the speaking tube that served the driver's compartment. I could imagine my partner nodding.

"And then what?" His voice was thin through the tube; my bodiless state muffled the sound almost too much to hear him.

"I'm to drop the money off the right-hand side."

"Very well."

We'd been on a merry little tour of Chicago for some time now, driving from phone box to phone box. Each time we paused, she had to rush out and wait for it to ring, then get fresh instructions from the kidnapper on where to go next. He said he was watching, so Escott faithfully followed instructions, just in case.

The big car eased to a halt, skidding a little on icy slush, motor thrumming impatiently. I hoped this wouldn't be another water-haul. Not waiting for Escott to come open the door, Vivian slid across the seat toward me. I kept my incorporeal self out of her way, clinging weightlessly to the suitcase she pulled along. It was full of cash meant to buy back her daughter's life.

The bridge didn't seem to be over water, a complication we could do without. I have a problem crossing the free-flowing kind. Vivian gave a small ladylike grunt of effort, lifting the case, banging it against something. I sensed the shape of a wide railing. Just as well I couldn't see how far the drop would be. I hate heights.

Wrapped around the case, I gave an internal wince for what was to come.

A shove, then a horrible, time-suspending plunge, truly awful. I couldn't force myself to hang on. It didn't matter that in this state I'd suffer no hurt from the fall; instinct took over. I whipped away a crucial second early and made a slower landing.

Oddly, there wasn't a lot of impact noise from the case when it hit. Just a soft thump. Maybe it was in a snowdrift. I sensed the ground and tried to figure out where the cash had gone. It would have been nice to be visible, enabling me to see, but too much of a risk. The kidnapper had brains behind his efforts. I had to respect that.

From what seemed like the far distance came the rumble of the Cadillac driving across the bridge above me. Escott would return Vivian to the Gladwell estate, and there they'd have a long, grim wait for news of the daughter's pickup location. Hopefully, it would come from me, not the gang.

I hovered, impatient, wondering if I dared move off, find a secluded spot to hide, and melt back into reality to get my bearings.

"Hurry!" called a man's voice. Urgent. Not close, but too close.

Someone rushed up, apparently grabbing the case. I shifted to wrap around him. He muttered a curse against the sudden chill but kept going. This was familiar. I'd had plenty of practice hanging on to people in such a manner.

He moved fast, puffing hard with his burden. I stuck with him as he ran, stopped, turned, and sat. We were in a car. A door slammed, the motor gunned, and away we went.

It seemed safe to flow clear and explore the confines of the vehicle. I reached out with what would be my hands and felt my way around, craving orientation. The buoyant freedom of this form was extremely enjoyable, but going on for this long was turning it into too much of a good thing.

The front seat held two men, the back was empty but cluttered with unidentifiable stuff. I bumbled my way behind the seat, down to the floorboards, and cautiously went solid amid a debris of cast-off clothes, musty blankets, and empty beer bottles. Drained and dizzy, I ached to stretch. It had been a while since I'd spent so extended a period in a formless state. If either of the two men happened to turn, they'd spot me, but I was willing to chance it for the reassuring relief of having my body back to normal again.

For the time being, the men were too distracted with jubilation to bother. They'd just picked up the ransom—a neatly packed hundred grand—and the guy on the passenger side was doing a rough count. Eavesdropping, or in this case backseat-dropping, I'd learned his name was Ralph; the driver was Vinzer.

Mine is Jack Fleming. I should mention that I'm a vampire. I drink blood and can hypnotize most people into doing what I want, but vanishing's one of the best aspects of the condition. No turning into mist or fog, but absolute invisibility, more presence than person, very handy in tight spots.

It made me the ace up the sleeve for the kidnap victim's family, so forget the stakes and garlic, I'm one of nature's good guys.

"Anyone following?" asked Ralph.

"No."

"Then let's go back."

"Dugan said to be sure. I'm gonna be sure."

A third member to the party? I decided to hold off breaking heads until we met up with this Dugan bird. Maybe the girl they'd taken away was with him.

Turns were made; so far as I could tell, speeding laws were observed; then Vinzer slowed and stopped, motor running. "There he is."

A window was rolled down. I felt a wash of icy air.

"Is it all there?" a man called to them.

Vinzer repeated the question to Ralph.

"Gimme a minute."

It took Ralph longer than that to count the cash, during which I remained absolutely still and quiet, easy enough with no beating heart or need to breathe. These clowns were in for a truckload of trouble. I could afford to wait before running them over with it.

Only a patch of night-gray sky was visible through a grimed window. I thought we were still well within the city, though, just not in an area with high buildings to give me a landmark.

"Yeah," said Ralph. "It's all here, Dugan, small bills. We're rich!"

"Right then," said the third party. "Lead on, and I'll watch your backs."

The window went up, and Vinzer shifted gears. We rolled forward, apparently on a more direct course to our destination. There were fewer turns, and I saw the rise and fall of telephone wires and passing streetlights. No way to tell where we were heading.

"Watch our backs," Vinzer muttered. "More like watching us so we don't run off with the dough."

"I'd do the same if I was him. Just makes sense. Dugan trusted us to meet up with him."

"Only after he told me how tough it would be to do anything else."

"What d'ya mean?"

"He didn't come out and say it, but he let me know."

Ralph persisted with the same question.

Vinzer snorted. "He told me it would be too bad if the cops got a description of us and the plate numbers of the car."

"So?"

"It was how he said it. Like he'd phone it all in if we didn't show."

"Well, we did show, so now it don't matter."

"He don't trust us, so I don't trust him."

"You worry too much. Dugan's been straight from the start, just careful, you know? This was being extra careful. I'd do the same if I was him."

"If you was him, you wouldn't need the money."

"He said he was broke."

"Yeah. He said. You ever once live in a place like he's got? I don't buy his story."

"Don't matter to me. This job worked out. That's what matters."

Vinzer muttered again but subsided.

The steady undulation of phone wires threatened to make me carsick, so I looked away. I'd materialized down in the foot well, which was unpadded, with a blackjack in one coat pocket and a .38 revolver in another. Both seemed to be burrowing toward each other as each bump and pothole in the road telegraphed through my long bones. I settled in as best I could for the duration and hoped my unaware companions continued to be preoccupied by thoughts of Dugan. He sounded to be the possible brains behind their operation and apparently lived somewhere nice enough to impress Vinzer. Maybe it was too nice and needed a lot of expensive upkeep, so he chose kidnapping over bank robbery to acquire some big cash.

As a crime, kidnapping used to be almost respectable, a popular, low-risk way of getting rich quick. All you had to do was walk off with someone's kid for a day or so, trade the tot for a box of spending money, then hope to lam it before the cops caught up. The American public had developed a sneaking admiration for such criminals, almost like for Robin Hood. It was a lark, an adventure, and no one was ever really hurt. Until the Lindbergh case showed everyone up. The fun had gone out of the game. Now it was as deadly as it had always been, maybe more so. Harsh federal penalties had raised the ante for the criminals, so the more ruthless ones made killing the victim part of the job. If they were really sadistic, torturing the victim's family with a mixture of hope and anguish kept things even more entertaining.

The family in this case was a widowed mother who had inherited a Great Lakes shipping business. Mrs. Vivian Gladwell, short, a little wide in figure, in her young forties, had been content to host bridge parties for her friends and attend church and charity events. Her only offspring was Sarah. She was physically sixteen years old. Mentally, she would never progress much farther than ten. She would always be a harmless, loving child. Vivian doted on her.

Two weeks ago, Sarah took her French poodle for a walk on the estate grounds, where she always stayed inside the wall and gates. The dog had come back to the house, but not the girl. A terse message was tied to its collar like a Christmas tag. In block letters it said Sarah would die if the police were brought in; the place was under watch.

My partner, Charles W. Escott, a detective for all his protest at being a private agent, had worked for Vivian on something minor a few months ago. He was evidently still fresh in her mind when she phoned with barely suppressed hysteria. He told her to bring in the cops. She refused and begged for his help. He reluctantly involved himself. He instructed her to send her chauffeur to his house with a spare uniform and to take a long, zig-zag route.

I'd just woken up for the night, emerging from my hidden sanctuary in the basement to find my sometime partner apparently changing trades in the living room. He said the chauffeur would be staying over a while, then explained why.

Escott's impersonation idea was good, allowing him to gain

unnoticed entry to the Gladwell house, but the flaw in the plan jumped right out at me. While Escott buttoned up the dark gray uniform coat and gave a last buff to his high boots, I took the chauffeur aside for a little chat. A short bout of forced hypnosis eased my worry that the man might be in on the crime. It wouldn't be the first time a servant had been turned by a bribe. Escott tipped his peaked hat in salute to my idea but showed a grim face.

"I've rather a nasty feeling I'm in over my head on this one," he said, his way of asking for help. Until now, the only kidnapping case he'd ever dealt with had to do with a pur-loined pooch he once stole back for a client.

"No problem." I got dressed, called the head bartender of my nightclub to tell him not to expect me any time soon, and we loaded into the Gladwell Cadillac. I invisibly smug-gled myself into the house, was introduced to Vivian, and made it my business to hypnotize all the rest of the staff on the sly. They were in the clear, which was too bad. A solid lead would have finished things right away.

For the next two weeks, Escott remained on the estate, phoning brief reports to me and the chauffeur just after sunset. The kidnapper called the Gladwell house several times, usu-ally in the middle of the night. Vivian's conversations were short and heartbreaking, pleading for her daughter's return and to speak with her; the muffled voice on the other end of the line hissed dire warnings against involving the law.

The man eventually lowered his ransom demand for a mil-lion dollars to a more reasonable hundred grand after Vivian swore she couldn't remove such a huge sum from her bank without drawing notice, which was true. Twice she'd gone out to hand it over. False alarms. Escott judged the apparently cruel ploy was to see how obedient she would be, and he assured her none of it was unusual.

"I do not think we're dealing with a professional," he confided to me in private.

"How's that?" I asked.

"A smart man would want to finish the job quickly. Keeping a person confined against their will is a difficult and consuming task. Delay increases the risk of discovery. This fellow makes me think he saw a film about the topic and took it as a pattern to follow. Amateurs are unpredictable, more dangerous. I don't hold much hope for Sarah."

It was rare for Escott to be pessimistic, but he was too well aware of the seriousness of this job, and the pressure ate steadily at him. Lean already, he lost weight, and from the hollow cast of his eyes, I was sure he wasn't sleeping. If Sarah came to harm or had already been killed, he would carry it the rest of his life.

But today the last post brought instructions. Escott phoned me just at sunset. I hurried over, again sneaking into the house.

In a plain envelope was a blurred, inexpertly shot photo of Sarah Gladwell staring in wide-eyed confusion at the camera, holding a two-day-old copy of the *Tribune*. The background consisted of churned snow and the white clapboard side of a building, with no other clue to her location. A block-printed card stated calling the police would get her throat cut. To bring home the point, the bottom corner bore a large red smear. It could have been ink, but I'd instantly picked up bloodsmell. No matter whether the blood came from Sarah or not, the effect on her mother was the same. She'd shown an astonishing amount of restraint so far, but she didn't have much control left. Tears streamed, but for the moment, she held off breaking down completely.

"We'll get her back, ma'am," I said and hoped like hell I'd be right.

No way of setting the odds for that, but they were bad. Unless the kidnapper wore a mask, the unblindfolded Sarah would have seen him. Maybe he thought a girl with her limited mental state posed no threat. Otherwise, he would kill her. He may have done so right after taking the picture, but there was no point saying that aloud to her mother.

Fortunately for me, he liked working after dark. Soon after I arrived, the hissing voice was on the line with directions and more threats. Escott put on his chauffeur's cap.

The first time we'd made a run, he'd told Vivian that my job was to trail the kidnapper from the drop. She'd objected, even though my sudden inexplicable appearances in her home with all the doors and windows bolted convinced her of my talent for getting around unobserved. This still wasn't enough for her to risk Sarah's life. Escott and I had exchanged a look. From that point forward, I'd pretend to stay behind but would vanish into the car, and off we'd all roll.

And this time, finally, it turned out to be the end of the line, one way or another.

"Wish it was closer in," said Ralph, sounding impatient. "I wanna cut free and leave. Is he still there?"

"Yeah," said Vinzer. "Right with us."

"You don't like him, do you?"

"That crap don't matter. You just do the job."

"He's doing the job. Job's done. Know what I'm gonna do with my share?"

"You only talk about it fifty times a day."

"I'm going to Miami," Ralph continued, ignoring him.

"Gonna get one of those fancy places on the beach, buy a joint with some good-looking girls, and have them do all the work. Have fun with 'em any time I want."

"Miami's too expensive. Go to Havana."

"But they got horse races, dog races, everything—an' they talk American."

"Once you hit the tracks, you'll be broke in an hour."

"Not if I win. Everyone knows when you lay down the big money you get back bigger money. No more stinking two-dollar windows for me."

"Same horses run at two bucks as for twenty-five Gs. Same horses lose."

By that division of the money, I could deduce there might be four in the gang. Three to make the pick up and one left behind to watch Sarah? I could hope.

I'd gotten used to thinking we were dealing with a single man. Not easy to tackle four, but possible by taking out one at a time, and only after I got the girl clear. If she was still alive. I was tempted to make my presence known to these goofs right now and hypnotize them into submission, but I'd tried a stunt like that once and had nearly wrecked the car and me with it. Besides, there was the guy following us. Dugan. Better to let things move forward, then jump in once I had the whole picture.

"You just don't want me havin' fun," Ralph grumped. "I got all the money in the world now and you act like it's nothing."

Vinzer sighed. "No, I'm acting like you're an idiot. If you played it smart you could make your share last the rest of your life. You almost got it right about buying a business, but go anywhere near the tracks and you'll be back here again."

"Holding a suitcase with a hundred Gs?" Ralph snickered.

"Aw, shuddup an' lemme drive."

One of them turned on the radio. We listened to Bergen and McCarthy fading in out of the static. I was too nerved to laugh at the jokes. Ralph hooted and repeated punch lines to himself.

After an entirely too long but favorably uneventful ride, Vinzer made a turn onto an unpaved road. We left behind the march of phone lines that comprised my only scenery except for occasional looming trees. I wanted to sit up for a look, eager as a kid for the end of the trip. They had the car heater going the whole time, and in my heavy coat and gloves, I'd grown warm, weary, and cramped. If I'd still been human, I might have disastrously dozed off.

The road got rougher; we skidded on icy patches. Vinzer grumbled under his breath. He finally braked and cut the motor. He and Ralph left the car. At nearly the same time, another car door slammed shut close by. The sound was flat, isolated. I counted a slow ten before raising my head in the hard silence.

Empty, snow-covered countryside, no lights showing except from a small clapboard house that had seen better days. Vinzer and Ralph went right in. I sieved-out of a fairly new Studebaker and made note of a battered old Ford parked next to it. No other cars were in sight.

Partially materialized, I floated lightly over the snow, drifting close to the building. Escott said I should rent myself to haunt houses for Halloween. The ghost gag was damned helpful for this kind of work; it made me harder to spot, left no tracks, and I could still discern things fairly well through the gray fog that hindered my sight.

The stark structure was no more than fifteen feet wide but went back three times that distance. I knew the type. If you stood at the front door, the hall lined up with it so you could see to the back of the house. Every window was shaded or thickly curtained, not one crack to peer through.

Going to the side, I went solid near a front window that served the living room. Within, the men whooped and laughed like Dodge City on a Saturday night. Vinzer and Ralph were the heroes of the moment with their delivery.

Guessing the presence of so much money would keep them occupied, I eased down to the next window. Less noise here, perhaps an empty room. As good a place as any to start. I had to brace internally. Sieving through the tiny spaces between wood and lathe was different from flowing through a gap like a mouse hole. It was more a mental than a physical sensation, not a favorite, but the unpleasant restriction was brief as I passed from outside to in, no invitation required. I listened for signs of company in the space around me, then slowly went solid.

Some nights it's great to get out of bed. Sarah Gladwell was fast asleep on an army cot shoved next to one wall. Her breathing didn't sound right, kind of hoarse, but she was breathing. She didn't wake to my intrusion. I hoped it meant she'd been drugged and wasn't sick. The room was cold; she had only one blanket.

The door was wide open to a narrow hall. Any second one of the men might walk past and look in. I couldn't carry her out that way. They had to be taken care of before I could get her clear.

Barging in on them like a fist-swinging gangbuster had appeal. Even at four to one, I could win with my strength, but fights were unpredictable. If the men were armed and quick enough to shoot, the walls were too thin to risk having bullets flying around. I could survive getting shot, but not

Sarah. She was going back to her mother in one undamaged piece.

Getting the gang separated so I could more easily take them was best. I just had to figure out how. Making a racket to draw them to the rear of the house would put them on guard, bring them running, alert and suspicious. If I waited, something would turn up in my favor. They wouldn't stay in the front all night. My betting money was on the bathroom. Sooner or later, someone had to use the toilet. Did this old place have one? No matter, an outhouse would work even better for me. I wouldn't have to worry about making noise during the bushwhack.

Hiding behind the open door, I went still again and paid attention to the conversation in the next room. The guy named Dugan seemed to be in charge. His accent was from Chicago, and he spoke like he'd had some education. He praised Ralph and Vinzer for a job well done, then announced it was time to pack up and leave.

"Aw, but it's late, and we been on the road all night," Vinzer objected. "My ass is numb from all the driving."

"Your posterior got paid enough for it," said Dugan. "We've been here too long. I want us away before morning. You and Ralph go over the whole house, clean it thoroughly. Should the police find this place and find even one fingerprint, the game is over, so dust like your grandmamma used to."

"I ain't doing no woman's stuff."

Dugan's tone was patient. "Very well, you and Ponti finish the job in the yard. Ralph and I will clean house. Where are the gloves?"

"In the kitchen. I wanna beer."

"Then get your beer and let's all get to work. The sooner it's done, the sooner we may leave."

There were some vague noises, then two men clumped past, going toward the back of the house and outside, slamming a door. I went invisible, waiting to see where Ralph and Dugan would start. Dugan, I presumed, also went toward the back, seeking gloves.

"Hey!" Ralph called after him. "How 'bout we have some fun first? Work out the cramp from that sittin' an' drivin'."

"Fun?" Dugan slowly returned. They stood almost in the doorway, perhaps looking in at Sarah. "What on earth do you mean?"

"You know."

The dawn came. "Are you mad? She's just a child."

"So? Her body's full grown. Female is female."

"That's disgusting."

"She won't even notice, Ponti's stuff has her out cold."

"Why not wait until she's dead, then? The effect would be about the same."

"I ain't kiddin' here. You gonna stop me?"

"Just make it quick. I am not cleaning this pigsty on my own."

Ralph laughed, short and ugly, came in, shut the door. Even in this state where most sounds were muted to me, I could hear his breathing. The boy was worked up plenty. Must have been the influence of the cash that put him in the mood. I floated close as he moved toward the cot, materializing in time to see his pants drop. Not a pleasant sight. They remained at half-mast after I clocked him from behind with the blackjack, catching him before he made a noisy crash to the floor. I wanted to put in a strategic kick to discourage future amorous ideas, one brutal enough to last him a lifetime, but that could wait. Such lessons worked better when a man was conscious. Instead, I used his belt to tie his hands and wasn't careful about leaving slack for circulation.

One down, one to go in the house. Dugan made an easy target. He'd begun cleanup in the front room and never saw me coming, never knew what hit him. Brains of the outfit or not, he dropped just as fast. He wore suspenders, but they served just as well as a belt for tying him up. Better. I had plenty left over to loop his ankles together, leaving him trussed tighter than a Christmas turkey.

Two to go, outside. I hurried past empty rooms, pausing in a dark kitchen to look out a window. The yard job, whatever it was, had taken Vinzer and Ponti out of sight, but I heard thumping and hammering. They were making too much rumpus to hear the back door open; I went through the normal way. From the high porch I was able to see an outhouse off to one side, what was left of it, anyway. The two men were busy dismantling it by lantern light. The roof was off, lying in dirty churned snow. They were busy pulling the walls and plank seat apart. The wood was old, easy prey for their mallets and crowbars.

I couldn't understand right away why the hell they were doing such work. Just as well my mind doesn't go to places like that without some effort. It took a minute, but realization finally came. We were smack in the middle of winter. The ground was too hard to dig a hole for a grave, so why not use one already dug? They intended to drop Sarah's body into a pit where it would never be found, probably filling the rest in with the broken wood. If they left the intact roof on top of the mound, people would guess what had stood there and avoid the area. Dugan or one of the others had some brains to have thought this up. No heart, but lots of brains. I felt like beating them till gray juice leaked out their ears.

Taking on two surprised men while I was this pissed off

was effortless. The hard part was holding myself in check so as not to kill them. I'd spared the near-rapist, Ralph; I could spare these undertakers. For what they'd planned and what they'd put Vivian and Sarah through I wanted them to live long, miserable lives in a federal lockup.

I left their unconscious bodies in the snow, returning to the house to make sure no one else lurked behind the doors. All was quiet. I checked Sarah more closely this time. She wore the same clothing from the photo, and when I happened to take a breath, it was plain she had on the same outfit as when she'd been grabbed two weeks ago. Didn't matter to me, I only breathed regular when talking. God knows, Vivian wouldn't care so long as her girl came home.

Sarah refused to wake. Disturbing, but perversely convenient if she slept through the trip home. Pushing her sleeves back, I found needle marks on the inside of her elbows and sniffed the bruised area. There was a taint to the bloodsmell under her skin. Morphine. Jeez, if they'd turned her into an addict . . .

Couldn't worry about that now. Her mother was waiting. Wouldn't you know the damn place didn't have a phone so I could tell her to relax. All the calls had to have been done from booths to make them hard to trace. Smart, smart boys.

I wrapped the blanket close around Sarah, then went out to the car. It had plenty of space once I'd thrown the junk clear. I shoved Dugan and Ralph into the trunk. Tight fit for them, they might smother or freeze, but life's tough. After tying Ponti and Vinzer up, they got the back seat to themselves along with the suitcase of cash.

Sarah I eased onto the passenger side, where she slumped down with a sigh. Poor kid.

With no idea where I was, I started the car and followed

its tracks in the frozen mud until reaching paved road. Since we'd turned right on the way in, I turned left and kept my eyes peeled for a clue to our location. The stars were out; I found Polaris and drove toward it. Soon a garishly painted road sign urged me to Phil Your Tank at Phil's Phil-Er-Up! only half a mile ahead. At this hour the place was closed, but it had an outside booth. The phone book hanging from a chain in the glass box was a skinny volume for Lowell, Indiana. The name didn't mean anything to me. Maybe Escott would know.

I got a handful of change ready and asked for the long-distance operator. She told me how much for three minutes. My hands were shaking. I dropped more coins than I put in. Not a lot of traffic on the lines; she got me straight through. Vivian Gladwell answered before the first ring had finished.

"Yes, yes? Where is she?" she blurted. "Please give her back!"

God, what a terrible mix of agony and hope was in her quavering voice. A big load of weight slipped from my hunched shoulders as I identified myself and delivered the good news. She let out a scream that nearly broke my ear-drum, but it was one of joy, not anguish; then she started sobbing in relief. The next voice I heard was Escott's.

"Mrs. Gladwell is rather overcome," he stated, his British accent very pronounced. It made him sound lofty and calm, but I knew better. Inside his head he was probably grinning like a chimp. "I expect once she recovers, she will have questions."

Anticipating what those might be, I supplied answers, which he relayed to her. Most of it was reassurance that Sarah was alive and well, what her mother needed to hear the most. Such was Vivian's state that she forgot to ask how in hell I'd managed to pull off this stunt after being left behind in the first place. Later on I could hypnotize her into forgetting that detail completely.

The operator interrupted, wanting more money. I dropped in change.

"I'm in Lowell, Indiana," I said to Escott. "Where is that from Chicago?"

Over the wires, paper rustled. He'd kept maps ready by the phone. "You're about twenty miles due south of Gary, twenty-five more miles from there to the house." He gave me highway numbers and directions to follow.

"I'll get Sarah home as soon as I can. Have a doctor on hand; they pumped morphine in her to keep her quiet. You calling in the cops?"

"That's up to Mrs. Gladwell. I shall recommend it, though."

"Convince her. These bastards need locking up. Hard time."

"I trust your judgment, old man. In the meanwhile—"

"Already on my way."

The reunion was a real heart-warmer. Vivian, a couple of housemaids, a medical-looking man, a nurse, and even the French poodle swooped on the car before I'd quite stopped, accompanied by tears, gushing, shouted orders, and excited barking. I carried the still-sleeping girl upstairs to her room, then got out of their way so they could take care of her.

Escott had hung clear of the circus, waiting in the entry hall for me to return and give him the details of my outing. He was a great one for self-control, but the dam finally burst. His eyes flashed a smile, and he wrung my hand and thumped my shoulder a few times.

"Bloody fine work, Jack. Bloody fine!"

"Not bad," I said, but I couldn't help grinning, too. It would have been good to have a drink to celebrate, which, of course, was impossible. My body refused to take in booze anymore, but old habits, customs, what have you, die hard. I settled for a cigarette. Couldn't inhale, but it was something close to what living used to be like.

"It would be for the best if you avoided telling Mrs. Gladwell of Ralph's carnal intentions toward her child," he said after he heard the short version of my outing.

"No problem. He can do that himself when he and the others go before a judge, anything that might get him a long sentence. That is, if she's willing to prosecute."

"She is, now that Miss Gladwell is back. I'm to phone the police. I take it you intend to persuade the gang to make a full confession of their misdeeds?"

"Every last one of those bastards is in for my special evil-eye triple whammy. Once I'm done, Clarence Darrow couldn't clear them if he brought in Jesus H. Christ as a character witness."

Escott bounced one eyebrow. "You seem a touch peeved."

I jerked a thumb at the stairs. "I got a sister with almost the same name. Sarah Jane. She's older than the kid and got all her brains, but still . . ."

"Quite," he agreed. "Thank you for saving her."

"Anytime." I'd saved him, too. He had very much been in over his head, had needed me and the advantage of my special condition to change the odds. He wasn't shy about asking for help, but we both knew I was the one who made the miracles happen. There was no competition going on; neither of us was stupid enough to go down that road. Without him there would be no jobs; without me on some of them, no successful finish. We each contributed, so far as I was concerned, an equal share of effort. Corny as it sounds, what really mattered was looking out for our clients.

He fished a cigarette and lighted up, a sign of a shift in his mental gears. After inhaling a deep draught of smoke, he nodded toward the car. "Well, shall we see to it?"

"Yeah, but include me out of the official investigation." My condition precluded all daylight activity; when the sun was up, I was literally dead to the world, meaning I could never testify in a court. Too bad, but the hypnosis would make that unnecessary.

We briefed the now-happy household to forget about me, but it was a headache-making hour before we were set to call the law. I'd knocked the gang out good, and it took a while to bring them around. Their collective grogginess helped shove my Svengali act on them, though. My kind of hypnosis works best when the subject is off guard and sober. Escott saw to it I had plenty of privacy to prime the boys to be chatty as parrots for their confessions. His contribution was evidence: the notes, shorthand transcriptions of each phone call, along with his exhaustive report on the whole business. He'd been waiting for my arrival to type the last of it, but legally it was very thin pickings. Circumstantial, unless Sarah could identify her abductors, and any lawyer could muddy that up. The confessions were crucial.

"This is the tricky bit," said Escott. "What made them turn themselves in?"

I'd thought that through on the long drive back. "A two-fisted Good Samaritan happened to stumble across their country hideout, caught on to their game, and tackled the gang. He slugged information about the girl from them, dropped them off here for the law, then vanished into the night. That's the story they'll remember. None of them got a look at me, and neither did you. You only just heard the car drive up and went outside. I kept my gloves on, no prints for the cops."

"Most dramatic. Let's hope the authorities don't assume you were a member of the gang who chose to remove himself."

"They won't. The girl's back, the money's back, the bad guys are marching themselves to jail, nice, neat, tied with a bow, and you'll be the hero of the hour."

"I hope not." He seemed alarmed at the prospect. Couldn't blame him. The bulk of his trade depended on keeping his face out of the papers. His clients liked their privacy; a too easily recognized detective—or private agent—didn't get a lot of business.

Escott would soon have his hands full, but it'd give him a chance to work off all the nervous energy he'd bottled up. He was an expert at showing a poker face but couldn't quite keep his fingers from twitching. He'd taken on a hell of a responsibility and had felt its bone-breaking weight, though he never said anything, always projecting a staid, confident front to Vivian. Once the matter was over and done, he'd probably sleep for a week.

"Eat something," I told him by way of farewell. Don't know if he heard me.

Like my mythical Samaritan, I faded into the night, taking a casual exit down the driveway, guiltlessly pleased to be clear of the approaching mess. I'd just left the front gate behind when a cop car zoomed past, heading for the house. More cars followed; some were police, others could only be reporters.

Blocks from the hubbub, I flagged a cab and went home. The Gladwell chauffeur was gone from his guest room by then. Escott must have told him the coast was clear. Fine with me. I don't mind company, but I have to whammy them so they don't think it odd about my snoozing all day in the basement and not eating. Not a whole hell of a lot of people believed in vampires anymore, but why take chances?

After a shave and a change of clothes, I was ready to get back to my own trade, that of being a glorified, high-hatting saloonkeeper, loving every minute of it.

Time to go see Lady Crymsyn, the second most important woman in my life.

2

THE building housing my nightclub took up its own small block. Once in a while I had to remind myself that this was indeed my place. So what if the bankroll had come from stolen mob money? I'd more than earned it, washed it clean, and was an honest, taxpaying citizen, or so my accountant assured me. People treated me like I was important and called me Mr. Fleming. Stuff like that made me stand straighter to fill the role.

A wreck when I found it, I'd turned a burned-out hulk into a palace. Since opening last summer, business had been good enough to put a down payment on the next structure over, which had been empty for years and likely to stay that way. I had that knocked flat and paved into a much-needed parking lot. The only complaint I ever got from customers was over where to leave their cars. I grumbled, on occasion, myself, but no more. The expense of the lot had been worth it the first night I glided my Buick into its own specially reserved space. So far, the satisfaction had yet to wear off. It always put me in a cheerful mood no matter what awaited inside the front door.

Tonight it was the smile of greeting from the doorman, the hatcheck girl who took my things away to the cloak room, and the bartender standing at his post behind the lobby bar. I smiled back, stepping into the tall, wide space with its polished marble floor and touches of gleaming chrome trim. On the wall opposite the entry, marking the route to the main room and stage, was the larger-than-life portrait of Lady Crymsyn herself. Deigning to smile mysteriously down at lesser mortals from her canvas perch, she was the figurehead for the club, giving customers someone to focus on that wasn't me. A few thought she must be a real person, the true owner of the place hiding behind a stage name. There was no reason to disabuse them of the notion; it made for good business to keep them guessing. On special occasions I hired a look-alike actress to put on a red dress identical to the one in the painting and mingle with the crowds. Believers and those who knew better loved the gimmick.

The second show was nearly over; it would soon be time to close out the registers and count the receipts. When I first opened, I had an excellent general manager to sort out those important details. He left town, though, and I'd still not found quite as competent a replacement. One of the bartenders took on some of the run-of-the-mill tasks like ordering supplies, another man saw to the building maintenance, and a girl I knew who was a genius at accounting came in three times a week to keep the books straight. Still, there was always a big stack of paperwork and decisions only I could see to, which often meant scarce free time to play host, my favorite part of the job.

Real work could wait though; the band was into a hot number backing a woman's strong voice. I passed under the portrait, going into the red-velvet depths of the main room. About a quarter of the tables were occupied—busy for this late on a weeknight—people were on the dance floor trying to keep up with the fast rhythm the drummer had set. It seemed like business as usual and felt like home sweet home. I couldn't have pulled the smile off my face with a tow truck.

It turned into a grin (no doubt on the sappy side) when I spotted Bobbi Smythe, the number-one woman in my life. For a change she wasn't belting out the song onstage but directing the show. Instead of a spectacular sparkly gown, she wore a plain dark suit so as not to detract from the current star. Not that she didn't look great; in a potato sack she was a stunner. It made no difference to me. Whatever clothes she wore never failed to inspire in me an overwhelming urge to help get her out of them.

She was at the bar across the room, watching the singer and likely thinking of ways to improve the staging. Bobbi had initially begun booking acts and directing to help out at the club's grand opening and developed a real taste for it. Once she got herself noticed enough by the right people, she had plans to sing and act in Hollywood, though. She'd been brushing close to it for over a year now; with her talent, it was only a matter of time.

I tried never to think about that. It made my heart hurt.

She glanced toward the doorway, spotted me, and raised a hand in greeting. The way the place was laid out, everyone could see newcomers, a design I'd purposely worked into the plan of the room. Some customers were more comfortable sitting with their back to a wall, having a view of the door, so I obliged them. The booths were set out on three levels in a wide horseshoe shape marching down to the dancing and stage area. Plenty of walls to go around for everyone.

I took stairs to the topmost level, which was empty. Bobbi came up from the opposite side, meeting me in the middle for a big kiss and hug.

"You're feisty," she observed when she surfaced for air. "Does that mean good news?"

She knew all about the kidnap case. "The best. Over, done, happy ending." I had a bear hug left in me yet and lifted her up, slow dancing in a circle while her heels dangled. She made an oofing sound but no other protest.

"Good, I was getting tired of that long face you kept making." Feet on the floor again, she drew me toward an empty booth. "Gimme."

Okay, I was as fond of necking in the back row as any other red-blooded guy, so . . .

"Not that!" she fiercely whispered, squirming and trying not to giggle lest we upstage the singer.

"I know." I reluctantly turned back into a gentleman again but couldn't shake the smirk.

"Tell me what happened on the case," she said, clarifying the vague "gimme" demand.

I told her, keeping it short, light in tone, and modestly heroic. With the danger past and the pressure off, I even felt heroic about having rescued the maiden and captured the villains. No one else would ever hear of my derring-do, but it didn't matter, not when Bobbi looked at me like I was Galahad and Tarzan rolled into one.

"You should use that stuff for one of your stories," she suggested when I finished.

I shrugged. "Charles seemed to think the gang saw a movie and stole the plot. It's probably already been written into a book. Just about everything else has."

She patted my hand sympathetically. I harbored forlorn hopes of turning myself into a fiction writer but had so far failed to sell anything or work on much lately. Maybe those years of hammering out news copy when I'd been a reporter tapped me dry. I was also damned busy running the club, and so on and so forth. One of these nights I'd get tired of hearing my own feeble excuses and get back to wordsmithery in earnest. But not tonight.

"The show going well?" I asked. "Adelle's in fine form."

"She's always better for the second set, warmed up. Once she gets the measure of the crowd she plays 'em like a banjo."

Adelle Taylor, one-time silent movie comedienne, now a well-known radio actress, could put a song across and then some. She had a great voice and would have done well when the talkies came in, but by then she had grown tired of getting hit in the kisser with pies. There was also her looks. Nothing wrong with them, she was a classic beauty and kept herself trim, but Hollywood scripts rarely had a part, good or bad, for a woman in her thirties. Adelle read the writing on the wall and skipped over to stage work, where lighting and makeup could take off the years, and to radio, which didn't care how you looked. I'd heard her play Juliet and Lady Macbeth equally well.

She had a local following of admirers I'd hoped to lure through Crymsyn's doors, so she was booked for the weeknights, leaving her free on weekends for radio work. Then I advertised big. The ploy seemed successful; new faces appeared at the tables, perhaps to become regulars. When not sidetracked by Escott's cases, I did my best to assure that by personally greeting as many as I could when they first came in the lobby. A handshake, a smile, a look straight into their eyes with a confident statement they would enjoy themselves had done much for my business.

I cheated, of course, using hypnosis to plant the suggestion. Not a lot, just a gentle nudge. If customers had a good time, they'd return for more. My conscience was only a little tarnished. The only time I really dirtied it up was the night an entertainment reporter came in to do a review. I made sure he loved the place and consequently got a great write-up in his paper. All's fair in love and liquor sales.

The supernatural edge was probably why I had a decent house even on weeknights. An astonishing number of other clubs in Chicago needed slot machines, tables, and other illegal advantages in their back rooms to stay alive. I could have made a hell of a lot more profit taking their road but didn't want the bother of cop raids during election years and payoffs the rest of the time.

Speaking of those clubs, the owner of the Nightcrawler was seated on the lowest tier of the horseshoe, closest to the stage. You couldn't miss Gordy Weems; he was like the portrait out front, built on a larger-than-life scale. He'd been squiring Adelle Taylor around town since summer, having snagged her on the rebound when something bad caught up with her last escort that took him out of her life. She'd been bruised by the experience, but had apparently found in Gordy a bit more than just a massive shoulder to cry on. He was pretty well gone for her. Despite the fact he was one of the major names in Chicago's mobs, he proved a remarkably stable influence.

It was odd, though, that he should be here, even to catch Adelle's act. He had his own place and a lot of other businesses to run; usually you couldn't blast him out of the Nightcrawler. He was always there. Period. His bodyguards were scattered at surrounding tables, so this wasn't a spur-of-the-moment outing for him. He had company along.

"Who's the guy with Gordy?" I asked.

Bobbi barely looked at him, as though to remind herself of someone she'd already seen but forgot was there. "I don't know. Probably mob. Generally is with Gordy. They came in an hour ago. Adelle sat with them a while, then had to do her set. They've been talking nose-to-nose a lot. The guy likes whiskey straight, and Gordy's kept even with his usual."

Which was tonic water and a shot of lime. Some kind of business was afoot, then. He never drank when he worked, but why here instead of his own place? Maybe he needed my special talents. It wouldn't be the first time. I didn't mind. His mob authority made mine one of the few joints in town exempt from paying the usual protection money. He owed me a few big favors but was also a friend. I was always ready to lend him a hand and vice versa.

"Guess I better find out if I'm supposed to be there."

"He'd have sent one of the boys for you then," she said with a nod toward the bodyguards. "They would have seen you coming in."

"True." If it concerned me, I'd be notified. For now, I was more than content to relax in a booth with my arm around Bobbi. "How's the night been in general?"

"Good business, about half a house. We lost a few between shows. Some people have regular jobs in the morning. The whole band remembered their instruments and showed up on time, even that drummer who's usually late."

I smiled.

She caught it. "Jack . . . did you do anything?"

"I had a little talk with him." It left me with a headache

afterward because the man was fond of drink, but some of my influence must have seeped through the booze into his brain. He seemed bright and sharp of eye tonight.

"What kind of talk?"

"Just a recommendation he go easy on the bottle and pay attention to his job so he could keep it."

"Must have been some kind of recommendation."

"Irresistible."

Her lids went to half-mast. It made her more cute than threatening. "Uh-huh. I thought you weren't going to risk messing up peoples' lives with that Svengali stuff."

"You think he's helping himself much?"

"No, but the road to hell and all that."

"It's only temporary. He can get himself sober and stay that way with my help, but unless he wants it on his own, it'll eventually wear off. I can't change a person's basic nature; that's up to him. The door's open, though."

"So long as you're not too disappointed if he doesn't go sailing through it."

I lifted a philosophical hand. "No skin off my nose. After all, I only throw myself off bridges in the line of duty."

She quirked one corner of her luscious mouth. "Ain't that the truth and a half?"

I'd told her about my hurtling ride over the railing with the ransom suitcase.

The band played on; Bobbi announced she had things to look after backstage and went off to track them down. I had work as well, helping to close out the lobby register and send the doorman home. The hatcheck girl had her area in order, ready to go when the last customer came to collect. The bartender had everything cleaned up except for a dark red stain on the floor behind the bar. Nothing would ever clean that.

Years ago when this place was a different kind of a hot spot for booze, it became the site of a mob war skirmish. Someone lobbed a grenade through the front door, and a lady bartender named Myrna caught shrapnel in the throat. She dropped in her tracks and bled to death. The stain behind the current bar marked the spot where she'd fallen and died.

My maintenance man had chiseled out and replaced the tiles several times, but they'd always stain again in the same pattern. We finally gave up. Vampires I believed in, but never ghosts. Myrna's sanguinary presence in the club had changed my mind.

"Any problems?" I asked the bartender, Wilton. He was the only one in the joint willing to work the front alone. Oddball things went on here, but he didn't mind. Jobs were scarce, and not having a pay envelope was more frightening to him than going partners with a ghost.

"She keeps switching the vodka with the gin," he said, jerking his chin at the rows of bottles lining the thick glass shelves. "Trying to be funny, I guess."

"Maybe that's how she kept them when she was alive. Try leaving them in place."

"I did. She switched them back."

Myrna had a sense of humor. "Anything else?"

"She sliced up some lemons. I had them set out with the knife, got busy, and when I went back, they were all ready in their bowl. What gets me is I never see any of that happening."

"Shy girl. It bother you?"

"Nah. I kinda like the company. I been—don't laugh, okay?—but when no one's out here, I talk to her sometimes."

"Makes sense to me." I talked to her, too.

I'd gotten Myrna's name from a young woman who impersonated Lady Crymsyn for special events and shows. Along with being an actress she was also psychic and rattled on about mystical type stuff in the same matter-of-fact tone other people used when commenting about the weather. She was used to dealing with ghosts and assumed others were the same. Escott dated her for a while, but I don't think he was too easy with that facet of her talents. Hypocrite. He could share his house with a vampire but got cold feet with a ghost-seeing girl.

"How are you, Myrna?" I asked.

No response. One of her favorite gags was to flicker the lights or turn them on and off, which is what I half-expected to happen.

"She must be someplace else," said Wilton.

We counted money and totaled tabs and tips. He signed out, gave me a list of supplies we'd need, and left for the night. I wrote the numbers on a clipboard, bagged the cash, and went upstairs to my office. Just as I turned the doorknob, the lights inside came on for me.

"Funny girl," I said to the empty air.

I'd done myself right with this room, making it comfortable. Most of the time I was allergic to paperwork, but nice surroundings reduced the symptoms. Bobbi had picked out a couple of the luxury touches like the heavy, light-blocking curtains and an extra-long sofa but hadn't gone overboard with pillows and frills. Some club offices looked like a brothel parlor; I didn't want that. Besides, fancy stuff didn't combine well with multiple locks and bolts on the steel door or the wire-meshed, bulletproof glass of the windows. The room was as secure as a giant safe because occasionally I'd sleep the day through on the sofa. When the sun was up I was dead—or something close to it—and thus vulnerable. In that state I needed all the sanctuary I could afford.

I shoved the money bag into a safe disguised to look like a drawer-front on my massive desk, locked up, and returned to the main room. I put the light out myself, thinking Myrna wouldn't mind.

Adelle had finished her set, taking her last bow to applause. She threw a smile at Gordy and went backstage. He was still busy with his friend, who didn't appear too friendly now that I got a good look at him. A wide man with a red face, pronounced jowls, and a bad haircut, his suit was on a level with his hair, the coat too narrow for his frame so it stretched tight across his shoulders.

Some kind of serious dealing was going on with them. They both seemed tense. I walked past, but Gordy didn't give any high sign to come over, his focus on the man.

Fine with me; I could ask him later or maybe find out what Adelle knew. She'd be in her dressing room. The band had two more numbers, a moderately fast dance, followed by a slow swing version of "Good Night, Sweetheart," which told the customers the place was about to close. Some of them were already settling money on the waiters, gathering up to leave.

I took the long away around to get backstage. There were four dressing rooms here, men on the left, women to the right, each side sharing its own small toilet and shower in between, an unheard-of luxury for the talent. Bobbi had helped with the layout, insisting the expense would be worth it. She had plenty of show biz know-how and knew what was needed, so I gave her a free hand. Since the opening the artists had only wild praise about their accommodations. I finally got it: that if they were happy, they'd make the audience feel the same.

Adelle had the celebrity room, a red-painted door no different from the other three, close to the stage with the number one engraved into a chrome star mounted at eye level. A slot beneath had a card with her name on it in curlicue writing. Come the weekend, someone else's name would be in place, but for now she was queen of the show.

Her door was wide open, and I heard her inside, apparently with a guest. "Oh, for crying out loud," she exclaimed, sounding pleased.

Her back was to me as I came even with the opening. She'd plastered herself to the body of a tall, strongly built man, kissing him like tomorrow didn't matter. He returned the favor with interest, his arms wrapped tight around her, hands firmly cupping her butt.

I kept going and hoped Gordy stayed the hell out front.

The band finished their last number and began packing instruments and filing out, passing me where I stood just inside the red velvet stage curtains. I had a nod and smile for them, a word of thanks, good nights, and see ya laters, all the time with my brain churning over Adelle's little love scene.

I'm in favor of affection of most kinds, and had it been anyone else, I'd have shrugged it off, since this was none of my damned beeswax, but she was Gordy's steady date. Though he was a good friend, I didn't know him well enough to guess how he'd react to her running around on him. The way that kiss had gone, there was no chance the handsome guy could have been a long-lost relative, not unless Adelle came from one seriously unhinged family.

I pressed the button that drew the curtains. They rattled smoothly along their tracks. Another high-hat expense, but otherwise I'd have had to pay some union man to do it manually. Once they were shut, I slipped out front by way of the side stage stairs, crossing the dance floor. All the customers had departed except for Gordy, his guest, and the bodyguards. The grim discussion was still going strong.

The last bartender and a couple waiters who were stacking chairs on the upper-tier tables looked toward me. They were familiar enough with Gordy's face and reputation to give him a wide berth, but at the same time they wanted to close things out and go home. I motioned them to come down, meeting them at the bar on the far side of the room.

"We'll shut out the register," I said. "If those guys want anything more, I'll take care of it. You know what they're talking about?"

"No, sir," one waiter volunteered. "Don't wanna know, either."

I chuckled once so they could see I wasn't worried. It only reassured them a little. They felt better once their tips were divided and they could escape out the rear exit, following the band.

The bartender and I did the final money count, then he gratefully left as well. I wanted to go backstage again and find Bobbi but had to park myself here until Gordy finished his talk. The staying open later than usual didn't bother me; whatever Adelle was up to in her dressing room did. Fortunately, Gordy was too involved to go look for her.

With everyone gone, it was nearly quiet enough for me to listen in on him, even at this distance over the hum of the beer cooler. They kept their tone low and droning, though. I caught a few words, but not enough to figure out what they were talking about.

Then Bobbi emerged from backstage. She'd probably been having her nightly chat with the band leader about tomorrow's music. She had company with her, a petite, elegantly slender woman dressed to the nines, with some tens and elevens mixed in. If Bobbi hadn't possessed a strong presence of her own, she'd have looked like a dowdy shop girl in comparison. The woman had white blond hair under her velvet hat, which sported a diamond-crusted pin holding spiky feathers. Matching bracelets were on one black-gloved wrist; the other was hidden inside a fur muff. A thick fox fur lay around her shoulders like a safari kill. There was a very exotic cast to her face, high cheekbones, full lips, long, dark, slanted eyes. She had a stately walk, chin elevated like royalty. You went at her speed or you went away.

Bobbi seemed immune to that inherent command, going at her usual sprightly bounce, yet both women arrived at the bar at the same time. I wondered how they did that.

"Jack, this is Faustine Petrova." Bobbi's expression telegraphed that I should overdo the manners.

I came around the bar to take Faustine's regally extended hand. In no wise could I convincingly bow and kiss it. Only Escott could get away with that, so I settled for a gentle double shake and release, adding a nod and welcoming smile. "A pleasure. How do you do?"

"Berry vell, t'ank you," she replied in a rich contralto, lips carefully outlining each word, teeth showing.

"Miss Petrova was a member of the Moscow Ballet not long ago, but decided to leave," Bobbi explained.

"Eet vas pol-i-ticks, my dear. Peasants who think they know daun-ce." Faustine Petrova sniffed her disdain. "Now because of that Austrian 'ouse painter an' that pig of a fascist train conductor, there is no place in all Europe safe for the true ar-teest."

I didn't know if the accent was real or not, but I could

listen to it for hours. "Yes, things are very miserable over there."

"Indeed. Zo I come to vonderful Amer-i-ka in hope to be free to do az I pleaze. Eet iz a great country." Her approving gaze swept around the interior of the club, as though it embodied the best of corn-fed, homemade ideals.

"I won't argue with that, Miss Petrova."

"An' zo, in the spirit of all t'ings good in my new 'omeland, for verk I am look-ink."

"Indeed?" I glanced at Bobbi for enlightenment, having no idea what the hell kind of "verk" I could provide a ballerina in my joint. The hot jazz, blues, and swing I showcased wouldn't mix well with her kind of training.

Bobbi's eyes sparkled. "Miss Petrova is here with her partner, Roland Lambert. They do exhibition dancing, specialty number stuff."

Faustine lifted a lazy hand, palm up. "Eet pays the rent."

That kind of act I might be able to use, depending how good they were. "Well, the band's gone now, so an audition isn't possible—"

"I've already seen them," said Bobbi. "They're terrific, like Astaire and Rogers but at a higher temperature. They know what they're doing."

I trusted Bobbi's shrewdness about all things related to the stage. "I suppose we can work out a contract, do a trial run for a week, and see how it goes. You know the requirements?"

Faustine nodded. "Daun-cing wit' the customers after show. I have no problem wit' that. Neither does Roland. I enjoy mingl-ink wit' the people. Amer-i-kans are zo charm-ink."

It was too much for me to picture her bouncing a fast fox trot with some Midwestern businessman in search of a foreign thrill, but if she didn't mind, I was willing to give it a try. "When do I meet your partner?"

"Roland's backstage," Bobbi answered for her. "He's old friends with Adelle."

Really close old friends from the look of things, if he was the man I'd seen with her.

"He heard she was here and decided to look her up. We all got to talking, one thing led to another, and they asked about working here. Before you arrived, they did a free show early on as their audition. Went over great."

"Roland's still talking with Adelle?"

"They had some catching up to do. They used to be married."

I blinked. "Married?"

"It was years back. They're all over it now."

Apparently not quite. Was that going to be a problem? The none-of-my-damned-beeswax tune played through my head again. I'd have to talk to Bobbi about this.

She beamed a smile at Faustine. "When can you come by tomorrow? We'll have to sort out the contract, schedule, rehearsals, and get some publicity photos for the ads and so on."

"Roland takes care of those t'ings. He come in vhenever you vish."

"One o'clock, then," Bobbi said decisively, softening it with an ingenuous smile. She seemed extremely pleased with herself. They must have really impressed her.

"Before you leave, I'd like to meet him," I put in.

Faustine favored me with a smoldering eye. "I vill get him. Once he is talk-ink, is difficult to drag avay, but I know how." She made a smoky smile and a sly wink, then undulated off. Hopefully, Adelle and Roland would be able to pry themselves apart before she walked in on them. The fewer people to gossip, the better. I stifled the urge to glance over at Gordy, waiting until Faustine was out of earshot.

"Iz that for reeel?" I asked Bobbi.

"Who cares? It works. Had you drooling."

"I was not drooling, just slightly fascinated. I never heard a Russian speak like that before, like Bela Lugosi crossed with Garbo. What's the real story?"

She shook her head. "What I told you is what I know, and they really are good dancers. Roland used to be in Hollywood, that's where he and Adelle met. She vouched for him so far as his talent goes. He sings and dances, has done plays and musicals. He got supporting romantic roles in some smaller films but never really hit the big time. Drink, according to Adelle. That's why she went to Reno a year into their marriage. That was ten years ago. He swears he's cleaned up his act since."

"I hope so. No room in this place for booze hounds breathing sour on the customers."

"Like that drummer?"

"He's at a safe distance and sober for now. What do they expect me to pay them?"

"The standard rate."

"Faustine won't be buying diamonds on that."

"You thought those were genuine?"

"I guess the accent blinded me. Won't hoofing in a night-club be a comedown for them?"

"It's work. There's not a lot of it around these days, and there's always been more actors than acting jobs. I think they're trying to build up a grubstake before moving to New York or to Hollywood. That or hoping to carve a place for themselves in this town."

God, I wished Bobbi would listen to herself. She might

think twice about going into the movies. There was plenty for her to do in Chicago. It wasn't that I wanted her to give up her dream, I just didn't want to lose her to it. We'd had that conversation more than once; this wasn't the time to go through it again. I shoved the old ache back into its rickety box and slammed the lid.

"Something wrong?" she asked.

It was terrifying how well she could read my face. What was unsuccessfully hiding there must stay put. I had a different problem all primed, anyway. "Listen, I saw this Roland with Adelle in her dressing room wrapped in a clinch that looked a lot more serious than old friends saying hello. They were more like honeymooners than a divorced couple."

"You sure?"

"I know a love scene when I see it. That one would have Will Hayes dropping dead of shock."

She shook her head. "But they only smiled and shook hands earlier."

"Saving the best for later. What with Adelle and Gordy doing a two-step for all this time, I thought one of us should—"

"Jack, it's none of our business."

"So I tell myself, but Gordy might not care for a moocher on his territory."

"That's Adelle's choice," she said archly.

"Not really. Gordy's not just any guy. You know what that means."

She started to say something more, then visibly changed her mind. When we first met, Bobbi was mistress to a mobster and had had very damned little choice about much of anything in her life. "Okay. I get it. But Gordy's a friend."

"Who kills people. Don't ever forget that. Adelle can't be

completely ignorant of what he does, but she may need reminding. If she's going to run around on him, she won't like
the consequences when he learns about it, and don't kid yourself that he won't."

"You wouldn't tell him."

"No. But he'd find out. It's what he does his whole life:
find out things. Sometime soon take Adelle aside and give her
the straight on what it means to date guys in his line of work."

"She won't believe it."

"Give her a chance; she might. For her own good, she has
to."

"And if she doesn't . . . you'll talk to her?" Bobbi knew
what that involved.

"I won't tell her who to be with, just help her understand
things."

"I don't like that."

"Me neither. I can also talk to this Roland, suggest he make
himself scarce around Adelle, but one or the other has to lay
off before there's a disaster."

"Why not talk to Gordy?"

She caught me flat-footed there. It never once occurred to
me that I could also do a Svengali act on Gordy, and I didn't
like it any more than she did. "All right, touché, ya got me
square in the gizzard. I don't wanna interfere with any of
them, and this ain't anything I should poke my nose into,
but when I see a train wreck about to happen . . ."

"Okay, I'll give Adelle a heads up, pretend I was the one
who saw her with Roland. Maybe there's a perfectly innocent
reason why they were kissing."

She wouldn't have said that if she'd seen their level of osculation. Roland looked like he'd been mining for tonsils.
"You could drop a hint to Roland about Adelle dating one of

this town's top mob kingpins. Mention the possibility of broken legs."

She relaxed a little. "I could work it into a conversation. . . . I don't want anyone hurt, but getting involved without an invitation is always a mistake. For all we know, there's nothing going on."

"All the same, I wanna avoid trouble. There they are. Introduce me, my sweet."

Bobbi made a sound suspiciously like a growl. When we turned to face them, we were close enough side by side for me to give her an easy-does-it pat on the rump. A little one, just to let her know that everything would be all right, no hard feelings. The growl abruptly choked off. She shot me a "don't be a wiseacre" look, recovered, and did the formalities. I shook hands with Roland Lambert.

3

ROLAND was in his late thirties, matinee idol looks, a steady, honest eye, and a firm hand. I wanted to not like him, but his smile exuded the sort of winning charm politicians tried to project and so often failed to fulfill. It wasn't anything you could fake; you either possessed cheerful, wholesome sincerity naturally or you didn't. This man looked like he'd never had a bad day in his life and never would. Formal in an impeccable tuxedo, I could tell he was also careful about details. There wasn't one trace of Adelle's lip rouge or face powder on him.

"Faustine tells me you're going to give us a trial run, Mr. Fleming," he said. "I can't tell you how grateful we are for the chance."

"We'll see how things work out. You planning to stay in Chicago?"

"For the time being. We've only just come from Europe, and this is Faustine's first time in the States. She's hardly had a chance to see anything. Soon as we were off the boat, we got a train out here to look up one of her cousins from the old country."

"Did you find him?"

"Yesss," said Faustine. "Ve talk of dead family an' bad times since death of czar. So bourgeoisie of him to live in past, so bor-ink, zo ve leave. Some family is better at distant, yesss?"

If she'd said elephants were purple, I'd have agreed with her. "How did you two team up?"

Roland beamed down at her. "We met at a backstage party." He put an arm around her waist. "It was love at first sight."

Faustine beamed up at him. "Roland iz such a roman-tik. He sveep my feet out."

Until now I thought they were just working partners. They didn't seem a match, him being so all-American and her being . . . her. I glanced at Bobbi, but she kept her smile firmly fixed in place, and it looked genuine. She liked a good love story.

Roland went on. "I'd made a niche in English theater play-ing Americans, but we couldn't stay, the way things are go-ing. Soon as my latest play's run ended, we hopped a boat. The captain married us right after we cleared port."

"Zo roman-tik," Faustine added, tilted eyes glittering.

With her gloves on I couldn't see a ring on her finger, but Roland sported a discreet gold band. Had Adelle noticed, or did it matter to her? Bobbi didn't seem surprised at this news. Maybe it had come up earlier in the evening.

"What a trip, too," said Roland. "Cold as hell, everyone seasick with the high waves, and they ran submarine drills the first day out. Didn't call them that, of course, people were nervous enough. We all crossed our fingers against being another *Lusitania*. There's going to be war in the rest of Europe soon, not just Spain, you mark me. We got out just in time."

"I've seen the newsreels," I said. "Hitler's full of a lot of air, but that'll be the limit. He won't be so stupid."

Roland shook his head. "They're taking him very seriously over there. Have those reels shown the English parents training their kids about wearing gas masks?"

"Yeah, but that's an overreaction. The news plays it up because it sells papers and packs the theaters. Don't know why they're worried. Hitler would have to fight his way through France first. He's not going to risk going up against the Maginot Line. He just likes to hear himself talk."

"But too many others are listening to him. Lemme tell you about the German influence on—"

"Pol-i-ticks." Faustine sneered. "Are an utter bore, dar-link. Let us speak of more pleasant t'inks."

He shot her a rueful look. "You're absolutely right. I forgot that ladies are less devoted to America's other favorite pastime than are gentlemen."

"Vat more other pastime? Zex?"

I liked her way of thinking.

"Baseball," Roland answered, unperturbed.

"Ah!" she brightened. "I berry much vould like to see a baseball game. Iz possible?"

"In a few more months when things thaw out. You're going to love Wrigley Field."

"And hav-ink a hot dog? More months to vait?"

"I'll buy you one tomorrow."

"I loff Amer-i-ka!" She didn't beam so much as glow. Very easy on the eye.

By the time they were ready to leave I certainly didn't believe in Faustine's accent, but listening to her was too much fun. Bobbi's entertainment instincts were exactly right; these two would draw people in and keep them happy. Roland would get the women to swoon over his grin alone; Faustine would flatter the men into jelly just saying, "Good even-ink."

We said farewells, and I escorted them out, unlocking the front door. They'd been in the country long enough to buy or hire a car, a new-looking green Hudson. Roland handed Faustine into it, and off they drove. I went back for Bobbi and to see if Gordy was close to shutting things down.

Adelle Taylor emerged from her dressing room, having apparently been busy changing. I never understood how women could switch stage costumes in a few seconds but take half an hour to put on regular clothes. It was a nightly ritual for Adelle, but she was beautifully turned out. Her dark hair was drawn up under a fancy hat; gloves, bracelets, coat, and all the things in between were decked out better than a Macy's window. She was enough to distract Gordy's attention from his guest. His otherwise impassive face shifted into what for him was a big, approving smile. He was gone on her, all right.

I hoped Bobbi was right about me keeping clear. Adelle, seeing Gordy wasn't ready, went over to the bar to talk with Bobbi. They were both acquainted with the basics of mob etiquette, and interrupting a private powwow, as Escott might have said, was "not the done thing." I hung by the entry under the portrait and hoped Bobbi would take the opportunity to let Adelle in on the specialized etiquette of dating mobsters. Gordy would never do anything against his girl, but Roland was fair game for rough stuff. I'd not been kidding about broken legs.

Gordy turned back to his table company, said something I couldn't catch, then they both rose, the man unsteadily, but sweating hard to master himself. All six bodyguards rose as

well, regarding one another with restrained distrust but be-
having. I had the feeling that if I coughed too loud, a shooting
war would break out.

Anticipating their departure, I'd left the front open and
followed them. Gordy's boys went along outside with the rest;
Gordy hung back. His guest glared at him, reddened eyes
annoyed.

"What gives?" he demanded, his gaze shifting suspiciously
from Gordy to me. "You two conniving?"

"I'm driving my girl home," Gordy replied evenly. "She's
waiting for me."

"The canary?"

"The canary."

The man snorted disgust, then rounded fully on me. I got
an up-and-down and didn't impress him. "Who's the snot-
nosed kid?"

I was thirty-seven; I just didn't look it. A mixed blessing
at times. Certainly I was old enough to know better than to
react. He was throwing out a challenge to see which way I'd
jump, but my night had been busy enough. "I'm Jack Fleming. This is my club."

Another snort. "Who bought it for ya? Some kind of bar
mitzvah present from your daddy?"

I smiled as though he'd been witty. "No, I earned it.
Thanks for asking." He was too drunk to be hypnotized or
I'd have given him a flying start on his future hangover. With
enough emotional force behind the suggestion, I could drive
him or nearly anyone else insane. Having that kind of power
and having seen its effect on others usually kept me from
getting pissed with people, even the ones actively seeking a
kick in the ass. "I hope you enjoyed your evening."

"Go to hell, punk." He waited, maybe thinking I'd take a

swing at him or at least frown. When I didn't, he threw a puffing laugh of contempt at my face and left. I was glad about not needing to breathe. His secondhand booze would have put W. C. Fields on his ass.

"Should I lock it?" I asked, once the door had him on the other side with the bodyguards.

Gordy seemed pleased. Since nothing had happened, that made two of us. "Nah. My boys will see him off."

"Good."

"He's a bastard." Gordy's way of apologizing.

"In two minutes he won't remember any of it."

"Don't underestimate him."

"Who is he?"

"Hog Bristow."

"His mother hated him that much?"

"Got the name when he worked in meat packing, killing the pigs. He liked it. Word got around, one of the old bosses asked if he could kill men just as easy. He could. He liked that, too. His other name is Ignance."

"His mother *did* hate him."

"Don't ever let him hear you call him Hog unless he likes you."

Gordy knew some real pips. "What's he doing here?" Meaning in Chicago over New York. There'd been a Hell's Kitchen accent under Bristow's drunken slur.

"Business."

Which could be just about anything in the rackets. Gordy frequently kept me wise to what was going on, simply because I was on the outside of his mob-centered world and determined to stay there. He knew the value of a neutral ear combined with a shut mouth. "Why at Crymsyn instead of your place? Not that I mind the extra business."

"Whole town knows you're not on anyone's side but your own. It's safe to come here."

"Safe?"

"For talk. Started when this joint first opened. You invited everyone to the big party. It crossed borders. We found we could do stuff here and not have to worry about trouble."

Good grief. Lady Crymsyn as an underworld League of Nations. Not something I'd planned on. I'd noticed a lot of gangsters coming in, but until now thought it'd been for the shows and quality booze.

"The boys in the business agreed to keep the shooting in the streets. Place like this is too useful to mess up."

There were times when I couldn't tell if he was kidding or not. This was one of them. "Bristow coming back?"

"Tomorrow."

"What's his problem?" With that kind of man there was always a problem.

"He wants a piece of my territory. I don't want to give it to him."

"Doesn't New York decide those things?"

"He's got ambition. Figures if he can take it, he can keep it. They're letting him try because they like him. He's a funny guy. They think."

"Because he's funny they're going to risk a war if you slug it out with him?"

"He's got ideas, too. Told them I'm too soft, don't make as much money as I should. There's a depression going on, what the hell do they expect? NRA programs don't go to booze, houses, and gambling. Bristow says he can change that, bring more cash. He harped for too long. You harp too long on something, they either shoot you or listen. They didn't shoot him."

Regrettable. "What are you going to do?"

"Talk him out of it."

"Just talk?" Gordy was a persuasive man with a subtle intellect, but Bristow didn't look the type who would hear anyone but himself. Drunk, he struck me as having less brains than your average rabid dog.

"Not much choice. I can't scrag him for no reason. They like him too much. So long as he behaves himself, I gotta put up with him telling me what he wants."

"Which you won't give to him."

"I can't. I do that, it proves to New York he's right about me being soft. If I keep turning him down, sooner or later he either goes away—which means he loses face with them—or he takes what he's after. He ain't taking squat from me."

"But he'll try?"

"Maybe."

"How?"

He lifted his wide shoulders a quarter inch. "He'll think of something. But not tonight. I got him so drunk he won't be able to move. If I keep him drunk, he might forget why he came to town in the first place."

"I can do that for you, if he's sober. Send him off to Havana for a long winter vacation."

"I just might ask. In the meantime I'm learning plenty from him. He don't know that I'm learning, either."

Gordy's hobby, passion, vocation, specialty, and profession was information. For him, knowledge truly was power; he had an unofficial Ph.D. in the collecting of anything worth knowing where it concerned the mobs. He had good reason for putting up with Bristow, then.

"I can help you there, too." I didn't mind making the effort if it sped the man on his way. "He won't recall a thing, either."

"I might ask you that, too. But it can wait."

We ambled back to the main room and the bar on the other side. Adelle greeted him in what had become her usual affectionate manner; bestowing a peck on his cheek and taking possession of one of his arms.

"All done?" she asked.

"With business," Gordy replied. "Home?"

"Yes, please."

"See you, Bobbi. See you Fleming." He escorted her out, a grizzly bear picking his steps carefully with a swan.

"All done?" Bobbi asked in turn.

"Just about." I collected the register money, tips, and clipboard record and took them up to the office safe. The light was on for me, and I remembered flicking it off before. When I put it out again, it stayed out. Myrna was tired, too. I left the light behind the lobby bar burning, though. She liked it that way.

"Busy night," said Bobbi once we'd settled in my car. She'd wrapped up deep in her coat against the damp chill coming from the not-too-distant lake. It would take a few minutes before the heater warmed up enough to blow more than freezing air.

"You pooped?" I backed from my parking place and headed toward her hotel apartment.

"Not that much, but I can tell you are, mister gangbuster man."

Sadly, that was true. Now that the excitement was over, I was dragging like a sleepwalker. "It's been a hell of a night."

"A two-week-long night for you."

Again, true. Escott hadn't been the only one made crazy

tense over the Gladwell case. I wasn't in much of a mood for what relaxed me best. The only real recovery, mental and physical, would be resting the day on my home earth and visiting the Stockyards for a long drink. That I would do tomorrow. Though there was plenty of time for a stop before dawn, I wanted body rest first. Just sitting on the couch with my feet up and staring at nothing in the quiet of the house was what I craved more than blood. I'd used a lot of myself up this long night. Escott called it "mental digestion," where you don't think of anything, yet do a lot of thinking all the same.

I escorted Bobbi up to her hotel flat, parting with a chaste kiss good night and got myself home a couple hours before dawn. Not too surprisingly, Escott wasn't back. He was either tied up with talking to cops or still providing support and advice to Vivian Gladwell. Maybe more. She was a pretty good-looking woman, and he had plenty of charm stored away for when he felt like using it. The last couple weeks must have thrown them into the same room a lot, and now that the crisis was past . . . well, I knew firsthand how a surge of relief could affect one's libido. For both of them.

Since resolving some problems out of his past, Escott had discovered girls all over again and seemed to be making up for lost time. Not that he was gone every night, but now that he'd opened his door again to romantic possibilities, he had more social invitations. The women couldn't get enough of him. Must have been his English accent.

I might introduce him to Faustine and see what he made of her Russian inflections. That reminded me of the Roland-Adelle duet.

Collapsed on the parlor couch with the big radio playing low, I stared at my feet propped on the arm and considered a possible triangle with Adelle, Roland, and Faustine. Include Gordy and it made a cockeyed square with all the weight in his corner. A dangerous balance. Bobbi was right about me butting out, but I didn't care to stand by when I could head off a disaster. Me talking to Adelle—or Roland—would help. It seemed the safest road, especially if no one remembered anything, and what Gordy never found out wouldn't hurt anybody.

But tomorrow was soon enough already to work things. I shut the radio off in mid-tune and went upstairs for a quick bath and fresh pajamas, then down to the basement for sack time.

Soon after my change from being living to being Un-dead, I was stuck for a safe place to hide from the day. I needed a totally private, fireproof refuge that wasn't a mausoleum. Closed-in, dark, airless places full of coffins and skeletons gave me the heebie-jeebies same as anyone else.

Then Escott invited me to move into his old brick house. The building had once been the neighborhood brothel, with lots of big rooms divided into little ones to accommodate the business. Escott's sporadic but ongoing campaign of restoration compelled him to take a sledgehammer to those interior walls. The ground and second floors were finished, but the third floor and attic work had been interrupted by a surge in his private agent business. I told him to bring in people to complete the job; he could afford it, but he preferred doing things himself. It apparently reminded him of his days on the stage. Along with acting, he'd picked up plenty of carpentry skills.

Escott had kindly walled up an alcove in his basement, creating a very secure and secret lair for me to pass my daylight oblivion. It wasn't flood-proof, as we'd found out last fall. During the season's first hard freeze, a kitchen pipe cracked, and as my chamber was underneath, I had a hell of an awakening. My first alarmed thought was that the house had caught fire and the two inches of ice water covering the floor was leakage from the fire hoses.

Thankfully, it wasn't, and it could have been worse, but the flood was calamity enough. A plumber took care of the pipe and a mop and bucket took care of the mess, but I'd had stacks of books and papers lying around, most ruined or nearly so. It prompted a new habit in me to keep things up on tables and shelves from then on.

Vanishing, I let myself sink down through the small gaps in the kitchen floor where Escott had hidden an emergency trapdoor. It was under the table, covered by a rug. Directly below was my walled-up chamber with a few homey necessities: table, chair, a lamp I always kept on, my typewriter, and an army cot. On the latter was a length of oilcloth stitched into a long, flat bag that held a quantity of my home earth. It was both creepy and comforting. I'd cheated death but still had to bed down on a reminder of the grave. I didn't know how, but its gloomy presence kept me from being aware of the passage of the hours. Without it, days were excruciating jaunts into purgatory because of the bad dreams between sunrise and sunset.

I had other places to flop, but they weren't as comfortable. Those were strictly for emergencies. Once in a while I'd mull over the possibility of fixing up a second permanent spot at the club, something even more secure than my locked office. Lady Crymsyn's basement was clean, dry, and bright with electricity, but someone had died very horribly in one of its far corners years back. No ghost haunted that area, but the still-fresh memories of what I'd seen and imagined about that death lingered. Also, a couple of idiots had tried to kill me down there, so I took the hint that Fate had dropped and kept clear of the area.

Superstitious? You bet.

With a grateful sigh, I lay on my creaky cot and waited for the dawn. A silent, lonely pause, but brief if I timed it right.

Through the walls, I felt the sun creeping up and fought to stay awake. Pushing sleep off for as long as possible caused it to take hold more suddenly. I went out quick, then, one second awake, the next not. It was better than the alternative, which was a gradual, unpleasant sinking into paralysis, eventually followed by a slow loss of consciousness. The progression was too much like dying, and I'd had enough of that for several lifetimes.

I was awake. Then I wasn't. Good.

My "morning" started at close to five in the afternoon. Winters could be pure hell, especially in Chicago, but I welcomed them for the extended hours of darkness. The equinox had turned, though, each new night a minute shorter than the previous one. I'd learned the value of not wasting them as they dwindled.

I woke up hungry, my corner teeth out. Nothing surprising, I'd used a lot of myself last night. My body was never too subtle when it came to its need for blood, but would have to wait a little longer. Dark as it was, there'd still be plenty of activity going on at the Stockyards, and my feedings were better done alone. Most people were apt to find my need to open a vein in an animal's leg to drink down the fresh, warm blood flow revolting. Though normal to me now, turned into a pleasurable necessity, I couldn't blame them for their reaction.

Escott was back, his long form reclining on the couch much the same as I had done. In his case, half a drink waited on the table, and newspapers were scattered to hell and gone on the floor. He was usually much more orderly, but he had earned time off. His eyelids were sealed shut, and a soft snore originating from his ample beak of a nose made the paper on his chest flutter a little.

I was about to ghost upstairs to dress, allowing him to continue undisturbed, but the damn phone rang. He jerked awake with an exasperated groan.

"I'll get it," I said, guessing this must have been going on all day.

It was a reporter for a paper I'd never heard of, and when I repeated his interview request aloud, Escott shook his head and waved off the prospect of getting his name spelled right.

"He's left for the week," I told the receiver. "Don't call back." I dropped the earpiece on its hook and went to the front room, dropping into my usual chair by the radio.

Escott sat up wearily. "There are occasions when I quite envy your ability to sleep through rows."

"It's not exactly sleep, but I know what you mean. Why not leave the thing off the hook?"

"Actually, I arranged for my answering service to take calls over the next several days. They're only to put through Mrs. Gladwell, the police, yourself, Shoe, Gordy, and Miss Smythe, of course. How the devil did that reporter get past, I wonder?"

"Probably pretended to be a cop. I've done it myself. The trick is to sound bored and keep talking."

Escott rubbed his face. "Perhaps I should go back to the

stage. There wasn't as much money, but it was less nerve-racking."

"You should take a vacation. All the papers talk about now is Palm Springs. Nice and warm there. The women are in swimsuits year round."

"Tempting as that is, I'm required to remain in town until this case is concluded."

"That won't be long. The cops have the guys."

"For the time being. One of the men you caught is the last scion of a very old, respected, and influential family."

"Which one? Dugan?" He'd been better dressed than the others, better educated to judge by his speech.

"Indeed. One Hurley Gilbert Dugan."

"So? He's still a kidnapper and was all set to murder that poor girl."

"Ah, but you've not heard that it was a terrible mistake, that he was forced into the crime by bad companions."

"What?"

"My dear fellow, please don't shout. It won't improve the situation."

By now I should have been used to the world spinning screwball into daily disasters while I lay insensible. I wasn't. In a quieter tone: "What the hell is going on?"

"I have no doubt that Dugan was the ringleader, but he's claiming to be as much of a victim as Sarah Gladwell. He's spun a very convincing story of being too easily influenced by some questionable types who befriended him in his friendless isolation, then threatened to kill him if he did not aid them in their nefarious kidnapping scheme. It's in the papers." He gestured at the drifts of newsprint lying all over the place. I caught a few of the more creative headlines. A *lot* had been going on, and none of it made sense.

"And people are swallowing that crap?"

"If one shouts a lie long and loud enough, it tends to be believed. I think Charlemagne began a rumor that a queen he once proposed to killed and ate her own children. Helped him save face when she refused his marriage offer. Many believed him because of who he was."

"Charles . . ."

"I know, but the distraction of pointless trivia keeps me from smashing things. Besides, this is certainly a similar situation of someone shouting a lie to save himself. It's so completely outrageous that the papers are listening. Only the first day, and they've generated miles of print slanted in his favor. By the time the trial comes up, it's likely Dugan will get naught but a slap on the wrist, then off he goes back to his sad isolation, wiser for the experience."

I'd seen lies work before but could not understand it happening in this case. "What about the confessions?"

"His three companions have willingly owned up to their share of guilt so as to obtain mercy from the court. They maintain Dugan was their boss and directed them in the crime, but Dugan holds to his story, saying they vindictively want to drag him down as well. I've a friend in the district attorney's office who let me know on the sly."

"That can't be possible. I primed him same as the others, gave him the works, the same confession to say. I know he was under."

"We may venture to speculate that in this instance your hypnosis failed for some reason. If he was intoxicated, you'd have had little effect on his mind. He was either drunk or . . ."

"Insane," I completed.

"Indeed."

Oh hell.

4

"WAS he drunk?" Escott asked.

"No. I'd have smelled it on him. Sensed it in other ways. He went out just like the others." Or so it had seemed.

Damned few people were immune to my kind of hypnosis. Drunks were difficult, but I could eventually get through the booze by either taking it slow or just waiting for them to sober up. With crazy people, waiting didn't work. They tended to stay crazy and not go under at all. Their minds were somehow resistant to my will, and it showed. But not this time with Dugan. He'd played me and played good.

"So the guy is nuts?" What a perfect pip. Loony bin cases I didn't like one little bit, too unpredictable.

"He's moneyed and probably unbalanced," said Escott. "I'm quite terribly shocked. No, I take it back; I'm bloody tired. Been at it all day. The Gladwell estate is under siege by the press. Mrs. Gladwell has hired bodyguards to keep out the riffraff. Some of the more vicious members of the populace are accusing the poor woman of staging the kidnapping herself, either as a means to get rid of a mentally defective child—"

"Oh, good God."

"Or as a publicity stunt. Of course, they're vague over exactly what it is she wishes to have publicized. It's sickening."

"This changes things."

"Indeed. There is a serious likelihood that a clever lawyer could get Dugan free."

"No," I said decisively. "I'm not going to let that happen. How can it happen with the other members of the gang talking their heads off?"

"They're seen as lying about his part in the crime to make things easier for themselves. If they implicate Dugan, perhaps they will have shorter sentences to serve. They all have records for various offenses. Dugan's is clean—officially—so with—"

"Officially? What's he not done, then?"

"Interesting chap. Took me a bit of digging, but I found a few choice items in his far past to consider. When Hurley Gilbert Dugan was ten, there was an incident involving the death of a governess. She was found in her room with the gas on, but nothing was proven one way or another. It could have been murder, suicide, or an accident, but after that, he was packed off to a boarding school. In the time he was there, another student died of an apparent fall down some stairs. Dugan was removed soon afterwards, taken home again, and taught by private tutors. That was years past, though. I found nothing of further interest unless you want to count deaths in the family, which seem to be legitimate heart failures and disease."

"What was he, a one-man crime wave?"

Escott shook his head and sipped his drink. "One should

not leap to conclusions. Though they are suspicious, neither of the episodes are necessarily connected to him. I've witnessed stranger examples of coincidence in action."

I was less ready to give Dugan the benefit of a doubt. He'd not actually discouraged Ralph from his intent to rape Sarah— only called it disgusting. He and the rest had been industriously preparing to dump her in that pit afterwards, dead or alive.

"Look, if he's got money, what's he doing pulling a kidnap job?"

"The very point he's raised time and again to the press: that he has no motive. He's stood on the front entry to his venerable family mansion, grandly pointing out to the photographers that a man in such a home has no need of mon—"

"He's not in jail?"

"His lawyer managed to get him out after posting bond. I'm told the show before the judge was most convincing. At least the other three are where they belong."

"Not good enough!"

Escott finished his drink, hanging on to the empty glass, running one long finger around the top the way you do on crystal to get it to sing. This one remained silent. "With Dugan's lack of reaction to your intervention, he likely is insane but able to behave normally most of the time. We've both met that type before."

"Have you talked to him?"

"Only to my friend on the inside, who was present during an initial interview session. She described him as being 'very charming' for what that's worth, but sensed there was something 'off' about him that she couldn't describe."

"What was she doing there?"

"Taking stenography notes for the district attorney's office.

With my direct connection to the victim in this case, the lady could lose her post for merely wishing me good evening in the street. It's extremely unethical, a jeopardy to the DA's case, but this young fellow put the wind up her, so when I telephoned, hoping for a hint or two of how things were progressing, she fairly gushed."

"She owe you a favor or just like you a lot?"

He lifted one hand from the glass in a demurring manner. "Bit of both, as well as her interest in seeing Dugan put away. She's not above bending rules in a good cause and knows I can keep a confidence."

"My lip's buttoned, too."

"Never crossed my mind to worry about you."

"What did Dugan do for a living before he took up crime?"

"Very little. His uncle's family has something to do with ball-bearing manufacture. It mostly runs itself under a board of directors, so Dugan devoted himself to educational pursuits."

"Smart?"

"Graduated with honors from the University of Chicago. A business degree of some sort, quite in keeping with his class."

"Any mention what he does in that free time when he's not kidnapping girls?"

"You'll hate this: charity events. Before her demise last year he would squire his aging mother to such things."

"Doesn't support him being very isolated."

"No, but it does give him a point of connection to Sarah Gladwell. She and her mother often attended the same affairs. I've not yet been able to establish a similar connection between him and his tarnished companions in crime. I should like to know how they met."

I went over my memory of Dugan from last night: knocking him cold, shoving him in the car, bringing him around, finally hypnotizing him. He'd been the last in line for his turn, no special reason. He was older than the others, in his young thirties, which had struck me as odd. Most people that age were more or less settled into routines established years earlier. He'd had a pale, good-looking face, mouth quirked in a kind of secret smile. It was his natural expression, his lips shaped that way, not fading even when I had him under. Usually people go all dead-eyed and slack-jawed. His eyes had glazed during his turn, but it's easy enough to fake. Could he have wakened sooner than the others, have heard things, been quick enough to understand what I was doing? If so, then that made him far too smart for my peace of mind.

I flipped through the newspapers. Their pages had photos of the gang, Vinzer, Ralph, and Ponti, the bearded scruffiness of their mug shots in stark contrast to a handsome society portrait of Dugan. Also included were pictures of him escorting his sweet-faced, white-haired mother to past charity events, evidently plucked from the papers' archives. He looked very benign indeed.

Several papers had sent photographers out to the small house in Indiana to get shots of the kidnappers' country retreat. Captions for the scene of the crime pointed to significant sites like the bed where young Sarah had lain and the partly destroyed outhouse. I'd stopped the cleanup before it had begun; hopefully there were still plenty of Dugan's fingerprints to be found there.

I looked at Escott. "Does Dugan have a story on where he spent the last two weeks?"

"He claims he was a prisoner to the other three, too fearful of his life to chance trying to escape."

"Bullshit. He was in a car right behind Vinzer and Ralph the whole trip back to the house."

"Pity you can't testify to that."

I grunted agreement, skimming the papers. The articles varied wildly on angles. Though all were anti-kidnapping, very few were anti-Dugan; the rest annoyed me. Were they that impressed by his wealth? Understandable in these hard times, but hardly rational. A couple of the more thoughtful ones reported on and speculated thoroughly about the mysterious Good Samaritan who had foiled the plot. They called for him to come forward with his testimony. I would have loved to oblige them, with or without their offered reward. It was hefty enough to attract plenty of phonies. They'd all have to get through the coming dog-and-pony show without my help.

"Bored rich guy," I stated, shaking my head at the follies of the world. "Maybe he's trying to top Leopold and Loeb by getting away with it, skipping jail altogether." That was a lot of conclusion-jumping, but it nettled that the guy might have put one over on me. I wanted him to live down to those conclusions. "He didn't need the money, so the kidnapping might have been an experiment to him, a thrill crime to see if he could do it."

"He very nearly did, if not for your intervention."

"He still could. I won't let that happen."

"Jack . . . it would be best to deal with this before it ever goes to court."

"I'll try the evil eye again, really press things. See if I can make it last long enough for him to sign a confession."

That snagged me a doubtful look. "If you think it worth the effort."

The idea behind the confessions was to wholly eliminate the need for a jury trial. The kidnappers were supposed to admit their crime, tell the judge to throw the book at them, and bring the mess to a swift end. But it promised that Dugan and his family would fight and fight dirty, and with enough money thrown around, even this serious a charge could be dodged.

Thinking of Sarah Gladwell on the witness stand turned my guts. A halfway good lawyer could make mincemeat of any sixteen-year-old, but one with Sarah's mental state had no chance at all. He could play up the fact that she'd been drugged, was too feebleminded to be believed, or make it look like she'd been in on the crime herself as a prank, not knowing any better. The star witness against Dugan and the rest would get pity or sympathy but no justice.

"It'll be worth the effort," I said. "Let's call it eliminating a possibility. I was tired last night. The work I did on the other guys gave me a headache. Maybe I was punchy by the time it was Dugan's turn, took things for granted, got sloppy with the work. I'll give it another try, see what happens."

"And if it doesn't work?"

I didn't want to think about that. Escott apparently read it in my face. We went quiet for a while, not the comfortable kind. I cleared my throat and stood. "Well, I got a saloon to run. Why don't you come over? See the show, blow away the cobwebs. Bobbi would love to see you again. She thinks I'm a big hero on this case; you can tell her different."

He shrugged, not saying one way or another, frowning at his empty glass.

The phone rang again. I answered it. Another reporter who'd bluffed his way in. Jeez, when I'd been one, I had no idea how irritating we could be. "Wanna do an interview?" I called toward the front room.

Escott barked a short laugh. "I've left for London. A flying visit to see a certain Lady Crymsyn."

I told the man Escott was off crime-busting illegal pinochle games in Timbuktu and hung up.

As the evening settled firmly on the city, lights kindled bright in the houses and stores, making me feel less alone in my head. People and cars clogged the streets. It would be hours before they thinned out and finally emptied, and by then my club would be hopping, a second home to other night people.

We took my Buick to Lady Crymsyn, arriving an hour earlier than necessary. After parking in my slot, we walked a short block to a diner where I bought Escott a decent meal, keeping him company. The smell of cooked food tended to inspire nausea in me, but the only way I could be sure he'd eat was to watch him. I was hungry myself, but that feeding would have to wait. To look normal, I ordered a cup of coffee, stirring a spoon in it whenever the waitress passed by.

Once Escott started on his plate he didn't stop, packing the stuff away like a starved miner. The last couple weeks had left him gaunt; I encouraged him to a second dessert. I did the talking, avoiding the subject of Dugan, keeping strictly to business about the club. This included a lengthy mention of Roland, Adelle, the exotic Faustine, and the so-far-unaware Gordy.

"Bobbi said to keep my nose out of it," I told Escott. "And I know she's right, but I don't like the potential for trouble."

"Then you'd best retire to a very distant and deserted island. Any patch of earth on this planet with people on it has that potential."

"Screwy world. Why can't we be more sensible?"

"I'm sure the Almighty has been asking that very question for several ages now. We are creatures of spirit and body, both in frequent conflict for supremacy, when we should seek a balance between the two."

"Where'd that come from?" I'd never heard such ideas from him before.

"Mrs. Gladwell and I had some rather remarkable conversations about many things, including certain forms of philosophy. I tried to get her to talk to pass the time and keep her mind from dwelling too morbidly on the fate of her daughter. It seemed to help her bear up under the burden."

"How's she doing now?"

"Oh, worlds better with young Sarah back."

"Is she all right? Those drugs they gave her . . ."

"The doctor is optimistic about a complete recovery. Fortunately, she remembers little of her ordeal, though the poor child has had nightmares. They moved her bed into her mother's room for the time being. She feels safer there. I dare say Vivi—Mrs. Gladwell is also the better for it. She never lets Sarah from her sight. There's a nurse with her at all times. Mrs. Gladwell is taking great pains to keep the troubles of the outside world distanced from the household, the best thing for them. She's remarkably perceptive. And erudite. Some people have libraries for show, but she's read hers. All of it. Quite an achievement with that many volumes."

I made noises like I was interested and got another earful about Mrs. Gladwell's virtues. Escott was impressed with her mind, which was a rarity. Usually a woman's looks first hooked him, then if she had some kind of artistic talent like singing or acting. He had a mile-wide streak of frustrated creativity with no time to indulge it because of the demands of his agency, but he liked talking shop. A woman who appealed to him on an intellectual level was a rarity. There were brainy women all over, but those who crossed his path in business never hung around long enough for anything to happen.

He seemed more relaxed and less exhausted when we strolled to the club, and I unlocked the front. The staff was already at work; Wilton had let them in by the back door, and Myrna was there, of course. The lobby bar light didn't go out, but it did flare inexplicably brighter for a few seconds.

"Hello, Myrna," I said, looking toward the bar. I never saw anything, but it was a general point of focus.

"That's damned unnerving," said Escott.

"You used to say that about me."

"Only when you abruptly appeared out of thin air. She's not appeared at all."

"Would you be happy if she did?"

"I doubt it. Have you thought of hiring a ghost-breaker?"

Before I could reply, all the lights in the place went out, and I mean all of them. Only a little street glow filtered in from the red, diamond-shaped windows high above, plenty for me to use, but no one else. Startled exclamations came from the staff in the main room. I shot a sour look at Escott that he couldn't see, so I put it in my tone of voice. "That ain't gonna happen. Myrna stays."

He shifted. "Jack, have you just vanished?"

"No. Why?"

"Because I'm bloody freezing all of a sudden."

I addressed the general air, which had gone strangely cold. "Take it easy, Myrna, he didn't mean it. You're welcome here for as long as you want."

"I'm very sorry, Miss Myrna," he added, sounding humble.

"That was unconscionably rude of me. I apologize."

It was hard not to laugh. I held it in and waited. Eventually, the lobby bar light came on. None of the others, though.

"It seems there are good reasons not to speak ill of the dead." Escott had gone bone white, and I could hear his heart thumping. What I had come to take for granted had left him seriously shaken.

"Mr. Fleming? Is that you?" Wilton came out of the main room, his flashlight beam bouncing as he walked. "What happened?"

"Mr. Escott just has a misplaced sense of humor."

"Huh?"

"You know where the switchbox is?"

"Yeah. Reebie's down there now. Good thing you got these everyplace or we'd be breaking our legs." He lifted the flash. It had only been prudent to keep several scattered throughout the joint; all the bars had at least two, and every fire extinguisher had one next to it mounted on a clip.

The lights came on again. Escott remained pale and chagrined. "I think I should like a short walk," he announced. "Work off this chill."

"Chill?" said Wilton. "It must be thirty degrees outside."

"Thirty-four. Should warm me up nicely. Back in a tick." He turned on his heel and all but bolted out the doors.

"What's with him?"

I shrugged and took off my coat and hat. "Let's open."

Wilton followed me upstairs for the register cash, then left me to wrestle with last night's paperwork. It didn't take long; out of pure self-defense against being shown up too often by my bookkeeper, I'd bought an automatic calculating machine, which speeded things. Escott said I'd lose the ability to add sums on my own, but I wasn't overly bothered. Anything just so the books balanced, and more often than not they did. With a warm feeling of triumph, I wrapped the cash, clipped the checks together, and sealed both in a heavy envelope. There was a bank with a night-deposit box only a block distant. When I had a spare moment, I'd walk over. I never worried about thieves, though Wilton had other thoughts.

"One of these days you're gonna get clobbered, Mr. Fleming," he'd say. "Take your car and one of the guys along."

"I'll be fine. This way only one man gets clobbered." The would-be thief if he was dumb enough to tangle with me.

As I slipped the envelope into the desk safe and locked it, heels clacked purposefully upstairs. Her color high from the cold, Bobbi burst through my office door, wrapped tight in her fur-trimmed coat, a funny kind of hat slouching all over her blond head. Her arms were full of the latest papers, which she plopped before me. She came around my desk for a kiss and hug hello, then pointed to the newsprint.

"Have you read those? What they're saying about the kidnap case?"

"Charles did. Gave me the lowdown."

"It's infuriating! Doesn't anyone remember the Lindbergh baby?"

"Apparently not today. Why don't you write a letter to the paper?" I held up the worst of the stack. Its headline proved muckraking was still alive and kicking, high circulation being the owner's golden calf.

"I should have dinner with the editor of that rag, then hit him in the face with the main course. Gordy knows him; maybe he can get him to write sense. What is this world coming to? How did this happen? I thought the gang were all going to confess."

I gave her a short version of what Escott and I had speculated about Dugan's hypnotic resistance throwing a really big left-handed monkey wrench into the works.

Bobbi paced up and down the office, picking her gloves off with short, jerky movements. "If that Dugan gets away with it—"

"He won't. I promise."

A pause in her course. "Really?"

"Scout's honor, spit in his eye."

That pleased her, and a lot of the tension went out of her body. "Good. I'm glad there's someone around like you who can fix messes like this."

"Just the few that sock me in the face. Charles came over tonight, but took a walk. When he gets back, would you keep him company? He can use cheering up."

"I'd do that anyway." She opened the liquor cabinet by the windows, poured a small liqueur into a shot glass, and sipped delicately from it. "How is he?"

"Tired and antsy. Myrna spooked him." I told her what happened earlier.

Bobbi thought that funny but was sympathetic. "How is it he can room with you but have problems with a ghost?"

"Ask him sometime. I've wondered that myself." When she came close enough to my chair, I pulled her onto my lap. She finished her drink, putting the glass on the desk, and draped her arms around my shoulders. Very chummy we were. "You smell good."

"I should, I pay plenty for it."

But what I wanted was under her perfume. Intense hunger plucked at me on several levels. I forced it off to the side. "Did you talk to Adelle?"

"Not yet. No opportunity today, and I'm not going to bother her with this before her show."

"How about after?"

"If and when the time's right."

Her voice told me I should back off and let her figure it out. No problem. "How did things go with Roland and Faustine?"

The after-lunch meeting with Roland Lambert had been on time and was all business, which impressed her. Completely professional herself, Bobbi looked for it in others and respected the ones who came through. "We're set up for the weekend. The band has copies of their dance music, and I've got ads placed in tomorrow's paper announcing them."

"Remind me to put you on the payroll."

"Already am." True. She was on the clock like the rest whenever she came in to help.

"Then I should give you a raise."

She squirmed on my lap. "Feels like you've given yourself one already."

"Oh, no, that's your fault." I kissed the inside of her wrist, lips lingering on the pulse point, eyes closed to better listen to her heart. Its dark rhythm was inspiring in all kinds of ways.

"Hey, you're not giving me any chance to seduce you."

I pulled back, more than ready to cooperate. "A woman with ideas. I like it."

She moved off me, going to the windows. The curtains were open, as were the blinds. The glass was an inch thick, layered with wire mesh. It distorted the view of the outside a little, but after an incident last summer involving a grenade being lobbed through, I didn't mind the warping. Bobbi let the blinds down.

"I thought you were the exhibitionist type," I said.

"Only when the audience is blocks away, not just across

the street." She shut and locked the door. "I wanted you to see my new dress."

"Sure." I looked forward to getting her out of it.

Coat flung off, she did a turn. "Isn't this just the cutest thing?"

Her new favorite movie—which we'd gone to see three times now—was *Snow White*, and the dress was covered with colorful pictures of all the film's characters. I'd never seen anything like it: cockeyed, but on her, terrific.

"They had it in brown silk with the prints, but I thought the white background worked better. You don't think it's too springtime?"

"On you it's good for any season." She did look cute. "Now I get the hat."

"You noticed? It's called a Bashful hat."

It did resemble the hood things the dwarves wore. "You, my dear, are anything but bashful. C'mere."

"I should eat an apple first so you can wake me from the spell."

"We only have lemons on hand, but if you want I can go find—"

"Nah, stay here with me. It's cold outside."

She came over and pressed me into the chair. It was the plain, straight-backed kind with no arms. Bobbi hiked her new dress up and straddled me where I sat.

God, I loved it when she got new clothes.

She had on a slip and a garter belt to hold up her stockings, but nothing else underneath; any encumbrance between us came from my side of things, but she was already helping to loosen my pants. We'd discovered that making love while still partially dressed was very arousing for us. Once in a while I wondered why, but not to the point of trying to figure it out. It worked, and that's what really mattered.

With some shifting, we got my pants shoved down; the activity, along with quick, anxious kisses stolen in between, proved to be more than inspiring. She laughed softly, eyes bright and wicked, and eased onto me, going slow now. Her position put her throat at just the right level for more kissing. She had a thin silk scarf wrapped there to hide the marks I'd left from past encounters. I unwound it and held her steady as she rocked against me, taking her time. My corner teeth were out, but it was better when I waited. Not long, though, the way she was riding, her moves speeding up, her breath deepening for that final release.

She didn't have to tell me when. I sensed it, felt it, pulled her close, and seized it. She covered her mouth to muffle her cry, then went still, panting a little, her whole focus on what was happening to her body as I supped on her blood. It filled me, completed me. I had a different set of sensations, no less euphoric, and gave myself up to them for an unguessable time.

Bobbi gradually slumped. Worn out from the pleasure, I lazily thought. The liqueur she'd drunk imparted a unique taste to her blood, and I relished its rarity. It went to my head, as though I was slugging it back straight from the bottle. Filtered through her body, taken from a living human vein, there was nothing else quite like it.

But she wasn't dozing. Something was wrong. I made myself wake from my own ecstatic trance and stopped what I was doing. Her head lolled, eyes shut.

Oh, damn.

My heart swooping with near panic, I got us untangled and carried her over to the couch. She was completely limp, passed out. Blood seeped from the wounds I made. Too much? I didn't know. I pressed my handkerchief against them and said her name.

"C'mon, honey, don't do this. Bobbi?"

She was a long, long, awful minute coming around. In that time I got the office liquor cabinet open, grabbed a bottle, and returned to kneel next to her. My fingers trembled as I smeared brandy over her lips, touched a few drops to her tongue. She moved a little, making a face.

"That's it, sweetheart. Come back. Wake up."

"Mm?" She tried to move her head away.

"It's all right, you're all right." Please, God I hoped so. "Just stay put, and you'll be fine."

Her eyelids fluttered but didn't come all the way open. She looked sluggish and puzzled. "What . . . ?"

I caught up her hands. They were icy. "I'm sorry."

"Why? What's going on?"

"I took too much from you. Made you pass out."

"Oh, don't be silly." But she saw I was serious and tried to sit up. "Jack, it's nothing, don't make a big fuss."

She wasn't in the mood to listen, so I stood and put my clothes into order again, needing the distraction. My hands shook so hard I could hardly tuck in my shirttail.

"I'm fine, Jack. Really I am."

Impossible to look her in the face. "I could have killed you."

A pause. "No, you wouldn't."

She didn't understand. Once with another woman I'd come close to going over the edge by taking things too far. I'd been so lost, was so drunk with the feeling of it that I very nearly—

Bobbi didn't know about that. She never would. "Look, it got out of hand. I should have gone to the Yards last night. It keeps my hunger in check, keeps me safe with you."

"Safe? What the hell are you talking about? I'm perfectly

fine. I just passed out from it is all, I've done it before."

"Not like this."

"Jack, it's nothing to go crazy over. Will you settle down? Please?"

I sat on the couch next to her, staring at the floor. "I think you should have a doctor check you tomorrow."

An exasperated sigh. She reached for my hand and held tight. "What's going on?"

"I just had the bejesus scared out of me. Scared to death I'd hurt you."

"Well, I'm not hurt."

I resolved to never forgo future trips to the Stockyards to feed. Even if things were as she said, I would never allow the risk to recur. No more complacence.

She moved closer and held me.

I grabbed her back as hard as I dared. "God, if anything happened to you, I'd lose my mind."

"I know," she whispered. "But the bad old days are gone. Nothing's going to happen to either of us. The bad stuff's over now. I'm fine. What we were doing was completely wonderful and just overwhelmed me is all, and let me tell you, I love it. So stop being afraid."

Fear was a good healthy thing to have, so long as it didn't paralyze me. It was my changed nature that was so terrifying; no escape from that. If I respected the rules and kept my head, she'd be safe. If not, then I had no business being with her. Animal blood fed me, but human blood held so much more: nourishment, intoxication, addiction, the potential for obsession. Give in to it, and the woman I loved would die.

"Hey." She gently tapped my nose. "Wake up; you're too quiet."

"Fear and guilt," I said. "They'll talk to me all night if I let them. They make a hell of a team."

"There's no room for them in this league. Tell 'em to take a hike."

Her hazel eyes could see more inside me than I ever could. They saw all of it, accepted, loved. She made me want to be a better man, made it feel like I'd already gotten there. "Do you know how much I love you?"

"Yeah." A smile, a little crooked, warm as heaven. "I do."

About half an hour later, I was in the lobby, trying to get back to business as usual by glad-handing the first customers coming in. The normality of it helped push my fear away, but not too very far. I wanted to atone, apologize, grovel, whatever it took to make it up to Bobbi. Except she didn't want any of that. All right. I'd play it how she wanted, but I would be more careful. Before I touched her again, I'd go to the Stockyards and take care of my deadly appetite.

It was still only a weeknight; I wore a dark suit, not a tuxedo, but Bobbi said I looked flashy as a new car. Mirrors being useless to me, I relied on her judgment when it came to clothes and grooming details.

Along with some new faces, a few regulars turned up, delighted to see me. Each and every one of them got the smile and handshake, and the brief instant of eye contact where I told them they would have a great time here tonight. Hypnosis stuff made my head hurt, especially when I was hungry, but it was worth the discomfort for the boost in business. I gave a nod to Wilton to confirm drinks were half price until the show started.

Bobbi had gone to the backstage area to make sure the band

and the rest of the talent were ready. If she hadn't had aspirations of her own to look after, I'd have hired her permanently as my general manager. More often than not, she had singing work at other clubs but was happy to help with bookings when she had the time. Otherwise, it was up to me, and I didn't have nearly her experience, nor was I up and about during the day for auditions. Things would run more smoothly if not for that restriction, but my alternative to having half a life was being all the way dead, so I never complained, even to myself.

She came out front, still amazingly fresh in her *Snow White* dress with the cartoon characters all over. I'd never look at that movie the same way ever again.

"We're all set to go," she said, slipping an arm through mine.

"Great. The drummer still sober?"

"Like a judge on election day. Roland!" She smiled past me as the doorman ushered in Roland Lambert. He was natty in a vicuna overcoat and a big smile, his hair lounge-lizard slick. You could read by the shine on his shoes. "You didn't say you'd be by again."

"I wanted to get the lay of the land," he said as we shook hands. "Always helps the act to know the routine of a place."

"Where's Faustine?" I asked.

"At our hotel, resting. She spent the day shopping and wore herself out. I slept late, so now I'm ready for something to do. We'll be neck and neck again for our debut, though. Will you be at our rehearsal tomorrow?"

"Tied up elsewhere, but Bobbi said you were great, and that's enough for me."

He cut her a little bow. "I'm honored and forever grateful, good lady."

"Hm, you have been in England, haven't you?" she said, pleased.

"For far too long, I'd forgotten just how charming American girls can be." He served this up with a smile and an eye twinkle. The way he did it made it more flattery than serious flirtation. Bobbi seemed to like it just fine. I wasn't worried about her falling for his line, but had it worked on Adelle?

"Before things get too crowded, let me find you a nice table," she said. She slipped an arm through his and led him off. I had a feeling she'd work Gordy and Adelle into the conversation at some point. Hopefully, he'd get the right idea from it.

Escott came in, his face red from the cold, which suited him more than that sheet-white he'd shown earlier.

"Feeling better?" I asked, as he shrugged from his coat and handed it and his hat over to the check girl.

"Much improved, thank you. I just wanted a bit of air."

"Sure." Might as well pretend to go along with him. He'd been gone nearly two hours, which is a hell of a lot of air for anyone in Chicago in January. "Like a little something to warm up?"

"A small brandy would not be unwelcome. Thank you."

I gave Wilton a high sign, and he poured out a generous shot of our best. Like the rest of the staff, he knew Escott's drinks were always on the house.

"It will be a bit of a wait warming this," he said, cupping the snifter in his hand. His fingers and nails looked blue. "Left my gloves at the Gladwell house. I'll call and ask if they've been found. May I have the use of your office phone?"

"Help yourself."

He gave a genial nod and went upstairs, almost as at home here as in his own place. Apparently he'd forgotten Myrna's not-so-subtle presence for the time being. I wondered about the gloves business, whether it was genuine or just an excuse to talk to Vivian. Probably both. I silently wished him luck and shook hands with the next group of customers coming in from the cold.

Right behind them were two of Gordy's top bodyguards, Lowrey and Strome. Well, I'd been warned there would be more talks tonight.

They weren't as big as Gordy, few men were, but they made up for it with weapons and they would have some brains. Normally, I don't welcome guys wearing overly padded suits meant to hide their shoulder holsters, but these were almost family. In a sideways kind of direction.

" 'Lo, boys. Anything up?"

"Just checking things, Mr. Fleming," said Strome. He'd been with Gordy for a long time and had early on learned to call me mister. He didn't know about me being a vampire, only that I now and then helped his boss out on special jobs, and that I was extremely dangerous to cross. Gordy had passed on to me the gossip about my reputation with the gangs. I'd found it to be both amusing and daunting. I liked their respect but didn't care for the possibility of having it tested by some wiseacre. Strome was a prudent sort with nothing to prove.

"Gordy on his way?" I asked.

"Yeah."

"Bristow, too?"

"Yeah." Strome was as loquacious as his boss.

"How are negotiations going?"

Lowrey shrugged. Cut from the same block of granite as Strome, his dark eyes both looked made of glass, the effect reinforced by the fact they were not quite in line. It was a subtle thing; sometimes I didn't know which eye to look at.

They checked their heavy overcoats, the girl staggering off under the combined burden. The doorman ushered in two more men of the same type, Bristow's boys from last night. The four bruisers looked at one another, faces dead, arms loose at their sides, with me in the middle like the referee at a free-for-all match. You couldn't cut the air between with a diamond drill. I almost heard growling. No love lost among this bunch.

The girl came out again and read the mood right. Her big-eyed gaze hit me with a question on what to do; I smiled and jerked my chin, silently indicating for her to scram. She scurried back to her checkroom. Wilton seemed ready to duck behind his marble bar.

Hog Bristow chose that moment to bull in, making everyone jump. He instantly noticed the tension and settled an accusing, bloodshot glare on me.

"What the hell is this?" he demanded.

The lobby lights flickered and went out.

5

I HAD enough street glow to see by, but not the other guys. For them the place was pitch black. Both sides stepped away from each other and drew guns.

"Wait—" I began, then the lights flared on again, the sudden brightness making me wince. I was still in the middle, looking everywhere at once and hoping to God no one got stupid.

"What the hell . . ." said Bristow, his hand inside his coat.

"Not now, Myrna," I muttered through clenched teeth.

"Who's Myrna?" he demanded, pulling a semi-auto clear of its shoulder holster. He aimed it square in my direction.

The lights remained on, but no one relaxed.

"Who's Myrna?"

"Someone with a sense of humor." *And bad timing,* I silently added. In the past when there was trouble, Myrna played with the lights as a warning to me. I could appreciate her concern, but things had been under control without her help.

"Where is she?"

"Backstage. We got electric problems, crossed wires. Throw a switch the wrong way, and this happens. It's nothing to worry about. You can put away the heat."

He threw me a glare, then nodded to his men. I sent the same message to Gordy's crew, and everyone eased back. They were all walleyed now, trying to look around the lobby while keeping watch on each other. Wilton had vanished behind his marble-topped bar. I could just hear whispering and thought he was praying until I caught Myrna's name in his litany.

"Get your wires fixed," said Bristow, holstering his gun.

"I certainly will."

He looked hungover and bloated but sober. If Gordy kept on with his plan to keep the man drinking, there'd be no need to put him out of the way; his liver would do him in. None too soon. These guys were far too edgy. Other things were going on under the surface, and I could guess it meant tough times for Gordy. I fastened Bristow with a not-too-evil eye and a warmly sincere smile, desperate to calm things down. He was the key. "Nice to see you again, Mr. Bristow. Sorry about the rough start, but I'm sure you'll have a fine time here tonight."

Hostility melting away, his expression went blank for a few seconds. With his men frowning, we shook hands; his grip was reassuringly lax.

Bingo. I'd pinned him square and had to fight to keep from visibly sagging with relief. There would be no gunplay, at least not from him. "I think you'll be able to work things out with Gordy as well," I added, softly confidential with no threat in it, nothing to alarm his guards.

"You do?" Sleepwalker voice.

"Gordy's a stand-up guy, runs things great. No need to make changes, don't you think?"

He had no time for a reply; Gordy came in, two more men along, one of his own and the other with Bristow's crowd, creating a distracting shift in the men already here. The hypnotic priming was over, but even this small touch would be sufficient for the present. If Gordy wanted more, with specific instructions, I could oblige later. For now I was just grateful to get the burning fuse out of the powder keg. Neutral territory my ass.

"Fleming," he said. A greeting with an infinitesimally raised eyebrow. He'd picked up on the leftover tension.

"Gordy. Good to see you." I held onto the pleased-host face. After all, I was just a saloonkeeper. "Is your party all here? Ready to go in?"

Bristow came more alert but with only a shadow of his initial belligerence. "Yeah, let's get this show on the road." He led the way in, his men following. The first two shot me a fishy glare, suspicious that I'd been up to something. They'd have a fine debate trying to figure it.

"What did you do?" Gordy wanted to know.

I kept up the innocent act. "Just greasing wheels. You may find him in a better mood than before, but I can't promise how long it'll last."

The corners of his eyes crinkled. "Thanks."

Wilton rose from behind the bar. I made a thumbs-up at him, but it didn't do much to clear his worry. The check girl ventured to poke her head out. I signed for her to come take Gordy's things. He granted her a benign smile and a twenty-dollar tip. She nearly floated away. Chances were she'd risk coming in again tomorrow.

I wanted a change of subject. "You follow that kidnap case

in the papers?" Gordy got updates about the job from me as part of our usual shop talk. "The one Charles has been working on?"

His attention shifted unhurriedly from the girl to me. She had great legs. "Yeah. Bad deal on that society bum getting clear."

"Dugan's not clear yet."

"Oh, yeah?"

"I'm going after him."

"Sounds good." No need for him to ask for details. He knew I'd fill him in after the dust had settled.

"I may want particulars on the rest of the gang. Stuff the cops wouldn't have."

"Whatever you need."

"You know any of those guys?"

"Not personally. They're nothing. Some theft, some hot checks, one guy shoots morphine. Small-change chumps. My people wouldn't use 'em for anything, especially the doper. I can have 'em all bumped if you want. Even the fancy-pants." Gordy could arrange a hit on anyone, any place, especially if they were in jail.

"Don't think that will be necessary, but I'll keep it in mind."

He gave a minimal shrug. Offering helpful information or death were all one to him. Guards before and behind, he lumbered off to the main room just as the band warmed into the first dance number for the night.

Wilton's smile was fixed and brittle. Gordy had been speaking low, but perhaps our conversation had carried.

I went over. "You okay?"

"I guess." He didn't sound convinced.

"Did I hear you talking to Myrna?"

He nodded. "Seemed the thing to do. Told her to stop with the lights. She's a great kidder, huh?"

"Yeah, so's a lot of people who come in here. You know?"

"Yeah, sure, Mr. Fleming," he said slowly. "Everyone's a kidder."

"Glad you understand that."

His gaze flicked behind me. Another party coming in. Good, we could both do with something normal. "Back to work," I said, cheerful again.

They were high-hat types I'd not seen before, three couples, very well-dressed and young, but old enough to drink or they'd not have gotten by the doorman. There were too many at once for me to deal with, but I managed to snag the first man with my usual welcome speech and beamed charm at the rest. They were oddly tight-lipped as they took in the lobby; it usually inspired approving murmurs.

"Oh, do come along, Anthony dear," said one of the girls to the man. Her eyes were bright and guarded, passing right over me. Her message was clear: stop wasting time with the servants, dah-ling. No skin off my nose, their money spent as good as anyone else's, and they generally had more to throw around.

Anthony dear took her arm, and the group wafted in, keeping their hats and coats. Barhoppers sampling a new place, I figured. They'd have at least one drink then decide where to go afterwards, but the breed was more common on Fridays and Saturdays. This bunch either kept bankers' hours at work or didn't work at all.

The main room was about a third full, very good for the middle of the week. The high-hatters were clumped at one of the lower booths just inside the entry. They were trying to figure out the drinks order with the waiter while shedding their coats. Anthony dear saw me, then looked elsewhere a little too casually. What was his game? Order pad in hand, the waiter hurried off to the bar.

I made the rounds, stopping a few moments with the regulars, making sure everyone had what they wanted. Gordy wasn't at his down-front table tonight. He and Bristow were high on the third tier, removed from the noisy crowd and music, the better for talking. They seemed to be deep into things, heads forward, faces unreadable. I couldn't tell how well my influence was working on Bristow, but I expected Gordy would let me know.

By the time I reached the bar, the waiter was back from serving his posh table. "Those new ones in the far booth," I said. "What did they want?" You can tell a lot about people from their choice of drink.

"Four martinis, a horse's neck, and a Four Roses. A triple."

"Which one got the whiskey?"

"Skinny guy on the end."

That was Anthony dear. What had him so nervous to want that much ninety proof? The booths each had a small lamp; the low light picked out the red flush of his skin from the booze he'd busily slugged back. If he kept up that pace, he'd put himself in a coma.

Roland Lambert and Bobbi had a table close to the stage. As a matter of habit I noted their drinks: grape juice on the rocks for her, coffee for him, apparently still on the wagon. Not many were up to resisting the call of demon rum and its many cousins, so I gave him credit for that. I wanted to like him, and would have, had I missed seeing him fooling around on his new wife. Maybe he and Faustine had a free-love kind of marriage, if that's what those were called. I didn't get it. If you don't plan to stick with your one partner through thick or thin, then why bother to team up permanent?

Bobbi laughed in response to whatever Roland was telling her. They seemed to be getting on fine. Show-biz chat probably. His past experience in Hollywood would be irresistible to her; she'd want to know everything as part of her preparation for breaking into movies.

She rarely talked about it with me anymore, knowing how I usually reacted to the subject, which was to clam up. She sometimes mistook that for anger, but it was my way to avoid saying anything stupid—like asking her not to go. That was a tiger trap I wasn't about to drop into. She'd helped me realize my dreams with this club; it was only fair to do the same for her, even if my heart wasn't in it.

Part of me tiredly repeated I wouldn't lose her; another part tormented with the likelihood that she'd leave and never return. It had happened before. No matter that the circumstances of losing Maureen—the woman who gave me this dark change, a woman I'd loved just as much—had been very different; the scars were in my memory. On bad nights they still bled. If I didn't watch myself, Bobbi would suffer from my past pain. Neither of us needed that.

Bobbi saw me watching her, smiled, and waved. I smiled back, not quite ready to join them. It was close to show time, anyway.

Consciously shrugging off the mood, I strolled to one side of the dance floor where a microphone was set up. I used to be awkward, but coaching from Bobbi and plenty of practice turned this aspect of my job into an enjoyable boost, just the thing for a sagging spirit. Applause helped, even if it was only a polite smatter.

I caught the band leader's eye partway through the current number. The music slowed and softened, and a blinding spotlight smacked me hot in the face. I switched on the mike and introduced myself. The regulars clapped; the high-hatters gave curious stares. I thanked everyone for coming in, told them they were lucky to be here tonight, then explained why by introducing the lovely and talented star of stage, screen, and radio, Adelle Taylor.

The band boomed her lead-in fanfare, the house lights dimmed, and the spot swung to fix on her as she glided from the wings, taking center stage for her first song. I made an unobtrusive exit, job finished for the night. Anyone could have done it, but I'd grown to enjoy those few seconds of attention, playing the good host.

Now I was free to invite myself over to Roland's table, gesturing him back as he started to rise. "We're informal here. Is Bobbi treating you right?" I took a seat next to her, getting comfortable.

"I'm learning plenty about Chicago," he said, pitched barely loud enough to be heard over Adelle's voice. Dancers sifted by, pairing up on the floor in front of the stage. "I used to only pass through here between Hollywood and New York. Seems I missed a lot."

"You planning to stay?"

"We haven't decided yet. Faustine and I want to look around first. I need to get used to the U.S. of A. again, and she needs to meet it, period. She's looking forward to working again, if she can find any in her line."

"Isn't there a ballet company here in town?"

"She's checking that, trying to get a decent agent." He pulled out a gold cigarette case with his initials on it and offered us a smoke. Bobbi declined, thinking it was bad for her throat. I tried one. It was black with no filter. The taste was strong and exotic, reminding me of Faustine.

"They should be glad to have a Russian-trained dancer around," I said.

Roland shrugged. "Anyone would be, but there might not be much open for me here as an actor. I'd thought I'd talk with Adelle, find out what sort of opportunities are in radio. God knows I can fake nearly any accent in the British Isles by now." His gaze rested fondly on Adelle as she shimmered in the spot, her rich voice rising with the music. "If there's some Shakespeare afoot, I'm sure she'll help me get in."

I kept my face frozen as best I could, but Bobbi shifted next to me; she'd have to trust that I'd keep my yap shut, and I would. For now.

A waiter came over, wondering if we wanted anything. I gave my usual negative reply and asked Roland if his coffee needed hotting up. He asked for a large glass of ice water. The waiter nodded and left.

Bobbi said, "I was just pointing out local celebrities to Roland, but I don't think he believed me."

"How so?"

Roland indicated a direction with his cigarette. "That big guy up there, he really is with the mob?"

There was only one truly big guy in the place, so I didn't have to turn to know he meant Gordy. "Let's just say he's a businessman and leave it at that." I gave a quick wink and smile.

"But he's a friend of yours?"

"And Bobbi, too. Gordy can be a good friend."

"He's like Al Capone though?"

"He's a businessman. Chicago style."

"And Adelle's seeing him?"

"They like each other fine. He respects her. Treats her right. Looks after her very closely. Like the army at Fort Knox. Smart men don't cross him." Bobbi tapped her foot warningly against my ankle, but I judged I'd dropped enough hints for Roland to think about.

"But a gangster?"

"Love's screwy, and you can't argue with it."

Finally Roland seemed to catch what I was throwing and eased back. "True. I count myself quite lucky Faustine felt inclined toward me in that way."

Except, apparently, for those hot moments in Adelle's dressing room last night. I hoped bringing Gordy so firmly into the picture would spark some common sense in Roland, keep him from a repeat performance. Much of that would also be up to Adelle, it taking two to tango and so on. Hopefully, Bobbi could take care of that part of the job a little later. I planned to keep Roland busy telling me about European politics during her set break, giving her a chance to go backstage for a girl-to-girl chat with Adelle.

"Who's the college crowd?" Roland asked, his focus shifting to the high-hat table. "They don't seem to be enjoying themselves."

I'd noticed. They had their drinks, but no smiles to go with them. Anthony showed a very red face, having drained his triple in an amazingly short time, but was still upright and responding to conversation. "They're new. Probably still getting used to the joint."

"I've seen them at other clubs I've worked," Bobbi put in.

"Oh yeah?"

She shrugged. "I don't know the names, except for the black-haired girl next to the skinny guy. She's that society deb, Marie Kennard. Oh, don't worry, Jack, she's allowed to drink now. Her coming out was enough years ago. I was with the band singing at her big party. Thought she'd be married by now. They usually are."

Roland chuckled. "My dear, by now she could have done that, gone to Reno, and shed her husband like an old skin. It's embarrassingly easy these days. Ask Adelle."

Bobbi's mouth popped open with shock. "Roland, I didn't mean—"

He stubbed out his cigarette and patted her hand, eyes twinkling. "Of course you didn't, I'm a poltroon, but I wanted to see the look on your face. It was darling. I promise to behave in the future. Actually, Adelle and I are quite easy about those times. I was a perfect beast and had it coming. We've forgiven and forgotten. Certainly she deserved a better man than I was back then. I hope she's done so with that gangster fellow, but one can't help but be uneasy. I still care for her—as a friend."

"She's never been happier. I heard her say so."

He pantomimed being shot in the heart. "Oh, a mortal wound to my vanity, but you can heal it in an instant if you'll honor me with a dance."

He was smooth. Great delivery. He swept Bobbi onto the dance floor before she knew what hit her. I should have been jealous, but wasn't. She'd get her balance back soon enough, then he wouldn't know what hit him.

Young Anthony dear of the high-hats had left his group. I wouldn't have noticed his absence except for his friends staring my way. Soon as I looked, they went into a too-casual huddle. They must have been talking about me, but I couldn't imagine why. The only notoriety I had was over six months out of date, having to do with a murder victim found in Crymsyn's basement. It got my picture in the papers, but the case was long over and done.

I thought about vanishing and drifting over for some eaves-dropping but couldn't risk it. I'd pulled that stunt plenty of times, but only in places where I never expected to return. Lady Crymsyn already had a resident ghost; no need to start rumors that the owner was one as well. Instead, I smoked Roland's exotic cigarette, deciding I liked my own home-grown brand better, and stayed put. It was good not to be doing anything strenuous. Despite the blood I'd taken from Bobbi earlier, I wasn't fully revived. Last night had been a lot of work. Very shortly, I'd make a bank run to deposit receipts, then stop at the Stockyards for some serious restoration. Until then, loafing was allowed.

Roland and Bobbi finished their turn on the floor and came back. She asked him to repeat a story he'd related about danc-ing with Marion Davies at a Hearst mansion weekend party. He had my full attention, since I'd always had a soft spot for that actress.

Apparently she was a good egg with a better sense of humor than William Randolph. She'd been in a costume epic and wanted a sword-fighting lesson from Roland, since it looked like fun. He'd managed to smuggle a good supply of liquor onto the teetotaling grounds of the estate at San Simeon, though, and had been drunk as a skunk at the time.

"I dimly recall chasing her around the swimming pool with a dessert spoon instead of a sword," he said. "We didn't want to do each other an injury, you see. Marion was laughing so hard she fell into the pool, and it was only gentlemanly that I jump in to save her. We were having a fine time splashing about until Hearst turned up. Seemed he didn't care to have his lady friend dripping wet with her clothes clinging to her, not with all the other guests to see, anyway. Marion laughed it off, but the next morning I woke up on an airplane heading back to Hollywood with no idea how I'd gotten there. She later sent me a note, apologizing. I still have it somewhere. Lovely girl."

Bobbi asked him to tell another one, but Escott came in and walked over. Whatever his phone call to Vivian had been about left him in a good mood. He bowed over Bobbi's hand, smiling warmly and complimenting her on the *Snow White* dress. That made her sparkle a little brighter. If I had a soft spot for Marion Davies, then Bobbi had one for Escott. Must have been his accent. I introduced him to Roland. They said the usual things, sized each other up, then Roland asked what part of London he was from.

"Oh, several places at least," was Escott's light but gently discouraging reply. He didn't talk much about his past. "I understand you had some success on the stage there. Quite an accomplishment. May I inquire what productions and theaters?"

Roland was more than pleased to share stories about past triumphs, then with a prompt from Bobbi, talk changed to the Gladwell kidnapping. Escott kept things on the most general of terms, but she wanted details. He seemed ready to supply them. Then Anthony dear came back to his friends.

"Good lord," Escott muttered under his breath.

"Something wrong?" Bobbi asked.

He wore a peculiar, stretched smile. "A slight digestive upset. I think I'll see if the barman has something to help." He excused himself and walked unhurriedly away, his back firmly to us and the other table.

Roland looked puzzled. "That was a quick onset of symptoms."

"I'll see if he needs a doctor," I said, excusing myself, too. Careful not to make a beeline, I threaded between tables, playing host, until reaching the bar. Escott had a brandy instead of a bromide in front of him.

"What's up?" I asked.

The left side of his mouth twitched, and he remained turned from the room. "That young fellow with the large group is related to our infamous Hurley Gilbert Dugan, that is what's up, old man."

It was a struggle, but I resisted the urge to check over my shoulder at the high-hatters. "You're kidding."

"I assure you I am not. He's one Anthony Brockhurst, a distant cousin. His picture was in the papers, those society events Dugan went to with his late mother. This is no coincidence. What the devil could he be doing here?" he wondered, irritated.

"Following you."

"Or you."

"How would he—oh." If Dugan remembered our hypnosis session he'd be curious and ferret out my partnership with Escott pretty quick. Part of that could be asking a few staunch supporters to go to my club and play spy. Now I understood the stares and backhand talking. How much had Dugan told them? Were they in on the kidnapping? I got an itch to corner Anthony dear for a private "chat." The rest of them, too. They couldn't all be as crazy as Dugan.

"This is not amusing," said Escott, his face sour.

"Dugan probably had you under a microscope within an hour of his arrest. Those birds will know we work together. No sense staying glued to the bar, so relax."

"I suppose not. I just hadn't expected this, particularly from a pack of bloody amateurs."

It did rankle. Usually we were the ones shadowing people

and making them nervous. "Well, I wasn't exactly watching for tails when we left home tonight."

"I advise a change in that for the time being."

"No kidding. Think Dugan's got a real detective after us?"

"It's a possibility to consider. I would, in his place." Escott turned around, one elbow casually resting on the bar. Despite his tense mood, he showed nothing of it in his posture or expression now, which was that of a man free of cares, in a celebratory mood, even. He was one hell of an actor.

Still too pissed off, I knew better than to try mimicking him and stayed in place. "You see any contenders?"

After a few minutes, during which he would take a mental picture of everyone in the room and compare it to the filing cabinet in his brain, he said no. "None that I know or have seen, at any rate. There are none here with the look."

I could trust his conclusion. He was better at spotting cops or PIs than Gordy, which was saying a lot. "So we just have the society types to worry about, huh?"

"Indeed. They're amateurs, which is something of a relief, but one never knows what tomfoolery they could get up to."

True. This wasn't our usual kind of opposition where we could swap fists in a back alley with mugs who knew the ropes. Anthony's well-scrubbed and perfumed bunch seemed fit for nothing more harrowing than a college fraternity party. They were playing way outside their field.

Escott pretended to watch the dancers as they swung in time to Adelle's latest song. "I'm getting the impression they're waiting for someone. Dugan, perhaps?"

Hell. I didn't want him here dirtying up the place. "Maybe. I can find out. If any of them leaves for the john, they'll have a detour they won't remember."

He puffed a laugh.

"Take your drink back, make like everything's normal, and lemme see how this plays. Tell Bobbi I'm working, whatever's safe to say in front of Roland. She'll get it. Gordy's here—"

"I noticed. Isn't that Hog Bristow with him?"

I'd not mentioned him, but I wasn't surprised he knew the man by sight. Escott was a walking encyclopedia when it came to crime bosses. "Yeah, they're talking business, though, Gordy's gonna be working on that."

"Just as well. No need to trouble him with such a minor annoyance."

Minor? I hoped he was right.

We went our separate ways. I took my time, again stopping at tables, but managing to miss Anthony's. Carefully not stealing a glance at him or the rest of his crowd, I felt them watching me as I left.

Between the lobby and the main room there's a small blind spot in the passage, just this side of the portrait. It wasn't anything planned by the designer, just turned out that way, and at times like this it was very useful. Once there, I vanished and streamed quickly back toward the party.

I hovered over Anthony's table but only picked up a word or two; it was hard to hear with Adelle's singing going on. They were a sulky bunch, not saying much.

Then a woman, Marie Kennard by the bored tone of her voice, said, "I think he's gone for a while, Anthony. Time for another call."

"Right," came the reply. I sensed Anthony's slow exit from his seat. "I'll be a minute."

"We'll keep what's left of your drink warm."

He grunted. I tagged along as he walked. The music faded, replaced by the brief creak of hinges as he closed us into the confines of the lobby phone booth. Coin in the slot, dialing, then he greeted whoever was on the other end of the line.

"Hello, hello? Gilbert? . . . Yes, it is I, who else?"

I experienced a warm feeling of satisfaction, slightly marred by the frustration of getting only half the conversation. I'd have given a lot for Hurley Gilbert Dugan's side.

Anthony went on. "He's left. . . . No, I don't know where. . . . Follow him? But you told us to stay together and not draw notice. . . . Oh, bother this. Why are you so interested in him? . . . Well, be that way. We're only trying to help. . . . All right. All right. . . . No, I'm not drunk. . . . Yes, I'm sure I haven't the least idea where he's gone. Probably in the building if you've not seen him. His friend is still here. I think they spotted us, though. . . . No, we did not do anything; he's a detective and must know his trade. . . . All right. Yes, I'll call again if I see him. . . . Well, don't let yourself freeze. . . . Yes, good-bye."

He snorted and hung up in disgust.

"He's completely mad," he said, apparently to himself, then shivered. I'd not been careful about avoiding contact with him. He shoved the folding door open and slipped clear. I trailed again; he headed for the main room instead of the john, which was too bad. Not that he was in any condition for hypnosis. His slurred speech told me the futility of that ploy, but there are other ways of getting information that don't leave marks. I intended to ambush him in the passage, but he moved too fast for me to materialize and grab him.

Damnation. Aiming for his table, I got there just as he sat down. He repeated his private comment to his friends.

"He's going through with it?" a girl asked. Marie Kennard again. She sounded less bored now.

"If that Fleming fellow ever decides to cooperate. Blast. Gilbert will catch his death out there waiting for that fool."

Interesting. So Dugan himself was on the watch for me? I didn't want to miss him, but I also didn't want to miss whatever else this pretty crowd might have to say.

"Oh, Anthony, don't make such a face," Marie said, petulant. "Gilbert won't blame you if the man doesn't cooperate. He'll just go home."

"Be sure to remind him of that, won't you?"

"I'll write a note in my diary. How much longer must we endure this place?"

"At least an hour more."

"So long? How perfectly dreadful."

Now, that just hurt my feelings.

"Marie, it's not as though we're on the front lines in a trench, so put on a brave face and think of how this is helping Gilbert. We're spies in enemy territory, sacrifice is de rigueur, and it is in a noble cause."

"I'll feel more noble after another drink."

They impatiently called for a waiter. I waited for more information, but they seemed to be stuck in their collective sulk; Anthony ordered another Four Roses triple. Hardy type. Might as well leave and see what opportunities Dugan presented, if any. I felt my way back to the blind spot and hoped no one would be there when I materialized again.

It was clear, and just as well. Dizziness struck with a vengeance, sending me staggering as though I'd been blackjacked. I swayed against the wall like a drunk, both hands on it to steady myself. Hot and cold shakes waved over my body, retreating slowly and leaving a clear message: get to the Stockyards before the hollow ache inside went out of control. I couldn't push further without risking all kinds of grief. When my version of hunger got too serious, common sense and restraint were the first to go. Food now, fun and games later.

No activity in the lobby. The check girl chatted with Wilton; both stood a bit straighter when the boss appeared, but I didn't mind so long as their work was caught up and the customers were promptly served. I gave the girl a message to repeat to Escott: that I'd be gone for less than an hour and to keep an eye on our special guests for me.

"An hour?" Wilton asked when she'd left.

"Got an errand."

"You okay, Mr. Fleming? You don't look so good."

"Just a little warm. You remember that fancy-suit stick who was just in here using the phone? Look out for him, see if he makes more calls, and write down when. If he or anyone else asks for me, I'm still around but unavailable."

Wilton nodded, and I went upstairs. In the office I got the cash envelope from the safe, locked the door, and avoided the lobby by using the back alley exit to leave the club.

A slow walk around the building to the parking lot didn't flush any obvious stakeout. I fully expected one. Anthony gave me to understand Dugan might be lying in wait. I'd be pleased to find him, but only after I was in better shape.

Eyes peeled, I gave everything in view a good scrutiny, but the street looked the same as ever, no unfamiliar cars at the curbs or extra shadows in the doorways, just the wind blowing stray paper around. Nothing conspicuous here but myself, doubled by the fact I'd left my hat and coat behind. The cold didn't affect me as much as it had before my change. On a run to the Stockyards outer coverings weren't necessary; I moved faster without them.

If Dugan was on watch, where would he be hiding? My skin prickled as I imagined the kinds of things that could go wrong. Did he have a gun aimed at my chest? Hard luck for him if he fired. Metal bullets, whether silver or lead, can't kill me, but they hurt like hell, and getting shot would put me in exactly the right mood to break his neck. With Gordy's help, disposing of a body was no great challenge.

But all was quiet. I almost wished otherwise. It would bring an end to the matter for damn sure.

Uneasy but not able to wait, I got in my Buick, the cooled-off motor obligingly turning and catching on the first try. We'd not had any really bad weather lately, and it was still holding in the low thirties. Moderate for this time of year. That had been of great concern to Vivian Gladwell in her worry for Sarah. The girl's wasted, sleeping face kept popping to mind as I backed from my parking spot. It was depressing, made me feel like I'd failed her by not completely removing Dugan as a threat. I'd done my best, but would just have to try again.

For distraction I put the radio on loud and caught Fred Astaire in the middle of "The Way You Look Tonight." We didn't share the same key, but I sang along for the hell of it and wondered if I could get him and Johnny Green's band to play at the club. They were famous and likely pretty busy, but it was worth a try. I'd ask Bobbi to look into it.

No one seemed to be in my wake on the short drive to the bank. They were either very good at tailing or didn't exist. The rearview mirror remained clear of anything troubling, though there was plenty of traffic. A disappointment, but not much of one. This wouldn't be the first time I'd gotten things wrong, but it always was better to err on the side of caution. I took a careful look around when I left the car to slip the money into the night deposit, but I was quite alone.

I was more cagey on the second leg of my trip, making a lot of turns and double-backs. A couple times I thought someone was following, but I shook them too easily for it to be anything but my imagination. After ten minutes of circling blocks and beating out stop signals, my guts gave a sharp twist as a reminder. My corner teeth were beginning to bud all on their own. Next would come the tunnel vision. After that, a strange, lightheaded kind of insanity.

Hitting the gas, I endeavored to outrun it.

In order to feed the country, the Stockyards had to run day and night, but some areas slowed down sufficiently to allow me to get in without drawing notice. My being able to vanish was a big help, allowing me to remain out of sight the whole time except for those few moments it took to feed. I knew the place so thoroughly by now that I could get around quite well in that state. It made things easier on the shoe leather, too. Less cleaning.

No such convenience tonight. I'd stretched too thin. Sure, I could still vanish, but coming back would mean another bout of sickness and having jelly for legs, not something I wanted to go through again. Playing ghost could wait until after I'd fed.

I had plenty of physical strength left, though; boosting over one of the fences was easy, and again when I found a pen full of prospects. Now all I had to worry about was keeping some cow from bowling me over on my ass. I'd done the milking plenty of times growing up on the old family farm; cattle could be skittish but were generally cooperative if you knew what you were doing.

Picking an animal in the small enclosure, I calmed it to my presence, knelt, and went in quick and clean on a leg vein, supping deeply. The lush red stuff filled me with vast warmth and reassurance. Weariness melted from my bones. Before my change, no food ever had this profound an effect. Drink came the closest. A shot of booze was remotely comparable, but that had dampened the senses; this brought energy and rejuvenation, pulsing life into a body with no beating heart. I drew on it, exulting in the primal joy of satiation.

Once again I speculated about taking away extra to store in the refrigerator at home. Escott and I had talked about it; he didn't mind, even suggesting placing it in beer bottles so their amber glass hid the telltale color. The scare with Bobbi earlier resolved me to figure out something. Blood wouldn't keep for long, but even if it lasted a few nights, my trips to the Yards would be cut by half. How much better to squelch around here only once a week instead of every second or third night.

It would also lower the chances of my being caught by one of the workers. That had happened a few times. I'd dealt with it, hypnotically convincing them they'd seen nothing and to go on with work. The encounters had put the hair up on the back of my neck, and made me wonder if there had been others I'd not spotted.

That prickly feeling was on my neck again, but I was inclined to put it off as more imagination. Just thinking about a threat could bring out the heebie-jeebie sense. I'd been extra careful tonight.

Replete and restored, I pulled away, pinching the vein to slow the flow. The cow showed no great concern. It remained in place a moment, then abruptly snorted and moved off. Time I did the same.

On the other side of the fence, I fished out a handkerchief and swabbed my mouth for stains. God, that had tasted good. I felt ready for anything now.

Until I heard something toward my right, toward the street where I'd parked.

A narrow pass-way ran between the high enclosures, just wide enough for one animal at a time. Pelting down it at full speed was a man. It was a good assumption he'd seen something very disturbing. Like me.

I ran after. With the advantage of strength and speed, I closed up his lead. He didn't make a sound when I caught his shoulders and hauled him around. Not wanting to hurt him, I went easy on the spin, backing him against the fence. Cattle on the other side milled, alarmed.

It took me a long second to recognize him because he was so completely out of place. He was taller than I remembered and lot more animated, his pale face distorted by emotion, chiefly fear. But Dugan's mouth was the same, with its built-in smile. He showed teeth in that instant, then I felt him bury a solid fist in my stomach accompanied by some short, sharp pops. His punch hurt. Continued to hurt. Far too much. Only after seeing the blood did I understand the meaning of the close-in pops and realize he'd shot me.

6

HE stared, wide-eyed, as my legs went out from under. Gray mist clouded my sight. I fought it, grunting against the pain, reaching for him. He backed nimbly clear as I fully collapsed, shuddering into the mud.

"Come on," he whispered. "Show me."

Show him what? I had no breath for swearing but thought of several ripe words as I clawed at fence rails, trying to pull myself up again. The wounds were beginning to knit, but they burned like a fury, made movement difficult, thinking damn near impossible.

"Show," he repeated impatiently. He kicked my hand, knocking it from the wood rail, then hooked his foot under my arm and flipped me on my back. I'd break his leg. Both legs. I'd break one now if he'd just let me. . . .

He stood off exactly one pace too far, teeth showing, eyes

bright, and aimed the gun at my chest. A revolver, small caliber, but large enough for the job.

"Wait—" I started.

"No." He fired. Twice.

My last view was his exultant face as the gray mist abruptly wrenched me clear of the razoring agony.

Release from the burden of a body was the ultimate blessing. Until you shed it, you're unaware of just how truly heavy and awkward it is being encased within clumsy, vulnerable flesh. The ease of nothingness, the simple floating . . . here was I truly safe from all harm, all physical ills. But emotions were harder to cast off. Especially anger. I owed that son of a bitch.

I went corporeal as soon as I was able, rolling disoriented in stinking slush.

The pain was gone. Vanishing gave complete healing, this one faster and less tiring since I'd just fed. The shock was more mental than physical. Recovery from that would come from beating the hell out of Dugan. Except he'd left. He'd sprinted for the fence, topped it, and was just dropping to its street side.

Pushing up, I stumbled a few futile paces after, then went invisible again, seeking an easier method to give chase.

I rose high over the pens. In a way, I could fly, not like a bat as in Stoker's book, but by simply willing myself in any direction. Because of a profound hatred of heights, I rarely did this. If I wanted a view of the city, I'd take an elevator to the top of the Wrigley Building and look through a window the same as any other sane person. For the moment, I was too pissed to be terrified.

The wind buffeted my amorphous self; there was no cold or warmth to it, never was in this state, just the force of the flow. It wasn't too bad; I could hold in place with a little effort. The effort increased when I partially materialized. The more solidity to enable me to see, the harder it was to stay up, the more I wanted to vanish again. That's a lot to juggle while trying to float forty feet in thin air. Really, really thin air. This was taking too damned long.

Rising and dipping on its current, I caught fast glimpses of the overall area, looking for movement in the grayness. The pens were like a huge crossword square, some of the boxes filled with livestock, others empty and waiting. Sounds were distant; all I heard were agitated cattle making commotion. I pushed toward the boundary line of the fence.

The bastard was fast. Dugan had made it across the street and was in my own car. I'd taken the keys, but he'd somehow gotten around that problem. Not bothering with the lights, he gunned it and took the first corner on two wheels. Though quick enough in this form, I couldn't hope to follow. I let myself ease back to earth, went solid, and labored very hard at not ripping one of the pens apart. Smashing things would have felt good, but there was no point to it; I had to think.

Dugan had seen everything. He must have been watching the whole time I'd fed. But how much did he really know?

I had to assume the worst. Anyone who'd bothered to hear even a garbled summary of *Dracula* would have enough to reach a fairly accurate conclusion about what it means when a man drinks blood right from a vein. If Dugan didn't accept the reality of vampires, at the very least what I'd done made me some kind of repulsive lunatic to be avoided.

But he'd shot me, had been quite deliberate about it, had expected something out of it. "Show me," he'd whispered, as though he'd known what would happen if I got a serious enough injury. That grin . . . Had he been wanting me to disappear? Apparently.

But did he think he'd killed me?

No answer to that one. His hurry to get away could have had as much to do with escape from discovery as escape from me. Until I learned more, staying out of sight seemed the safest course.

This time my shakes were not from hunger but from impotent rage and—goddammit—fear.

I went back to the pens to restore what had been lost in the shooting. Things might get busy; I needed to be prepared and drank my fill, drank until it hurt. The red flood made me sluggish, but the feeling wore off as I walked clear of the Yards area, seeking a phone, finally finding one inside a closed gas station.

No one would be in my office to answer, so I dialed the number for the lobby pay phone. After a lot of rings, Wilton hesitantly answered.

"It's Mr. Fleming. I gotta talk with Escott. Get him. Now."

Wilton sounded surprised I was on the line but made an admirable job of doing what he was told. Not too many moments later, Escott came on.

"Is there a problem?" he asked.

"I'll say there is. Gilbert Dugan saw me going on a bender in the Stockyards."

"What?"

I repeated the bad news, adding details about the shooting. Escott asked the same kind of questions I'd thought of, none of which I could answer. "I don't know how he could have followed me. I was careful the whole way. I did enough turns to lose a school of lampreys."

"Yet he departed in your car, not his own. Interesting." He sounded thoughtful, which was annoying.

"What d'you m—oh, hell." I didn't want to believe it. "You think he was in *my* car the whole time?"

"It's a possibility to consider. The only likely one at this point."

"Son of a bitch." And a lot of other colorful descriptives. Dugan could have hidden on the floor down behind the seat. Hell, he could have gotten the idea from me. Escott and I had talked openly of my cramped trip to the country hideout in front of him and the others, thinking them safely hypnotized. Why had Dugan risked it, though? Several reasons came to mind, and I didn't like any of them. "I'm cabbing back to the club. Keep that Brockhurst bird under watch. Do whatever it takes, but don't let him leave. He's my lead to finding Dugan tonight."

"I'd be glad to, but they've gone. About five minutes ago."

I took a breath for another explosion, then stopped. There was nothing remotely foul enough to suit the situation. They'd have to invent a whole new language to cover it. "All right. Hold the fort 'til I'm there, then we'll figure out something."

"Should I relate any of this to Miss Smythe?"

"If she's alone, yeah, she needs to know what's going on. Keep an eye on her, would you? Bodyguard stuff, but not so's she'd notice."

"Of course."

Another call to a cab company got me a ride back to Lady Crymsyn. The driver gave the filthy state of my clothes a suspicious double take and balked at the stink, but I showed enough money to keep from being stranded. He wasn't much for conversation, though I did catch him trying to use the rearview mirror to check on me. At this point, I didn't give a damn. When we arrived, he got a decent tip and a whammy to make him forget how he got it.

I went in the back way, wafting invisibly through the stage area to an empty dressing room. The mud stains on my pants weren't beyond cleaning, but the coat was ruined from all the bullet holes and blood. The lead had torn right through my body and out. God knows where the bullets had ended up. Probably embedded in the thick wood fencing and the mud. I hadn't thought to look.

My shirt was also a loss, front and back, but easily replaced. I kept spare clothes here in case I needed to sleep the day over or had an accident. The latter had been based on the possibility of a spilled drink, not my surviving a murderous assault by an armed lunatic.

I washed up in the small shower, accompanied by the band's music filtering through the walls. Donning a fresh shirt, I had assurance that the evening was still going smoothly for the club. Adelle's first set was over; she'd be on her break, perhaps out front with Roland, Bobbi, and the rest of her appreciative audience.

Then the romantic melody softened and slowed for a pause in the phrase, allowing me to clearly hear what was going on in the dressing room across the hall. There's never mistaking that particular series of rhythmic sounds for anything else. Apparently Roland and Adelle were in the midst of a very intense nonverbal reminiscence about their honeymoon some ten years past. It was definitely them; I recognized the voices—or rather the breathy groans and whispered endearments.

Oh, brother. I didn't need this.

Eyes rolling skyward, I gave a long-suffering sigh and re-solved to stop being such a naive optimist, thinking people would learn simple common sense without the benefit of a sock in the kisser. Roland had gotten fair warning about Gordy, and Adelle should have known better.

Later. I'd fix things later, the both of them, with or without Bobbi's approval of my using the evil eye to do it.

I put on a spare suit, not my best, but more fitting than the white tuxedo still in its paper wrap from the cleaners, then vanished to float into the main room.

My heart didn't work anymore, but it still shifted enough to lodge in my invisible throat as I glided toward the ceiling. Though a much lower height than I'd attained at the Stock-yards, it seemed worse for being indoors. Materializing a little at a time in the shadows of the black-painted rafters, I made my way to a row of hanging lights aimed at the stage and hovered there a moment, secure that no one would notice me behind their glare. From this vantage—and I hated having to look down—I spotted Escott. He was at Bobbi's table, seated next to her and across from Faustine Petrova. Oh, brother, again. What a rotten time for *her* to show up.

Fixing the direction in my mind, I vanished and descended. Faustine's accent was going strong as she related some story about Roland. I brushed close enough by Escott to give him a good chill, then swept toward the lobby, re-forming in the blind spot.

He was delayed a few moments, probably had to wait for Faustine to finish. His face was grim when he stalked toward me, and we didn't say anything, just turned and marched up to my office and its privacy. Once on the other side of the door, I gave him all the bad news about the Stockyards debacle with Dugan. My anger and fear returned afresh with the recounting, but I spoke in a calm tone while pacing around.

"Okay," I said at the end. "Where do I find him?"

From the sofa, Escott lifted one hand in a throwaway gesture. "You don't expect he'll just wander home after such an adventure, I hope?"

"It's a place to start. If not there, then I'll find this cousin Brockhurst and track him from that angle. Dugan saw too much for me to let him run loose."

"I've a rather unpleasant thought about that fellow. . . ."

"Only one?"

"Indeed. What if prior to what he witnessed in the Stockyards he was already aware of your condition? The hypnosis . . ."

"It had crossed my mind." I rested my duff against the solidity of the desk.

"From what you say, it seems he had a specific understanding of what you are."

"Yeah. Like he knew what might happen when he shot me. Now he knows for sure. You'd heard or read about that kind of stuff, chances are others have, too."

"Remote chances."

"Not remote enough."

Escott rose and took a turn pacing the room a couple times, visibly thinking, then sat at my desk, pulling out the phone book. "What good does it do him?"

"I don't give a damn. I'm more worried about the harm it can do me."

"To go to all that trouble and hazard, he'll be after something. It's one thing to read an ancient report about vampires by Montague Summers or labor though some lurid Byronic-style tale in a dime magazine from a drugstore, but quite another to come face-to-face with the reality. This assumes Dugan knew to connect the forced hypnosis of his gang to your specific aspect of the supernatural. Otherwise he might think you're a jumped-up stage mentalist."

"So he reads a lot. It doesn't matter what he knows about folklore or vampires or tap-dancing leprechauns so long as he's shut down for good. Maybe no one would believe him if he started sounding off about me, but I sure as hell don't want to go through the aggravation. I have to find him and make a serious try at putting him under so he can forget everything."

Escott scribbled lines on some notepaper. "Here's Dugan's address. There are two A. Brockhursts listed. No way to tell if either is the man you want, but you can proceed to them if you've no success at Dugan's home. How will you get there?"

"I'll ask to borrow one of Gordy's men. He'll keep his mouth shut."

"Your car. Will you report it as stolen?"

"I'll have to if I want it back. If there's a God in heaven, Dugan will still be driving it, but I'm not counting on that."

"He may think he killed you."

"I won't count on that, either, but I'll stay out of sight for the time being. Aw, hell . . . if I'm dead, I can't report on the car."

"Leave that to me. I can say it was taken from the parking lot and give Dugan's description as the driver. It would be very convenient to have him red-handed for grand theft. He couldn't wriggle so easily from that charge. Blast, what was his game hiding there in the first place?"

"To get information about me." I'd thought it out during

the cab ride. "If he was curious about the hypnosis, he might have wanted to corner me alone for a little chat. He was carrying heat, either to force answers or put me out of the way. Or both."

"Or shoot you to see if you'd vanish. Your trip to the Yards was a bonus for his collection of incriminating evidence."

"Hey, I'm not the bad guy here," I grumbled, mostly to myself.

"Rather determined of him to sit in your car on a chill evening in the hope you'd take a drive."

Too determined, I thought. *Was it a sign of his craziness?* "He was near a phone earlier, though. Had to be waiting someplace else. Anthony got up twice to make calls before I left the club. I listened in on the second one when he told Dugan I was out of the main room. Maybe they knew about my regular runs to the night deposit at the bank, though I usually walk."

"In which case, I'd recommend you make those less predictable."

"No problem. If Dugan isn't home to visitors, then I'll locate Brockhurst. There was a girl in their group, Marie Kennard, who was chummy with him. Don't know the names of the rest."

Escott flipped pages. "There are several Kennards, but nothing under M. I can check things more thoroughly tomorrow."

"Except I'm not waiting that long. Don't know when I'll be back. Can you help Bobbi close this joint?"

"Certainly—"

Someone knocked on the door. The hatcheck girl was there. "Got a message for you, Mr. Fleming." She handed me an intricately folded bit of paper. Writing was visible on some sections. "Isn't this the cutest thing? I never seen anyone do that to a note before. The man said it was gravely important. He said to be sure I said 'gravely' to you."

I felt cold. "What did he look like?"

"Nice. About as tall as you. Light eyes. Nice smile. High-class kind of gentleman. Well dressed."

"He still here?"

"Came and went. In a hurry, y' know?"

"Okay, thanks."

She left. I shut the door and put the paper on the desk as though it might burst into flames. About three inches tall, it was shaped like a bird with a long beak and uplifted wings, and it looked fragile.

Escott frowned. "Origami," he said.

"That Jap paper-folding stuff?"

"Yes. Apparently this was done to catch your attention."

"Meaning I should read it right away." I carefully demolished the bird figure, flattening the paper so we could both read the neat, block-printed lettering it bore.

Mr. Fleming,

You have my sincere apology for the unfortunate exchange between us earlier, but I deemed it necessary in order to confirm the full truth about you. I hope once you are recovered we might have a private talk. For that I will take precautions to ensure my complete safety, and advise you not to indulge in any reckless behavior against me. The consequences would, I guarantee, be absolutely disastrous to you. As a sign of my good faith, you will find your vehicle returned to its usual spot.

If a meeting is amenable, please signal by going out-side to look at your car. Light a cigarette, then throw it

*into the gutter. Go back inside the club. I think you will
be wiser than to try seeking me out.*

You will be watched.

Yours truly . . .

He'd not signed it. No need for names.

"I guess this answers the question of whether or not he
thought he'd killed me."

"Bloody hell," said Escott.

Not having much choice or a brilliant idea to get out of
it, I left by the front door, thoroughly checking every inch
of the street and the surrounding buildings for any sign of
Dugan. Nothing. No one loitering in doorways, no vehicles
unfamiliar to the neighborhood, but he could be parked at
a safe distance, keeping an eye on me with field glasses.
It's what I'd do.

My car was in place as promised. I found it had been
hot-wired. Dugan must have done that before following
me into the yards. I could imagine him crawling into the
front seat, doing the job, and leaving the motor running,
ready for a getaway. Again, he must have suspected what
business I had in the cattle pens. I didn't like that he was
that smart.

I lighted the cigarette, took a puff, and threw it arcing
into a gutter. Tiny sparks of smoldering tobacco scattered.
It streamed smoke a moment, rolling in the wind, then
went out when it hit a patch of slush. There was no reaction
to this that I could see, and no one shot me again, so I
went back to my office where Escott waited. He'd traded
the desk for the sofa. We didn't say much, just listened to

the distant band music filtering up from the main room. About five minutes later, the phone rang.

"Hello, is that Mr. Fleming?" Cultured voice. The one I remembered giving instructions to the other kidnappers about how to clean up their hideout.

"Dugan."

"How do you do?"

"What do you want?"

"To set up a meeting time. Will tomorrow evening at seven be convenient?"

I listened for a clue to his location. The clink of dishes could mean a nearby diner or drugstore, but nothing came though but the usual line static. For all I knew, he could be downstairs in the lobby box.

"Mr. Fleming?"

"Come over now. Let's get this out of the way."

"Sorry, but I'm busy. Tomorrow at seven? I can make it earlier or later if you like. I'm not unreasonable."

"Seven," I said.

"Excellent. Just the two of us, your office."

"Yeah. Private."

"I look forward to it, but please, and I cannot stress this enough, do not take action against me of any kind, you or your friend the detective. Do not involve the police; there is to be no discussion of this with others. No investigations, no violence. Do nothing. Otherwise, the repercussions will not be to your liking. That's not a threat but a warning. You get only the one. Don't test it. Are we clear on that?"

"Yes."

"Very good. In the meantime, go about your normal routine. I shan't bother you, though you will be under watch."

He hung up.

I dropped the receiver in its cradle and repeated to Escott the half he'd not heard.

"I think the last bit about being watched is a bluff," he said. "Dugan seems rather snagged on the topic. The calls made to Mrs. Gladwell, the notes, always reiterated she would be watched."

"So he's a frustrated Peeping Tom. He wants to spook me. It's working. You can figure he'll want you to stick to your routine as well."

"Of all the bloody cheek, ordering us about."

"Repercussions," I said. "What's he got in mind?"

"I can think of several hundred disasters. Better not to speculate. Best to plan out how to deal with him once he's here. Knowing what you are, he will arm himself to the teeth since he's essentially taking himself into the lion's den."

"You did the same thing." On the night we met, Escott had prepared defenses that included a supply of garlic and a cross, which I'd been able to ignore, and a crossbow, which I had not. I could expect similar measures and more from Dugan.

"Actually, the invitation was for *you* to come to *my* office . . ." Escott continued thoughtfully.

"After you swiped my home earth to get me there."

"I have apologized; besides, it all turned out well enough."

"Yeah, but you're one of the good guys. Dugan's a kidnapper, has attempted murder, maybe has murdered, and is probably a prime candidate for the booby hatch."

"But curious. That could work against him. So . . . I return to the question of how any dealings with you could benefit him."

"Too easy, Charles."

"Oh?"

"One visit to the district attorney and a few other key people, and I can make them forget all about Dugan's involvement in the Gladwell case. He'd like that to happen, don't you think? He'd carry it all the way to Mrs. Gladwell to get himself clear."

Escott's mouth sagged open, and for a second or three, it looked like his brain had steamed to a complete halt. He eventually recovered. "Well, we can't allow that."

"Nope. I'll have to see him, try to put him under. If that doesn't work, I try to find out what his precautions are and make them go away. He'll want to talk about them to keep me in line. Did you let Bobbi in on what's going on?"

He shook his head. "We were never alone long enough. First Mr. Lambert monopolized her, then Miss Petrova arrived—"

"I saw. She's something, isn't she?"

"Indeed she is. A touch theatrical, but of an agreeably ingenuous variety. Intoxicating in small doses."

Whatever that meant. There was no such thing as a small dose with a gal like Faustine. "I'll have to talk to Bobbi. I'm going to need her help setting things up to welcome Dugan."

"Not putting her in the middle of this, are you?"

"Brother, she is essential. You, too."

"In what way?"

I told him my idea.

"Bloody hell," he said again and broke into a rare laugh.

* * *

We split up. Escott made his way to the club's basement where the carpentry tools were stored. He wanted to know what kind of drill bits I had on hand and was intent on locating extension cords, yardsticks, plaster, and other odds and ends. He'd be happy and occupied for hours. Nothing like a fresh problem to solve to cheer him through and through.

I went down to the main room to rejoin Bobbi at her table. Roland Lambert and I would have a man-to-man talk, but it seemed better to wait until he was alone. If he and Adelle were still unavailable, I had no wish to break in on them. Bobbi and I had once been interrupted like that, and it's not fun for anyone.

"What's with the different suit?" Bobbi asked.

"Had an accident," I answered. "Spilled something."

She could read on my face there was more story to tell, but she'd have to hear it later.

I smiled at Faustine and told her how delighted I was to see her again. She purred something similar in return. Then I asked where Roland had gone.

"Een the back of the stage, I t'ink," she said, sipping from her glass. It held something clear with an ice cube. I couldn't tell if it was water, vodka, or gin. She'd dolled herself up in more safari kills, leopard and sable draped over a black, clingy gown. Instead of a hat, she had some kind of bandage thing rolled around her white blond hair. It looked like a screwy war-wound dressing, except it seemed to be made of satin with lots of rhinestone trim.

"He said you'd tired yourself out shopping today."

"How droll of my dar-link to say so, but yes, I did do

much buying of t'ings. I vish to look berry Amer-i-kan. Success? Yess?" She gestured to indicate her ensemble. I knew a whole lot of *bupkis* about women's fashion but had enough brains to express appreciation for the view. She did look impressive.

"We're doing more shopping tomorrow," said Bobbi. "I'll make sure she gets to the best places."

"An' a luncheon wit' the hot dog," Faustine added.

"Chicago style, I promise. Then maybe we try to find you an agent."

"Roland vill be look-ink. He said Adelle would be help."

From what I'd heard, they couldn't have had much opportunity or inclination to discuss Faustine's interests. I held to a neutral face. "I'm sure she'll have something useful for him."

Bobbi shot me a what-the-hell-does-that-mean look. It was pointless hiding anything from her, but this wasn't the time for shocking revelations in front of the guy's wife. I made an uninformative smile, then asked how things were going for Gordy and Bristow up on their third-tier perch.

She took the change of subject in stride and shrugged. "Hard to tell. The mean-looking guy kept the waiter busy bringing drinks until he finally ordered a whole bottle. He's doing most of the talking; Gordy listens."

No gun fun. I liked that. How would Bristow's booze consumption react against my influence, though? It gave people a certain immunity from me; would it also erode the effect of the suggestions I'd already planted? I had often wondered about it.

"What's going on with them?" she asked.

"Negotiations. The guy wants Gordy's territory."

Bobbi sat up a little straighter. She was aware of what

that meant and where Bristow's ambitions could lead. "How serious?"

"Gordy's got things in hand."

"Gordy is friend?" Faustine wanted to know.

"A very good one."

"Vhat matter is eet?"

"They're a couple of salesmen trying to divide up the city," I said. "One guy wants another guy's customers. They'll work things out."

"Amer-i-kans, always the beez-nuss. I like eet. Here anyone become the million-aire, yess?"

"Rags to riches is our favorite song."

"I vould like hear'ink that sometime."

"Of course, things haven't been so good since the crash—"

"Poof," she said dismissively. "You vant to see big wreck of the crash, go to Continent, go to Russia. Boom, crash, boom, all over there. You here have no idea. Zo innocent. Yess, you have the soup kitchens, Roland tell me of them, but you have soup. Places over there, a potato feed village for a month, if they lucky to have potato. I am beeg coward; I get out." She looked at Bobbi. "Tomorrow I vish to find church to light candle for those behind, yesss?"

"Sure," Bobbi agreed, impressed by Faustine's social spirit.

"Is good. I should ask my cousin, but he annoy me with talk of the dead and days gone by. Days are gone—poof—vhat more good to vish them back? Most I never vant to remember." She lightened this with a self-deprecating smile and a flash of her eyes. She lifted her glass. "To good days that come, yesss?"

"To better days, yes," said Bobbi, lifting a glass of her

usual grape juice. I had no drink but murmured approvingly.

The bandleader struck up Adelle's fanfare just then, signaling the start of her second set. She emerged from the wings, introducing herself this time around. She beamed in response to the applause and, with a completely straight face, smoothly launched into "Ain't Misbehavin'." I damn near choked, turning it into a cough.

It couldn't have been too convincing. Bobbi read me better than a book and kicked my ankle. I took it like a man, giving her a short nod and a thin smile so she wouldn't do it again. She arched one eyebrow. I offered another smile, trying to look like I'd had enough, which was true, but jeez, I needed a laugh. Must have been reaction to getting shot and worry over what Dugan's game might be. I'd tell Bobbi about it later. For the present, I liked it that her biggest concern was keeping me in line.

Roland Lambert came out the backstage area door, looking fresher than next week's paper. His tux was in perfect order, hair still slicked down, not even a sheen on his upper lip to betray his recent physical effort. He raised a hand in our direction, then paused at the bar. The man there served him a tall glass of ice water with a twist of lemon. Roland made his way toward us but was stopped by a woman at another table. She asked him a question, and he broke into a grin designed to charm. She seemed delighted in turn and hastily scrabbled for a paper cocktail napkin. The man with her produced a pen, and Roland obligingly signed his autograph.

"Eet sometime happen," said Faustine, who also watched the interplay. "People remember him from cinema. He adore the notice."

That was apparent. Roland seemed humbly grateful for

the attention. He bowed and kissed the woman's hand—
she looked ready to offer to bear his children—then made
his way toward us. Other patrons saw and were speculating
on the handsome stranger's identity. I heard some of it over
the music, including a fiercely whispered, "No, he did not
use to be Ramon Novarro" from a nearby table. Their interest sat well with me, anything to keep them coming
back for more.

Roland arrived, put his glass down, and picked up Faustine's hand to kiss. "How are you, darling?"

"I am vell. Vhat vas that?" She indicated the table he'd
just left.

"Haven't the faintest who she was, but she'd been in
London and remembered me from that production of
Springtime for Flowers. Dreadful comedy," he explained to
Bobbi and me. "Critics roasted it, but it went over well
with the regular populace. I played the rich American in
love with the gardener's daughter who turns out to be the
impoverished contessa in disguise. I don't know where the
playwright got—"

"That is lovely, dar-link," said Faustine shortly. She
made to stand up. Roland did his gentleman's duty with
her chair, pulling it back.

"Something wrong?" Roland asked.

"Da! All is the sssame." Her tone was a few dozen degrees
below freezing. "Always sssame, wit' the ss-same."

"Beg pardon?" He was honestly puzzled.

"Clear I am mak-ink wit' you!" She picked up his water
glass and flicked her wrist, dashing the whole of its con-
tents full in his face. "You are a peeg!"

Eyes blazing, she hurled the glass at his feet with a
skilled flourish. It shattered completely and with much
noise, then she sailed toward the lobby, head high.

THE sideshow was enough to stop Adelle's performance in mid-verse. Some of the band had seen it, and their focus on the song flagged for a few seconds until the leader hauled them back to business. Adelle gamely returned but forgot her place and belted out the wrong repeat on the chorus. No one paid much mind; most of the joint was riveted on Faustine's exit. It was a doozy. If she'd been a ship, icebergs in her way would have been the ones to break up and sink.

Bobbi shot me a look; I nodded agreement. She hurriedly followed after Faustine.

Roland held to a nonplussed reaction, freely dripping. The twist of lemon clung to one of his lapels like an eccentric boutonniere. I signaled toward the bar, and a waiter hurried over with a clean towel.

"I'm most dreadfully sorry, Mr. Fleming," Roland finally said, accepting the towel and dabbing at the damage. "I assure you that this is . . . is . . . oh, hell." He sat down rather heavily.

I gave him a minute to sop up the worst, then rose. "Come on, Roland. We'll dry you out backstage."

He let me take his elbow and guide him away. Lots of eyes on us for the trip. Not the sort of publicity I wanted, but bearable. Things like this happened in bars.

I showed him to a dressing room not in use and handed him another towel, then returned to the main room long enough to make sure the broken glass was picked up. The waiter was already there with a broom and pan. When I got back to Roland, he had his jacket and tie off and was undoing his white silk shirt. The fine fabric stuck transparently to his wet skin, showing a solid spread of shoulder muscle. No wonder he was so popular. He peeled the shirt and hung it on the corner of the bathroom door. I was out of fresh shirts, or I'd have offered him one.

"I am truly sorry about this," he said, and he did look very repentant.

"Tell that to your wife, not me." I hung back by the door, keeping clear of the dressing table mirror.

"She won't hear it. Too angry. It's my own fault. She's the jealous type. I shouldn't have paid so much attention to that autograph seeker—"

"Save the bull. Faustine knows about you and Adelle. That's what she's mad about."

Roland stared up, horrified. "But she couldn't."

"She's female. Of course she damn well knows. They all got a built-in sense about men. They always know when a man's being stupid. Sometimes they ignore it and hope the guy will smarten up, and sometimes they don't bother. Faustine won't put up with it."

"But . . . but I love her." He made that seem like the cure-all for everything.

"Apparently not enough."

"She knows I love her!"

"Actions speak louder than words, and the little dance you had with Adelle"—I jerked a thumb toward the star's room across the hall—"was a kick in the teeth to your wife."

"How did you—?"

"This is my place. I know everything."

He scowled, like the bad news was my fault, but I was unimpressed, having had worse from lots tougher mugs. "You going to fire us?"

"Nope. You come in to work like everyone else. If you two can't work, then you'll get fired."

That perked him, but it didn't last long. "We'll patch things up. We *need* this job. I'll make her see that it was nothing, that it will never happen again."

"Let her cool off first. You chase her down now, and she'll skin your face with a spoon."

"But I—"

"Roland . . . listen to me. . . ."

It took a little longer than usual, he had a lot of emotion to cut through, a lot of protest, but I got to him, and we had a fine chat. My favorite kind. I did all the talking.

While the newly penitent and temporarily wiser Roland flapped his damp shirt over an electric heater, I took the back way behind the stage to get to the lobby. Bobbi wasn't in sight; Wilton said she was in the john.

"The other blond with her, the one in the furs and oddball hat?"

"Yeah," he replied. He looked as though he'd seen such performances before. "She was plenty upset. Rattled some lingo I couldn't make out and kept saying, 'Peeg, peeg, peeg.' What's that?"

"Her husband."

"She don't like him much tonight, huh?"

"Not much." I cooled my heels in front of the ladies' room, reluctant to breach its sanctity. Though I'd been through it on inspections during the building of Crymsyn, once we opened, I kept clear. You had the men's and the ladies' and never the twain shall meet, nor shall such havens ever be violated. A sensible code to follow, apparently based on the tribulations of real life.

The place was full of mirrors, too.

After a few minutes I put an ear to the door. I heard contralto sobbing echoing off the marble interior and "Peeg, peeg, peeg," and what sounded like babbled Russian. Bobbi's lighter voice crooned sympathetically along. "I know, honey, they're all the same, every last one of them."

I hoped she didn't include me in the crowd and made a mental note to send her flowers. The two of them would probably be there for a good long while. I could have shortened the time, using my special talent to get Faustine to forget her anger and make things up with Roland, but judged it would work better after she settled down. Whenever possible, I tried to keep hypnosis sessions short and easy. Less of a disturbance to the subject and less of a headache for me.

The hatcheck girl was more interested in the floor show than Wilton and very pleased to participate. All she had to do was let me know when Bobbi and Faustine finally came out, but she eagerly watched the rest room door like the fate of the nation depended on it. For her, this was better drama than *One Man's Family*.

In the main room I propped up the other bar, which was only open when we had a bigger crowd to serve, and surveyed things. Conversation was back up to normal, the waiters were busy, the dance floor in use. Good. Adelle had reclaimed her composure and was cutting through "Have You Ever Met That Funny Reefer Man?" She didn't deliver as fast a ride as Cab Calloway, but she kept it jazzed enough to get away with it. Odds were that most of my patrons had no idea what a reefer was and why this was such a popular number with the grinning band members. Nearly everyone was either dancing or at least tapping their toes to the beat.

Gordy was the exception.

He and Bristow looked a lot more serious than before, and their bodyguards seemed to have been drinking lemon juice, straight. They were eyeing one another, hard-faced and tense. I debated whether or not to make the climb up there and pretend to play host, perhaps calm things between them a little. It was fifty-fifty whether such an interruption would hinder or help.

Escott appeared just then, saw me, and came over. Dust smeared his lapels, cuffs, and knees, indicating he'd been happily grubbing around in the club's tool storage.

"Everything I'll want is on hand," he announced. "No need to send out for supplies. You've also plenty of wire, though cobbling the more specialized electric bits together is not my strong suit. I can repair a lamp, but for what you have in mind—"

"Bobbi will know what to do, or know someone who does who can bring in whatever we need."

"What did she think of your idea?"

"Haven't told her yet, she's talking with Faustine, who's having a nervous breakdown." I gave him the short version of the melodrama.

"Dear me. Where is this Mr. Lambert? I didn't want to interrupt his talk with Miss Smythe and missed meeting him."

"Drying out backstage. We had a discussion. He won't be any trouble in the future. Tomorrow night will be better for socializing. He and Faustine should be back together by then. I'll see to it."

"Handy weapon, that."

"What?"

"Your hypnosis. There are occasions when I could find it quite useful, like waiting in line at the bank. It would be most handy persuading those ahead of me to seek other queues for their business."

"Don't forget traffic tickets." I'd been stopped a few times but always got the cops to forget whatever problem they had with me. It didn't work for parking violations, but I avoided those.

"Indeed. Have you noticed what's going on?" He indicated the top tier.

Bristow was on his feet, looming over a still-seated Gordy, face red and eyes blazing. All the bodyguards looked ready to erupt.

"Yeah. 'Scuse me."

Moving quick, I got up there. Gordy and his people saw me coming; so did Bristow's guys. Their notice telegraphed to him. He threw a glance my way with enough glower packed in to confirm my influence had worn right off. He was too drunk now for a second attempt to work.

"Mr. Bristow—" I began.

"Can it, punk," he snapped. "Get the hell out of here."

Gordy remained in place, his expression even more hooded than usual; I didn't know what he wanted done. I wanted there not to be trouble. "Siddown, Hog," he said, barely audible over the music.

"Screw that." Bristow turned full on him. "I'm telling you how things are gonna be, and you sit there like a pile of shit and don't say nothin'. What're you gonna do about it?"

"I will think things over."

"You think faster—no—you don't think, you just do what I say. That's New York givin' the orders. They don't like how you're doin' things, so it's me taking up the slack. You got no choice; you get outta my way, or you get run over."

Gordy didn't respond with so much as a blink. "Sorry you feel that way, Hog."

"It ain't me—it's New York. You don't like it, you just try talkin' with them an' see how far you get."

"I'll check first thing in the morning."

"You'll just do as you're told. You hear me? Do you? Say something!" Bristow was louder than the band, and other patrons stared curiously. My hired help, a little more knowledgeable about the situation, seemed ready to duck under the nearest tables.

"It's late, Hog," Gordy said evenly. "Real late. It's even later in New York. The bosses there don't like this kind of interruption to their sleep. I'll call in the morning and fix things. It'll be made right, I promise."

"My way. You do as you're told."

"Everything."

Bristow didn't seem the type to accept such an easy victory, but he couldn't do much else with Gordy agreeing with him. Neither spoke for what seemed like a couple of hours; then

Bristow jerked his chins, and his men slowly rose. Gordy's remained seated, taking their cue from him.

"First thing," Bristow repeated. "By noon I'm in charge, or you're dead."

Gordy made no reply.

"Say something!"

I don't know what Gordy might have said. The little lamp on the table suddenly flickered, forestalling his response. It was an instant's distraction, throwing all of them. The light flared, dimmed, then exploded, glass flying.

Of all the rotten times for Myrna—

The two men closest to Bristow saw and knew it was nothing to sweat over, but the third one only heard something like a shot. His gun was out, and he went for Gordy.

Things blurred; I seemed to be the only man moving; the rest were statues. Before the others could react, I was on him, dragging on his arm with one hand and wresting the gun away with the other. When the world started rotating again the would-be shooter was facedown on the floor, holding his arm and cursing.

"What the hell . . . ?" began Bristow, just becoming aware something had happened.

Another of his guys started to reach inside his coat, but I had his friend's gun aimed at his belly. He changed his mind, showing it by holding his palms wide. The third one found himself surrounded by Gordy's men.

"Everyone take it easy," I said. We did just that until I was sure they would be sensible without the threat of me putting holes in them.

"Put that away," said Bristow. He didn't look quite as drunk as before.

"When you leave."

"You don't order me around, punk."

"You're in my place, Hog. I don't allow this crap here." I tried to capture his full attention, but despite the shift in his manner, there was still too much booze in the way. Fortunately, his remaining guards were stone sober. "Clean your pal off my floor, then take your boss home and put him to bed."

The one I was ready to belly-shoot woke up quick and did as ordered. This didn't go well with Bristow, but he couldn't figure how to fix it. He made noises, snarled a final order at Gordy to do as he was told, and backed away. His men got the fallen to his feet, and they unsteadily departed, working their way to the stairs and down, hands inside their coats. Nearly the whole place saw the parade, and even if my customers didn't have the full story, they were able to recognize trouble on the hoof and get nervous. Once Bristow was out of sight, people visibly sagged and resumed talking. I expected many would wait a few minutes, then leave. It must have showed when I looked at Gordy.

He gave a small shrug. "Sorry for the trouble."

I shoved the gun in my pocket where its weight messed up the hang of my coat. With the table light gone, we were in a shadowy patch, giving me a small hope that few had seen the finer details of the incident. "What now?"

"I call New York. Tell 'em their boy is annoying people."

"Then what? That noon deadline—"

"I'll think of something."

Which was Gordy's way of telling me to butt out. Fine, so long as whatever he thought of didn't take place on my doorstep. No need to ask if he understood that. Since Lady Crymsyn was supposedly neutral territory, he'd be careful to respect it. I got the impression he was highly embarrassed about Bristow's behavior. Drunks in clubs were normal, a familiar difficulty easily handled, but edgy guys like Bristow and his pals had too many added complications.

"You need anything?" I asked, so he'd know there were no hard feelings.

"A phone."

"My office or the lobby booth."

He looked at Strome. "Lobby. Call the other boys. Meeting tonight at the Nightcrawler. They go there and wait for me."

"What about Bristow?" Strome asked.

"We're mostly safe 'til noon, but we keep our heads down."

He nodded and left.

I said, "You want me along, too?"

Gordy made one slow shake of his head. "Thanks, but we're covered. You don't need to be in this mess."

Very true. Better to stay clear and let Gordy fix the problem. I had more than enough to keep me busy. Annoyed with the weight of the gun, I gave it to him to look after, wished him good luck, and followed Bristow's route down. Escott was still parked at the bar on that side.

"Negotiations fail?" he inquired, keeping a bland face. He'd have seen everything.

"You're a mind reader."

"Bad timing with that light."

"Myrna was trying to be helpful, I think."

He took that in and chose not to comment. "I heard Mr. Bristow's rumblings of dire threats against Gordy and all his relations as he and his men made their departure. It does not bode well. I say, you're rather more pale than usual."

"No kidding."

"And your shoulders are up about your ears. Relax, old man, before you frighten the whole room. After all this time, you should be used to such rows between rivals."

"Don't mean I like 'em."

"No, of course not."

Until now I'd not realized just how stiff my neck and shoulders had gotten. I told Escott what I'd heard. "Hope to God we don't have another damned war."

"Bristow's forcing the situation. Very foolish of him. One must wonder why."

"He got drunk, got pushy, then couldn't back down."

"Perhaps. Or his position is so secure he's confident of his success."

"Either way or whatever else, Gordy's not letting him take over."

"Then a war is inevitable."

More likely it would be a very carefully accomplished, well-concealed execution. Though there were still spectacular exceptions, a lot of the truly violent mob games were more often than not played on the quiet. It was bad for business to leave bloody corpses all over the city sidewalks.

"So long as they include us out."

He went with me to the lobby, which was thankfully clear of Bristow and his friends. The check girl was on watch, shaking her head to indicate Bobbi and Faustine were still in conference.

"I'd really like a drink," I announced to no one in particular. Before my change, I'd have had several by now. At times like this I really missed the booze.

"Yes, sir," said Wilton. He was ready to serve up anything. I waved his offer down. "I'd like one. I could use one. Doesn't mean I'll have one."

"A typical night at Lady Crymsyn," said Escott.

"Jesus, I hope not."

* * *

Escott and I were in my office making a practical start on my plans for Gilbert Dugan when Bobbi and Faustine finally emerged from the ladies' lair. The check girl came to tell me, but by the time I made it down again, Faustine was gone.

"Where is she?" I asked Bobbi. She looked tired.

"I put her in a cab and sent her back to her hotel. No shopping tomorrow. We'd only end up in a hardware store buying axes or shotguns or something. Where's Roland?"

"In dressing room three the last I saw."

"I wanna murder that son of a bitch. Do you know what he's done to her?"

"Tell me all about it, but not here." I took her to the main room and an isolated table, disappointing Wilton and the girl. They'd just have to speculate.

Bobbi gave me an earful, none of it too original, the gist being that when Roland went on the wagon, he substituted women for drinking. To him, they were even more addictive than booze. "He just can't keep his pants buttoned," she said. Several times.

"Faustine didn't know that about him?"

"She thought he'd change for her. She thought marriage would make a difference. Poor kid."

This didn't sound like a curable problem, no matter how many times I slapped a whammy on Roland. "She gonna divorce him?"

"Not with her religion she won't. There's the other thing, too. She wants to be an American. She pretty much admitted it was one of the reasons she married him. She loves him and all, but . . ." Bobbi trailed off with a drawn-out growling sound, replete with disgust. "Men," she said in conclusion.

I remained diplomatically quiet. Now was not the time to remind her I was a member of the opposing party. "I had a talk with Roland. He's going to behave himself for the time being if he wants to keep their job here."

"You're letting them stay on?"

"Why not?"

"It's pretty generous of you."

I shrugged. "Everyone needs to work. I recommended plenty of groveling, apologies, and that he not beg for forgiveness."

She clouded over. "He should. Why didn't you?"

"First he needs to say he's sorry a lot. Asking to be forgiven lets him off the hook. To forgive is to forget. He needs a dose of responsibility along with the kick in the pants."

After thinking it through, her face cleared. "You're pretty damned smart."

"I read it in a magazine."

"Which one?"

"The kind you find in a dentist's office. Years ago." The story had ended with the forgiven two-timing husband running off with his secretary and his wife drowning herself. None of it had been too satisfying. After that I decided to stick to mysteries and stories like those in *Weird Tales*, where the bad guys generally got what they had coming. "You okay?"

"After listening to all her stuff about Roland, I feel like a punching bag. Poor Faustine. She doesn't have any friends here. Looks like I'm elected."

"You can't expect her to be pals with Adelle."

"God, no. Remember when I didn't think it'd be a good idea for you to get in the middle of this? I've changed my mind."

"No problem."

"Can you talk to Faustine tomorrow night?"

"If there's time. Something's come up."

"With Gordy?" She glanced toward the third tier where Gordy was still parked.

Flanked by two of his men, he sat well away from his table, back firmly against the wall. Though the exploded lightbulb had been replaced, he was in shadow. Apparently he was taking Bristow's threats seriously. There was no sign of Strome, in here or at the lobby phone.

"Nothing like that," I said. "Gordy's got some business going, but he's taking care of it. This is to do with me. The brains behind the Gladwell kidnapping is getting cute."

"That society guy, Dugan?"

"Yeah." I told her everything. It took a while, but she was a patient listener, and it provided a distraction from the triangle crisis. She went a little sick-looking when I told her about getting shot. She didn't interrupt, only put her hands over mine.

"That explains why you changed suits," she said when I'd finished.

"Are you all right?"

"Mostly. I'll be fine once I turn Dugan inside out a few times."

"What does he want from you?"

I shrugged. "Charles and I worried that one to death. We'll know tomorrow night at seven. Between now and then I need the both of you to do me a favor."

"Name it, sweetheart."

I named it, going into detail. "It should work, but you know more about that stuff than I do. Will it?"

Her eyes were bright. Really, really bright. "Jack, that has got to be the craziest thing I've ever heard of—and yes, of course it'll work!"

"You know how to hook things up? Have you got enough time to do all that?"

"I'll call a guy I know to help. He'll have the equipment we need. Between him, me, and Charles, we can have everything ready for you in a couple of hours."

It sure felt good to grin again.

I wasn't as skilled at carpentry as Escott, but made up for the lack by carrying tools and other things up to my office for him. This I accomplished by sinking straight through the floors to the basement and back. It was work and didn't feel good, but neither of us wanted people noticing extra activity on the chance that Dugan might learn about it. We'd spotted his cousin Anthony and his friends, but there might be others lurking around we didn't know about.

Escott got busy drilling holes in the walls, writing out measurements, and muttering to himself a lot. I was used to it from the times he worked on the house and stayed out of his way so he could concentrate.

Bobbi came in to watch, and he paused to consult with her. They had a mild debate about drilling holes in a side table. She was against it, but I said it was okay. I could always buy another one.

If some parts of the evening were rough, the remainder was nearly business as usual without additional floor shows, impromptu fast draws, or the lights going funny. I stopped to visit customers, smiled to everyone, and fended off questions about the tough guys they'd seen leaving.

"Just a misunderstanding; you know how it is," I'd say, which seemed to work since no one wanted to admit otherwise.

Adelle closed with her usual song; the band played "Good Night, Sweetheart" to a nearly empty room. Strome returned since the last time I looked and was talking with his boss. If I'd not been occupied with my own troubles I've have tried to listen, but instead went backstage.

Roland was gone. No telling when he'd taken a powder, but it was convenient. I knocked on Adelle's door, which was half open. She said to come in.

As with Roland, I lingered out of range of her dressing table mirror.

"Hi, Adelle. Good show tonight."

An elegant woman with dark hair, milky skin, and an understated manner when not performing, she turned at my voice, a touch startled. Maybe she'd been expecting Roland or Bobbi. "Hello, Jack. Thank you."

I gave her a moment to say more, thinking she'd ask about the water-throwing, glass-breaking blowup that had interrupted her set, but she didn't, which told me a lot I already knew. "You handled the disturbance very well."

"What distur—oh, that. I was hoping you'd forget it. I certainly wish I could. Dropped a whole stanza. What an embarrassment. It won't happen again."

"I know," I said amiably.

And about two minutes later I left, absolutely certain of that fact.

By the time Gordy came down from his perch to collect her, she was in a great mood. They said good night to me, and off they went in his bulletproof car. Adelle was wholly focused on him.

Two down, one to go in my brand-new triangle-busting business.

At dawn I went to bed; at dusk I was back from the dead again, having no conscious memory of the short winter day's passage. I was rested and ready to start the night and wasted no time getting to my club. The parking lot had only one other car in it, Escott's big Nash, slotted in next to my re-served spot, meaning he and Bobbi were already there, which wasn't part of their normal routine. If Dugan saw and ob-jected, he could take it up with me at seven. I let myself in and trotted up to the office.

"What do you think?" Bobbi asked brightly. She was at the desk, fresh-faced in one of her severely cut business outfits; Escott lounged on the couch. He was in his usual banker's clothing, not a speck of sawdust marring the sober lines of his dark suit.

I looked around the room and didn't see anything different except for a bunch of hothouse-grown flowers in a vase on the side table. Usually it only held an ashtray. "What's with those?"

"Disguise stuff," she said, glancing impishly at Escott, who nodded satisfied agreement. He had his pipe fired up; the place was thick with the fragrant tobacco. I checked the flow-ers more closely. They were packed tight with lots of green leaves mixed in, the better to hide my surprise for Dugan. The vase held no water and never would since it had no bot-tom.

"This is a disguise as well," Escott added, lifting the pipe. "The air."

"Air?" I sniffed. It was pretty dense. He must have been

smoking for hours, but it was a pleasant, sweet mixture.

"Do you smell anything else?"

"That's kinda impossible."

"Exactly. No fresh paint, no drying plaster."

I gave a short laugh. It was a detail I'd have overlooked. "Great, but couldn't you have opened a window?"

"Not without drawing notice; it's too bloody cold out. I brought a fan from the basement to help air things. Fortunately, very little paint was required, only a dab or two, but it is such small giveaways that can make or break a scene."

"Charles has been telling me about when he used to be on the stage," said Bobbi.

"Those days are not over yet, my dear. The performance has merely permutated into something considerably more interesting." He was extremely pleased with himself, so much so that he seemed ready to pop a vest button if he didn't get a chance to talk.

"Okay," I said. "I'm impressed. Now show me what's been done, and I'll give you a standing ovation."

"Hah!" he said and proceeded to point out everything. The three of us went to the next room over, which was ordinarily a storage area, and I got a look at the specialized equipment. It was bulky, but Bobbi assured me that it arrived in a plain crate by way of the delivery doors opening on the back alley, the same as the club's other supplies. Anyone on watch wouldn't know what was inside.

"You can work this?" I asked.

"We both can," she said. "Tested it out today. Here, listen." She flipped a switch.

I listened. And got impressed all over again. "Jeez."

* * *

There wasn't much to do until seven. The normal ritual of opening the place dragged like a snail, but I got through it, and none of the hired help picked up that anything else was going on. In a perverse way I was looking forward to my meeting with Dugan. Escott had the addresses of Dugan's friends for me to tap if things went wrong, but I was feeling optimistic.

The papers wrote nothing new on the Gladwell kidnapping case, just stirring what they already had into a different order to fill the columns. There was still staunch support for Hurley Gilbert Dugan, with quotes from his lawyer and Cousin Anthony. They both agreed that Dugan was a victim of the gang as well and agreed about it to every paper that would listen. He was nowhere to be found, having secluded himself from the hubbub. His lawyer read a statement from him that expressed his sympathy and regret to the Gladwell family with the hope that they would hear his side of things and know he also suffered. It was enough to choke a goat.

Escott said things were quiet at the Gladwells'. Reporters yet hovered by the closed gates, but it was a cold, fruitless, wait. Vivian was content to look after Sarah, who seemed to be recovering, patiently teaching her how to play cards. Apparently the girl was fast becoming a killer at "go fish."

With some satisfaction, Bobbi reported that rehearsals went well for Roland and Faustine's exhibition dancing. They brought their music on some records and with those playing over the club loudspeakers were able to work out what was and wasn't possible on the dance floor. They showed a civil face to the world, but it was clear that Faustine was still mad. Roland was the soul of contrition, very attentive to her, focused on the job, and stayed within her sight the whole time. I did not envy either of them.

Adelle turned up for work on time, along with the band, and Gordy was with her, which surprised me. When she went off to her dressing room, I took him up to his table. Strome and Lowrey were with him; the third guy was off parking the car.

"I thought you'd be busy," I said, once Gordy was settled.

"I was," he said back.

"What about that noon deadline?"

"It didn't happen."

"What did?"

"Nothing. Bristow had too much to drink and too much hangover. He forgot about it. He's coming back tonight for more talk."

I didn't care much for that.

Gordy accurately read my expression. "Don't worry, we ain't wrecking the joint."

That was for damned sure.

Keeping to my routine, I stood post in the lobby, greeted customers, saw to minor problems, and otherwise did my job. When Bristow came in, he was as abrasive as before, but I got around that for a few crucial seconds. He went into the main room in a remarkably good mood, which again puzzled his men. One of them hung back from the rest to have a private word with me. He was the one I'd had the gun on last night, and from the hang of his suit was still packing heat.

"What was that about?" he wanted to know.

"What was what?"

"You looking at the boss like that. What did you do?"

I gave him a demonstration—which he wouldn't remember—along with some very specific instructions on how to behave in my place, then told him to send his buddies out front to see me, one at a time. Even the guy whose arm I'd damaged fell into line. Gordy could wheel and deal all he wanted and any way he liked, but there would be no trouble here tonight.

When the time came, I introduced Adelle to the audience, and she launched into her first set. Couples got up to dance, and the rest enjoyed their half-price drinks.

At ten to seven, Anthony Brockhurst, Marie Kennard, and the other high-hatters unexpectedly came in. They all gave me the eyeball and got one right back, but without any whammy behind it. Time enough for that later. I wanted to save my hard-hitting for their resistant friend. They reminded me of a bunch of college kids crashing a party at a rival fraternity house, smugly daring their disinclined host to do anything about it. I chose not to; they weren't worth the effort, and for the moment were likely part of Dugan's strategy to protect himself. If anything bad happened to him, he had six witnesses on hand to swear that I'd been the perpetrator.

At five to seven I went outside and pretended to smoke in the windy cold, but it was really an excuse to check the street. It was still early enough for traffic; any of the cars parked in front of the shops and the diner could belong to him. He could have ridden along with his cousin's party. I tossed my cigarette at the gutter and went back in.

Seven o'clock came and went; so did five after seven. By then I was convinced he was pulling the same thing with me that he had with Vivian Gladwell and the ransom drop water hauls. At ten after I went up to my office, thinking he might phone.

The upper hall was dark, but my office light was on, the glow seeping from under the door. I distinctly recalled turning it off, though. Either Myrna was having her fun or someone more corporeal was where he shouldn't be. Listening, I heard enough to decide it was the latter. Myrna played with lights and swapped bottles of booze around on the shelves when no one was looking. She'd never shown any interest in opening and shutting desk drawers.

I twisted the knob and went in.

A familiar face. Dugan was at my desk, working with a lockpick on the panel that covered the built-in safe. He managed to jump less than a mile at my abrupt entrance, but he was definitely caught flat-footed and red-handed.

"Ah," he said. A smile came and went, seeming to linger because of the shape of his mouth. He had one of those innocent faces, the kind people automatically like and trust on sight. "Hello, there. I suppose you'll want an explanation."

I shut the door behind me with a good loud click. "I don't want anything. What *you* want is to give me a reason not to break your neck."

"Ah. Well, yes, of course." The smile flickered again. He gestured at a chair in front of the desk as though he was the host. "Won't you sit down, Mr. Fleming?"

The bastard had nerve. And arrogance.

I didn't like either one. He'd recovered his full composure lightning fast. Was that naïveté, stupidity, or lunacy? I'd dealt with crazy guys before, but each one had been different.

Dugan watched me, probably waiting to see what I'd do. Most guys would have a pretty strong reaction to being invited to sit in their own place by an unwelcome intruder. I kept cold and tried to imitate one of Gordy's dead-eyed stares. It was usually an effective ploy. You wait long enough, and the one you're staring at gets uncomfortable and starts talking to fill the silence. This was also the perfect time to attempt hypnosis again.

It's a potent power. Even when weak and on the edge of death, I'd been able to trust its strength over others.

Providing they were susceptible.

I focused hard, concentrating until a band seemed to constrict around my temples. There was no sense of contact with Dugan, no change in his eyes. I kept at it, time and silence stretching between us, kept at it until my head felt ready to explode. He returned my look, fully alert, perhaps even amused. That made me mad, helped me to press harder. Emotions fed the force of it.

But this time . . . nothing.

The only others immune to it besides crazy people and drunks were my kind, vampires. Dugan had a strong heartbeat going, though. His lungs pumped away nice and regular; he wasn't in the union. What I had not six feet in front of me was some not-so-ordinary two-legged insanity.

"Please." He gestured at the chair like he owned it. "Let's be civilized about this."

From a standing start, I moved faster than he could react, taking the distance and the desk in between in one flying lunge, hitting him square. He slammed bodily against the wall with a grunt and dropped on his face. I was set to throw a sucker punch or three to soften him some more, but he was too busy gasping for air to fight.

"Let's not," I said, standing up and brushing my knees.

8

"THAT was," he finally groaned out, "completely unnecessary."

He was in pain. Good.

Downstairs, the distant band struck up a dance number, and Adelle Taylor sang about love and loss to lure couples onto the floor. Perhaps Anthony dear and his friends would join them. More likely not. I figured they were here to back up Dugan in some way. The last thing I wanted was anybody walking in with a gun and interrupting. I snicked the lock shut on the door and rounded on Dugan.

I dragged him up by his fine blue suit and swung him around, back to the wall, until we were nose-to-nose. He didn't fight, even when I made a quick search for weapons and whatever else he carried besides lockpicks. He had a wallet, keys, a gold pocket watch, and a plain white envelope fat with papers. The wallet held eight dollars in cash and a driving license. I tossed everything on the desk and turned my full concentration on Dugan, whispering instructions for him to listen, bolstering it with the force of my long-suppressed rage. The latter I was always careful about; I'd once driven a man insane with it. Tonight I didn't bother holding back . . .

And it still didn't work. Time stretched, my headache worsened, and Dugan remained fully alert and aware, even amused, meeting my gaze look for look.

"Take your hands off me," he said evenly.

I did. By throwing him over the desk and across the room. He landed on the couch, hitting hard, the breath knocked right out of him. I stayed behind the desk. In my mood, I could forget myself and send him on a one-way trip to the cemetery. Damn, my head hurt.

"You shouldn't have done that," he said a moment later, once he'd struggled upright. He was rumpled but strangely serene of face.

"You break into my office for some burglary and think I should . . . what? Why don't you tell me?"

"I was just filling the time until your arrival. Simply an exercise to learn more about you. Besides, you're late. I said we would meet here at seven. You didn't think I'd come in by way of that lobby, did you? You might have made a scene. The stage entrance is much more discreet." He straightened his clothes, composing himself next to the table with the cut flowers. "You should show much better behavior than this."

"Guess again. This is no Sunday tea party. You're in my place. Expect mayhem."

"Which is going to shortly change." He shot me a smug look and another damn smile. "We really do need to talk."

True, but I wasn't going to make it easy for him. I opened

the envelope, pulling out papers. A quick glance showed them to be carbon copies of letters.

"Again," I said slowly, spotting my name, home, and club address on each page along with their phone numbers. My guts twisted like a snake. "Convince me not to kill you."

"It would be a great inconvenience. To yourself, I should clarify." With casual dignity he stood and retrieved his other property, then returned to the couch. "I did not take the risk of coming here without some insurance, as you're about to discover when you read those through. If I disappear or am further harmed, you will find yourself to be the focal point of a meticulous and far-reaching investigation conducted by various law enforcement agencies and other interested parties."

The letters were addressed to the Chicago DA's office, the Internal Revenue, J. Edgar Hoover, three major newspaper editors—the works, up to and including Walter Winchell. Anyone who could possibly turn my life into a living hell was formally notified of my existence and that I should be in jail. That was the short version. There were more details, and specific questions were posed, like how a guy working part-time for a detective was suddenly able to afford a fancy nightclub without bothering any banks for a loan.

I'd taken great pains to cover and clean up certain earnings for the tax man, but a really close look at my business affairs could create a lot of unfixable trouble. My work with Escott had put me in the middle of more than one murder case best left unsolved; my friendship with Gordy and ties to his mob would come out of the shadows. If even one of those resulted in a court case, I was sunk. Daylight appearances were impossible.

"I haven't mailed the originals," said Dugan. "Not yet. But be assured that should you choose to indulge in your baser instincts, there will be serious and permanent repercussions."

The letters were concerned with ordinary matters; no mention was made of my supernatural difference from the rest of humanity. If worse came to worst I could find a way out, even if it meant running off to parts unknown, but I'd worked too hard to casually walk away from what I'd built here.

"Those are," Dugan continued, "what I could put together in just one day. I have additional resources. I know many important people. You would not be the only one affected. Should you try to leave town, your family and friends will also find themselves similarly inconvenienced, all of it perfectly legal. My lawyer tracked down many of their names for me. I have dozens of similar letters ready to be sent out—anonymously—for each of them. I was creative with my accusations, but it's of no import, the effect of a lie can be just as damaging. Your detective friend could lose his license, that blond singer with whom you keep company will never get decent work again. That large gangster will have no end of grief with federal investigators and could shortly find himself heading for prison—"

"Okay, I get the picture. What do you want?"

He sat back on the couch. Smiling. Really enjoying himself. "Just answer a few simple questions. And perform a small favor."

The kind of questions and favor he'd have in mind could never be simple or small. I dropped the letters; they slewed across the desk. One sheet slipped clear and drifted, zigzag, to the floor. "Such as?"

"This may take a while. Please, be seated."

"Just ask."

Dugan gave a little shrug. "Very well. Our *initial* meeting was a *bit* one-sided. We had no real opportunity to talk. I will confess I was rather disturbed to find myself tied up in the car, then carried into the Gladwell house like so much luggage. Once that passed, I soon worked out that you were the one who spoiled my experiment—"

"That's what you call kidnapping, extortion, and attempted murder?"

"Oh, no, it was an experiment."

Jesus, he was absolutely serious.

"You may think I was after the money, but not so. That was just a little research in human behavior, which meant I had to work with people instead of mice," he explained, as though that made it all right. "The ransom was only a means to involve the other men in the operation, a way to success. I planned every detail: the sort of men I would need, the choice of victim. It was something entertaining and challenging to fill the time."

"Dugan, just what kind of sick bastard are you?"

His eyes twinkled. "I rather expected such a reaction. It's nothing new to me. I'm insult-proof. Try to calm yourself."

I calmed myself with the idea that he must have been lying. Nobody could be that crazy.

"Thank you. Now, I was just closing that experiment down when you halted the works. At first I wondered how you managed to follow my men. They're not up to my level of intellect but do possess a sharp instinct for survival; that's why I chose them. I couldn't accept that you'd suborned them by threat or bribery in so brief a time. It was quite a puzzle. Since you were unaware that I'd woken up from your most brutal assault, I continued the pretense of being unconscious. Once my initial confusion passed, I was able to study your interaction with each of my men very closely in the Gladwell parlor. Without the use of any drug you managed to sway them all to your will. It was fascinating and alarming, particularly when my turn came. I braced myself for some sort of mental shock, but nothing happened."

"Nothing at all?" It'd be a shame for my head to hurt so much for nothing, not to mention annoying the hell out of me.

"Do give yourself some credit for the effort. I will confess I was truly fearful of succumbing to whatever spell you put upon them, then delighted to find an immunity to it. Obviously their weaker minds made them easy prey. To assure my continued good health I wisely agreed with all you told me. It was a very macabre situation, especially when I came to realize just what sort of man was before me."

I kept quiet, wondering if he'd say "vampire" aloud.

He only showed his damned smile again. "You are a most unusual specimen, very rare. I've read a lot and know a great deal about all sorts of things and at first couldn't bring myself to believe the evidence. For instance, I'm not unfamiliar with hypnosis. I've seen it done to others. I have never once witnessed an adept *forcing* it upon an unwilling subject as you did to my men. You had a very special power at your command."

"They were off guard. You weren't by the time I got to you."

"Yes, but when you came in here, you tried again. You tried very hard and failed. That was quite evident. What I gleaned from that first encounter was that you fully expected it to work on me. Perhaps a talented stage magician or mentalist might be able to force his will upon a weaker, more receptive mind, but hardly—"

"Dugan, cut the crap and get to the point."

That hit a nerve. His mouth snapped shut, his eyes going

hard for a second, but he didn't give in to temper. "Well, well, someone's mother forgot to teach him good manners. Please, let's be civil with each other."

"You're a murdering son of a bitch who kidnapped a helpless girl and came that close to killing her, so don't talk to me about how to behave."

He waved one hand dismissively. "Very well, though your sentiment for that creature is misplaced. I chose her quite carefully, you know. I would never remove a contributing member of society, but she was nothing. Hardly a contributor; on the contrary, she was and continues to be a waste of resources."

"Her mother doesn't think so."

"Well, mothers are dominated by an instinct to protect their young, whether or not that offspring is worth the trouble. Things are different in the wild, where the weak are sensibly culled from the herd by nature's many checks and balances. Oh, please, do not counter with the judgment that we are not animals. We really are. The vast majority of humans are so complaisant in their superiority over animals that they don't consider the scientific fact that they are just another species among thousands. When it comes down to the basics, we are little removed from the brutes who grubbed around in caves not so very long ago. It's a great astonishment to the populace when a truly superior intellect comes along to show them their place in the scheme of things. That's why genius is so frequently misunderstood, mistrusted, mercilessly exploited by lesser men, or stamped out."

"You like to hear yourself talk, don't you?"

"Ah, by that I can infer that you wish me to move on to other points."

"Any point at all. Like what do you want? You said you had questions."

He made a little frown. "You're a very rude man. Were you always this way, or is it a result of your condition?"

"It's a result of you being in the same room."

"I'll just have to suffer through, then. I do assure you that your show of contempt is wasted on me."

"I'm heartbroken. Just get on with it or get out, I got a saloon to run."

The frown deepened. "I was hoping for better from you. You seemed a likable sort from your interaction with that detective fellow. By the way, where is he?"

I looked at my watch. "You got one minute, then I'm kicking you down the stairs."

A definite flare of anger in his pale eyes. "I remind you that I am the one in control here. I will send those letters out if you don't—"

"Yeah, yeah, and my whole life is ruined. Listen, Gurley Hilbert, I've had to deal with dumber mugs than you, but at least they got down to business. I never heard such a bum for listening to himself gabble."

His face went red. Apparently I wasn't the first who ever made fun of his name in that way or suggested he talked too much. "You will regret that."

"You got half a minute, then it's headfirst into the lobby."

He snorted. "Very well. I know exactly *what* you are. I only suspected at first and made a bold effort to confirm it. You must admit it's a compliment to you that I borrowed your method of pursuit, though the car ride was not at all easy or comfortable—"

"A quarter minute."

"—nor especially agreeable. You have a terrible singing voice."

That sidetracked me. "What?"

"During the trip you sang along with the radio, if one can call such an off-key yodel singing."

Now I really wanted to punch him inside out. I was well aware I couldn't hold a tune in a bucket, but the performance hadn't been for him.

"Anyway," he said. "I'd intended to make my presence known to you at some convenient point and ascertain one way or another your true nature. Imagine my elation when you stopped at the Stockyards and I was able to witness at first-hand the proof of my supposition. The follow-up was, of course, when I put you to the test with my firearm. I'd not intended to do it there, but you forced the issue with your attack. There was a risk you might be killed, but it all worked out."

"You could have been killed yourself."

"I didn't think that at all likely. I got confirmation; the stories I've heard about the abilities of your kind are true."

"Heard from where?

"A source meaningless to you. The public library."

As with Gordy and Bristow, the more Dugan talked, the more I learned about him. What little I picked up made my flesh creep. I'd encountered a similar type before during my days as a reporter. That other man had been a killer heading for death row and not a moment too soon. He'd been friendly, even charming, but gave off a sick emotional stink that made you want to run far and fast. I got the same feeling from Dugan. Whatever it was inside a person that my hypnosis could grab and exploit was missing in him. It felt like I was looking into a face where the eyes had been scooped out, while the body still lived on, unaware of the horror.

"You tell your friends here what you know about me?" I asked.

"You noticed them."

"Hard not to."

"They're here as part of my insurance; they've only seen your sort at the cinema. I can count on their loyalty."

"What lies did you tell them last night to make phone calls to you?"

He was unsurprised I knew. "Oh, that was nothing, and no huge lie was involved. I only said I wanted a quiet word with you in person so as to arrange a meeting with Escott. They accepted it."

"What about your 'experiment'? I doubt you gave them the real dirt."

"Of course not. They are convinced of my innocence. Nothing you say to them to the contrary will be believed. They are not aware of what you are, but I'll also warn you against harming or attempting to hypnotically influence them." He gestured at the carbon copies. "Any action on your part that I do not approve will result in all of these being dropped in the post. Please be assured, they are real; this is no bluff."

He had a kind of gun to my head, but there was only one bullet in it, and I was really good at ducking. He didn't need to hear that, though. "I can return the favor, you know. Winchell wouldn't find me nearly as interesting as you."

"That would be unwise, Mr. Fleming. I already have sufficient notoriety but am well able to withstand its blast. You cannot. I am certain because of what you are you would shun official notice of your existence. You can't hypnotize every bureaucrat, every reporter between Chicago and Washington."

"Sure about that?"

"Yes."

No need to disabuse him of that idea.

"Also, you have too much to lose." He lifted a hand to indicate my nightclub. "I don't. I have the kind of connections and money to allow me to leave this country and enjoy all that the world has to offer. If it looks like circumstances will shift against me, I'll simply move on. With all that you have invested in this place you don't have my sort of freedom. Should you try to leave, it will be in the knowledge that those you leave behind will suffer for it."

"What do you want?"

"Nothing major. You have only to talk to my men just as you did before. This time you will convince them to adjust their confessions slightly. They are to provide the police a story that will guarantee my exoneration from their crimes. I have one prepared that's a bit more detailed than what I've told the papers. It will serve to free me."

"You think I can do that with them wide awake and on guard?"

"Yes. I saw how you operated that night. You demonstrated such complete confidence that your hypnosis was obviously routine. You have evidently used it so many times before that failure was not even a remote consideration."

He had that pegged to the wall, but if I gave in too quick, he wouldn't believe me. "Suppose I fix them for you. Then what?"

"Another experiment, of course."

"What kind?"

"I'll let you know."

"Not good enough. You tell me now."

"Or what?"

"I don't cooperate. I'll have a few nights feeling bad about what you did to my friends, and I'll be mad about losing the club, but it'll be from miles away where you'll never find me."

Dugan shook his head. "I think not. You risked life and limb and your great secret to find that girl. What I overheard between you and Escott informed me that you are good friends, and you exhibit the unmistakable signs of possessing a sense of honor. Your anger at me for what you perceived to be a crime is one of them. Those are fatal flaws."

"I can get over them, but you won't get over being dead."

"Then my many letters will be mailed, and you will have six unimpeachable witnesses testifying that I came to this club at Escott's invitation. I left a note in a safe place outlining the whole business. My story is that Escott wanted to have a private meeting with me here to discuss matters to do with the Gladwell kidnapping. In the company of my friends I felt safe enough, you see. If you do anything rash, I guarantee he *will* be implicated in my death or disappearance."

"I'll talk to your friends before that happens."

"Perhaps, if you found them all in time. They'll have left by now. If I'm not away from here by nine o'clock at the latest, they are to contact the police, then scatter—after dropping my letters in the mail."

"Just a chance I'll have to take."

"But the letters will create a devil of a mess. It's unavoidable, no matter what efforts you make to the contrary. But think carefully on this: three of the kidnappers will still go to jail, and the girl's alive and well. What I'm asking isn't much. You need to be pragmatic. Balance a few hours of your time against months if not years of dealing with a host of very unsympathetic bureaucrats, police, and so forth. You can't bend all of them to your will. Truly you cannot."

I could if I had to, but the bastard had the high hand for the moment. I let him see me thinking it over. "What's this other experiment you got in mind?"

The smile tugged at him, as though he knew I was over the last hill. "When the time comes I'll tell you. I promise that it will not be morally abhorrent. I prefer to maintain businesslike conduct in all things whenever possible. You recall that I did return your car as a sign of my good faith; take that as an example of things to come. We've had a rather rough introduction to each other, but it need not have an adverse effect on our future dealings."

"I don't want any dealings with you. Here's how it works: you get this one favor to get you off the hook and out of my hair, and then it's good-bye. You go your way, I go mine."

His smile was patient. "Impossible. You are unique. I have to know more. How did you acquire this condition?"

"You tell me."

"Well, perhaps we can discuss it later. You have a very important errand to run tonight. I'll contact you tomorrow evening to ask after your progress with my men."

"Yeah, sure, now get the hell out."

"How delightful. However, I can't help thinking that you're giving in much too easily."

"I'm a fast thinker; it comes with the condition."

"Oh, really, come-come."

"What are you looking for, argument and hair-tearing at how unfair the world is? I'll do what you want. Now get out so I can call the fumigators."

"It's to be done tonight."

"Too soon. Those friends of yours are in jail. The cops don't let just anyone in for a visit, especially at night."

"Actually, they will. With your abilities, it should be very easy for you to get through to them."

"It'll take time. I don't even know which jail they're in."

"But I do." He pulled a folded paper from his wallet and held it up, then delicately straightened it with his long fingers until its intended shape was restored. It looked like the note he'd sent last night, a bird with raised wings. "How do you like my little cranes?"

I made no reply.

"One of my hobbies. I know dozens of patterns. Something to fill the time." He offered it to me. When I didn't come around to fetch, he gave a small shrug and set it on the table by the flower vase. "This has the necessary information and the new story the men are to provide to the police. You will persuade them to it."

"I have my limits."

"You will overcome them. You will also be watched. Don't mistake my pleasant manner for softness. I don't trust you."

"That makes two of us." I unlocked the door and held it wide. "Out, before I change my mind."

He stood and went to the desk, gathering his hat and the letter copies, not forgetting the one on the floor, then walked past. I sensed his tension, his bracing for another assault, but neither of us got stupid with the other. He paused. "One last instruction. Go to the front windows there."

"Why?"

"I want to make sure you don't invisibly follow me. You are to open the blinds and stand before the window for ten minutes. You will be watched."

He sure loved playing that tune.

"If you move from that spot before time, I will mail the letters."

That one as well.

I did as he said, making it clear that I didn't like being ordered around. I pushed the curtains wide and pulled up the blinds. Standing like this raised my hackles, but I could trust that the bulletproof glass would do its job in case Dugan or one of his friends thought to take a potshot.

He smiled one last time, put on his hat, and finally left, his steps unhurried on the stairs.

"Charles," I said, not too loudly. "Get your ass in here."

The next door down the hall opened, and Escott rushed in, alert.

"You hear what he wanted?" I asked.

"Everything. Miss Smythe and I have—"

"Great, we'll get detailed later, swap places with me, quick."

He caught my intention and we smoothly switched. We had nearly identical builds and frames; silhouetted against a window, we were twins.

"Face the street for ten minutes and don't show a profile," I warned him. Our heads were shaped a little differently, and that big beak of a nose of his would give the game away. I moved toward the door as Bobbi came in, looking excited.

"Jack, we got all of it, but I don't know if the band music might—"

"Later, sweetheart," I said, brushing her forehead with my lips as I zoomed past. "Keep away from the window!"

"You're welcome!" she called after, but she sounded amused.

Before I reached the stairs, I'd turned incorporeal, moving fast and silent, confident of the territory. At the landing I sensed what I hoped was Dugan walking away. I couldn't get close or he'd feel the chill of my presence. There was a chance he was aware of that giveaway. He headed toward the front. I heard the doorman say, "Good night, sir." The muttered response confirmed I had the right guy.

He paused on the sidewalk, perhaps looking both ways like any careful pedestrian, then trotted across the street, me close on his heels. A car door was opened and he slipped inside. I risked contact and slid in, too. From the feel of things, it was the backseat and otherwise empty. Taking no chances, I oozed up into the dead space of the rear window ledge and parked there.

"How did it go?" a man asked. I identified the voice. Anthony Brockhurst was playing chauffeur. He shifted gears, and we moved off. So much for keeping watch, though there might be other people around.

"Very well," Dugan replied. "I'm most pleased and very relieved. Mr. Escott, Mr. Fleming, and I have cleared a lot of misunderstandings away. They're going to cooperate with me."

"You managed, then?" This from a woman. Bored-sounding. Marie Kennard.

"Very well," Dugan repeated. "I convinced them of the error of their ways. They will be on my side from now on."

"Just on the threat of a few letters?"

"They're only hired help for that Gladwell harridan, after all. They're also very adverse to disagreeable publicity, especially Escott. He's been involved in more than one case of a dubious nature. He'd rather not lose his license to practice his trade should an investigation into his business affairs be launched."

"Seems a bit of a low blow," said Anthony. I couldn't tell if he'd had anything to drink or not. That would affect how to proceed this evening.

"This is my very life at stake," Dugan admonished, sounding wounded. "Those hooligans who trapped me in their filthy scheme . . . well, you know all that. Mine is a desperate situation because of their lies. It requires desperate measures to extract me from it. Besides, after Escott and Fleming got over their anger at the letter threat, they came to see the truth of things. I had to practically tell them my life story, which is what took so long. It wasn't cheap, but we've got it all worked out now."

"Thank goodness for that. You'd better call the others so they don't worry or drop the things in the mail."

"Then find a telephone."

"What were they like?" Marie asked, meaning me and Escott.

"Rough sorts, almost as bad as those criminals. They wear better clothes, but at heart . . . well, you'd not want to meet either of them in a dark alley. Thank goodness you won't have to go back there again. I was worried you might come to harm."

"I saw Fleming at the club. He didn't seem rough."

"Ah, but 'the devil hath power to assume a pleasing shape.' Fleming is the worst of the two. He has a particularly violent temper, keeps it hidden. Gave me some bruises."

Violent temper? He'd only seen me being mildly cranky. Wait 'til he saw when I really got pissed.

"You're hurt?" she sounded concerned.

"Mostly my pride. I've had worse on the polo field, my dear. Escott calmed him down. He's the brains of their unholy partnership. Once I got him to see reason, it sorted itself out."

"How much did it cost?"

"It's not good news. He wants ten thousand. Cash."

"That's an outrage! You've the threat of the letters to hang over him!"

"One has to compromise on certain business dealings. He's putting himself at risk on my behalf. He's wants 'a fair payment,' to use his words. Yes, I can hold the threat over him, but he promised to be less acrimonious and considerably more cooperative about it with a nice fat bribe to sweeten things. He was the one to raise the topic, not I, but it's a good thing we three talked about it beforehand, or I'd have been caught off guard."

"It's too much," she stated.

For once Dugan kept his mouth shut. I was fascinated by all the smart dealings Escott had accomplished without being in the room. He'd pulled in a hell of a profit. I wished that I'd thought of asking Dugan for hush money.

"This *is* Gilbert's freedom," Anthony ventured. "We can't let him down, Marie."

She must have stewed a little; there was a pause before she spoke again. "Oh, very well, just stop looking at me like that. I'm not going to scrimp, but I thought the letters would be enough to control him."

"As did I," said Dugan. "We had a long exchange about it, but he insisted he was willing to face whatever trouble came and the devil take me unless he got something advantageous out of it. It's like bribing a maître d'for a better table; bothersome, but we each get what we want. You're lucky I managed to bargain it down from twenty thousand."

"My God! He wanted *that* much?"

"Fleming did. I think he intended to pay off his club, but Escott was more reasonable. He could see I wasn't going to go that far."

"Here's a drugstore," said Anthony, slowing. "They'll have a phone booth."

"This will take a few minutes; it's four calls."

"Have you enough nickels?"

"I think so. . . . Yes, thank you."

I heard the door open and slam shut. Dugan could look after himself without me.

Anthony and Marie didn't talk much until she asked him for a cigarette and then a light.

"Ten thousand," she grumbled. "How is he ever going to pay me back?"

"You don't have to loan it, you know," said Anthony. "I could probably work out something with my family, but Father would be very difficult. He's none too pleased with this mess."

"He can never raise that kind of money on his old railroad stock. Even if he does, the lawyers will probably take it. I'll come to the rescue, but why, oh, why was Gilbert stupid enough to get entangled with those thieves? He might well have known it would turn out badly."

"We all make mistakes."

"This is a very costly one. I don't see how this detective can help him."

"Gilbert explained it all to me. Escott will forget important evidence, remember certain details differently. When he gives a formal statement, it can be in such a way as to support Gilbert's story. That's what they were working out up there, exactly what to say."

"What slimy, horrid people detectives are. Peering through keyholes for money. Was that man up in the window Escott?"

"I never met the fellow. It could have been Fleming for all I could see. As overdone as the club is, he obviously put a pretty penny into it; you'd think he'd have gotten better quality glass, not that murky warped stuff."

She agreed with him.

Overdone? What the hell is he talking about? Lady Crymsyn's perfect. Damned snobs. I should materialize now and scare the crap out of them.

Dugan returned before I got too steamed, sparing his friends some well-deserved terrorizing. I wondered if Cousin Anthony was in on the scam being pulled on Marie or if both were dupes in Dugan's game. Later I might find out. He seemed cold sober tonight.

"All taken care of," Dugan reported, apparently happy and relieved. "Let's go celebrate."

"Let's not," said Marie. "I'm ready to faint I'm so tired. Just take me home."

"Of course, darling. See to it, Anthony; the lady needs her rest."

Anthony did his chauffeur work. I couldn't tell how long it took to get to her place, though from a strong tug that went all through me, we crossed water, probably the Chicago River. It seemed to take forever to get over the bridge, but my presence didn't affect the car's progress.

Talk was at a minimum until Anthony finally slowed and stopped, cutting the motor. Dugan got out, apparently to accompany Marie to her door. If she was going to give him ten grand, he'd have to show her plenty of consideration. I hadn't figured out the relationships between the three of them yet, but it looked like she might be Dugan's girl rather than Anthony's. He was gone a while. When he returned, he got in the front seat. I moved down behind them to hear better but remained invisible.

"You've a long face," Anthony said, starting the car.

"She's upset about the money, but I let her know how grateful I am for her help. It's just very hard. I can't tell you how humiliating it is for a man to have to ask a woman for this sort of help."

"You've little other choice. I'd help if I could, but Father has everything tied up in trust and refuses to break it, even for family. I wager if *I* was in your place he'd still refuse."

"Well, you wouldn't have gotten into this stew at all. It's my own fault, I own up to that. How could I—oh, never mind."

Dugan sounded convincingly upset. I speculated just how much lying he'd done during our talk.

"It will be all right, Gil. You made a mistake, trusted the wrong sorts, got in over your head. Could have happened to anyone."

"No, only me. I don't have many friends, you know. I'm not the sort people take to, so when those men invited me to have a drink, well, I was ripe for the picking. I had no idea they were going to use my connections to get to that girl, that they were going to use me. My God, they'd have killed me, too, if that mystery Samaritan hadn't shown up. I'd like to thank him for saving my life."

"Did you ever see him?"

"No. Certainly he mistook me for being part of the gang, else he'd not have knocked me cold. Can't blame the man. Pity he's not come forward; he might have valuable testimony."

"Nothing good for you, though, if he thought you were in on things."

Dugan gave a heavy sigh. "I suppose so. I just thank God for you, Marie, and your friends believing me, or this would be utterly unbearable."

I was ready to hand him a violin so he could squeeze out even more sympathy.

"Are you going to marry her?" Anthony asked.

"I don't think she'd have me. Certainly I don't deserve her."

"Well, brace yourself, but I'm fairly sure she expects you to at least propose."

"Why should she want a penniless scholar facing a jail sentence? I've nothing to offer her but a drafty old house with two mortgages on it."

"She can help you out of that."

"It's asking too much."

"Ask her to marry you and find out if she thinks so."

Dugan seemed to mull it over. "All right, but only *after* this problem has been settled and sorted. Only then."

"Good man. You won't regret it. She's a wonderful girl. Well, here's the old homestead, drafts and all. You'll be all right? There's a man out front."

"Probably a reporter. They're terrible pests, always ready to believe the worst. I'll go in the back way. Thank you, Anthony. You're a godsend, you know."

"Don't be silly. Go get some rest; you must be done in after all that."

"Indeed I am. I'll see you tomorrow sometime." He got out. The door thumped shut before I could get clear, forcing me to push through the window to escape. I hated how that felt.

Anthony drove away. Dugan walked quickly. The wind was strong, wherever we were, pressing against me and probably chilling him right through. He was trotting, but I kept up easily, a very silent companion.

Through a gate, some steps, the snick of a lock, a door creaking open. I went high and gusted through near the top of the jamb. Once inside, I rose higher still to hover by the ceiling.

He clicked on lights as he went through the place. It seemed to be pretty big and, so far as I could tell, was empty of company. After some moving about, he finally paused.

"What a day," he said to himself, then gusted out a pleasant laugh. "What a perfectly *wonderful* day!"

I chose that moment to materialize right in front of him. God, but all the hoop-jumping crap I'd gone through was *worth* it to see the look on his mug. Appalled astonishment didn't begin to cover it.

"Glad you had such a good time," I said, cheerful, too.

Then I decked him, dead square in the jaw.

9

HE dropped straight back and down. No frills, no flourishes, and best of all, no talking. He sprawled on a worn-looking Persian rug, a lead brick in a nice blue suit. Slightly rumpled now.

I rubbed my knuckles out of habit. My hand didn't hurt. Hell, I could have used Dugan for punching bag practice the rest of the night and not felt anything but the warmth of righteous satisfaction.

God, that had been *good*.

Since he was out for an undetermined count, I took a look around what he called home. He must have been very secure indeed about his control over me to have come here. Maybe he thought I couldn't get inside a dwelling without an invitation, but he didn't seem the type to swallow all the old folklore and superstitions whole. More likely he just couldn't believe anyone would cross him once he'd decided things for them.

The room we were in served as a parlor and study in one. It was crowded with old furniture, expensive a couple generations ago, gone shabby in the years between with moth holes in the musty upholstery. Stuff made of wood had aged better, but the varnish had gone black. He had one big table covered with books and papers, the latter mostly bills, the top layer was legal documents. A few mismatched chairs, lamps, and shelf clutter filled up the corners, with nothing new to relieve the drab except for a cheap radio.

Scattered around were *hundreds* of his origami pieces. Literally hundreds. All kinds of animals, paper boats, planes, other objects not readily identifiable, they were everyplace. It was like I was being watched by them. A few quivered in unseen drafts as though they might start walking toward me any second. I quelled two urges: either to leave fast or smash the moving ones flat.

The rest of the place was big and pretty thoroughly cobwebbed, and if not already haunted, then it should have been. I wasn't much for figuring the date of a house, but this one seemed on a level with Escott's old relic, only he took better care of his home. The modernization here must have stopped when Queen Victoria died.

The other rooms were empty or down to a couple pieces that were too big to move. I got the impression he'd sold off stuff to pay the bills. He'd left the dust-coated curtains, probably to keep neighbors from seeing where all the echoes originated. Faded wallpaper bubbled or peeled quietly in the damp. The floors creaked or crunched from dry rot. I could see why he'd tried kidnapping as a source of income. Of course, he *could* have cut his losses, moved out, and gotten a job like a normal person.

Upstairs was more of the same: only one bedroom next to an aging bath was in use, the rest were gutted, their heating grates sealed up by rags and yellowed newspaper. He did have a nice clothing collection in his closet, enough to hold his head up at society events. So long as no one saw the inside of this dump, he could blend.

Back where I left him I found his phone and noticed the first two letters shared the same exchange as Vivian Gladwell's. Her house couldn't have been far. I didn't believe in coincidence. Going to the window, I checked the street. Big yards, posh homes, familiar neighborhood. A little more checking, and I found a second-floor room with binoculars on the sill. The window was on a straight line of sight through bare-branched trees to the Gladwells' front gate. You could just see the house beyond.

"You son of a bitch," I said, then went to call Lady Crymsyn's office, picking up the receiver using a handkerchief and dialing with the eraser end of my pocket pencil. I'd been careful not to touch anything, having left my gloves back at the club.

Escott caught it before the first ring died. "Yes?"

"I got him," I reported with no small triumph.

"Where are you?"

"His house. Wait'll you see this place. Talk about not very *Great Expectations*. Miss Havisham would feel at home."

"I look forward to it. You still wish to proceed as planned?"

"Yeah. You got everything set?"

"They're waiting and ready for us."

"Great. Where's Bobbi?"

"Downstairs running things."

"Any problems?"

"None of which I am aware."

"Great. Tell her I'm okay, then come over, and let's get this show on the road."

"Immediately."

It took him about half an hour with traffic. He used the back door, which opened into a badly kept kitchen. By then I'd found rope and other things and had Dugan trussed up tight, blindfolded, with a gag in his mouth. He lay on the floor like forgotten laundry, still unconscious to judge by his heartbeat and utter immobility.

"You're not taking any chances, are you?" Escott observed.

"You heard him talk. Wanna listen to more?"

"No, thank you."

"He didn't seem to be expecting any visitors after his cousin dropped him off. We have the whole night to go through everything.

"It may take longer than that. This place is enormous."

"He doesn't live in all of it."

I took him into the living room zoo. He paused, staring at the countless paper animals populating every horizontal surface.

"Good God."

"Yeah. That's what I thought. Must be a couple of reams' worth here."

"Are the other rooms . . . ?"

"No, just here."

He looked relieved.

Taking off his regular gloves, he pulled out a pair made of thin rubber, the kind used by surgeons, then gave me an identical set. Neither of us wanted to leave any sign we'd been near this place. "Tell me what happened after you left."

It was my pleasure. While listening, Escott poked, pried, sifted papers, rummaged drawers and cabinets, and generally turned the house inside out for information about Dugan. We found it impossible not to knock over or displace the origami pieces, but there were so many, chances are even anyone familiar with the place wouldn't notice the added disorder.

"No personal journal," he said a couple dusty hours later. "A pity. He seems the sort who would want a record of his accomplishments."

"Not that he's done much. He called himself a scholar, but I don't see many books." We did find a stack of old *Police Gazette*s and crime magazines, all with articles on famous kidnapping cases. "He should have gotten rid of these."

"He'll probably claim the gang brought them in for him to study."

"No doubt. Still, it's a damned fool thing to have those lying around."

I dropped a magazine with a torn cover onto the pile. Its lead was about the Lindbergh baby. "Yeah, of course only an innocent man would keep them. 'See what they forced me to read, Judge?' What a crock."

"To be expected. He's obviously a chronic liar."

"Only when his lips are moving. He should be on the stage, but I don't think too many people would believe him; he just expects them to."

"That expectation is a weakness. Let's hope he keeps it. You'll dissuade his friends from helping him further?"

"So long as they're not crazy."

"There's nothing to prevent him writing more letters, though."

"Won't matter if he's in jail. Look at this." I held up a letter. "He's supposed to be in court tomorrow. Ain't that too bad?"

Escott chuckled. "How convenient. And now you've an address for his lawyer."

"Yeah. By tomorrow night, Dugan won't have anyone on his side, and the law will be after him. Life is sweet."

"Still, it's a bit of chance we're taking."

"Safer than having him run loose. He can do with a dose of poetic justice."

"You're certain hypnosis won't work on him?"

I let the letter fall and picked up one of the origami animals, fiddling with it. "I did my best. It had no effect on him except give him a laugh and me a hell of a headache. We'll do it this way, then when the time comes, let him twist in the wind."

"As you wish."

"Something's missing," I said. "You find a typewriter here? Carbon sheets? Typing paper?"

"No. Nothing like that."

"Then he wrote the letters someplace else, or got one of his friends to do them for him."

"Where are those letter copies?"

I patted my inside coat pocket.

"But we've not found the originals. Perhaps one of his freinds has them."

"His fingerprints are all over these. If it ever comes to it, they can make a good case against him for blackmail by intimidation. It shouldn't get that far . . . oh, hell." Something about the paper animal caught my eye, got my brain to working.

"What's wrong?"

"Nothing. Just take a look." I unfolded what first appeared to be only scrap. Flattening it out on the table revealed writing on one side, all done in a distinctive dark green ink. Very oddball. I read some of the ruler-straight lines. Dugan had no scratch-outs, no botched lettering. The writing was so even it could have been done by machine.

Sentiment is our greatest hindrance to true progress. Think of the scientific advancements we could have by now had our ancestors been able to rid themselves of the more impractical emotions or at least better control them. We have twisted what should be simple survival and improvement of the species into a complicated tangle.

From the moment we're born we are driven by instinct to find a mate and through her propagate offspring, a laudable goal unless the mate is of a mediocre intellect, bound by the limits of emotions, which are passed on. The greater part of humanity is mediocre because we tend to be attracted to mates similar to our own background and place in society. There is safety in the familiar. Thus do we continue to hold ourselves back. We could progress to a higher level more quickly by a judicious program of breeding. If we have bred lesser animals to our purposes to produce cattle with more milk or meat on them, why not do the same for ourselves? The mating of two brilliant people would likely result in a brilliant child, and he in turn can expect to produce . . .

"Oh, brother." I said.

Escott puffed out a single laugh. "His journal. And I'd been looking for a notebook."

"This is more like an editorial than a diary. When I was

reporting, there was a guy on the staff who would write out whatever was bothering him that day. Sometimes they'd use it for an opinion piece."

"Dugan has a good point, but I doubt a practical application will ever prove to be popular." Escott collected more animals, lining them up, and we unfolded several. Each animal represented a specific subject. All were covered with the same machinelike writing, recording all kinds of observations about people and life, mostly the shortcomings. What a complainer. Giraffes were concerned with sociology, cranes were history, pelicans current events, boats were about euthanasia of inferior human specimens as a means to improve the breed. Chronic criminals, the mentally ill or retarded, those with hereditary afflictions or abnormalities were on his list. He had quite a fleet of boats.

"This is the damnedest filing system I've ever seen," I said, standing away from the remains and staring at the ones yet untouched. Just thinking of the hours he'd put in writing all that crap made my guts twist.

"Do you think there's any symbolism involved in his choice of animal for each topic?"

"Ask Dr. Freud."

"He is very consistent, in his own way organized, very prolific. An acute case of overthinking and too much time to do it. Could this be only window dressing intended to make one conclude he is less than rational? Or is he really like this?"

"I *know* he's nuts. Doesn't matter much. Once we're done, he'll have plenty more time to write his novel or treatise or whatever he thinks he's doing."

"Indeed. We should wind things up, then. I'll phone and let them know we're on the way."

* * *

The driveway to Dugan's garage led from a side-street entrance around the house to the back. There it was secluded, surrounded by trees and a high fence, and completely concealed the presence of my car. No one saw as we lugged Dugan's unresisting body down the kitchen steps and dumped him in the trunk, dropping his coat and hat on top.

"You're sure he's all right?" asked Escott.

I could understand his concern. Once, before I'd gotten used to my preternatural strength, I'd killed a man with a single punch to the face. Not that he didn't deserve it, but I hated being the one to deliver his fate. Sometimes, when mired in a dark mood, I could still feel the bones giving wetly under my fist. Not a memory I wanted to double. I listened to Dugan's heart and breathing. "He's just out. Smelling salts should bring him around."

Escott slammed the trunk lid shut.

Dugan's house keys in hand, I went back for a last look, making sure we'd covered everything. Propped against his phone was a single sheet of paper, the letter notifying him of his court date tomorrow. On its back Escott had block-printed "Good-bye," using one of the fountain pens on the table so its green ink would match up with the other written things. We left the essays lying around open so anyone who bothered to read them could draw their own conclusions about their writer's mental state.

Last of all, in the kitchen, I picked up a sizable suitcase we found in Dugan's bedroom. Personal stuff from his bedside table was in it, along with his shaving kit and toothbrush, and we filled the rest up with clothes and a pair of galoshes. We emptied hangers in his closet and enough underwear was missing from his bureau to indicate he'd packed for a long absence. Escott had found Dugan's bank- and checkbook and put those in, too. There was less than a hundred in the account. Added to what was in his wallet, if that was all he had in the world, he must have been desperate for cash.

He'd have other things on his mind soon, though.

I locked the house, put the suitcase in the backseat, got behind the wheel, and took the long way around to our destination. Eventually I found another side street entrance to a long driveway, this one in better repair with a gate made of tall iron bars with spikes on top. At one in the morning it was locked. Escott jumped out with a key, pulled the gate wide so I could get though, shut it, and rode the running board on the trip up to the big, dark structure ahead. He seemed to be thoroughly enjoying him- self.

Only one light showed at the servants' entry to the Glad- well mansion. As I set the brake, Vivian Gladwell herself came out to meet us. At this very late hour she was fully dressed and looked wide awake. If she was nervous, it didn't show. She went to greet Escott, giving him her hand. He took it in both of his—he'd removed the surgical gloves—and cut a little bow, looking pleased to see her.

"Hello, Mr. Fleming," she said as I got out. "Is every- thing all right?"

"Copasetic," I replied. "There's still time to change your mind, you know."

She shook her head, turning to Escott.

"Jack's right," he said. "This is a dreadful risk for you if word got out."

Another headshake, with a warm smile. She did have a nice face. "I trust my household. We're all in agreement."

Escott shot me a look of confirmation, nodding. He knew the people better. I could rely on his judgment of them and the situation in general.

I opened the trunk, and Vivian stared down at Dugan, getting her first sight of him outside of newspaper photos. His bindings didn't seem to shock her.

"To think I was at the same parties with him," she said. "He makes my flesh crawl."

"You and me both, ma'am." I grabbed under his arms, folded him forward, then heaved him up over one shoulder like a sack of flour. "Lead the way."

The physical effort impressed her. She recovered quickly, and with Escott behind carrying the suitcase, ushered us into the house.

The place was as silent as Dugan's aging white elephant but much warmer and missing the dust. He might be grateful for the switch in accommodations. Maybe he could write an essay about it if Vivian had some green ink lying around.

She went to a broad door under some stairs, opened it, and yanked on a light cord. Bare wooden steps went steeply down to the basement. Dugan wasn't especially heavy to me, just awkward. I was careful about balance on the descent. At the bottom was another cord, this one controlling several lights. We were in a big, dim, low-ceilinged area, chilly compared to the rest of the place. Here the laundry was washed, Christmas decorations were stored, and unfashionable furniture ripened into antiques. It was the Ritz compared to Dugan's place. The pitch-black dusty-museum cellar there would have scared Frankenstein into next week.

Vivian walked ahead, gesturing toward a sturdy door with a serious-looking bolt lock on it. The room behind it was a dozen feet square and very, very quiet, the result of solid concrete walls. It was lighted by one unshaded standing lamp on the floor by the threshold. On the far end was an army cot, several blankets spread neatly on top, with a pillow. Under the cot was a chamber pot discreetly covered by a square of cloth, a roll of toilet paper on end next to it. She'd thought of everything.

I rolled Dugan off my shoulder onto the cot and stretched my cramped muscles. "Is he in for a surprise." He'd wonder how the hell he'd gotten here. Most people knocked unconscious don't remember how they got that way.

Escott put the suitcase on the floor and opened it. He removed the safety razor and anything else that might be made into a weapon, including the toothbrush. "He only gets this when he is actually brushing his teeth," he said to Vivian. "The handle can be filed down to a point, you know. Wouldn't want anyone to get punctured."

"Goodness," she said. "I wouldn't have thought of that."

I went through Dugan's pockets, taking stuff he wouldn't need, like his wallet and a pencil. I judged his handkerchief to be fairly harmless . . . unless he twisted it into a garrote. On second thought I took it, too. He could use the toilet roll to blow his nose. Of course, he could rip his clothing up to make the same sort of weapon, but maybe it wouldn't occur to him. He'd be pretty damn muzzy. Vivian had an ample supply of sleeping pills to put in his food and drink.

We took his shoes and suspenders, the belt on his overcoat, and double-checked the room inch by inch, making sure it was completely bare of anything that would be used for a weapon or a means of escape. Vivian's people had been thorough. There wasn't so much as a used toothpick left forgotten in a corner.

"What was this before?" I asked her, wondering how an ideal prison cell happened to be in her basement.

"It used to be the wine storage. The lock prevented temptation for the servants. When we married, my late husband installed a special cooler on the ground floor for his stock, which I still use. It's more convenient than coming all the way down here, and electric, so the temperature is controlled winter and summer."

"I got something like that at my club. I'd like to see yours, though."

"Certainly," she said. "But, please, let's get him . . . well . . ."

"No problem."

Escott had been over earlier in the day with a special drill and hardware. He said it had only taken him a few minutes for the job, which would have done the Inquisition proud. Set deep into the concrete floor next to the cot was a very heavy-duty ring bolt made of steel nearly an inch thick. Threaded through it was an equally heavy chain, the ends joined by a big padlock. I tested the strength of the chain, yanking hard, trying to pull it apart or shatter the lock. No chance that Dugan would break it if I couldn't. I did my best and failed. It made me very glad not to be in Dugan's socks.

Escott wore something close to a smirk, his eyes twinkling with unsuppressed good humor. He *was* having a ball.

The weakest item were the handcuffs, but Escott had turned up a set of grim manacles that Houdini might have hesitated trying his luck against. They were padded to minimize chafing marks but would fit snug as a friendship ring. Escott looped these through the doubled chain and clamped them on Dugan's wrists, locking them fast. Only then did I cut the ropes. When Dugan woke, he'd have about a six-foot radius for exercise and wouldn't be able to come within four feet of the door. In planning it out, we tried to think of what we'd do in his place to escape. It only seemed prudent to be overcautious.

"He won't be able to change his shirt with those on," Escott pointed out.

"Too bad," I said. "Sarah wore the same clothes for two weeks. Do him good to find out what it's like."

"There's that, but I was considering the sensibilities of the people charged with looking after him."

"He can make do with a washbasin, and we can hold our breath," said Vivian. "He won't have visitors except to bring him food and—er—remove the necessary."

"How many are actually in on this?" I asked.

"All of us. The butler, maids, cook, the chauffeur—"

"That's a lot of mouths to keep quiet."

"I *trust* them, Mr. Fleming. Not many people are able to accept my daughter or treat her like an ordinary human being. It took me years to bring together a staff that would care for her as much as I do. Charles will tell you how hard it was for everyone when she was kidnapped and how incensed we all were when this—this *animal* began throwing out those horrid lies to the papers to talk himself free. We all want him to pay for what he's done. This is a start."

A start and a half, I thought, deciding that Vivian did indeed have the guts to go through it. "How's Sarah?"

Her face softened. "Improving. She has nightmares and won't let me out of her sight, but she's begun talking more freely again."

"Does she talk about what happened to her?"

"She doesn't recall much, only a little about 'the bad men' scaring her. I want to be able to look her in the eye and truthfully tell her that they will never scare her again."

"You can now. Make sure she doesn't come down here."

"Oh, that won't be a problem. Sarah hates the basement. Doesn't like the closed-in feeling. She thinks basements are where monsters live."

I looked at Dugan, gathering up the last scraps of his bindings. "She's right."

We went out, leaving Dugan alone in his cell.

"She fully understands the precautions she must take," Escott said about Vivian as we drove away. "Her butler and chauffeur will do the looking-after, bringing food and such. No eating utensils allowed, and always with at least one other man on hand to back them up. We've had a very somber chat about safe procedure and caution. I'll go over every day to check on things."

The way he'd looked at Vivian gave me the idea he would have done that with or without a prisoner to watch.

"I doubt they'll have difficulties, but can't say it will be pleasant for them."

"Less so for Dugan. He's still got better than what he gave Sarah."

"They're well aware of that. I think the household's outrage will be more than sufficient to carry them through, however long it goes on."

"Hope so. He may be tougher than we think. He could crack tomorrow or never."

"Either way, he will be subject to a manhunt. Once the authorities realize he's truant, they will have to assume it's to avoid prosecution. Even the worthies of the misled press will eventually see the truth."

"If it sells papers, yeah. Maybe Gordy can put a good word in for us. He's chummy with some of the crime beat guys. Did you see if he came in tonight?"

"Yes, along with several bodyguards and Hog Bristow. He showed no sign of remembering last evening's dustup or his noon-hour ultimatum. They were at that high table as usual."

"It's taking too long. Gordy should have gotten him out of the picture by now." He probably had his reasons for letting this drag, but I didn't like it dragging all over my place. Things had come too close to disaster with the near gunplay, and I wanted no more of the same. If he didn't resolve things tonight, I'd offer my services as interrogator the next time Bristow was sober, get what was needed, then pack him off to Cuba. This was the right time of year to enjoy Havana's climate.

I peered ahead, trying to blink my way past a light mist that had begun falling just after we left the Gladwell house. Though not cold enough for snow or sleet, it did slick the world up and obscure the view. The wipers would swipe the windshield clean, then squeak protest against the streaked glass, so I had to keep turning them on and off.

Driving in a full rain was easier; this stuff created too many shifting reflections.

"We anywhere close yet?"

Escott checked a map by flashlight. "One more street."

We went one more street. There was no parking to be had; the people living in this area had grabbed every legal space. We wouldn't take any illegal spots. This foray was meant to go unnoticed by the law. "Take it around the block a few times, would ya?"

"My pleasure."

I paused across from a venerable-looking apartment hotel and got out. Escott slid over to the driver's side, put my Buick in gear, and cruised off. He'd be gone about twenty minutes, plenty of time for my errand.

We'd debated on whether I should see Marie Kennard or Anthony Brockhurst, and Anthony dear won out, based on what I'd overheard in his car. He seemed to be second to Dugan in the hierarchy and the one most likely to know interesting things.

At this late hour there was no night man; you needed a key or to be buzzed in by a resident to gain entry. I wafted through the cracks, went solid, and used the elevator the rest of the trip. Counting off the door numbers, I found Anthony's flat at the far end of the fifth floor's hall and sieved inside.

Solid again. In a stranger's home. Me failing to suppress a big grin.

Damn it, it was *fun* to break into places, especially without performing any actual breakage and with *no* chance of getting caught. Not that I sneaked into just any house that took my fancy—I'd been taught better manners—but the ones in the line of duty were fair game. Unless required by the needs of a case, I never stole anything, so my conscience was fairly clean. I was just naturally nosy and liked looking around other people's lives because I suspected they were doing a better job of living it than me.

If his father controlled Anthony's money, he was generous, to judge by the surroundings. Everything was expensive and new except for what appeared to be family pictures dotting the walls. The Brockhursts looked to be a large and well-to-do clan. I didn't recognize any of them but did spot a formal studio portrait of Marie Kennard standing alone on a baby grand piano in the living room. Perhaps Anthony, the helpful cousin and unsuspecting best friend of the bad guy, had a crush on her, choosing to be chivalrous and stay quiet about it. I could imagine him at the keyboard practicing love songs while looking at Marie's photo. Close up and with time to study, she was a dish, but not to my taste. The studiously bored manner I'd overheard in the club and the car made her sound spoiled, not sophisticated. World-weary people who had never been near a real crisis weren't worth my time, but she was perfect for the likes of Dugan and Anthony. They were welcome to her.

This place was easy to go through; Anthony's life was uncomplicated. The usual trappings of modern living were in their usual places, including a very well-stocked liquor cabinet. No surprises there. Except for the piano, he didn't seem to have any creative leanings. I found some check stubs in his desk indicating that he had a job at a place called Brockhurst and Sons and damn near blanched at the amount he made. I couldn't imagine anyone being valuable enough to a company to deserve a sweet and cool hundred a week. Not unless they were in the movies or the mobs.

That was obscene. When I'd been reporting I counted myself lucky to pull in seventy-five a *month* and thought myself well off.

The desk was the kind with a hinged trapdoor on top. Lift and fold it to the right and a counterbalanced shelf within raised the hidden typewriter up level with the rest of the work area, which was now doubled. *That* was a very handy thing to have. Maybe I could get one of my own.

Used carbon paper was crumpled in the wastebasket, along with early versions of the letters Dugan intended to send out. Keeping company with them were two origami animals, a giraffe and a pelican, made from discarded drafts. He'd probably amused himself folding them while Anthony typed.

I found Anthony in his bedroom, snoring obliviously away in fancy red silk pajamas. There was a taint of booze on his breath, mixed with mint mouth gargle. That told me he'd had something to drink but not enough to make him forget to brush. This would be slow going, but hopefully not impossible.

Turning his night table light on, I loomed over him, tapping his face a couple times to haul him from sleep. Once I captured his bleared and dumbfounded attention, I was able to give myself another headache.

"You're sure that's all of them?" Escott asked after picking me up.

"The ones he had." I fanned the crisp envelopes full of potential grief, holding them like a card hand. They were stamped, ready to mail. None had a return name, but the delivery addresses were neatly typed, including one on top for the FBI. I ripped it open. It was indeed the original to what I'd seen earlier. "How could Dugan think J. Edgar Hoover would ever bother himself with me?"

"Because he likely would. I understand he is a very persistent investigator and a great one for collecting information, rather like Gordy. What about the other letters at large?"

"Brockhurst will get them for me." I shuffled this batch together and stuffed them in my coat pocket. The mist had grown thick and fast enough to qualify as rain. Tiny drops dotted the windows, and the wiper thumped back and forth without squeaking. I was glad not to be driving. "He was pretty cooperative once he was under."

"You're certain of that?"

"Slack face, eyes like a dead fish, and a suddenly slow heartbeat. I'm certain. He couldn't have faked the last." I'd also pretended to take a swing at him. He didn't blink, even when the breeze of my passing fist ruffled his hair. "He has the day to get the rest from the other four people in his little circle, then come by the club tomorrow night to deliver them. I told him to say he found out the truth about Cousin Gilbert, that he really had been the mastermind in the kidnapping, his motive being the money. Brockhurst will look shocked and grieved by the betrayal."

"Let's hope they accept it."

"If not, then I got their names and where they live. I should visit them anyway, make sure they're set straight about Dugan. This will save Marie Kennard ten grand. And from a disasterous marriage." Not a bad night's work. I felt positivly chivalrous.

"Was Brockhurst possessed of further useful information?"

"I asked about family history. Their paternal grandfathers way back when were brothers. Both did pretty well for themselves and their descendants until the crash. By then Dugan was the only one left of his branch. He lost his shirt. The Brockhursts had gone into ball bearing manufacture, so they weathered things better. Anthony seems to idolize Dugan, thinks he's a deep thinker, and he's given him financial help on the sly. He's got an open offer for a job at the family business, but he's much too sensitive for the harshness of the cruel world."

"Indeed?"

"My translation: Dugan's too lazy or thinks he's too good for regular work."

Escott nodded, thoughtful. "Yet he will put weeks of effort into committing a crime and lie his head off to con a young woman out of ten thousand dollars. The mundane bores him. He likes challenge to lift him from his ennui. Danger, too. He didn't bring a gun to your little meeting, did he?"

"Nope."

"And at least twice he mentioned doing various activities to 'fill the time.'"

"Boredom. Now that's a hell of a motive for kidnapping."

"I can understand him, though."

I snorted. "He's crazy. You're not. Don't go scaring me."

Escott chuckled.

It was great to walk into Crymsyn again and see everything running normally. The doorman told me we'd had a good crowd, people grabbing an early piece of the weekend by starting on Wednesday. They'd mostly gone home by now. I was just in time to close and felt like I'd missed a lot by not being here. Tomorrow would be less worry-making. With Dugan locked away, I could immerse myself back into my favorite routine.

How long he stayed chained to that floor was up to him. His only way out of his cell was to write and sign a full confession. Then I'd take him to the cops. He could scream all he liked about it being obtained under duress, but everyone in the Gladwell household would lie themselves blue denying that they had anything to do with holding him against his will. We knew who would be believed in the end. Especially if I had anything to do with it.

I had a lot of respect for Vivian for going along with our dangerous game. Escott had confided the general idea to her earlier today. All of it was based on the calculation that Dugan fully expected to leave his meeting with me alive.

We figured he'd have prepared some pretty serious insurance for that, and it would have to be blocked by us in some way. I had to play the business very much by ear, let him tell me what he thought I should know, let him think he'd won, then follow and look for a weakness.

Which had worked out very well, up to and including the possibility of putting him on ice. He had plenty of brains, just not a lot of experience playing with the big boys. Good thing for him that he'd tried blackmailing me instead of Gordy; otherwise, Dugan would be fish food by now. Gordy was more practical about disposing of annoyances. More final. Not that I hadn't killed before myself, in the heat of rage, cold-bloodedly, and out of my head with insanity. But I had enough deaths hovering over my shoulder, bleak company when in a gloomy mood. Maybe Dugan deserved to die, but I didn't care to be the executioner.

We'd intended to store him in the far end of Lady Crymsyn's basement, hidden behind a bank of crates and old scenery flats, and take turns keeping watch. But once she heard these tentative ideas, Vivian volunteered her place and staff for the job, and the devil take the law if she was caught.

Escott tried to talk her out of it. Any other client he'd have turned down flat, and devil take their bruised feelings in the matter. He failed with Vivian, which told me a lot about how far she'd gotten under his skin. Maybe he could bring her to the club some night to meet Bobbi, and we could all double-date like college kids.

Bobbi was in the main room, seated by the near-side bar. It was the best place to keep an eye on the patrons, the entry, and the show, which was winding down. She saw Escott and me come in and immediately got that things had gone well. I'd have done it all even without a hug and kiss at the end, but I wasn't going to turn down what was offered.

"So?" she said as we shed our coats and sat at her table.

"The good guys won."

"A tremendous success," Escott added.

Adelle was done for the night, probably backstage changing. Gordy and Bristow were still talking, which astonished and annoyed me.

"How much longer is that gonna go on?" I asked.

Bobbi leaned forward, impatient. "Who cares? Tell me everything. I'm ready to chew glass from all this waiting."

She got the short version; details could come later if she

wanted them. Escott let me do most of the talking, lounging back in his chair to load and light his pipe. He looked contented.

"What if he doesn't confess?" she asked when I was done.

"That, sweetheart, is the flaw in the plan. We're going to ignore it."

"*What?* Oh, you stinker, don't pull my leg."

"Well, not here and now. We could go upstairs . . ."

"Oh, hush!" she said, going a little pink.

Escott, more of a gentleman than I, pretended not to have heard.

I went on. "Anyway, a signed confession is the frosting. The cake is good all on its own. We don't count on him to crack, but the longer he's disappeared, the worse it'll be for him with the law. Then it won't matter."

Escott nodded. "If and when he emerges from his durance vile, he will find himself without friend or ally between him and a lengthy prison term."

"I was against this, you know," she said. "Until I heard him talking to you. What a creep."

"How *did* that go?"

"Perfectly."

"So it turned out?"

"Clear as a bell. Wanna hear?"

We went upstairs, and once more I got a good look at the stuff she and Escott had worked so hard to arrange. Wires threaded from holes drilled in the wall between the storage room and my office led to a simple-looking box with a brushed chrome face. The innards were probably stuffed with tubes and a spaghetti twisting of more wires and unbelievably complicated electrical tubes and other stuff. The box was linked by cables to other devices, and it was all very intimidating to unfamiliar eyes. Bobbi worked switches and dials easy as stirring a cup of coffee. They hummed, warming up. Then she went to a large turntable spinning an ordinary-looking seventy-eight record and set the needle on it to play.

Dugan's voice spoke from the grill of an amplifying speaker. He was underscored by static and distant dance music but perfectly recognizable to anyone who knew him.

". . . damaging. Your detective friend could lose his license, that blond singer with whom you keep company will never get decent work again. That large gangster will have no end of grief with federal investigators and could shortly find himself heading . . ."

"Oh, brother, that's great!"

She shut him off and grinned. "That's just the first one. The second's still on the recording table. It does fifteen minutes a side. We lost a little when I had to put a fresh blank in, but not much the way that joker likes to talk. I was worried the background noise of the band would ruin it, but you can make out every self-damning word he says. Even if you don't get a confession out of him, he can't deny any of this."

"I don't know if it will be allowed as evidence in court, but it would be a treat to have the DA in to hear it," said Escott.

"But I thought you didn't want anything to do with a court case."

"We make sure it doesn't come to that. If Dugan is stubborn about accepting his fate, we see to it he has a chance to listen to himself. I should like to be present to enjoy the look on his face."

"Won't it be a bad thing for Jack, though? They might want to know what his big secret is."

I lifted a hand. "No problem. I just whammy them into disinterest. Now, how about we put that in a very safe place?"

"After I make some copies." Bobbi fiddled with a knob and the hum of power from the machine diminished. "I'll take the originals to a place I know and have them turned into more records you can play on any phonograph."

"I should like to make a transcript first," said Escott. "I'll start right now. If the unthinkable should happen and either of those are broken . . ."

"Yeah, I guess I could slip on some ice on the way over."

"I'll need writing materials."

"In my office," I said. We went there. I got Escott a freshly filled fountain pen, some pencils, and a thick pad of paper. He knew shorthand nearly as well as I but I was better at typing. When he was done, I'd use my spare time to translate his scribbles into readable English.

He poked at the vase of cut flowers. "These will want water." He pulled the flowers and their greenery clear. Some stems remained behind, snagged on the microphone they had concealed. It was small, maybe as big as my fist, held by a short stand that fit into the bottomless vase. The cord ran through a hole in the table, down one of the legs by the wall, and then on through the wall. You had to know where to look to see it, and I'd kept Dugan plenty busy looking at me.

"I'm going to leave things set up," I said. "Never know but we might have a use for it again."

"But the recording equipment has to go back tomorrow."

"I can buy my own later sometime. Business is pretty good. Until then I can cover the mike with the vase, put some paper flowers in it."

"The curtains, too?"

"Yeah." Hidden in the curtain folds were two more microphones, hanging from either end of the rod at eye level. We couldn't be sure if Dugan would stay in one spot and had allowed for his moving around the room.

"You know . . . I could make something better for the one on the table." Escott stared at it, probably seeing something not yet there.

"Oh, yeah?"

"What about a lamp? I could fashion a pedestal base out of thin wood, drill holes in the sides, back them with black gauze . . . It would be like a radio speaker but in reverse. The lamp would even work. Of course, there might be an echo effect with the wood around the mike . . ."

"Talk it over with Bobbi."

He started sketching at the desk, focused on his new idea. "Um-hm."

Bobbi came in. "I got it ready to play. Talk what over with me?"

"I'll tell you; let's leave him think." Escott would be preoccupied for a while. I recognized the signs. I also had an idea about gutting a radio and putting the microphone in the speaker, but then someone might try turning the radio on, and that would raid the game. Arm in arm, Bobbi and I went downstairs. "How did the show run?"

"No hitches."

"Good. Anything from our dancing newlyweds?"

"Roland called to say they'd be rehearsing tomorrow. That's a good sign. You probably should talk to Faustine, though. Smooth things out for the duration."

"I'll do that the first—"

Hog Bristow and his three apes emerged into the lobby like a rockslide: not much speed but plenty of force. Bristow was red-faced, his shoulders bunched high, his head low, unconscious imitation of his nickname. The four of them saw me on the stairs where I'd paused in mid-step. Bobbi went still, her hand tighting on my arm.

Bristow pointed at me. "You tell 'im! You tell 'im good! No one messes. Goddamn bastard. Thinks he. Thinks. No one! You tell!"

The lobby lights flickered warningly, dimming, then snapping bright.

"Goddamn," said Bristow, glaring up at them. "Goddamn dump!"

With that, they rumbled over my floor, Bristow cursing and weaving so much his boys had to hold him up. The doorman hastily went to work and seemed relieved not to catch their notice as they passed by.

"Good night and little fishes," said Bobbi, breathing again. "What was *that* about?"

"At least one bottle of booze too many." This had to stop. I'd had enough. "Let's see if Gordy can enlighten us. Wilton, start closing up."

Wilton, pale behind his bar, visibly swallowed and nodded a lot.

Strome and Lowrey walking ahead, the third guy trailing, Gordy was just descending from his table. We met up at the bar on the far end.

"Guess you saw him," he said to me. He signed for Strome to keep going. "Bring the car to the front."

"What happened?" I asked, keeping my voice even.

There were no bodies lying around, but the last straggle of customers were hastily gathering up to leave. The band wouldn't have to play "Good Night, Sweetheart" this time to get them out.

He shrugged, a little sheepish. "Hog lost his temper."

"I think he was born that way."

"Maybe. He got loud. His boys talked him down, but not by much. He's plenty sore. Finally figured out that I'm not cooperating and never will. Tomorrow I'm supposed to let him take over or else. He won't forget this one. He talked to New York today. They want him to finish things."

"What does that mean?"

"What do you think?"

"Where will you finish it?"

His mouth twitched. "Not here. I like this place."

I was going to second that opinion, but Adelle came out, back in street clothes and ready to go home. She was all smiles for Gordy, unaware of Bristow's drunken wrath, but she picked up on the tension. Her smile dampened slightly.

"Anything wrong?"

Gordy shook his head. "Nothing to worry about, doll. Later, Fleming. 'Night, Bobbi."

Adelle seemed to want more information but had to walk out with him to get it. She sketched a puzzled wave over her shoulder at us and went along, taking two steps to Gordy's one. He must have been plenty upset; he usually walked at her pace.

I looked at Bobbi. "Wanna close this bar while I take care of the front?"

"But . . . that is . . ." She gestured after them.

"Nothing we can do. It's business."

"Business. And I know what kind. I sometimes forget that with Gordy. What he has to do to hold on to what he's got."

"Me, too." I was glad my responsibilities were more mundane. And mostly legal.

"I hope he keeps Adelle out of it."

"He will."

We split up. We'd meet later in the office to bag the cash and total receipts, then on the way to her flat I'd make a stop at the bank. I liked the routine; it got my attention off less pleasant matters like Gordy's pending disposal of Bristow.

In the lobby, the hatcheck girl had retrieved Gordy's overcoat, and he was just pulling it on. Adelle's face no longer seemed puzzled, only somber. Gordy must have told her enough so she could pack her curiosity away. She was well aware of his work beyond running the Nightcrawler Club and knew when to back off.

The lobby lights dimmed again.

Wilton stopped counting his register money and looked up, frowning.

"I get you, Myrna," I muttered.

The remaining two bodyguards noticed but didn't take any meaning from it. I went past them and the doorman, signing for him to stay put, and opened the front door myself.

Empty street, wet and cold, still raining steadily. Gordy's big bulletproof car growled quietly next to the curb, chugging out exhaust, Strome at the wheel.

"Bristow gone?" I asked, stepping out from under the

entry canopy. Rain sifted onto the back of my neck.

He leaned across the seat to the passenger side and rolled the thick window down. "Hah?"

I repeated the question.

"Yeah. He's gone."

Good so far as it went, but I took Myrna's fun with the lights seriously. She was quite a girl for spotting trouble. I left the canopy shelter and trotted toward the parking lot. There were few cars remaining, most likely belonging to the band members. I didn't know what make Bristow would have but could assume it to be a new model. Nothing fancy here. Musicians tended to earn squat, and their transportation reflected that.

The most likely hiding place checked, I hurried back. The other side of the club was bordered by a narrow street, clear of traffic. I carefully looked over the buildings opposite the front. All the windows were dark and closed tight. No one on the roofs. Unless they were down behind the facades. Cold perch.

Still bothered, I returned to the lobby. No one was hiding behind the bar with Wilton; the rest rooms—for once I broke my rule about invading the ladies'—were clear. Gordy waited near the door. Maybe he didn't know why I was running around, but he understood I'd have a good reason.

"Anything?"

I shook my head. "Not offhand." I still had the heebies and went to the light switch panel, cutting off power to the entry. It was sensible not to have everyone brightly picked out as they left. I'll see you out."

He sent Lowrey ahead, the other guy behind and close

to Adelle, and I held the door for them. Once out, Lowrey went to open the car's rear door. Gordy was just handing Adelle in when firecrackers went off. Three or four short, flat bangs. Gordy grunted and stumbled.

10

THE noise galvanized Lowrey and his partner. They went for their guns but couldn't pinpoint the source of the sound for the echoes.

Gordy shoved Adelle the rest of the way into the car but faltered in his dive to cover. He faltered so much he pitched facedown onto the wet, cold sidewalk.

Another couple shots sent the rest of us down with him. I flinched out of pure instinct and recent memory, but had my head up first.

"The parking lot!" I yelled at Lowrey, pointing.

He got to his feet, dragging his buddy along with one hand and snapping a shot off randomly with the other. It was stupid, but would maybe make the shooter duck.

Gordy let out another grunt of pain. I'd been torn between helping him and giving chase, but that decided me. I heaved him into the back seat. Adelle gave a startled cry as he fell heavily across her.

"What's wrong, what's wrong? Gordy?" panic raising her tone.

I pushed in next to him and yanked the door shut. "Out of here!"

Strome got over his surprise, forced gears, and gunned the accelerator. We lurched from the curb, skidding on the slick road, tires spinning, taking hold, spinning. I caught only the barest glimpse of the parking lot and saw only the cars, no shooter. I should have gone in, looked between them, under them.

"Shit," said Gordy, arms tight around himself.

"Where?" I asked. Couldn't see the blood for the dark color of his coat, but the smell was all over him. "How bad?"

"Donno. Hurts like hell. Club, Strome."

"Forget that. We're going to the hospital."

"Can't. They'll be there."

"You think they won't be at the Nightcrawler?"

"Can't have cops in. Gun wounds bring the cops."

"Okay, okay, I got a place then. Bristow won't know about it, I promise. They got a doctor keeps his yap shut."

Gordy shut his eyes. "I guess . . ." He gave a long sigh.

Adelle had been frozen, her face dead white. "Gordy? Say something. Gordy?"

I listened. Heartbeat. "He's just passed out. Take it easy. Strome, head south at the next corner. Make sure we ain't followed."

"But the boss said—"

"I'm taking over until he tells you different. Go south and step on it."

* * *

A tough trip for us all. Strome questioning every direction I
threw at him, Adelle fighting panic, blinking tears, and me
dreading that Gordy wouldn't last out. To give her something
to do, I had Adelle clamber over the seat to the front so I
could lay Gordy down flat. I crouched in the foot well and
told her everything would be all right.

Gordy opened his eyes a few times but didn't say anything.
He seemed to be drifting in and out.

"Here?" asked Strome in disbelief.

"Here," I stated. "Pull in and park. Adelle, you get out and
come around. If Gordy wakes up, you let him know we're
getting a doctor. Don't let him see you cry."

She nodded, eyes swimming. The last was more for her than
Gordy. If she thought it would help him, she'd keep control.

Soon as Strome braked and parked, I hit the door handle
and backed my way out. I'd located one bullet wound and
had a handkerchief pressed to it. Adelle took over; I sprinted
up some old stairs and banged loud on a door with a glass
panel. It rattled, came close to breaking. I kept hammering
away, calling loud, my heart clogging in my throat. God,
wasn't anyone *home?*

Finally a light came on past the frosted glass. "Who is it?"

"Jack Fleming. I'm a friend of Shoe Coldfield."

"Okay."

The Negro man on the other side unlocked and opened the
door. Dr. Clarson was small-boned and fine-featured, his short
hair peppered with gray. He wore a bathrobe and slippers but
didn't seem unduly disturbed by so late a visitor. "What's the
trouble?"

"Gunshot, maybe more than one. We gotta keep it under the table."

"Can you bring him up? What are you waiting for then?"

Down again to roust Strome from behind the wheel. We were smack in the heart of Chicago's Bronze Belt, and he didn't like it one bit. Couldn't blame him. The white and colored gangs had no love for one another, even against their common enemy, the law, but too bad, this was an emergency.

I got Gordy under the arms and dragged him from the car, Strome caught his feet, and we lugged him up the steps with Adelle anxiously following. We got through Clarson's tiny reception area; he directed us to an equally tiny examination room smelling of carbolic and alcohol. He'd changed his bathrobe for a doctor's white coat, and once we had Gordy on the examining table, he told us to undo his clothes.

The bright light here showed the damage all too clearly. Gordy had taken two bullets, one in the side, another in the back of his shoulder. The holes weren't big, but they bled steadily and too much.

"I'll need help," said Clarson. "Wash your hands, pull on some gloves and masks. They're in that cabinet over the sink."

"All of us?" asked Strome.

"Young man, I am not Hercules. I will not be able to turn this man over like a flapjack. You two strong boys are to do that. Miss? You're not going to faint, are you?"

Adelle, who was now very gray, made herself straighten up. "No, Doctor."

"Know any nursing?"

"No."

"Well, you're gonna learn some. Wash up, too."

She threw her purse on a chair, shed her coat and hat, and plucked off her gloves in about three seconds and was at the sink scrubbing away before Strome and I even thought of moving. She hiccuped, gulping deep breaths, and sobbed twice. By the time she had the rubber gloves and sanitary mask on, she was in shaky control.

While we washed, Strome muttered, "Ain't there no other place?"

"No. Now shut up and cooperate." I gave him a look.

He shut up and cooperated.

Clarson was either too busy working to notice or pretending not to hear. He was quick and efficient, and his questions were strictly medical. He wanted to know how long since the shooting, Gordy's age, and if he was allergic to anything. Adelle answered those. I was surprised to learn Gordy couldn't handle strawberries.

"Then we won't give him any," said Clarson, winking, which seemed to reassure her. He did not ask for anyone's name. Mine he knew, but he'd "forget" it before the night was out, along with everything else.

I lost track of time. It passed slow and fast at once. Gordy remained unconscious, which was just as well, though Clarson had me standing by with some kind of knockout gas just in case. I didn't watch and wished I could shut my ears off. Despite the fact I drink blood and utterly relish the taste, seeing it pouring out of a friend set off a whole different reaction in my guts. I found myself gulping, too, fighting dry heaves. Strome was slab-faced, not one sign of worry or queasiness; this was just part of the job.

Adelle, holding up better than I, handed Clarson instruments and whimpered relief when one of the bullets clattered into a white-enameled bowl.

"Good," Clarson muttered. "Didn't fragment. Seems to have missed his liver. Lucky man."

Big slug. At least a .38, maybe a .45. Someone had meant business.

He continued working. Strome and I turned Gordy over when asked, and Clarson started on the shoulder wound. The bullet had struck his blade bone and didn't want to come out.

"This is the tricky one. I expect he'll want to use his arm when he's healed up."

"He'll be all right, then?" asked Adelle hovering on hope.

"Don't know. Lost a lot of blood. Have to watch for infection. He's lucky, but not clear of the woods yet."

Out in reception, someone banged on the door, then opened it. I thought I knew what it would be and had Strome take over with the gas. "I'll look after this."

Clarson nodded absently.

I went down the short hall but didn't make it to the final door. It was kicked open. I went still, hands away from my body, palms toward the tall, grim-faced colored man who came in. He had a .45 revolver aimed right at my chest.

"It's me, Isham," I said calmly.

He recognized me right off but barely shifted the muzzle, his gaze on my blood-smeared gloves. "What the hell are you doing here?"

"Had some trouble. Friend got shot. Figured Clarson could help."

"Shoe don't know this."

"Not yet. You can tell him for me." Isham was one of Shoe Coldfield's soldiers. I'd expected him or someone like him to show up before too long. Coldfield, who ran the biggest mob in the Belt, kept a careful watch on his territory, and four white people in an expensive car stopping in the middle of it at this late hour would draw all kinds of attention.

"Who's the friend?" He started to move past me.

I blocked the way, not making a challenge of it. "You can look later. I don't want to distract Clarson." Keeping him and Strome apart also seemed like a good idea. "It's Gordy Weems."

Isham didn't quite rock back on his heels. "North Side Gordy? What the hell's going on?"

"Thug from New York's trying for his job, which would be a very bad thing to happen."

"You know that for a fact?"

Mob politics in Chicago were a very delicate balance of territory, power, and a kind of backhanded trust that it made lousy business to rock the boat unnecessarily. Lately things had been even and peaceful. But Isham might think a new boss taking over from Gordy would improve his own boss's position. "Yeah, for a solid fact. You don't want Hog Bristow coming in and throwing his weight around."

"Never heard of him."

"You will if he gets hold of things. A little war's been declared. Gordy needs to keep low in a neutral place until he can stifle this guy."

Isham didn't want to go along, shaking his head. "Not here, he can't."

"Call Shoe, let him know. I'll talk to him."

He frowned. "I don't wanna wake him up."

"Then don't, but leave us get on with things for the time being." I put my full concentration on him. "You can tell him in the morning if you think that's the right road. What would *he* want done?"

Release.

Isham blinked, resumed frowning. "Guess I'll call him."

I went back to the impromptu operating room, a pain between my eyes.

About half an hour went by, and Coldfield came in, a big, deep-voiced man who hated surprises. I was a major one. He looked like he'd been awake anyway, but I apologized for the intrusion. He shook my hand and told Isham to find another place to park Gordy's car. Strome would have taken the keys along, but Isham didn't mention a need for them.

"Is Charles in on this?" Coldfield asked.

"He's at my club. I called and told him what's happened and where we went." Escott had taken the news, passed it to Lowrey, and calmed Bobbi down. She'd been ready to go through the ceiling with worry. Gordy was a big brother to her. I had no good news on him but nothing bad, either. "He'll keep quiet."

"I know that. Who's this Hog Bristow?"

In a few words I outlined what I knew of the man and the general situation. "I had to get Gordy someplace safe where Bristow wouldn't look or could bribe or beat it out of people."

"Oh, yeah, a bunch like you coming here, no one'll pay mind to *that*."

He had a point. Coldfield called the shots for many in the Belt, but not everyone could be counted on to back him. There was always a small player looking to move up in the game. "Yeah, we'll get out soon as Clarson says. Gordy wouldn't want to impose."

Coldfield, who had been giving off tension like heat from a fire, nodded and seemed to ease back. "Don't worry about it. We can look after him. I just want to make sure there's no trouble coming my way. Is that something you can take care of?"

"As soon as possible. None of us wants trouble, but Bristow . . ." Until now I'd been holding a lot in. I didn't realize how much. "That son of a bitch."

"Easy, kid," Coldfield warned.

For the next moment I focused hard on not putting my fist through a wall or breaking furniture. I shook from it, though, feeling sick from the surge of adrenaline. Pacing up the hall, down, up again helped. Only a little. Smashing Bristow's wide mug in would cure it completely. In his case, I wouldn't mind the feel of shattering bone.

Other men might have stepped out of the way. Coldfield held his place, waiting as I worked through it. "Easy," he repeated.

I stretched out my stiff neck and shoulders. "I'm okay."

"Glad I'm not your enemy."

"Wish I didn't have any."

"Then you'd be deader than you are already."

That remark and how he said it hit me funny. I actually laughed. Soft, weak, and short-lived, but it cooled the rage to something manageable.

"Ready to talk some more?"

"Yeah. How long can we stay here?"

"Couple days, no more."

That was unexpected. "So long?"

He shrugged. "Gordy and I did some talking at your club's opening. Not a lot, but we got some things set straight. He gave me respect. I don't forget that. It won't do, me kicking him out when he needs a hand. Not good business."

"Glad to hear it."

"Besides, he gave my date a singing spot at his club. It's a big thing for a colored gal to sing at a white place. Especially the Nightcrawler. Got her some notice. You know what kind of a good mood she was in that week? If for nothing else, I owe him for that."

Strome came out, minus the rubber gloves. He and Coldfield sized each other up, but I'd already primed Strome to behave. "He's done," he said.

Coldfield and I moved past him.

Gordy lay on his side, his massive torso sporting more bandaging than a mummy. Adelle was adjusting a pillow under his head. Her face was pinched and tired, and I thought she'd shrunk a couple inches until I noticed she'd kicked off her shoes.

"He's stable for now," said Clarson, who was at the sink washing things. The front of his coat was all bloody, and the scent teased me. I shut that down fast. "I want to keep him put for a while. That okay with you, Shoe?"

"It's fine. How bad is he?"

Clarson shook his head. "He's a tough bird. I cleaned him good but need to watch for infection the next few days. I'm gonna put some blood back in him, have to arrange for it. If he wakes up while I'm gone, keep him still. He may not remember what happened. Tell him the truth if he asks, and assure him he's going to be all right. If he stays asleep on his own, fine."

"What about pain, Doctor?" asked Adelle.

"He'll have plenty. You know how to give a shot?"

She swayed a tiny bit. "No."

"I do," said Coldfield. "What should he have?"

Clarson indicated a hypodermic sitting ready in a glass dish on a table. "That. Meaty part of his arm. But only if he wakes up and would rather be out. He'll be thirsty. He can have chips of ice, no water. Got an icebox the next room over and a pick. Get it from there. I'll be back soon." He dried his hands and left, just starting to unbutton his stained coat.

"I'll watch the boss," said Strome, his hard face still expressionless.

"Where's Bristow?" I asked him.

"Huh?"

"Where's he staying?"

He shrugged. "Columbia Hotel, last I heard. He won't be there."

"How do you know?"

"Just makes sense. You do a hit, you lie low until things die down."

"What about him taking over at noon tomorrow?"

"He won't come out. He'll wait someplace."

"Just how much did he have to drink tonight?"

"A lot."

"I saw him and his boys leaving the club. He could barely talk. How could he have ordered a hit?"

Strome shrugged again. "Musta done that before he got drunk. Maybe one of his boys thought he should start the takeover early."

"Which one?"

"Who knows? They don't talk. All evening they don't talk. Just Bristow. He talks all night, every night, says the same thing again and again 'til I'm ready to plug him myself. Gordy sits and listens to it, then finally tells Bristow 'No, it ain't gonna happen,' and Bristow goes nuts. His boys got him outta there, but maybe one of 'em comes back to finish things. Just 'cause Bristow says noon don't mean he waits that long."

"When will Bristow show himself?"

"Who knows? He don't know if Gordy's dead yet. 'Less he hears different, he'll keep out of sight."

"Then let's give him what he wants."

His face almost twisted from the thinking. "You mean say the boss got scragged? No. I ain't gonna say it if it ain't true."

"Then Bristow won't come out of hiding."

"Don't matter. Sooner or later, we get him."

"Now you listen to me . . ."

"Jack." Coldfield interrupted. "Take what he says as right. 'Cause it is."

"I can smoke Bristow out this way. Beats turning over every hotel and flop in the city. Have him come to us."

"By saying Gordy died? You won't do him any favors with that game."

"Why not?"

"Because once a boss steps down—even if it's faked—he never gets back up again. Hell, I learned that in the play yard in grade school. So did you. Same thing would happen to Gordy."

"What do we say, then? That's he's on vacation?"

"Sounds right to me. Big Al would take off out of town all the time; no one thought twice about it because he left Nitti in charge to hold his place for him."

I didn't like the sound of this. "Oh, no, you can't be thinking—"

"No one crossed Nitti, because he was good at the job and had Al's blessing. No one will cross you, either."

"Oh, no, not me. I'm juggling too much right now."

"Makes sense," said Strome. "Better than your idea."

Of course it made sense to him since I, and not he, would be Bristow's next target.

"I'll back you to the other boys. You wanna get Bristow removed, this is how you do it. You get out front, say you're in charge, then wait."

"Oh, hell."

"You got some other stuff to back you up, too," Coldfield reminded me. I was starting to regret that he knew about my supernatural extras. Thankfully, Strome didn't inquire about what he meant; neither did Adelle. She followed all this with what looked like horrified interest.

"Jack, I don't want you risking yourself," she said. "Stay out of it. Have Gordy's men take care of things."

Strome looked like he wanted to tell her to butt out. Ladies and mob games weren't supposed to mix. He must have remembered she was still his boss's girlfriend. "We can take care of things better with Fleming running the show."

"But—"

"He's right," I said. "If Gordy wants his spot back in one piece, I'll have to step in. If it helps, I don't like doing it one bit."

"It doesn't help! I don't want him going back to that. If this Bristow man wants to take over, let him. Gordy and I can leave town."

"Adelle, it doesn't work that way, and you know it. Guys in Gordy's business never retire."

"I want us to be different."

"Me, too, but it isn't in the books."

"You'll do it?" asked Strome.

"With much reluctance and the proviso that I really am in charge."

"Huh?" This was news to him.

"What I say goes. The boys do the same for me as they would for Gordy."

"I donno about that."

"You don't like it, then you take over and *you* be the sitting duck for Bristow's shooters."

His eyes flickered. He must have been hoping I'd not have thought of that possibility.

"It's the only way. You want Bristow? That's the price. I'm

running the show—for real—for as long as Gordy takes to get well."

Strome looked at his unconscious boss. "What if he don't get well?"

"Worry about that only if it happens."

"It could."

"For God's sake, shut up!" said Adelle, hovering protectively over Gordy as he slept. "Don't say that; don't think it!"

Strome looked annoyed. "I wanna know."

He got some eye pressure from me. "Drop it."

And he dropped it.

Coldfield knew what I'd done and failed to hide his amusement. "Damn, kid. You'll do."

I pinched the bridge of my nose, suddenly tired. "That's what I'm afraid of."

Lady Crymsyn's ground floor was dark, but lights warmed the upper windows. My car was still in its space, gleaming from the persistent rain. The lot was empty now. Isham dropped me off at the curb, then drove back to the Belt. Strome was to watch Gordy and Isham to watch Strome. Hopefully nothing would happen. Adelle elected to stay with Gordy. There was no prying her away, and no one tried.

I didn't bother unlocking and sieved inside. The place was quite, quite empty, except maybe for Myrna, but hell, even ghosts have to sleep sometime.

Upstairs I found Bobbi napping on the office couch with three overcoats tucked around her: her own, mine, and Escott's. She looked so damn cute.

Dugan's voice droned from the next room over. I'd heard it all the way up the stairs. He'd say something, then stop, often in mid-word, then start again. Escott was hard at it, transcribing everything into shorthand.

"I'm almost done," he said when I walked in. I'd made enough noise walking up so as not to surprise him. "How's Gordy?"

"Still out. Clarson says he's holding his own. Shoe wasn't happy, but he did the right thing."

"Decent chap. Always has been. Both of them."

"Where's Lowrey and the other guy?"

"Left ages ago. Afraid they didn't say where."

"The Nightcrawler." I'd allowed Strome one call to Lady Crymsyn to talk to them. They got assurance that Gordy was alive, it was business as usual, and that I'd be doing some special work for him tomorrow. They could draw whatever meaning they liked from that.

Escott put his pad of paper to one side. "What now?"

"We get Bobbi home."

"She said she wanted to see Gordy."

"You can drive her over tomorrow. Maybe. He'll be at Clarson's, and you wanna watch for tails."

"Of course."

"And I'm taking over for Gordy."

Now he put down his pencil. He didn't say anything for the longest time, then abruptly chuckled.

"Hey, there's nothing funny about this! I could get punctured at any moment by one of those trigger-happy goons!"

"And you of all people would be able to survive it."

"Yeah-yeah, but I don't like tempting fate, she has a twisted sense of humor."

"Indeed. You have at last gone to the top in Chicago. You are now a bona fide American mobster."

I groaned. "Only 'til Gordy's on his feet."

"Will your official hat be a pearl gray fedora or a straw boater?"

"Wrong on both counts. A football helmet. We'll toss grenades instead of pigskins."

"What's going on?" Bobbi came in, eyelids puffy from interrupted sleep, one side of her face marked with pillow creases. She still looked cute. "How's Gordy? I want to see him."

I told her what I told Escott, adding, "Not until tomorrow, though, and maybe not even then."

"Why not?"

"Because visiting hours are over. The more activity at Doc Clarson's office, the more attention it draws. Adelle's looking after him. I told her to phone you."

"But I could phone her . . . Oh, all right." She correctly interpreted the look on my face.

"There's nothing you can do for him, honey. I promise. Let Adelle get some rest, let Gordy heal up. He's in good hands and will be much safer if we stay clear of him."

"What about the guy who shot him?"

"That's being taken care of."

"By you?"

Damn, she was far too perceptive. "Yeah. I'm running Gordy's operation. For as short a time as possible. But that's going to include finding Bristow."

It looked like she had a few objections to launch, then she sighed and shook her head. "Great. I'm back to being a gangster's moll. What ever will I tell Mother?"

"That the pay is the same."

"*You're* the one going after Bristow? No one else?"

"Have to. Gotta shut him down fast. You don't want him taking over Gordy's job. He'd turn the Nightcrawler into a crib house in half a week. Or less." I'd gotten that information from Strome.

In addition to earning his nickname by slaughtering hogs and later men, Bristow had worked his way up in the New York vice rackets. He was a good man at organizing pimps and their stables and turning a profit. Apparently he had dreams of establishing more houses in Chicago, an attempt to bring back the glory days of the old Levee when you couldn't spit anywhere between Clark Street and Wabash Avenue without hitting a brothel. There'd been some reform since then, so his attempt to turn back the clock would spark more trouble than it was worth. Why didn't New York realize that?

Bobbi did some teeth grinding but eventually shrugged. "How you going to do it?"

"I'll figure something out." My general plan was find Bristow, then send some of Gordy's torpedoes in to do the honors. That was how such things were usually accomplished. Then I had only to see to the daily running of everything else, keeping it steady until his return. I refused to consider anything else. Gordy *had* to come back.

"What about Dugan? You're busy with him, remember."

"Let him stew. He kept poor Mrs. Gladwell hanging for two weeks. Do him good to learn what it's like."

"And this club?"

"I can handle both, but I wouldn't turn down any offered help." I sounded hopeful.

She snorted. "Only because it helps Gordy. And I still wanna see him."

"Soon as we can. Let's get you home."

"Not yet, there's one more thing . . . Charles and I discovered it on the recording."

"Discovered what?"

"It's really weird."

"If Dugan said it, then I'm not surprised."

"Charles, would you play it?"

He nodded and worked the machine. The needle eased into the groove; the fuzz of static came through the speaker. Dugan talked about being civilized, then there was the sound of thumps, a fist against flesh, and me disagreeing with him.

A moment of silence, then not too distinctly a woman's voice faintly emerged from the background static and said, "Hit him again. I don't like him."

"What . . . ?" I began. Bobbi and Escott sharply waved me to be quiet.

Dugan groaned. "That was . . . completely unnecessary."

"Was so," the woman declared.

Dance music from the band, Adelle's muffled voice came through, picked up by the all-hearing microphone. More close to it a clunk and click of a door shutting—which was me locking the office—then some random thumps and scrapings when I'd hauled Dugan up for that last attempt to hypnotize him. My own voice was odd to me; I didn't care much for it, especially the kind of intense whispering I had to do when trying to put him under.

But on top of it, the woman said. "That don't work with his type. Bust him inna chops."

Dugan told me to take my hands off him, then yelped; there was a crash when he landed on the couch.

The woman laughed. "That'll show him!"

Escott raised the needle, then one of his eyebrows.

Bobbi looked at me expectantly.

"*Who* was *that?*" I asked. "There wasn't anyone else in the room."

"Perhaps there was," said Escott.

I got who he meant and shook my head. "Oh, no. No-nonononono . . . that's not possible."

"When one has eliminated the impossible"—he glanced at Bobbi—"and we have, then whatever remains—and we're very well aware that it *is* rather improbable—must be the truth."

I kept shaking my head. *"No."*

"Why not, Jack?" Bobbi asked.

Because I don't want it to be, that's why. "It just can't."

Escott played the piece again.

"Bust him inna chops," the woman urged, barely above the static but understandable.

He lifted the needle, put it on its rest, then pulled a box of matches from his breast pocket.

"No," I said firmly. "That's *not* Myrna."

The lights went out.

11

ESCOTT scraped a match to life. His expression was several miles past sardonic. Apparently this wasn't the first time the lights had failed.

"Now see what you did?" said Bobbi. "You hurt her feelings." A candle stood ready in an ashtray on one of the machines. She handed it to Escott, who obligingly lighted it. "I thought you liked Myrna."

"I do! But that *couldn't* be—"

"Shh! Don't you dare say another word."

"Charles?"

He blew out the match, dropping it next to the candle, and lifted his palm to my desperate appeal for sanity. "Believe or not as you wish, but the recording cannot lie. All we can do is try to correctly interpret what is on it. We've listened to it over and over. The voice is not a randomly picked up radio signal. No one else—corporeally speaking—was in the

room with you, nor was anyone nearby performing ventrilo-
quism or shouting up the heating pipes. The voice on this
record was specifically reacting to what you were doing, ergo
its originator was . . . well, I'm not sure 'watching' is the correct word. The originator was certainly aware of your actions."

"Couldn't it just be some kind of crazy static or an echo?
Some scratches on the record?"

They shook their heads in unison.

"But it's not all *that* clear."

"Clear enough," said Bobbi. "I thought you'd be happy
about this."

"Happy?"

"For proof of Myrna being here."

"We get proof every time she plays with the lights! Doesn't
mean I wanna——"

"Jack," Escott said evenly. "Before you get yourself in worse
trouble with our resident revenant, I strongly suggest you shut
the hell up."

I suddenly noticed the room was on the chilly side. For me
to pick up on that meant it had to be freezing. However,
neither Bobbi or Escott commented on the temperature drop.
No sign of goose bumps or shivering showed from them. This
must be how it felt when I invisibly clung to a some hapless
person. I used to think it was funny.

Bobbi addressed the air above her head. "He'll come
around, Myrna. He's just tired and upset about some other
stuff that happened tonight. Don't take it personal."

We waited, but the lights didn't return.

"I wanna go home," I said. "It's late. Even for me. And
that means *really* late."

Bobbi gave a sympathetic smile. "You're right. You sleep

on it, then we'll listen again tomorrow and see what you think."

I didn't want to think about anything for the next few *weeks*, much less tomorrow, not about Dugan, Bristow, and in particular Myrna the ghost. To tell the truth, she scared me more than the other two and all their friends and cousins combined. Until now she'd been interesting, amusing, but safe. Now she had a voice and an opinion.

"Best to lock the recording away," said Escott after a moment. "We've a full day ahead."

Bobbi brought out a flat cardboard box. She carefully lifted the record from the turntable and slipped it inside a paper sleeve, then into the box. "Open your safe, would you, Jack?"

That woke me up a little from my nonthinking, but not by much; it took longer than usual to twirl through the combination.

"There's just enough room if you move that stuff over."

I shoved tonight's money envelope and receipts out of the way. For a fleeting moment I considered making the bank run on our way out. Nah. It could wait.

Bobbi slid the box into the safe at an angle. I returned the money and clanged the door shut, spinning the combination, then locking its "desk drawer" facade into place. That had been what Dugan tried picking open with his burgling tools. Those were safely separated from him, hidden in a closet in the Gladwell house.

But I was determined not to think about him or anything else until tomorrow night at sunset.

And maybe not even then.

* * *

Not that I remembered sleeping, but I did feel better upon waking.

It had been one hell of a long night, and chances were the day had been the same. I'd prepared for it, bathing and shaving before retiring to my sanctuary, dressed except for my coat. That I'd hung over the back of one of the chairs in the kitchen a couple of yards above. I didn't want to go to bed with it on, not so much to spare it from wrinkles but from imagining that I'd look too much like a dead guy laid out ready for his casket. Why else would you lie down fully dressed in your best clothes? Of course, no one was around to see, but I just didn't like the idea of it.

Escott was at the kitchen table, pot of coffee before him along with an egg nestled in an egg cup. He had the top third of the shell off and scowled mightily at the innards.

"I timed it," he said, not looking up at my appearance out of thin air. "I bought a special timer in order to get it right. I got the water to a rolling boil, and I watched it like a hawk for the correct length of time. So why in God's name did the *bloody* thing come out overcooked?"

He didn't really want an answer, not that I had one. I'd given up trying to learn the mysteries of cooking back in my college days. My gut feeling was the egg had been on the small side, but this wasn't a discussion I wanted to get into.

"Did Bobbi call? Did you see Gordy? How is he?"

"Yes she did, and no we didn't. He's about the same as he was last night, which is no worse, so we'll have to take that as being in his favor." Escott gouged his spoon into his hardboiled snack and left the handle sticking up like a flag planted by a mountain climber. "I talked with Shoe, and he passed on that Dr. Clarson was cautiously optimistic. So far there is no sign of either wound going septic, and Gordy has been awake—briefly—and cogent. He's very weak and in pain. The soporific he gets for it keeps him asleep most of the time, which is likely for the best. Gordy's not to be moved. No visitors for now. Only Strome and Miss Taylor."

"I'm going to need Strome along with me tonight."

"I made that known to the gentleman. He had no comment."

"He talks even less than Gordy."

"Which says much about him."

"Eat your egg. What is that? A really late breakfast?"

He worked the spoon back and forth and mined a crumbling mouthful. "More or less. I stole a couple hours of sleep this morning, then went to see Mrs. Gladwell and her subterranean guest."

"How's that going?"

He chuckled. "Extremely well."

"What happened?"

"Around six this morning Gilbert Dugan woke from the clout you gave him and raised the most unholy row if one can trust the butler's and chauffeur's recountings. Apparently our intellectually superior gentleman went quite shriekingly berserk once he realized his predicament. Ten minutes or so of this tired him to exhaustion. He's loud but no stamina. This upset Vivi—Mrs. Gladwell, but—"

"Oh, jeez, Charles. Drop the front and call her Vivian. I know you like her."

"Oh." His ears went red, and he didn't do anything but eat his egg for the next minute. "Well. Then." When nothing remained of the egg but the shell, he put the spoon down and poured himself some coffee.

"Vivian was upset?" I prompted. God, some nights he was so damned *English*.

"Yes. She's had something of a sheltered life, and to hear that sort of unvarnished panic and rage coming from a grown man in such close physical proximity was quite frightening. But she held out. When it concerns the welfare of her daughter, she's adamantine."

That was a relief. Neither of us wanted her caving in.

"I was there when she went down to tell him the terms of his imprisonment. He got very foul with her, which we took to mean that he understood everything perfectly. He demanded to see first you, then me. I took care not to announce my presence, thinking he'd talk more freely. She said we were away on business and would be gone for an indefinite period. She said it in such a way that he'd know it to be false. He then complained piteously about the tightness of his bonds. She explained to him that they had to be snug because of the padding. If he tore that out, the manacles would still fit, only with more chafing from the rough edges. She warned him against that, being unable to guarantee the cleanliness of the metal. If he cut himself, he might get a case of lockjaw and die."

"Would he?"

"I really don't know. I only bought the things. I didn't inquire if they'd been sterilized."

"Where *did* you buy them?"

"From a blacksmith."

"He just had manacles lying around?"

"Yes. Along with horseshoes for the local farriers, he makes props for the stage, which is how I came to know him. He also runs a lucrative under-the-counter business for gentlemen with certain eclectic tastes that I shan't go into."

Fine, I'd ask more about the subject later.

"I stayed until luncheon, and heard how the butler and

chauffeur dealt with their charge. They worked out a method so they need not ever step into the room to deliver his meals and pick up the remains."

"What's that?"

"The butler found a coal shovel, the broad, flat kind. He cleaned it off and now puts the plates on it and pushes it only just within Dugan's reach. He's able to pull the plates off with his fingertips."

"Sounds good. But what if he makes a grab for the shovel?"

"They tied a very stout rope to the hand grip on the end. If by some mischance he should get hold of it, he would be in a tug of war against the chauffeur and the gardener, who are fit specimens. They gave me the impression they'd enjoy seeing him make the attempt."

"I hope they don't test it."

"Oh, no, they appreciate that the point of all this is to get Dugan's confession. There will be no larking about."

"Any sign of a confession coming?"

"Not for now. But this is only the first day."

A little disappointing but not unexpected. I'd hoped Dugan would crack right away, saving us all a load of trouble. Well, you can't have everything. Sooner or later he'd break. The packed heaviness, the ringing silence of those thick concrete walls would work away at him, along with not seeing any sky. I'd talked with guys who had been in solitary, and it left them scarred inside. They'd been in far worse conditions than Dugan, but the principles were the same. Isolation, silence, and nothing to do. I sometimes felt a hint of it myself while waiting for the dawn to render me unconscious.

"He'll capitulate. Eventually." Escott put his coffee cup in the sink, then cleared away the eggshell and wiped the table. He didn't know much cooking but could keep things hospital clean. "The last time I spoke with Vivian, he was in a sulk. His evening meal's to be a curry. The flavor should disguise the taste of the sleeping pills the cook is to mix into his portion. With what's going into his sweet pudding, he should sleep the night through with no incident. I wonder how he'll manage without eating utensils?"

"He say anything useful?"

"No, but he did try to warn the house that *you* were a mortal danger to them."

"What?" My nape hair went up. We'd discussed the possibility Dugan might play that card. I didn't think he'd show it so soon.

"Not to worry. As soon as he worked up to revealing that you were a blood-drinking vampire, it only confirmed to all of them that he was a raving lunatic. If you are worried that any might take him seriously, then I'm sure one of your little 'talks' will sort things to your satisfaction."

It seemed that an awful lot of people, myself included, were taking my acquired talent too much for granted. I was glad to have it, though. "Heard anything from Brockhurst?"

"No, but I've not been to the club or my own office today. I thought he wasn't due until nine."

"Yeah, I'm just nerved up."

"It's far too early in the evening for you to start that. While I'm thinking of it, I should call my answering service. There must be a perfect avalanche of messages piled up from the last few days. Also, Miss Taylor passed on a list of things she wanted from her flat, and Miss Smythe promised to have them ready at the club when we got there. I rather think she will insist on delivering them herself on the chance she can persuade the doctor to allow her at least a look through the door. One cannot blame her."

Hell, I wanted a look for myself. "Anything from Strome?"

"Shoe didn't mention him."

"I gotta talk to him, find out what's been going on with Bristow, if anything."

"Of course. My answering service can wait a bit longer."

I dialed a private upstairs number for the Shoe Box, Cold-field's nightclub, and interrupted his supper. He had no news of Gordy showing much improvement.

"Doc says he's holding his own. Best he can do is keep on resting," he told me. "That Miss Taylor's been watching him close. Hasn't budged since you brought him in."

"Is Strome still there?"

A heavy sigh that was more than half growl. "Yeah. Like a blister. Sure can tell he hates where he is. I think he's scared shitless, but putting up a show like he's not."

"What's scaring him?"

"Miles and miles of brown skin." Coldfield chuckled. "I think he's afraid it'll rub off. Isham hasn't helped much."

"What's he done?"

"Nothing serious. Just made sure Strome got a big plate of fried chicken three times today, along with some collard greens and such. Lord knows where he found those. If he could have located a watermelon this time of year, he'd have cut the guy a big, smile-shaped slice."

"He's not treating Adelle the—"

"Oh, hell, no. Isham's got better manners than that, but if someone's got a goat to get, he can't resist the challenge. That lady's so wound up about Gordy she's not touched any food at all."

That decided me about bringing Bobbi along. She'd be able to make Adelle take care of herself. "I'm coming by soon.

Have to pick Strome up for some work tonight. You hear anything about Bristow today?"

"Nothing. I've got my people keeping their eyes open, made some calls, and I know Strome's done the same. Bristow's yanked the hole in after him."

"If he's still in town. I'll be at Clarson's in an hour or so."

"Pull around back."

"No problem."

Escott followed in his own car as I drove to Lady Crymsyn, parking next to my spot in the lot. No rain tonight. A few puddles lingered in low spots of the paving, gradually shrinking in the cold wind. I gave myself a mental kick in the pants. If I'd just checked things more carefully last night . . .

What had I expected to see? A shooter standing up, gun extended like a duelist? That he'd have an arrow-shaped neon light blinking over his head saying, "Look here"? I should have—

"Jack?" Escott paused on his way to the front.

"Yeah, coming."

Bobbi must have seen us arrive; she unlocked the door. Sober clothes and a somber face, a brief smile for my kiss hello. Before she could ask, I relayed Shoe's latest report on Gordy.

"I'll take you over to see him," I promised. "Adelle's going to need a break, but I was hoping you could fill in for her here tonight."

"I thought of that already. If you get me back in time, I can do it, but I'm warning you I'm in no mood for singing. I talked to Roland and told him we had an emergency. He said he and Adelle could start their weekend show early. We can call it a sneak preview or something."

"You're a genius." I kissed her forehead. "Charles will manage the place tonight."

"Does it require doing that announcement?" he asked. "Introducing them and such?"

"Yeah."

"I'll want some lines to say."

"What?"

"Lines. To speak."

"You're an actor, make something up." I moved toward the stairs.

"Actor, yes, writer, no."

I stopped moving toward the stairs. "But you're *used* to being onstage."

"Indeed I am, but I always had lines. Usually written by Shakespeare."

"You don't have lines when you're in disguise and working a case."

"That's quite different. I'm pretending to be someone else."

This was making my head hurt, and I hadn't hypnotized anyone. Yet.

Bobbi waved one hand in my direction. "Oh, Charles. It's easy. Just pretend to be Jack."

He rounded on her, looking relieved. "What an excellent idea. Thank you."

"Pretend to be—now just a damn min—"

"No problem. I took your place in the window last night. Felt like a turkey in a shooting galley, I tell ya." His precise English accent was gone, replaced by . . . I don't know what. It sure as hell wasn't me.

"I sound like *that?* You're nuts!"

"Brother, it's close enough." He shoved his hands in his pockets, parked his duff against a wall, and crossed one foot over the other. Bobbi giggled.

"Oh, for God's sake, I'll write you something to say, just don't expect any Shakespeare. And don't go putting on my new white tux."

"Ya sure? I'd look pretty snazzy."

"Yeah-yeah. Now stop doing that." Jeez, it was creepy.

He straightened into his normal posture. "Very well."

Red-faced, Bobbi snickered all the way up to the office.

She'd recovered by the time I set the brake behind Clarson's building. The alley was barely wider than the car and full of potholes deep enough to make me anxious about breaking an axle, but we were hidden from the street. The hour was still early, and people were out despite the wind. It sliced through my overcoat, an icy, arctic knife with a serrated blade. Bobbi visibly shook and made *brr* sounds as we climbed outside stairs to the second floor, and she still had some shaking left even after we got inside.

"Anything this cold should be illegal," she muttered.

Clarson had opened the door for us and smiled. "I got a gas fire in my office if you need warming up."

"Thanks, Doctor." I said. "How are you?"

"Thawed and ready for the oven. How 'bout yourself?"

"Worried about Gordy."

"There's no change. No talking, but you can see him if you don't mind wearing a sterile mask."

Neither of us minded. I put down the small suitcase that belonged to Adelle and unbuttoned my coat. Bobbi also kept hers on but removed her gloves, hat, and a thick wool scarf.

Clarson gave us each a white square of gauze with thin ties dangling from the corners. We knotted them into place, and he took us along the hall to a different room from his improvised operating theater. This one was furnished with a high, hospital-style bed, all white enamel and crank handles. Gordy's unmoving form dwarfed it.

He was almost as white as the bed and lay completely inert. It hurt to see him like that. He seemed flattened. Frail. Like he wasn't Gordy anymore. I could still smell blood, tainted by the miasma of a sickroom. Despite the cold, I wanted to open the window wide and flush the place clear. Gordy's head and shoulders were partially obscured by an oxygen tent made out of thick cellophane. Maybe it insulated him from the smell.

Strome was in a chair by the door. He wore a mask, too, making his face even more expressionless.

Adelle rose from a cushioned chair next to the bed. She rushed toward Bobbi, arms out. They clung to each other, and Adelle sobbed a few times, and in a soft, controlled voice Bobbi told her everything would be all right. She told her that a lot until Adelle was able to pull away, wiping her eyes with a very crumpled handkerchief. She looked like she'd been holding in a lot of tears. Her sterile mask was askew after that. She tugged it back into place and motioned for us to retreat back to the hall.

"Bobbi brought your stuff," I said, lifting the suitcase.

"Thank you." Her normal throaty tone sounded rusted and clogged, as though she hadn't done much in the way of talking lately. "It's been awful, but everyone's been so kind."

Bobbi put an arm around her. "C'mon, honey, let's get you patched back together. Wash your face and change. Put on some makeup, or Gordy won't know you."

"I can't do the show."

"Forget the show, it's covered. You got more important things on your mind."

She got the case from me, and Clarson led them away. Adelle evidently needed to talk, and Bobbi was a good listener. They'd be busy a while. I went back to the room and signed for Strome to join me in the hall.

"How's it been?"

He pulled the mask down so it bunched under his long chin. "Goddamn dinge-town."

I was in no mood for crap. "Shut up about that and stick to business."

He subsided, and without any whammy work from me. "I made calls. Lowery's made calls. The boys are running all over town. Word came. Bristow says he didn't do it, but he has to say that."

"Who'd he say it to?"

"He called New York; they called the Nightcrawler. Boys there said that Gordy's alive and kicking, but New York wanna talk to him. Some of the boys here believe that, some think he's dead, the others are itchy, wondering which way to jump. We got a meeting like you want. Seven."

My watch read ten after six. "At Gordy's office?"

"Yeah. They ain't gonna like it if he don't show."

"I'll take care of them."

He grunted.

"Problem?"

"You ain't Gordy. It ain't me; it'll be them."

"I'll take care of them. You back me like you said last night, and you do it one hundred percent, or Bristow will be the last man you ever see. A mug like him moves into a new spot, he always gets rid of the old lieutenants."

He nodded. "I know how it works. You just don't get too cozy, yourself."

"Trust me, I'm the only man in this burg who *doesn't* want the job."

Strome nodded, eyes dead, like he'd heard that one before.

Bobbi elected to stay and be moral support for Adelle. She was just phoning the club to tell Escott as Strome and I made our way down to the alley. Isham came up the stairs, a grease-splotched bag in his hand. I smelled fried food on the freezing air.

"Don't you want no supper, Mist' Strome?" Isham drawled innocently. "Do you a pow'ful heap o' good to keep yo' strenth up, thas a fact."

"Knock it off," I muttered out the side of my mouth, but I couldn't avoid smirking. Isham winked once at me and leaned against the building so we could pass. "Shoe coming over?"

"Later on." His Southern accent had instantly dried up. "Doesn't want to draw notice here, y'know?"

"Make sure he calls Escott at my club, you keep them both posted about the patient."

"You got it."

Strome held silent all the way back to the Nightcrawler Club, which was quite a drive. The side streets were clogged with cars, the larger thoroughfares had even more cars, plus the traffic signals—all against me—horse-drawn wagons, and suicidal pedestrians. We arrived ten minutes late, but that's what I'd calculated as the perfect time. Late stragglers would be there, and the others would have worked into a grumbling restlessness, wondering when the hell things would start.

We went in by the back way again, this alley in far better repair, up a short flight of concrete loading dock stairs to a busy, steam-filled kitchen. Lately Gordy had been offering steaks and the trimmings on a very short, limited menu, but it seemed to be going over well. All he needed was one man out front as a food shill. His job was to sit in a central spot and be served up a slab of meat wider than my hand to tempt a dozen other patrons to do the same. It always smelled good, which accounted for most of the orders.

The profit margin was enormous since Gordy had a deal going with a meat-packer union boss. The boss got into the club whenever he wanted, no cover, no paying for shows, as many guests as he chose to bring along, and the first round of drinks free. His meals were free, too, and in return, Gordy got an unlimited supply of beef without having to pay.

Sweet stuff, and I could get in on it, but I didn't want the bother of a kitchen at my place just yet, if ever. Cooked food smells were nauseating to me. My customers would just have to make do at the diner down the street for the time being.

Through the kitchen, a hall, the back stairs. The band out front boomed away on a frantic number. It was still a little early in the evening to force that kind of speed-up on the dance floor. I had to remind myself this wasn't my club; I was just here to keep the muscle in line, not interfere with the show talent.

The upper landing, then left to Gordy's office. Its door was wide open, and a dozen guys were outside, watching my progress. Lots of hats and eyes and grim expressions. I knew many by now, all of them by sight and was on amicable terms with most, which didn't mean anything. In the rackets a guy could be your lifelong best friend but still order you killed or even do the killing if it was deemed necessary. The unpredictable

Dion O'Banion was executed in his own flower shop while shaking hands with a guy, the hit approved by two of his closest bootlegging partners, Johnny Torrio and Al Capone. Business was business.

This bunch looked worried and watchful. Once I went inside, I got why. At least another dozen boys were waiting, and none of them were my best friends and never would be. They either had a gripe against me or we'd traded fists at one time or they didn't like my looks or resented that I got special treatment from their boss. Despite the high-tone suits and dapper hats, it looked like a convention of junkyard dogs, even the handsome ones. I couldn't hear any actually snarling, but you could feel it strong in the air like the hum a radio gives warming up with the sound on full.

It was much as I'd anticipated.

I crossed the room, Strome a good three steps behind. So much for backing me. If anyone took a shot, he was in the best position to see . . . and duck from the line of fire.

Lowrey and a man named Derner sat at Gordy's desk; he was one of the more sensible lieutenants. I might be able to rely on him, but he'd go along with the majority. He was speaking into the phone, his gaze on me.

"He just walked in," he said. The room was quiet enough so everyone heard. Derner held the earpiece out. "It's New York. They wanna talk to you."

"I wanna talk to them, but in a minute."

"But—"

"In a minute."

Derner pulled his sagging jaw back into place, hastily mumbled into the mouthpiece, and hung up. He vacated Gordy's chair and got out of my way, but I had no intention of sitting there. Nearly thirty guys so tough you could ice skate on them were just looking for me to get stupid. Leaving that chair empty for the time being sent them a message about my intent but also left things open for misinterpretation. Instead of showing respect for Gordy, they might think I didn't have the guts to sit in his place. Those were the ones I had to watch for, and they all seemed to be in the front circle.

Lowrey glanced at Strome, then me. "Who's watching the boss?"

"A friend. He's in safe hands."

"Whose?"

"Wise up." There was no way I'd let that information drop here with all these ears. For all I knew, Bristow could have already recruited half of them with promises of better pay and positions when he took over. Which wouldn't happen if I could help it.

I parked my duff on the edge of the desk, recalling that Escott had adopted a similar posture. Just how close had he been to imitating me? I kept my hands out of my pockets, though; it spoiled the lines of the suit, which were very smooth. Whoever had eyes to see would know I wasn't packing anything more lethal than a handkerchief and loose change. Strome told me to carry heat, and I did have a gun. I had a couple of guns, picked up here and there on various cases with Escott, but left home or locked in my office safe. These guys wouldn't be impressed by firepower. It was too common, too easily used, too easily betrayed. On the other hand, they'd take me for an idiot, going unarmed.

"Here's the deal," I said, loud so the boys in the back didn't have to work to listen. "Gordy's been plugged, but he's all right. He told me to keep things running until he gets back."

"How do we know that?"

"Because Bristow ain't standing here, and most of you are

still breathing. If Bristow gets in, he will clean house. Those two go hand in hand."

"If Gordy's all right, why don't he call?" This from a big guy named Ruzzo. He wasn't the one to worry about, that would be his younger brother, also big. They were both called Ruzzo by everyone, with no additional name to distinguish one from the other; one man, two bodies, and two bad tempers if they thought anyone was shorting them on money or deference.

"I didn't ask why," I said. "That's how he wants it."

"He's dead," said Ruzzo the younger, "Like I thought."

"Like I thought," echoed his brother.

Fair fighting was for the boxing ring, and sometimes not then. With no warning and moving faster than they could think—not difficult—I darted from the desk, gut-punching once each, left, right. Not quite hard enough to rupture internal organs, but folding them down. Neither would be moving right away. I strolled back to the desk, shooting my cuffs.

Several of the guys blinked and maybe remembered why Gordy gave me special consideration, even though I wasn't on the payroll.

"Gordy says I'm in charge 'til he returns. If you're wondering about changes, I'm not making any. Everyone keeps doing what they do same as usual. Any problem with that?"

A gaunt man two steps from me pulled his gun from a shoulder holster with the same casual movement as lighting a cigarette. He was a heartbeat from shooting, but I slapped my hand over his, forcing it down, squeezing hard to break fingers. He got a fist in the jaw with my other hand and dropped. I plucked the gun free of his lax grip and, very purposefully, gave it to Strome. A message to him, too. He met my gaze steady for an instant. He was unreadable but didn't try shooting me, despite the offered opportunity. Whether it was because he knew better than to try or was genuinely supporting me, I couldn't tell. He shoved the gun into his belt.

"Everything runs the same," I continued, "except for you guys who are going to find me Ignance Bristow. He's the one who did the shooting or arranged to have it done. He was only supposed to *talk* Gordy into handing over the business. It didn't happen. Now I wanna talk to him. After I'm done, Gordy's gonna want to talk to him."

"He won't let us bring him in," someone said.

"You don't have to *bring*. You just *find*. Find him and tell me where he is. I'll take it from there. Make damn sure you're right, 'cause I don't have time to waste on no goose chases. When you're sure, you call here."

"We get paid extra for this?"

"Extra? Okay, who's the wiseass?"

General laughter. Not a lot, but a good sign.

"This ain't a hit, this is hide-and-seek. But—the guy who finds Bristow gets a grand as a bonus. You can buy your girlfriend something nice and something nicer for the wife so she don't mind you being out late."

Another laugh.

I pointed to the men on the floor. "Get these mugs outta here and set 'em straight. If you got work to do, go do it. The rest of you spread out and look for Bristow. Find him tonight, and I'll put another grand on top of the first."

"That's just for locating him? We don't do nothin' else?"

"Easy money," I said.

They all seemed to agree; I never saw a room clear so fast without a lunch whistle sounding first. They left behind the Ruzzos and the gaunt gunslinger. At a look from me, Strome called a few guys over for cleaning duty, dragging the bodies out.

The phone rang.

"That'll be New York again," said Derner.

"Who am I talking to at the other end?"

"Guy called Kroun."

I thought I'd heard of him. Gordy talked about lots of people, lots of names. "Who's he?"

"The fella who sent Bristow here."

Great.

12

"THIS is Fleming."

"And who the hell are you?" Ordinary voice, Hell's Kitchen accent. Definitely aggressive.

"Filling in for Gordy tonight. You Kroun?"

"Yeah. Where's Hog?"

"I don't know."

"What's this about him shooting Gordy? He wouldn't do that."

"Well, Kroun, you're in for a disappointment. Bristow was crazy drunk last night and plenty mad. He had a lapse in judgment. Gordy got away, and put himself where he can stay healthy."

"How you know all that?"

"I was there, saw everything. What the hell were you thinking, sending that brainless thug out here to take over from Gordy?"

Derner gave me a sharp look. Questioning the New York bosses was something you only did once.

"Hog says he can do a better job." Kroun sounded like he was simmering just short of boil-over.

"All he wants is a place to get drunk every night."

"The money's not like it was. Hog can do better."

"Check the paper, there's a depression on. Gordy's doing damn well, and a damn sight better than Bristow would. He keeps his head clear and has a brain inside it—"

"Aw, go buy a violin. So you're filling in? What're you going to do about this?"

"That's up to Bristow. He *will* be found." I hoped I wasn't talking too fast for this guy. "*How* he's found is his choice. He can be dead or alive. His choice."

"You bury him, you put yourself in the same box. He's got friends here."

"Then he should go back to 'em. I'm the *only* friend he's got here. Listen very carefully, Kroun. If I don't talk to him, one of the other boys will, and it'll be with a gun. They're plenty sore about what he did to Gordy."

"I don't hear no proof Hog did anything. You think I'm just gonna take your word for it?"

"Your favorite son will be explaining himself soon enough. If he lives that long."

"What d'ya mean by that?"

"Just listen: I'm the one man here with enough sense to keep him alive. If he should happen to call home to say hello, you pass that on. Every guy in this town wants to nail him to a wall. I'm the one man here who *won't* kill him. I know what's at stake." Not strictly true, but Kroun wouldn't be asking for a list.

"Hog won't believe that."

"Then he's dumber than he looks. Gordy has to have told him I don't care one way or another about how you guys run your business. It's none of mine, and I want to keep clear of it. But Hog comes in like a binging sailor, rocking boats, upsetting things—that's bad for everyone's business."

"So?"

"If you can talk him into being smart, I can clean up the mess he made and see to it he's happy with the deal."

"What d'ya mean by that? What deal?"

"Have him talk to me, and he'll find out. If he doesn't wise up, then you can't blame anyone but him for whatever happens. I don't like assholes coming into my town thinking they can kick my friends around and not catch one on the chin for it like a man. That kind ain't worth the powder to blow 'em to hell, and you and I both know it. If Bristow thinks he's got big enough balls to take on Chicago, he's got to prove it to me first. You got that straight?"

Silence on the line.

"I said, do you got that?"

"Oh, yeah. And Hog's gonna get every word." His voice was shaky. Mad as hell kind of shaky.

"Good. Now I have things to do." I hung up.

Strome didn't move or speak. Same for Lowrey, who looked out-and-out appalled for a second before covering it up.

Derner opened and shut his mouth a few times and finally said, "Where you want the funeral?"

"Mine or Bristow's?" I grinned.

"Both. What the hell were *you* thinking, kid? Talking to Kroun like that?"

"If I rolled on my back and pissed myself, would he have respected me?"

"I guess not, but Kroun—"

"Is probably calling Bristow right now and passing on my message just the way I want. I'll wait here for him to phone. Of course, if any of the boys finds him first, then I change my plans. I hope you got two grand in petty cash lying around." With the amount of gambling going on in the private casino downstairs, that's probably what they used for coffee and donut change.

"That's the boss's money you're throwing around, remember."

Just what I wanted to hear: guys in Gordy's organization talking like he could walk in any minute. "Gordy won't mind."

"Two grand? That's a lot, considering there's no hit on."

I was fairly confident that no one would collect. Bristow would call first. Not because he was smart but for a chance to let me know what he thought of me. After he was done spitting dust, I'd arrange a meeting with him and do my evil-eye "deal." In the meantime, the hunt for him kept a lot of dangerous, jittery guys chasing around and focused on something else besides me. Of course, if one of the boys accidentally killed him, that would change things, but I was optimistic about Bristow's ability to survive, even with a bounty on his head. His bodyguards would keep him safe if they knew what was good for them. "I think insurance people call it a finder's fee. Gordy can take it off his taxes."

"Taxes?" Derner spoke like it was an unfamiliar foreign word.

"Never mind. Anyone deliver a paper here today? I wanna read the news."

Strome found this morning's papers. I sprawled on Gordy's wide leather sofa and looked over the headlines. The others took the hint and parked themselves at the other end of the room to wait for Bristow's call.

The kidnapping case had faded from the front page, replaced by a milk fund scandal, union troubles in Detroit, and the latest load of woe from China. The Japanese were murdering them. The Chinese were in desperate need of pilots and people to teach them to fly, but not having much luck. The officers wanting to learn were from the upper crust of a very caste-bound society and took criticism from lower-rank tutors rather badly. If you gave your noble-born student a poor grade, you could have your head chopped off. Along with the war, they were losing flying teachers by the bushel basket. Though many outside the country were sympathetic, there weren't a lot of American or British fliers interested in taking their place.

I dug out the funny pages, finding them much more entertaining than usual. Having been walking on the edge for too long, I craved inanity. Strome, Lowrey, and Derner didn't hide their annoyance at my enjoyment, but damn it, the laughs felt good.

The crossword looked interesting, so I went to the desk— only then did I sit in the chair—and played at filling in the squares for a while. The phone rang a few times, but it was ordinary club business that Derner handled quickly to keep the line clear.

Halfway through the puzzle it hit me: I'd faced down all those toughs and hadn't once resorted to the evil eye. Hadn't even thought of it. I was faster and stronger than any of them and had used that, but it was different, seemed more square for some reason. And no headache from the effort.

But all the rest was *me*, not supernatural influence. For all the guff and gab I'd thrown out, I'd been rock steady and still was; it felt good, even. This ordinary kind of smoke and mirrors stuff agreed with me.

Well, well, Mrs. Fleming's youngest was doing all right for himself.

When I'd had enough of self-congratulation, I decided to check the inside headlines for that morning's latest about the Gladwell kidnapping. Escott had mentioned no new developments over his boiled egg supper, but then he'd slept in late and might not have read anything. Neither of us had listened to the radio, either. I shifted newsprint around on Gordy's desk.

The kidnapping had been relegated to page two, and I expected a much-truncated story rehashing everything, but there was fresh information after all. The first was Dugan's mysterious failure to appear in court. His lawyer gave excuses, requesting a postponement. The judge rescheduled things for tomorrow and sternly lectured the lawyer about the importance of not wasting the court's time.

By tomorrow, if not already, Dugan would be on someone's official fugitive roster. He'd be in jail now if they'd been doing their jobs. For crying out loud, kidnapping was a federal crime to start with, and he'd added to it by taking the girl across state lines. He should have been stewing in jail, not Mrs. Gladwell's basement. God save us from fancy-talking liars.

But tacked onto the bottom of the article was the real bombshell. My guess was the news had come in after they'd set up the front page. Rather than ripping everything, they'd made space for it on the already existing story. Under a smaller heading that read "Grim Discovery at Kidnap Hideout" was a report from Indiana. The cops there had done some digging—literally—at the farmhouse. Dumped in the cesspit under the partially destroyed outhouse were two bodies, an old man and woman, apparently the owners of the property.

I stared at the print a long time, then read it again, carefully, but the words hadn't changed. I stood, throwing the paper down, and paced a few times.

Derner looked up. "Something wrong, Mr. Fleming?"

"I want a new edition. The latest you can find. Now."

"Okay." He went to the office door and passed the errand to someone down the hall. About a minute later he had an evening paper taken from one of the boys.

The kidnapping was once more on the front page, this time with photos. The couple had been identified, their ages listed, with a truncated history of their lives. In summation, they were elderly, had no close relatives, and kept to themselves. Perfect for Dugan's purpose. If they disappeared from their isolated farm, no one would be likely to notice for months. Cause of death seemed to be gunshots to the head.

How had he found them? Had he and one of the other men, maybe Vinzer the driver, gone along the back roads looking for just such a setup? It would be easy enough to pretend to have a breakdown, stroll up to a house, and ask to use a phone. Dugan's polished manners and nice clothes would get him through any rustic door. Sooner or later, they'd find a place not on the phone exchange. Plenty of those in farming country. They'd narrow it to anyone who kept to themselves. No visitors, no family, no neighbors. They could find all that out over a friendly cup of coffee. Then Dugan or the other guy would take out a gun and with a couple of bullets claim the house for their own.

If I'd known that to start with, I'd have killed Dugan and his whole gang the first night and lived with a clean conscience afterward.

Mostly clean.

I'd killed before. It wasn't my solution to every problem, and I sure as hell hated what it did to me, but in this case I could honestly say their deaths would not have troubled me too much.

The paper played up the fact that Dugan was truly missing, from his court date and from answering questions about the murdered couple. A lot too late, the editors had come to realize their society pretty boy was a bad egg after all. The cops were again grilling family and friends for his whereabouts. Well, they wouldn't be lying when they said they didn't know.

I wondered if Escott had had a chance to read this stuff and reached for the phone, then changed my mind. That could wait until after Bristow called. I sat and stewed and thought seriously about killing Dugan even now in cold blood. There'd be nothing to it: just go up to a man chained helpless to a wall and snap his neck. Or use a gun so I wouldn't actually have to touch him and feel the life going out. I thought about that a lot, what I'd have to do to get rid of the body, how I would deal with the aftermath inside my head. As long as I slept on my home earth, there would be no nightmares, and if I stayed busy and distracted, I wouldn't have to think about it. For decades to come I wouldn't have to think about it for a single minute.

I wondered what kind of hole in the world he would make disappearing. It's a big thing to kill, not necessarily a bad thing, but a big thing, the old toss a rock into a pool kind of thing. Would the ripples be too much to handle? There would be a hellish legal fuss with the law looking for him, but beyond that . . . maybe it'd work.

But it wasn't practical. Too many witnesses. Vivian Gladwell trusted her servants, but I couldn't. I'd have to remove

Dugan to some other place. Escott would have to be told . . . or I could hypnotize him into forgetting. Not square, doing that to my best friend, and eventually it would wear off and he'd remember. Or, knowing what I had planned, he'd help, become an accessory to first-degree murder.

We'd been through a lot together, and I could count on him, but he didn't need this kind of burden. Okay, maybe I *could* kill Dugan cold, not something to be proud of, but in the end too much of a problem to drop on my friends.

I eased back from the idea. Things would serve as they stood; no need for me to step in swinging, all fired with belated vengeance. We'd continue as before: let Dugan rot for a time, then turn him over to the law. It was slow, and justice was sometimes uncertain if not completely absent, but better that someone else handle the problem.

Besides, if Dugan's trial didn't go the way I thought it should, I could always step in and have a "talk" with the judge, attorneys, and the whole damned jury.

I cut the article out, shoved it in my pants pocket, and pretended to read. Across the large room, Strome told the other men how he'd spent his day in Clarson's office, speaking soft to keep me out of it. He complained about the food, how he was treated, and I picked up plenty about him and how his mind worked.

There was no point reminding Strome that Coldfield's people had saved Gordy's life and were continuing to preserve it. Throwing it up in his face would not make our own uneasy collaboration any better, and he wasn't the type to learn new stuff, anyway. I'd make sure he wouldn't be going back to watch over Gordy. His Bronze Belt surroundings were too distracting to him. He'd be paying more attention to himself than outside threats. Better for Gordy that Coldfield's people played bodyguard. They knew the territory, what was normal, what wasn't.

When talk shifted to the present situation, I sensed a few looks thrown my way. Their voices got softer, but my ears picked up every word. Strome and Lowrey didn't think I could pull off running things, but Derner had seen me in action and thought I had a chance.

"He does something to people," he said. "I donno what, but he talks and they listen. The boss calls him in whenever he needs a special job. One minute a guy's all piss and vinegar, the next he's on a train to Florida and happy about it."

"So?" said Strome. "Ain't gonna work with Bristow. We listened to him all this time, and what he goes after, he gets. Even the boss wasn't crossin' him. Night after night we was listening to that crap."

"The boss was learning stuff," Lowrey put in.

"Ain't that much to learn. Bristow's taking over."

"Fleming'll kill him first. He an' the boss owe each other. He's stand-up. He'll back Gordy all the way."

"Fleming don't have the authority to do any killin'. I don't see that kid having the guts, neither. It's just show with him, nothing underneath. We've seen a dozen punks just like him come to town, gas loud, and then they ain't around no more. New York likes that loudmouth bastard Bristow. If anything happens to him, we all go, including Gordy."

"We go anyway if Bristow takes over," Lowery reminded him.

"You mean when. Gordy's not looking so good. Even if Fleming stops Bristow—which he won't—Gordy's dead meat.

I'm moving town. Plenty of places in Jersey or Florida to work."

"When you going?"

Strome seemed to consider. "We'll see how this punk handles a real piece of trouble, but I can promise you Bristow will bury him. When that happens, you better be packed and going through the door."

Gordy had some fine fellas working for him, but it was the nature of the business. When he was better, I'd let him know about Strome's flexible loyalty, though he was likely already aware of it.

"Strome! C'mere."

To give him credit, he didn't do a guilty start at my calling him over. He took his time, though.

I swiveled Gordy's chair to put my back to the other guys and gestured for Strome to pull another up close. "We gotta powwow about tonight," I said. "Make some plans."

Strome got a chair and sat. I leaned forward. He mirrored me to a lesser extent, but we definitely had privacy. I could be confident that Derner and Lowrey wouldn't overhear.

"Yeah, what plans?" His talk with them must have been fortifying to his self-assurance; after all, I was just a kid full of my own piss and vinegar.

I took care of his objections to me in about a minute, though it made for a good sharp pain behind my eyes. When I was done, we stood and shook hands. "Glad that's settled. Good luck."

His mouth twitched like it was trying to remember how to smile, and he left. No word of parting to his pals as he passed. I didn't do anything drastic, just told him to go home and sleep for a couple of days. By then things would be over, one way or another. By then Gordy would still be with us or not. I hated that latter possibility, but it had to be considered. One thing that would *not* happen was Bristow taking his place.

Derner stared after the departing Strome and muttered to Lowrey. "See? That Fleming guy *does* things to people."

As it ticked toward nine o'clock with no word from Bristow, I got antsy and phoned my club. Escott answered.

"Any sign of Brockhurst yet?" I asked.

"Not tonight. I think he took a powder."

What the hell? "Okay, you can lay off." Impersonating me once was funny, but not twice.

"Not my doing, bo. He's the no-show."

"Charles?"

"Yeah?"

"How's the dance act going over?"

"They're burning up the floor. That blond pippin's laying 'em flat. Wouldn't think the mugs would go for that snooty type, but they're eatin' it up. We're having grief from the damn lights, though. It's that short what needs fixing. You need to get here and do that."

Right. Well, he didn't have to hit me twice with a two-by-four. "I'll be over, but I can't leave just yet."

"Where are you?"

"Looking after Gordy. He's ready to chew nails over Bristow, but I talked him into keeping his head down a little longer." Escott knew as well as I that Gordy was still out. Now he'd also know that I'd caught his message.

"Maybe I should talk with him, too. Where's he parked?"

"Don't worry about it. You can see him tomorrow. He's in a bad mood."

"I can cheer him up," he pressed, still holding the American accent. Someone had to have a gun to his head. Certainly they were listening to everything.

"Look, I'm gonna wind some stuff up here and get to the club in . . . oh . . . about an hour. If Brockhurst comes in, tell him to wait. All I want is fifteen minutes with that jerk. Just fifteen nose-busting minutes."

"Yeah, but—"

"In an hour," I said, hanging up and bolting for the door.

I'd wanted to work in a stop at the Stockyards at some point tonight but had to nix that. Not that I was in dire need of blood; it was just to keep myself prepared in case things got rough. But events had bulled ahead and sideways of my feeble plans.

Risking notice from traffic cops and subsequent delays, I ran stop signals but got lucky, reaching Lady Crymsyn in twelve minutes flat. The only parking space was my reserved spot, and I wasn't using it in case someone was on watch. I drove around the block and backed my car into an alley, hoping the owners of the property didn't have any night deliveries scheduled.

The wind was still ugly but blowing in a favorable direction for me. It was strong at my back as I hurried along the nearly empty sidewalks. Cars growled past, snorting thick exhaust that the wind immediately shredded. I knew it wouldn't do that to me when the time came to go invisible, but it raised unpleasant mental pictures.

Before taking the last corner, I paused to check the front of my club. My office lights were on. One of the window curtains was held partially open; a man's form—not lean enough to be Escott—was silhouetted there, looking out. Very smart of them, but they didn't expect me for another forty-five minutes yet.

Peering narrow, I sighted a sharpshooter's bead on the entry, intending to bowl straight in. Not caring if anyone walking by noticed, I vanished and let the wind speed me along across the street until I washed up against the doors like ghostly flotsam. I hit so hard it nearly sent me solid, but the shock passed, allowing me to sieve under the cracks into the lobby.

Busy night. I sensed people milling about, couldn't tell how many. None saw me flowing across the lobby, though a few might have felt a passing chill. They'd blame it on drafts. I surged upstairs and down the hall, materializing in the room next to my office.

Dark and empty as I expected. The recording equipment was gone, only the tables, a couple chairs, and a phonograph on its stand remained. Excelsior scraps littered the floor, left over from packing the stuff off again. The wiring from the microphones was still in place but not hooked up to anything. I didn't need them, only had to press my ear to the adjoining wall.

I could hear just enough breathing to know more than one man was in the room. No one spoke. This was a rotten time for Bristow to play clam. I wasn't going to just walk in blind. Not in the strict sense. I wanted to know how many and where they were.

One way to find out. Damn.

To avoid the unpleasant sensation of pressing through the wall, I eased quiet into the hall and slipped beneath the office door, then had to try locating Escott among the several individuals here. Two were behind my desk, close together, another seated on the front corner of the desk near the door, one by the window, another on the sofa. They were too scattered for me to take on and be certain of no gunplay.

Guessing that the man in my desk chair was Escott, I moved in close to give him the shivers. He obligingly coughed and cleared his throat so I'd know his voice.

"What's with those lights?" someone demanded sharply.

"We got a short," said Escott. "I tol' ya. They flicker like that all the time."

"Goddamn it!" This was from Bristow. Unmistakable. He was on the couch. "They're out again! Someone get a flashlight."

I took a hell of a chance with Escott's life, but he knew I was there and would duck quick enough. Materializing in the dark behind the guy nearest him, I plucked his gun away and slammed home a kidney punch, dropping the thug almost instantly. He'd been aiming at Escott. Now the gun was pointed at Bristow, who was on the sofa, glaring impotently around and grumbling in what for him was near pitch blackness.

When the lights abruptly came on again, the men honestly didn't notice me right away. The guy I'd clobbered and I both wore dark coats. I stood in his exact same place. It was the change of the gun's direction that got Bristow's exasperated attention.

"Hey! Why are y——"

Oh, my, but he had a beaut of an expression on his wide mug once the bad news settled in and took root. His mouth made like a fish's. His brain had called a sudden strike and wouldn't be working for an indefinite period.

The other men were even slower to react. The one sitting on the end of the desk happened to notice something was off with his boss and tardily turned to look. He twitched at seeing me but didn't dare go for his gun, which was holstered under his arm. The guy at the window had his back to the room. It must have been the abrupt silence that caused him to drop the curtain and turn. He blinked, squinting at me in disbelief. Most importantly, he didn't move.

"Hands up," I said. "Nobody get stupid. I just want to talk." When they looked like they'd behave, I motioned the two on their feet over toward the sofa. The one I'd hit was still down, gray of face and breathing funny. He'd probably be peeing blood for a couple days.

Escott had sensibly leaned over and to the left, ready to slip from the chair if necessity dictated. He gradually sat up, sighing with relief.

"That was a bloody long fifteen minutes," he said, annoyed. He must have been pretty shaken. Usually stuff like this put him in a good humor. At least his English accent was back.

"How much longer did you have to wait?" I asked.

"Until you finally telephoned? They invaded here around a quarter past eight. The one chap had his gun against the back of my skull the whole time. They wouldn't let me phone out. They thought it would better lure you in unawares if you called first. I was to get you here or at least discover Gordy's location from you."

I was surprised they didn't try beating it out of him and said as much.

"Actually, they did indulge in a spot of uncivilized behavior, but nothing that would show. When you walked in, the plan was for you to see me here as usual, unmarked, then jump you. Fortunately, I persuaded them to my ignorance, that I was just a club manager not privy to my employer's secrets."

"He squealed like a pig," said Hog Bristow with satisfaction. "Told us everything."

Escott shook his head, not quite rolling his eyes. "One of my finest performances of utter capitulation, abject terror, and lying through my teeth. Quite wasted on this gathering. Shall I continue his porcine analogy by adding a remark about throwing pearls before swine, or would that be too trite?"

"It's just as well for you he fell for it."

"What's that supposed to mean?" demanded Bristow.

It was hard to believe this guy had any friends, much less people who thought him capable of taking over for Gordy. "It means you really are dumber than you look."

"Hey!"

"Shut up." I waved the gun, reminding him who was in charge. "Kroun in New York gave you my message, right?"

"Yeah. I got it. Why d'ya think we're here? You think I'd just walk into the Nightcrawler on your word? That *you* can keep *me* alive?"

"You're alive now, aren't you?"

"Enjoy it, you goddamn pink-eared mama's boy. When I'm done with you, they won't need a meat grinder to turn you into dog food."

"You still expect New York will protect you after trying to bump Gordy? Forget that."

Escott eased from the chair. He must have taken a few gut punches, for he moved carefully. Staying out of my line of fire, he disarmed everyone, taking his big Webley back from one of them. The lights flickered slightly but didn't go out. The men looked up, uneasy.

"Goddamn short," Bristow muttered.

"Myrna," I said softly. "Her name is Myrna."

"Who the hell is Myrna?"

"Resident revenant and guardian angel." I addressed the air. "Thanks, doll. You did good."

"Indeed. Extremely well done," agreed Escott, having apparently lost his nervousness about her. "You two gentlemen join your friend on the floor. Lie facedown and clasp your hands at the small of your back. A little more speed, if you please. I have a grudge against the lot of you and shall shoot the slowest in a very undignified and disagreeable location. That's better. Now lie perfectly still."

They were lined up side by side, even the guy I'd hit. He was the only one who didn't seem to mind being motionless.

"You're gonna die buckwheats, you son of a bitch," Bristow growled at me from the couch.

"Beg pardon?" Escott kept his eyes on the three floor goons.

"Nothing to do with *Our Gang*," I said. "It's killing a guy slow and ugly as a lesson to others."

"Interesting nomenclature. One wonders at its origin. I hope you'll take steps to change his mind about such an alarming course of action."

"Oh, yeah." Damn, it was a relief to have him talking normal again. "Hey, Ignance."

You could almost see the steam coming out of Bristow's ears. "Why you—"

"Yeah-yeah, I know, buckwheats with a beer chaser. You have anything to drink tonight?"

"What's it to you?"

"You'll find out."

Just then the office door opened. Anthony Brockhurst stood on the threshold in a dapper camel-hair coat, silk scarf, and topper. Marie Kennard was with him, clutching at her high fur collar and looking sullen-angry. They saw Escott standing over the men on the floor and me with my gun aimed at

Bristow. It must have been an impressive tableau.

Anthony's eyes popped, and he fell away half a step. "I-I can see you're busy. I'll just come back later."

Keeping my aim steady, I gave Anthony a look. "Oh, no, get your ass in here. You're late."

Marie let out a soft little moan of alarm and seemed about to bolt.

"You, too, sister. Inside."

Just the sight of the gun, though it was pointed elsewhere, put me in charge of them. They were almost too petrified to obey. Anthony gallantly stood in front of her.

"Let her go; you don't need her here," he declared, chin and voice high.

"*Both* inside. Now. Shut the door." They did exactly that. I made them stand well clear of Bristow and glanced at Escott. "What is this, bank night?"

"You didn't exactly plan it this way," he admitted.

And I couldn't deal with more than one at a time. I'd have to cut down the opposition odds.

Then Bristow, fast for his bulk, boosted from the couch and slammed one meaty arm into Escott like a club. Softened by his earlier pummeling, Escott grunted and staggered, tripping over one of the goons. He failed at catching his balance but kept a grip on his Webley when he fell.

Marie screamed and ducked; Brockhurst grabbed her out of the way, pushing her down, throwing himself on top, which was sensible. Hog Bristow had a gun in his other hand and used it.

The first shot was for me. I dove to one side, slamming smack into my chair. I heard him fire again as I pitched head-first toward the floor. The flash of agony ripped through my chest for an awful instant until my body ceased to be solid.

Though quick enough to avoid a tangling crash, I'd still caught a bullet.

Bristow rumbled something indistinct, and Marie screamed again, a good, long, piercing one. I got moving.

"Shaddup!" Bristow ordered.

"Boss, let's go," said one of his boys urgently.

Marie shrieked.

I materialized behind Bristow, grabbing his gun hand, twisting it down, not being careful about my strength. He cursed in pain and plugged a hole in the floor before I wrenched the weapon away from him. I hoped to God the bullet didn't crash through to the lobby below.

We danced around. I glimpsed Escott huddled to one side. Couldn't tell how badly he'd been damaged. Enough not to participate. Someone hauled sharp at my arm, and Bristow broke free and turned.

"Get him!" he bellowed.

Two of Bristow's men had recovered their feet and their guns. They leveled the latter at me.

Oh, shit.

The lights winked out. Now we were all invisible. At least until my eyes adjusted. I stopped being there. Fast.

Gunshots. Cluster of them. Impossible to tell how many. Surging toward the shooters, I tried to get behind them, but they were on the move.

"C'mon, boss!" one of them yelled.

"You kill that punk?"

"Out, boss! *Now!*"

They audibly bolted. I went solid again, kneeling by Escott. It was dim, but I could distinguish outlines and movement. "You hit?"

"No," he gasped. "Ribs." Bristow must have had an arm like a baseball bat.

"He's dead," said Marie Kennard, in a thin, funny voice. For a second I thought she'd misjudged Escott's condition until realizing she meant Brockhurst. She tried crawling out from under him. He wasn't moving.

I hurried over and pulled him off her. His head lolled as I checked for bullet holes. No bloodsmell, though. Marie scooted back against the wall, tucking her legs up close, a hand to her mouth.

"You killed him," she whispered.

But I heard a strong heartbeat. "Easy, sister. He's just fainted."

"Wh-what?"

"Fainted," I said more loudly. "Charles . . ."

He'd begun to sit up. "I'll watch these two. Go after the—"

I whipped out the door. In the lobby another woman cut loose with a scream. Bristow shouted. They should have left by now. Must have been hampered by the mug I'd punched.

Quick down the stairs, but I missed the gang's exit out the front and probably just as well; they'd have fired at me again. Disaster in this crowd, in this dark. Myrna had done her specialty number over the whole joint, God bless her.

Wilton had a flashlight and shone it around; people drifted toward him like moths. Focused on it, they missed my ghost-like passage tearing through the door.

Cold wind thrashed at me as I re-formed under the entry canopy.

Bristow and his mob pelted toward a big car parked across the street, nearly getting run down by a panel truck. He waved his gun at the heedless driver, who blared his horn, brakes squealing. Two of the bodyguards half-carried their boss and their faltering companion clear just in time.

I started forward, then had to pause or get hit myself. By the time I made it halfway across, the truck was gone and they'd loaded into the car. Bristow had the wheel.

He'd just got the engine started as I grabbed the door handle. He looked up, jaw falling as he recognized me, rage and disbelief in a dead heat on his face. I yanked the door open. Too hard. The hinges cracked and the thing came away in my hand.

Bristow glared at the impossibility. "Son of a bitch!"

Shot.

Goddammit—the thug next to him caught me in the same damned spot. I staggered away, dropping the door. The world faded. Another shot, but I was gone. The car motor roared, gears protested. I sluggishly moved toward the noise, trying to find the gaping opening where the door had been, but slammed against the metal side of the car instead. It was moving, tires screaming against the road.

Solid. Just long enough to get a bead.

Not solid. Hurtling after them, speeding low and fast, fighting the tumbling wind in the wake of their passage. I thought I felt the heat belching from the exhaust pipe; I was certain I felt the back bumper jouncing just ahead and streamed forward, reaching for it, searching out the trunk.

Something carried it abruptly away from my sense. He must have cut a turn. Sharp screech, skidding. I guessed a hard right, tried to follow, but trying to fix on anything, especially a fast-moving anything was damn near impossible. The hulking car was elsewhere. I'd have to go semitransparent.

And it cost time. Too much. When I materialized enough to see them, they were too far distant for me to catch up.

Fully re-forming, I tried to get a plate number. Couldn't.

They wouldn't be too hard to trace. There weren't a whole hell of a lot of cars running around Chicago with the driver's door gone.

They shrank in the distance and turned again. Out of sight. They'd be back for more, though, after a little regrouping.

I walked back to Crymsyn, overcoat collar turned up against the wind, pissed and wanting to punch things. Most of it wore off by the time I'd covered the blocks back. It surprised me how far we'd gone in what seemed such a brief time.

Very tiring it was, too. I was healed but drained. Passing under a streetlight, I found the only visible damage was to my clothes. Holes there, some bloodstains. Alarming to the uninitiated. Anger-making for me. I'd paid hard-earned bucks for this overcoat. Maybe a reweaving job . . . if only that was my biggest problem.

Damnation to Bristow. I'd have to find him quick. There was no doubt in my mind he would try to make good on his buckwheats promise. He might arrange the same for Escott just for the hell of it. I'd have to go back to the Nightcrawler and think up a brilliant song and dance for Kroun, start things over again, and try clearing this mess before it got worse.

Someone had apparently noticed the discarded car door lying in the street and thoughtfully moved it. Now it was propped against a shop building, left in plain view should the rest of the vehicle's owner return to claim it.

But I couldn't expect Bristow to oblige.

Lady Crymsyn's lights were back on again. Heartening sight: business almost as usual, no cops or sirens. Maybe the customers startled by Bristow's exit had chosen to leave rather than make a scene. I'd ask Wilton later. Not wanting to deal with comment from the staff, I ghosted in and didn't go solid until making the upstairs landing.

I pushed the office door open. Escott had kept the party going. Brockhurst, recovered from his ignominious faint, was huddled on the couch with Marie. He tried to stand up and face me, but she dragged at him.

"No, Anthony! Please!" she pleaded.

He was white around the gills, so he let himself be persuaded. Good. I was tempted to sock him one. He didn't deserve it, but he was handy, and life ain't fair.

Escott was just to my left, standing—sitting, rather, since he'd pulled my desk chair over—guard. He had his big Webley ready, which was enough gun to scare anyone sensible. It worked great on our guests, though he didn't have it aimed directly at either of them. Neither seemed to notice.

"Hallo," he said, giving me a once-over. He raised an eyebrow. "Been to the wars, have you?"

"Just the one and not for long."

"Long enough. You are in a state."

The holes and bloodstains looked worse in full light. The big one with the singe marks was right in front. A second hole with less blood was inches from it and slightly lower. Bristow and his pals had done some damn fine shooting. Lucky me.

Our guests goggled at the destruction.

"Are you all right?" Brockhurst ventured.

"Just peachy."

"That blood . . . you're hurt?"

"Yeah, in fact, they killed me. At least twice."

He put on an affronted face. Marie seemed ready to slug me. Good. They were busy being mad, which was better than thinking about the craziness in front of them. I peeled out of the damaged overcoat and left it on the desk, not without some regret. Maybe the laundry had delivered more fresh shirts earlier today, and—

"What happened?" asked Escott.

I gave a longing look at the open liquor cabinet and wished I could still have a shot of booze. From the glasses that had been used, all three of them had indulged.

"Jack?"

"Yeah. Bristow got away. I ain't betting money he won't come back. He'll be loaded for bear. Elephant, maybe. A whole damn herd."

"Perhaps we should remove from this place."

"You for certain. Disappear yourself to a hotel for tonight."

"At the first opportunity."

"Or better, go over to Vivian's."

He considered that one for a whole two seconds. "Normally I would not impose, but in this case I'm sure she won't mind."

"What is going on?" Marie demanded, her voice cracking. "Who were those men? Let us go!"

"When I'm ready," I said. I went to the cabinet, poured doubles into three fresh glasses and shared them around. Since I couldn't have a drink, I'd get my comfort vicariously. No one protested or turned down the offered hospitality, especially Brockhurst, who downed his in one practiced gulp.

Escott had a pointed look for me, and I understood him. If hypnosis became necessary later, I was shooting myself in the foot giving these two booze now.

"You okay?" I asked him.

"I should like a gallon of liniment, a few aspirin, and some sleep."

"How much damage did they do?"

"No broken ribs, though the one I cracked before is protesting the maltreatment. Much of the rest of my person has been thoroughly tenderized."

I wanted to ask if he could have talked his way out of being hurt altogether but figured Bristow would have had his boys roughhousing him just for the hell of it. They'd get their payback, but I should have anticipated something like this. All my smart-ass talk to Kroun was supposed to make *me* Bristow's new target, not anyone else.

Escott must have read my face. "Really, Jack, this was not your fault. Had I too quickly given in and told them what I wanted them to know, they'd never have believed it. As I'm sure you've noticed, Bristow has all the intelligence of a box of bricks. I discerned that he draws conclusions from a person's emotional reactions, not from what is actually said. That's how he understood we were insulting him without his having the least idea what the insult was about. Abstractions make less sense to him than hieroglyphs do to us. We see the pictures and know they mean something. He sees only a wall."

"Where'd all that come from?" This was new stuff from him.

He sketched a brief smile. "Vivian and I had a fascinating conversation about the workings and processes of human thought. Perception is a very subjective experience. She's interested in understanding how her daughter's mind works, the better to help the girl—"

"Oh, *God*," said Marie Kennard. She seemed less angry and frightened now, shifting toward impatience.

"It's all right," said Anthony, misinterpreting. "I won't let them hurt you." He took her hand.

"No wonder Gilbert got on so well with him, they talk exactly alike."

Escott looked insulted. "Young lady, *I* am not a compulsive liar."

"Let's not get into that," I said. "Brockhurst, did you bring the letters?"

His expression wavered an instant, a dredged-up reaction from the instructions I'd given him last night. "I have them here." He patted his inside pocket.

"Hand them over."

He did so. I put them on my perforated coat. They made quite a stack. Like the others I collected from Dugan, these were addressed to people of such influence and position as to make life miserable for my friends.

"That's all of them? You're sure?" I dipped back toward head pain again, to be certain he told the truth, and it got a little way past his drink.

"All of them," he whispered.

"Why are you helping them?" Marie asked him.

He blinked, coming out of it, unaware he'd even been in. "I have to. It will help Gilbert." His voice, but my words from last night.

"How? You said that before. *How* will this help him?"

"I can't explain yet, but I will later."

"It *is* later." She glared at me. "You got what you want, now let us go."

I wasn't holding the gun on them, but couldn't fault her assumption that they were prisoners. "Was it your idea to come up here with him?" I hadn't allowed for the possibility that any of his friends would tag along.

"Yes. I want to know why he's doing this, giving these to you. We can always write more."

"I know, but you won't. Where are the others in your band of merry makers? They downstairs?"

She didn't answer.

"Brockhurst?"

"They're not here," he said. Truthfully.

"That's good. We've got enough guests at this party."

"Let us go," she repeated.

"In a minute. I want to talk to you about your friend Gilbert and that ten grand he says we want." I jerked my head Escott's way to include him.

"What about it?"

"Deal's off. We don't want your money. In fact, we never wanted it. That was all Gilbert's idea. He was trying to shake you."

"I beg your pardon?"

"Last night? In the car? Anthony drove you away from the club. During the ride, Gilbert told you all about how he bought us off the kidnapping case with the threat of these letters and a bribe to sweeten things. He said Escott was the brains, and I was the crazy-mad muscle that roughed him up some."

She stared. "How do you know that? Anthony, did you tell him?"

"Yeah-yeah, he told me all about it. Well, sister, you need to hear the truth about poor, abused, misunderstood Gilbert."

"I don't know what you're—"

"Charles, are those records still in the safe?"

He nodded. "Miss Smythe wasn't up to dealing with the copying business today. However, I did transcribe the rest of it this afternoon. Only in shorthand, though."

"That's fine. Keep these birds here a second." I went to the next room, bringing back the phonograph, setting it on the desk, and plugging it in. Then I unlocked the false drawer front, spun the combination, and took out the flat box inside.

The top record had no label last night, but now sported a title, *H. G. Dugan—Part One*, and date, neatly printed on a small square of paper that was cellophane-taped near the center of the disk.

I tilted the record so Marie and Anthony could read it.

"What's that?" she asked, suspicious.

Escott answered. "When your friend Gilbert made his visitation here, presumably to come to an advantageous arrangement with us concerning the kidnapping, he was unaware we were recording him. I think you'll find his candor with Mr. Fleming to be remarkably enlightening."

"Lemme set the scene," I said, fitting the record onto the spindle. "When I came into this office yesterday for our meeting—that's me and Gilbert, not Escott and Gilbert like you were told—I found your smiling sweetheart trying to pick the lock on my desk. He's a bad kid. Too much time on his hands."

"Impossible," she said.

"Possible, and true. He had a set of professional lockpicks he must have gotten from those three criminal types he had helping him with the kidna—"

"They intimidated him into working for them! If he'd not done as he was told, they would have killed him."

"Honey, did you ever once ask yourself *why* a gang of toughs like that would think an upper-crust, high-hatting, fancy-pants double-talker like Dugan could *ever* be a help to them on a kidnap job?"

"He knew the family, had access to the house—"

"And in the entire two weeks of the kidnapping, and the time before that, did Gilbert show the least sign that he was under pressure or preoccupied by anything threatening?"

"They told him if he said anything, he would die."

"Gosh, and a brainy guy like him couldn't think of a way around that? But let's put it aside for the moment. Back to me coming in here and finding him impersonating Raffles on a bad night. I will admit to a certain amount of annoyance about it and threw him around. Anyone would. I also tried to persuade him to sense, which we need not go into; suffice to say it did not work. After that, things got really interesting, bang, crash, boom, because I was frustrated and Dugan, being the source, made him the logical target for my ire. I will point out to you that Mr. Escott was *not* in the room, and in fact never spoke to or saw Gilbert at all that night. So the stuff you heard in the car from dear Gilbert dealing with and finally bribing my partner here was just so much horse hockey."

She shook her head. "No, you're lying."

"Lady, I don't have to, but Gilbert does, enough for ten politicians. Just listen to what's here, and if there's anything on this that makes me a liar about him, I'll give *you* ten grand."

Record spinning, I put the needle in the groove and let Dugan damn himself.

13

DURING the course of playing both records of Dugan's un-witting confession, I was prepared to throw Marie and An-thony a little hypnotic punch into believing my side of things. Unfortunately, working a whammy that went against a per-son's ingrained inclination was always temporary. Without regular reinforcement, the persuasion I wanted would never stay in their minds until they realized the truth of it for them-selves.

Despite the distraction of Escott's Webley, Dugan's little helpers listened close and careful to everything. From their shared expressions of horror, they apparently understood what it meant.

Marie found a handkerchief in her purse and made use of it. Anthony seemed in about the same shape but being a man couldn't give in to tears. He looked grim and sad and restless. A couple times he asked me to stop the play, but I wasn't feeling softhearted tonight. Their friend was a bastard, and I wanted them to know that for a solid fact. But betrayal is a terrible thing to deal with, and when it was over, they tried to shove its reality away.

"You made it up," said Marie decisively. She straightened, showing a brave if sullen face to me.

I'd expected resistance. "I'm not smart enough or crazy enough to make up that kind of crap. You think he was reading from a script? Maybe you think he was blowing gas at me for some secret purpose. If so, then why did he tell you that Escott was the only guy he spoke to, or was that all part of some master plan Dugan couldn't reveal to his best friends?"

"Then that wasn't Gilbert."

"Wise up, lady. Who else talks like that? Well, maybe Escott, but they have totally different voices."

"You threatened him in some way," said Anthony.

"Does he sound like I was holding a gun on him? No one's that good an actor. What you heard was the real Gilbert, the side he makes sure you never see. That was him in charge, threatening me, telling me how things were going to go, threatening my friends with six kinds of grief unless *I* jumped through *his* hoops."

"He has to save himself. Those criminals put him into this position. Gilbert knows no one will believe him. He has to do whatever he can to preserve his freedom."

"You think blackmail's a nice, stand-up road to take? What would your mother say?"

He flinched. It had been a pretty low blow. I'd calculated it just right.

"How do you explain away that ten grand he says Escott insisted on for a bribe?"

"You just didn't record that part."

"Shall I play it again? From beginning to end? The whole thing is right there, starting with me coming in the door to Gilbert ordering me to stand in front of the window. This *is* the truth. Your friend is a liar, blackmailer, kidnapper, and would have murdered that helpless young girl with less thought than you put into picking out a tie. And . . . did you happen to read the papers today?" I pulled out the story about the dead couple found at the farm hideout. "The Indiana DA will start pressing for a murder charge on this. Unlike Dugan, he takes the killing of innocent people very seriously."

They looked at it; so did Escott, who shook his head, somber. I folded the clipping and pocketed it.

"Gilbert didn't do that," Marie whispered. "It was those other men. They just didn't tell him."

"What, and miss a chance to terrify him that much more into helping? It don't wash, toots. He was out there helping demolish the rest of the outhouse so they could dump Sarah Gladwell's body into it."

"How do you know?"

"You don't have to repeat this, 'cause I'll deny it, but I was the mysterious Good Samaritan who clobbered them all and brought them in for the cops."

She shook her head. "But you—if that's true, if you want Gilbert in jail so badly, why don't you come forward?"

"Health reasons. I also thought Dugan and his crew would have enough weight to hang themselves without any help from me. Too bad I was wrong, but circumstances seem to be catching up with him after all. He seems to have pulled a hole in after himself, too. Has he talked to either of you today? You'd think he'd call and get the bribe money business finished. Don't look good for him, does it?"

They had no answer for that.

"Dugan's doing everything his twisted brain can think of to get out of paying for what he's done *and* still turn a profit. You're damn good friends to be willing to give him ten grand; he doesn't deserve you. But he's very deliberately and cheerfully *using* you. Since he couldn't haul in twenty-five Gs from Vivian Gladwell, he'll settle for ten conned from his girlfriend. My guess is as soon as the cash is in hand, he's off to Brazil."

Marie shook her head "N-no, he—"

"Lemme ask you this: When's the last time you were ever in his house?"

Anthony blinked and didn't reply.

"Think he's a little embarrassed having people over? The place looks on the haunted side these days."

"He just likes to meet his friends elsewhere. Four walls closing in and all that," he offered.

"More like they're falling down around his ears. Appearances are important to him. He doesn't want you to see just how desperate he is. You know about his paper animal collection?"

"What?" The subject switch confused him.

I opened a desk drawer and pulled out some slightly crumpled origami animals. And boats. Last night I'd taken away a few samples, just in case they'd be needed. "Look familiar? He does this a lot. 'To fill the time,' he says. Sound familiar? Would you know his handwriting? You aware of his preference for writing in green ink?"

They stared at the pieces.

"Unfold one of those boats. I've not read what's on there, but I can guess it's pretty revolting. Read it, see the kind of crap's flowing through Dugan's mind. See the stuff he doesn't tell you because he knows damn well how you'd react. Go on."

They didn't move, so I picked up two random pieces and put them into their hands. Very reluctantly, Marie unfolded a boat. Anthony held his loose in his palm and read over Marie's arm. They didn't get far down the page.

"This doesn't mean anything," Anthony said. "A man has a right to an opinion. This is a free country."

"You got me there. But what's your opinion of a person who thinks people should be matched up to breed like a strain of cattle stock? Who thinks less-than-perfect children should be killed? Certainly Sarah Gladwell falls into that category. He said himself he carefully chose her. Come on, you two. Don't be so damned thick-headed. Dugan put one over on you and too bad, but—"

"No!" Marie tore the paper up. "He's just doing this to mislead people. Or it's forged—"

I caught her eye, freezing her in place. "Believe it," I said softly. "He used you. Used both of you. It's okay to be mad at him." I let her go, and she started sniffling.

"You're horrible. I hate you."

She was and wasn't talking to me. The turntable still spun; I put the needle arm over the record and dropped it in a spot I'd memorized.

". . . sentiment for that creature is misplaced. I chose her quite carefully, you know. I would never remove a contributing member of society, but she was nothing, on the contrary . . ."

I lifted the needle, reached into the safe, and pulled out a delicate crane, tossing it to Anthony. "Read that. You can see I didn't open it; they don't fold back quite the same. This is what he wanted me to get the other kidnappers to say to get him off the hook. You heard him tell me what he wanted done. His own writing."

He shook his head. "Never mind. I believe you."

About damned time.

"Who was that woman?"

"What woman?"

"The one in the room with you. The one on the record."

I risked having Myrna mess with the lights. "That was just background noise from downstairs. Dugan and I were alone. That's why he was able to gab so freely."

"But what is this 'secret' of yours he talked about? It's not you hypnotizing people. What did he mean about you invisibly following him? And that Stockyards business——?"

Headache time. "Don't worry about that. Forget that part. What's important is he really did kidnap Sarah, and he tried to extort money from her mother and from you two. He's a liar and all the other garbage. Are you both straight on it? Dugan's a bad guy."

"Oh, shut up," said Marie, kneading her handkerchief as though searching for a dry spot to use.

"Where is he?" Anthony asked.

I shrugged. "I haven't heard from him since last night." That was absolutely true. "My guess is he got wise and decided to lam it."

"But he was so confident——"

"Based on lies. Maybe he realized it wouldn't work or worried that I might not toe the line for him after all. He's got a big brain; maybe he thought himself into a corner and knew he'd have to run. Why don't you go visit his house? See if he left a clue."

"You've been there, haven't you? That's how you got these things from him. What have you done with him?"

"Nothing. I don't have to. He's done it all himself. If you hear from him, have him call me. He likes to listen to himself talk so much he'd probably love this." I nodded toward the spinning record.

Marie surged up, darting for the phonograph, murder in her eye.

Escott got there first. She slammed into him, but he held in place, arms up to deflect her fists. He dropped his gun on my coat, then grabbed her wrists. He spun her around quick as a jitterbug dancer, crossing her arms in front of her like a straitjacket, which mostly immobilized her. She struggled to get free, twisting and bucking. He tried not to wince.

Anthony was shocked for a moment, then stepped in and pulled her away. "Marie, please don't!"

She subsided into sobbing, falling against him. "You're horrid, all of you!"

"Not us. Gilbert," he said.

"You liar!"

"I'm sorry, my dear, really I am."

Escott got his gun and sank back on his chair with a stifled sigh. Marie went unintelligible for some while, her posing and apparent boredom completely gone. Her reaction told how deeply Dugan had gotten under her skin. He must have executed one hell of a charming performance for her, saying and doing all the right things, being the perfect gallant. The other night Anthony had been urging Dugan to overcome his reluctance and propose to her. How much of that had been inspired by Dugan's manipulations so he could laugh up his sleeve at them both? I could imagine him entertaining himself by setting all his friends up, then having them eagerly running around in response to every little thing he said. What a way to fill the time.

"Okay, Brockhurst," I said, "you think you can convince the rest of your pals that Dugan's guilty after all? I don't want any more letters being written."

"I don't know . . . possibly."

"Would hearing these recordings do the trick?"

He nodded, not meeting my eye.

"Fine. Maybe by tomorrow we'll have some copies for you to pass around. Phone here around six, and I'll let you know. You two scram."

He looked, startled. "Just like that?"

"Yeah. In case you missed it, I'm busy with another mess right now." I plucked at my bloodied shirt. "This has nothing to do with you, and I suggest you forget all about it."

Anthony hurriedly guided Marie toward the door, yanking it open and hauling them through before I could change my mind.

"You sure that's wise to let them run loose?" Escott asked. "There were things on the records that might raise questions."

"I'll deal with them then. My guess is those two won't be back if they can help it."

"One may hope. Now . . . what about Bristow?"

"He promised to buckwheats me, and it's a sure thing he'll invite you to the party just for laughs, but I don't particularly want to go."

"Indeed. I had quite enough of his hospitality." He went to the couch, sinking stiffly onto it. "I've an image in my mind of having an extremely hot bath and doing nothing at all for at least twenty-four hours, but rather think it will have to be postponed."

"Only until we get you to Vivian's."

"I shall phone her shortly so she may have some warning. How much about this Bristow business should I tell her?"

That was a change. The only cases he ever talked about with clients were their own. This wasn't exactly a case, though. On the other hand, maybe he thought Vivian should know what she was getting into if she granted him shelter for an indefinite period. "Use your best judgment," I said. I stabbed two fingers through the shirt holes. My jacket would have holes out the back as well. Another reweaving job. Or a new suit. "I wonder which of Hog's boys did the actual shooting last night."

"Does it matter?"

"It will to New York. Bristow was drunk enough then to step out of line, but maybe too far gone to be the triggerman. I can attest to some personal experience that he and one other of them is a good shot, though. They'll want the man who actually did it. I'm hoping it was Bristow. If Gordy's men find him first, he could maybe choose not to come quiet and end up dead. That would solve a lot of problems."

"Gordy's men?"

I gave him the short version of life at the Nightcrawler and how I'd dealt with Kroun. "He's probably already phoned Kroun to tell him what kind of a rat I turned out to be. All I needed was five minutes with Bristow to get the fuse out of the powder keg. That's in the toilet now."

"Then arrangements must be made to allow you to make a second attempt."

"How?"

"I haven't the faintest idea. If Gordy's men locate him, you can sneak up on him and bash him about the head and shoulders for a few hours. I'll be happy to hold your coat for the duration."

"Or I can try to set up another meeting through Gordy's people. I'll see what Derner can do. Bristow may think I'm dead, you know. His boy got me point-blank. With me out of the way, he may figure he can waltz in . . . except he doesn't know how bad off Gordy is. I let drop with Kroun that he was okay, just keeping low, but they won't buy that for long."

"Do you really think one of Gordy's people might have shot him?"

"It's a possibility I can't leave out. This is a tough business, and if any of them decides Bristow can move them up in it . . ."

"And you suspect—?"

"All of them. Maybe not Strome or Lowrey, not directly, but either of them could have gotten someone else to do the actual shooting. Then there's Derner. He's been second fiddle at the Nightcrawler for a long time. He might want more. Then there's all the other guys." The ones I'd dealt with earlier and sent out to find Bristow. "I don't want it to be any of them, though."

"Indeed?"

"I like things simple. Bristow being the shooter is best. If I end up having to question every guy in Gordy's organization, I'll have a headache the size of Lake Michigan."

"You'd do it, though."

I sighed. "Yeah. I would." I reached for my phone and dialed Dr. Clarson's number.

Bobbi answered.

"It's me," I said. "How's Gordy doing?"

Her voice was very subdued. "Still the same. He should be better, Jack. After all this time? He should. But he's not."

"He'll get better." But she was right. I'd seen guys shot in the war who either rallied early or gradually faded away after a long plateau of nothing happening, good or bad. "You know

Gordy, he thinks things over without saying anything, then suddenly goes to work."

"Yeah, I guess so."

An old war memory dredged up for me: being in one of the hospitals, seeing some of the wounded guys from my company. Remembering the ones who made it and why. "Do me a favor and talk to him."

"Talk to him? But he's supposed to rest."

"He's been resting. Maybe too much. You and Adelle talk to him, tell him what's going on, act like he's part of the conversation. Tell him about the weather, tell him stories, play the radio for him. He might be awake under his eyelids and just can't talk back yet." I knew what that was like.

"Okay. We'll do it."

"And you can tell him I'm taking care of things with Bristow."

"Oh, Jack, you got him?"

I hated disappointing her. "Well, not yet. We had a setback, but I'll be fixing things, then sending him back to New York."

"Even after he shot Gordy?"

"His mistake. They won't like him so much after I'm done."

"But will they not like him enough to keep him there?"

"I'm hoping they'll keep him there permanently." *Like under a highway or as part of a bridge.* "Pass this on to Shoe if you see him, and tell him I said to go on with keeping Gordy under wraps. He's safer there than anywhere else."

"Thank God for that."

"But I don't want to take any chances. If Strome or anyone else from the organization shows up that isn't me, don't let them in."

"Why?"

"Loose ends."

"What's going on?"

"Is Isham there?"

"Yeah. Him and another couple guys. I'll let them know, but you're scaring me."

"Don't be. I'm just being extra careful. Bristow might have had help I don't know about."

"Like Strome?"

"Yeah, but it's long odds. I'm only saying keep the doors locked for now. Old maid stuff, y'know?"

"You're sure?"

"Yeah, honey. I've got some more stuff to do tonight. Can you get a ride home in case it runs late?"

"Yes, but I think I'll be staying. Adelle's getting some sleep. Poor thing's worn down to the bone. Can't blame her."

"I'll call to check in. If I'm not in the office, do you know the number for the lobby phone? I'll have Wilton keep his ears open if it rings. And you can reach Charles at . . ."

She wrote down the numbers I dictated. "Where will you be?"

"Got some other business to clean up. Tell you later."

"Is it about Dugan?"

"Yeah. We just convinced his friends he's guilty, so that's finally over. I had them listen to the records. It wasn't fun, but they came around."

"They're all right?"

"Not happy, but breathing regular. I sent them home, too. Tell you later."

"Darn tootin' you will."

We said bye and hung up. I told Escott about Gordy's unchanged condition.

"Talking to him might help at that," he said thoughtfully.

"It can't hurt. C'mon, let's get you some aspirin. I think Wilton keeps a bottle under the cash register." I took the record off the player and slipped it in its sleeve and then the flat box with its brother, but not into the safe. That I clanked shut and locked.

"What are you doing with those?"

I grinned. "Does Vivian Gladwell have a phonograph?"

We didn't leave right away; I had to change clothes. There'd been a laundry delivery that afternoon, and along with fresh towels for the washrooms and bars, I had a clean suit and a half-dozen shirts stacked in one of the dressing rooms. After staring at the near-pristine suit for ten seconds, I decided not to risk it and hung it in the closet. That thing had cost nearly a hundred bucks—over a month's pay for my last regular job as a reporter. Though I was making much more than that in profits now, I hated wasting money.

Maybe I could hit Bristow up for compensation. Literally. A few socks to his wide kisser wouldn't improve his looks, but I'd feel better. While he lay all groggy on the floor, I could see what the inside of his wallet looked like.

Fresh shirt buttoned, tucked in, tie in place, and coat on my back—the holes weren't *too* visible—I was ready to make a quick check of how the evening had progressed without my supervision. I emerged from the backstage area, nodded to the bartenders, and surveyed the crowd. They seemed cheerful, tapping in time to the music, talking, smoking, drinking, and watching the show. Not bad, especially since I'd missed doing my usual light "enjoy yourself" whammy on them at the door.

Thankfully, the early debut of Roland and Faustine had

gone without a hitch, according to the waiters. The dance duet had gotten in sufficient rehearsal to be a real audience-pleaser. They had enough professionalism—or desperation for a paycheck—to put aside their big fight and focus on the job. I'd heard of couples like that who could brawl better than cats and dogs before and after a show but still deliver a flawless performance in between.

Escott and I walked in as the band struck up a tango. It was kind of old stuff, having had its heyday with Valentino, but the arrangement shifted back and forth between tango and swing rhythms, a contest to see which was better and both winning. One minute Roland and Faustine were smoldering eye to eye, the next they were up and spinning into a modified jitterbug. She wore a glittery silver gown with the hem high enough from the floor so as not to tangle her feet, and the shimmering skirt swirled dramatically with every turn. She had on heels but still managed to put in some ballet-style twirls. There was no toe dancing, but you could see the classical influence in her form. Roland moved gracefully, both supporting and showcasing her.

"Damn," I muttered to Escott, who had parked at the bar. "They're good."

"Excellent sense of timing," he agreed.

Escott had washed his aspirin down with a ginger ale instead of gin and tonic. He probably wanted to be sharp later on.

"I gotta play boss for a few minutes," I said, gauging the music. The number was about to wind itself up.

"Please proceed. It will give time for my medication to work."

The exhibition dance ended; Roland and Faustine made bows and collected a huge round of applause, which boosted my satisfaction. With this initial reception to judge by, they'd go over very well tomorrow night.

It was time for the patrons to join them on the floor. I had the jump on other guys since I'd known it was coming and reached Faustine first.

"How 'bout a quick turn?" I asked.

She granted me a pleased smile. "But ov course. You enjoyed our daunce, yesss?"

"Very much." The band did a slow waltz. I was no Roland Lambert but could keep up with this beat without disgrace. Faustine was a delight in my arms, like dancing with air. "I wanted to thank you for coming in ahead of time."

"Eet vas our pleasure. Tomorrow vill even better be."

"Are you two working things out? I know it's not my business, but I like my performers to be happy."

She stiffened only a little. "Yesss. Ve talk. He prostrate himself, as he should. I may forgive, but eez difficult."

"You can always talk to Bobbi if you need to, you know."

"Yesss, she is lovely-sweet to be zo nice in my troublings. I like not to impose, but in this only another woman understands. She is vhere tonight?"

"Looking after a friend who took sick."

"Nothing to be caught, I hope?" She looked alarmed. Bobbi was the same way about colds.

"No, stomach problems."

"Hopeful I am there is quick recovery, then."

"Thanks."

Across the floor, Roland squired an older woman around. She was elegantly dressed, well into the dowager years. He guided her majestically over the floor, and she seemed to glow from his twinkling attention. Faustine noticed, and her chin went up, eyes glinting. "He is being good boy tonight, yesss.

But I expect he must daunce wit' the pretty ones, too."

"I think he'll behave for awhile, even with them."

She made a small *humph* sound. "Some men should not marry. Perhaps eet vas a mistake for me, but he is zo handsome, such the charm, and I do love. I know he loves me, but sometimes he forgets. We shall see."

I could *make* the situation better for them, but so long as she wasn't throwing drinks in public, things were under control. It was better for them to work their marriage stuff out on their own.

An eager-looking business type cut in on me the moment the waltz shifted to a rumba. Faustine would have her hands full with him, but he'd behave. The waiters had been told to keep watch in case any guys got fresh with her. She had a high sign to give should things get awkward. This was a class place, not one of those dime-a-dance warehouses. Though not happy about dealing with mobsters, my staff could handle the regular sort of customer.

I went back to Escott. "How about a drive over to the Gladwell house?"

"I already telephoned and told Vivian we were on the way," he said, face carefully neutral.

And I thought that business type was a fast worker.

Escott got in his car, and I got in mine, and we didn't look over our shoulders more than a dozen times after leaving the club. My job was to trail him and watch the rearview mirror to make sure it stayed clear. We figured if anyone—meaning Bristow—followed us, they would be more interested in my car.

Escott had a talent for throwing a shadow and lost me in

ten minutes, and I knew where he was headed. He wound that big Nash around corners like it was a bicycle. I barely kept even with him, lost sight of him twice, then gave up and let him bull ahead. If Escott shook me, then he was safe. I was less safe but better able to handle trouble.

To make sure I was fully restored for whatever lay ahead, I took the long way around to get to the Stockyards, parking in a different spot from last night. Made wary by Dugan, I vanished while still in the car and ghosted across the street, not going solid again until far inside the cover of the cattle pens. Even then I had a good, careful look around to make sure I was alone and unobserved.

I hoped to settle things soon with Dugan, else I might always feel like someone was watching as I fed. Not exactly good for the digestion.

Business finished, I returned the same way and sped out, not stopping until I found an all-night drugstore. Its bright lights made me wince, but no matter, so long as the phone worked. I wedged into the narrow booth, unfolded the door into place for privacy, and dialed the Nightcrawler Club.

"Derner." He'd picked up before the first ring had finished.

"This is Fleming—"

"What the hell have you been doing?" he demanded.

I suppose he had a right to be worried. Not for me, but his own hide. If I didn't hold things together for Gordy, we were all up shit creek. "What have you been told I've been doing?"

"Kroun's heard from Bristow. They ain't happy. Said you tried to kill him."

"*He* was the one trying to plug me. Twice. He must have left that part out."

"You got hit?"

"He missed me, so I might forgive him. Where is he?"

"Kroun didn't say. On the move, probably."

"Think he'll come by the club?"

"There's a laugh."

"Can you get him there? Tonight?"

"I don't see how."

"Call Kroun. Tell him Gordy didn't make it and Bristow is free to take over. Tell him you don't care who runs things, that you can be a big help getting the other guys to cooperate. Tell them you can get *me* to the club so Bristow can—"

Derner audibly sputtered. "You're crazy! I can't feed them that crap! You know what they'd do to me?"

"I'll make it square for you later. The important thing is to put Bristow in a place where I can talk with him, and it's got to be tonight."

"You gonna kill him?"

"Of course not. I'm gonna be smarter than him, which ain't too hard. You just make sure you sell Kroun on the news."

"What about Gordy?"

"What about him?"

"They said he was dead. Is he?"

"You got told wrong. I saw him tonight, and he's still breathing. So long as he keeps breathing, you and everyone else stays copasetic."

"But—"

"Can it. Who do you want running things? Gordy or Bristow?"

"Gordy."

"Same here, so gimmie a hand on this."

He mumbled a reply. He'd cooperate.

"Great. Just get Bristow to the club and keep him happy. Cooperate with him, make him believe you. I'll check in later.

See to it you're the one answering the phone. Now . . . where's Lowrey?"

"He went home."

"What, not out on the big hunt for Bristow?"

"Not with *his* missus." By his tone Derner gave me to think Mrs. Lowrey had more in common with Marie Dressler than Greta Garbo. A hen-pecked mobster. What would they think of next?

"Okay, where's he live?"

"What for?"

"I got a job going; you'll hear about it later."

That didn't seem to satisfy him, but he gave me an address. I scrawled it on the back cover of the booth's phone book and tore it away. "There's one more thing . . . call off the hunt for Bristow. Tell the boys thanks and go home. Don't mention Gordy one way or another."

"They're gonna be sore. They'll think you took the reward."

"Give 'em each fifty bucks as a consolation prize."

"B-but that's nearly fifteen hundred! For doing nothing!"

"It's five hundred less than you'd have paid out before, and this way everyone gets something. Gordy will approve."

"You don't know that."

"Do I have to come down there? Just *do* it!"

After fishing a map from my glove box, I looked up Lowrey's street and drove over. He and I had some talking to do.

It was a surprise to learn he was a family man. He had a narrow house in a crowded neighborhood, filled with a wife and several kids to judge by the amount of toys scattered around the small, muddy yard. As it was late and a school night they were all in bed. I found this out by a silent invasion of their home, floating from room to room, ghostlike, which roused a couple of dogs. They gave sharp barks of alarm upon sensing me and rushed around sniffing like crazy and whining. This woke Mrs. Lowrey but not the mister. She grumbled at him for not getting up to look for burglars, going to see for herself.

I materialized at their front door and knocked. The dogs barked frantically. She told them to shut up, and I heard her slow approach.

"Who is it?" she called over the din.

"I'm here from Derner. Gotta see Lowrey." The idea of simply appearing in their bedroom did not appeal to me. I'd have to hypnotize her, which would happen only after I scared her half to death. Terrorizing housewives, even if they were married to gangsters, just wasn't a nice thing to do.

"Who are you?"

"It's business," I hedged. "Club business. Gordy."

That was enough for her to cautiously unlock and crack the door. It was on a chain. If anyone really wanted to break in, a halfway decent kick would do it.

"Yes? I don't know you." She had a fierce eye, peering sideways through the opening. One of the dogs forced his muzzle through and snorted mightily, growling.

"No, ma'am. I'm new. Derner sent me with a message for Lowrey."

Nodding like that was something familiar, she undid the chain. The dogs, a couple of big mongrels, charged up, wanting to see who the hell I was, and after one good sniff retreated, tails tucked.

"He's asleep. I'll get him." She stared at the dogs.

"Just show me where; Derner's waiting. This won't take a minute." I hoped.

A tired-looking woman in a sagging bathrobe, married to a gangland bodyguard, she understood not to ask questions or cause delays. For all she knew, I might have been sent here to kill her husband. It was all part of the job. She pointed, frowning. "Through there."

"Thank you."

I went in, flipping on the overhead light and closing the door. Up the hall I heard a drowsy kid ask his mom what was wrong. She told him to never mind and go back to sleep. Couldn't tell if she was scared or not.

Lowrey was sprawled in bed, down to a yellowed singlet and the start of a beard. I got him awake just enough to put him under again, and primed to answer questions.

"Who shot Gordy?" I asked, still trying to figure out which of his eyes to focus on. Either one seemed to work well enough for my kind of work. "Did you see him? Who?"

"Donno. Dark. Hadda be Bristow."

He was the logical suspect, but I wanted to cover all the bases. "Who's next in line after Gordy to run things?"

"Bristow," he mumbled.

"If Bristow ain't in the picture, who else?"

"Dunno. Fleming. He could do it."

Me? Holy moley. Who the hell did they think I was? "But Fleming helped save Gordy."

"He coulda got that English gumshoe to do it for him. He pretends to help Gordy, then Gordy croaks, then he—"

"Yeah-yeah, I got the picture. Well, forget it, powder puff, Fleming ain't playing that game."

"Okay," he said obligingly.

"Anyone else want Gordy's job?"

"Derner, maybe. Strome, too."

Now we were getting somewhere. "Think Derner would knock Gordy off to work for Bristow?"

"Dunno. Maybe."

"What about Derner knocking Gordy off to take over for himself?"

"Strome thinks he would." Lowrey shrugged. "Maybe. Ask him."

I planned to and got his address from Lowrey, writing it on the scrap of phone book cover. "Okay, you did fine. Now forget I was ever here and catch up on your sleep." I shut off the light on the way out.

Mrs. Lowrey seemed more awake and showing worry. "Anything wrong?"

"No, ma'am. All finished. Your man can take some time off."

"Husband," she corrected archly. Apparently she worked hard for that gold band on her ring finger. It and she deserved acknowledgment and respect from lowlife mugs like me.

"Yes, ma'am. Husband. Sorry to barge in." I got out fast.

Strome was next. I found the right residence hotel, the right number, and slipped under his door like an unwelcome bill.

He lived in an unprepossessing flat, just three rooms. Gordy's people were well-paid; Strome could afford better. He either spent the bulk of his time in other surroundings or the bulk of his money in the Nightcrawler's casino. I didn't see him as the type to send money home to his dear old ma.

In the combination living and bedroom, the Murphy bed had been pulled down from the wall. The sheets and blankets were messed around but unoccupied. No overcoat lying around. He was out, and I'd specifically told him to go home and sleep to keep him out of trouble.

Someone must have woken him up. Bristow perhaps. Or

Derner. And Strome knew exactly where to find Gordy. Either of them could get the information out of him, willingly or not.

There was a phone in the small kitchen. I used it to call Clarson's again. Bobbi answered again.

"Everything quiet?" I asked.

"Why? What do you know that I should?"

"My old maid stuff might have something to it. I want you should get out of there."

"Jack . . ."

I knew she wouldn't leave. "All right, there's a chance that Bristow might come by."

"Oh, damn. You better talk to Isham, then."

"And you *have* to get yourself and Adelle out of there."

"She won't go any more than I will."

"Persuade her, doll."

"We can't leave Gordy—"

"Listen to me a minute. You think Gordy would want either of you in the way if something happens?"

"But—"

"Isham and Shoe can look after him better if you two are gone. You know that."

She knew but didn't like it. "How serious is this?"

"I don't know. I'm playing the better-safe-than-sorry song. You and Adelle go back to Crymsyn or take Adelle to your place, I don't care, but you get clear. It's tough, but he'd want both of you safe."

"And then what?"

"And then nothing happens, if we're lucky, and you can come back. You promise you'll leave?"

Not happily, but she promised. I asked her to put Isham

on. Apparently he was hovering close, for he took the phone right away.

"Yeah, what's going on?" he wanted to know.

I explained a few things in broad terms. "Is Shoe there?"

"He can be."

"Let him know what I said. Beef up the guards outside. If you see Strome coming back with friends, you may have to nail them all. Keep your eyes peeled for a blue car with a missing driver's door."

"Huh?"

"Just what I said. Any chance of moving Gordy out of there?"

"You'd have to ask Clarson."

"Ask him for me. I'll call back in half an hour. If anything happens before then, you can reach Escott here." I gave him the Gladwell number. "Make sure Bobbi and Adelle get a ride to wherever they want."

He said he would and hung up.

I called Derner, knowing full well he might be working with Bristow. Or for himself.

"What'd Kroun have to say?" I asked.

Derner sounded unhappy. "Not a lot. I told 'em Gordy didn't make it and that Bristow should be told. I don't know that Kroun bought it."

"What's he going to do?"

"He didn't say. I think he'll talk to Bristow, though."

I wanted to be there in person to get the truth out of him. It'd be worth a headache to make sure of Derner's loyalty. "You heard from Strome?"

"No. Why?"

"I got an errand for him, too. If he phones or comes back, get him and keep him there. I'll be in later tonight."

"When?"

"Later. Is the hunt called off yet?"

"Mostly. Some of the guys know, others don't. Word's getting around."

If he'd passed it on. "Keep it moving. I'll call again shortly, and I want good news about Bristow."

I slipped back under Strome's door, heading out. The street seemed empty, but I took a moment longer than usual to check all the stray shadows before pulling into the thin traffic. I shifted gears, both in my head and with the car, and headed toward the Gladwell estate.

Until now, up to and including getting shot at, everything had been a relative cinch. Now I had to deal with Dugan. I liked mob guys better. They had certain rules and ethics I could at least comprehend. You knew where you stood with them and how to handle them. Dugan was the kind of mess you just wanted to scrape off your shoe and walk away.

No walking from this one, though.

14

I STOPPED at the Dugan house on my way over, still checking for tails and cutting unnecessary but reassuring extra turns before getting there.

The neglected pile looked forlorn, like an old lady left behind by careless grandchildren. I wondered if Dugan had some kind of sentimental attachment to the place or if it was pride that made him stick it out here. Of course, he might have had nowhere else to go, hanging on until his kidnapping gamble paid off or the bank foreclosed. I couldn't feel sorry for him, though. He was able-bodied and sharp-minded. Instead of taking a cream-puff job in the family firm, he chose to kidnap and terrorize a harmless girl and her mother for two long weeks, apparently enjoying himself the whole time.

Sieving-in, I looked around, found it mostly unchanged from my last invasion. The cops or his attorney had come by, for the note Escott and I had propped on the phone was gone. No way to tell who'd gotten it, though.

I picked up a few things, shifting others over with a gloved hand to close the gaps so they wouldn't be missed. Twice I heard creakings and froze, listening. After some repetitions, I decided the they were branches scraping against the wooden flanks of the house, a creepy sound when you're alone.

And damn, this place was cold. Even for me.

I got out quick, sought the familiar confines of my car, and didn't stop until reaching the Gladwells' back gate. Escott had left it open. Apparently the flood of reporters had eased since Dugan's disappearance. At this late hour—it was getting on to midnight—no one was likely to come knocking unless they had business, like yours truly. I drove through and parked next to Escott's Nash.

The lights were on in the back of the house, and Escott answered the door to my knock. He and Vivian were having coffee in the kitchen. I'd egg him about domestication later, when we'd all be in a mood for it. I took off my hat to Vivian, asked how she was, got a polite reply and a question of what I was planning to do. She didn't look worried, which I took as a good sign. Removing my overcoat—careful to conceal the bullet holes in the back—I explained a couple things, and she agreed and went off in search of help.

"What's up?" I asked Escott. "Servants' night off?"

"Most of them are asleep. Is that a problem?"

"Not for me. I was just by Dugan's place, and the emptiness gave me the heebies. A brass band and Billy Sunday revival meeting wouldn't cheer that dump up."

"You don't care much for darkness and silence, do you?"

"Who does?"

"Good point, it just seems an oddity, given your condition."

"Damn few nice things ever happen to people—supernatural or otherwise—who wander around by themselves in dark buildings."

"Even better point. Any sign of Bristow and his friends?"

"Not that I saw, and thanks for reminding me. . . ." I went to the kitchen phone and called Clarson's office. This time Shoe Coldfield answered.

"You sure put the corncob up Isham's ass," he said irritably. "What's going on?"

I told him, with more detail, what he should know and my worries about Strome not being home. Escott listened in, nodding approval. "It's a long shot," I said to them both. "Maybe one of his cronies turned up and they went out for a drink, but I don't want to take chances that Bristow got to him."

"That's two of us," said Coldfield.

"Are Bobbi and Adelle out of there?"

"Yeah. They didn't like it, but they're gone."

That was a big relief. "Where?"

"I sent 'em off to a hotel. Couple of the guys who work there also work for me. They can keep an eye open."

"Shoe, I owe you."

"You just get the next singer I date a spot in your club for a week, and we'll call it even."

"Deal. Consider that a handshake. How's Gordy?"

"The same. Doc Clarson brought in a nurse to look after him, what with the other ladies gone."

"Can he be moved?"

"Not unless you want him dead, but I just figured a way around that."

"Oh, yeah?"

He told me what he had in mind.

Grinning, I said, "For that I'll have spots open for the next dozen singers you date."

"I'll hold you to it, kid. What are you going to do about Bristow?"

"I got some stuff set up, hope it'll get settled tonight, tomorrow night for sure. I'll let you know if it works."

"You let me know if it doesn't. Until then you and Charles keep your heads down. I don't want to scrape either of you off any sidewalks."

"No arguments from us on that."

"On what?" Escott asked when I hung up.

"Shoe hates a mess, so we can't let Bristow kill us."

"Or anyone else, one would hope. What news of Gordy?"

"He's the same. Safe so far, but Shoe came up with something genius."

"Indeed?"

"One of his car repair shops has an ambulance in. It's supposed to go back to work tomorrow, but they're gonna put some extra miles on it tonight."

"I thought Gordy couldn't be moved."

"Not him. They're gonna bundle a bunch of laundry together under a blanket, strap it to a stretcher with weights, and take it downstairs to that ambulance. It's going to arrive, siren going, lights flashing, bigger than Broadway. They'll get the stretcher into it, then drive off the same way. Everyone on the street will see. Clarson will put some of Shoe's men into white hospital coats to make it look good, and all the while Gordy's still safe upstairs in bed."

"Heavens, that *is* brilliant. But what if Bristow isn't there to notice?"

"Won't matter, word will get around. My guess is Strome or Derner have already got people on the watch—from a respectful distance. They won't miss that. The ambulance proceeds to shake any tails and take itself far, far away. Shoe's people will seem to withdraw, and they'll douse all the lights at Clarson's place."

"I wish I could be there to see, but it's probably best to let things run their course."

Vivian returned, carrying a squarish box with a suitcase handle and metal latches. "Will this do, Mr. Fleming?"

Escott hurried over and took it off her hands, putting it on the broad kitchen table and opening it up.

I checked. "It's perfect. Let's get started."

Hurley Gilbert Dugan sat up straight on his cot as though this was a fancy parlor, not a dank and chill underground cell. I'd just unlocked the heavy door and stood on the threshold, peering inside. He looked tired and disheveled, his shirt buttons undone and a growth of beard shadowing up his face and jaws, but his dignity—or sense of superiority—was intact. Not a bad front to keep up with no shoes and those manacles clanking on his wrists.

"I expected you to keep me waiting much longer than this," he said.

"Unlike you, I have places to be and things to do. I had a minute, thought I'd get some small-fry errands out of the way."

He smiled indulgently, the way you do with self-important kids. "And what is going on in the wide world? They're not telling me anything."

His caretakers weren't talking to him at all except to give orders like "Take your food," and "Push that onto the shovel." I heard the rule of silence was practiced on Alcatraz to good effect. "It's spinning on as usual. Without any help from you."

"What time is it? Someone took my watch."

"It's after sunset." I thought he might like to confirm what day it was, but he didn't ask. Not that I'd have answered.

"I want my watch back."

"You don't need it."

"I won't turn it into a weapon or a lockpick, if that's what worries you."

"It wasn't, but I'm happy to hear it."

"That watch is a family heirloom. Is it in a safe place?"

"Yeah."

"You won't tell me where? Is it supposed to add to my punishment? I've read that such tortures are inflicted on prisoners to destroy their minds and spirits."

"If not knowing where your watch is makes for torture, wait awhile, you'll learn better."

"What are you doing there?"

"You'll find out."

I'd been uncoiling an electric extension cord; now I brought in the portable phonograph Vivian had brought to the kitchen, setting it just inside the room. Her own machine was part of a large radio model as big around as a refrigerator, not the sort of thing you could easily lug downstairs. This smaller one had been volunteered by her cook to the cause. I put the machine gently on the floor and hooked it up to the cord's plug, then went out again, taking a flat box from Escott. It contained the two records we'd made, and he had carried it away from Crymsyn for safekeeping.

He stood just out of sight, but not earshot, of the cell, Vivian right next to him. We'd all agreed that Dugan might talk more freely to me without any additional audience.

"Are we to hear music?" He was very successful at keeping

his tone neutral, with neither hope or dread attached. He must have been curious as hell, though.

Except for such faint sounds of the household that might filter down to him through the many walls, the utter silence here must have been having its effect. I know I'd go nuts in my sanctuary if stuck there indefinitely. Even with good light, the freedom to move around within, a radio to play, and books to read, in the end it was still a tiny, confining vault.

"Yeah, you're gonna hear some singing."

"I suppose the only people looking for me are the police," he ventured. "That's why you put me here. So they would think I fled."

"You're real smart."

"It won't work. I'll make sure it doesn't work."

"You think a lot of yourself."

"No matter how long you keep me here, I'll find a way to fight the repercussions."

"By sending out more letters? Sure, go ahead. I talked with my friends. They said they could take little heat for me."

"That's a lie."

"You should know. Truth is, once I'm done, you won't be able to get a priest in a confession box to listen to you with a straight face. Write all the letters you want to good old J. Edgar and see what happens. You'll have to write them from jail, though. That's gonna have an effect on their credibility."

"When my lawyer learns what you've done—"

"I'll have a little talk with him pretty soon. If he's still representing you. Lawyers like to get paid, and you're short of funds now and getting shorter. Must have pissed him off in a big way turning up in court with you missing, and after all those stories in the papers about your innocence. The judge read him the riot act."

Eyes narrow, Dugan listened, sucking in every word. He'd know at least one day had passed just from counting how many meals had been brought down and their type. I thought of asking the cook to switch them around, serve him eggs for supper and roast beef for breakfast. They could skip a meal or bring him several close together. Then he'd have only his beard growth to estimate the passage of time. That would confuse him eventually, but I didn't want this going on any longer than necessary.

The last thing I brought in was some paper and a pen, putting those aside. They were his own, taken from his table-turned-desk when I slipped into his empty house. The fountain pen was loaded with his favorite green ink, the paper his stationery.

I also pulled out a few more paper animals and tossed them within reach of his chain tether. One of the boats lay on its side, a fragile shipwreck on the bare concrete.

"All right," he said after staring at them. "You invaded my house, read my private thoughts and within your limited standards judged them, judged me and found me wanting. So?"

"I figured it shouldn't be too hard to find a newspaper editor looking to improve his circulation. This stuff isn't exactly a signed confession but would make for pretty interesting reading in light of the kidnapping. Since they're in your handwriting, some of them with dates at the top . . ."

"Yes, I see what the threat is. Publish and be damned."

"Sure about that?"

He tried throwing a withering look of contempt, but just as he was warming into it, I turned my back on him, crouching to fiddle with the phonograph.

I couldn't tell how well Escott and Vivian could hear Dugan. I talked loud enough, but his voice might not carry well and was a little distorted because of echoes off the harsh walls.

"Fleming."

"I'm still here."

"I understand what you're doing. If I write my letters against you, you send these in to the papers. Move and counter-move, we neutralize each other."

"Sounds about right. But I'm not interested in neutralizing, Gurley Hilbert. Only winning."

Flash of annoyance. He really didn't like that moniker. "Then what? What do you want?"

"You know. A written confession. I think Mrs. Gladwell may have mentioned it to you."

"Impossible." He laughed, and it sounded sincere. "Even were I to write such a thing, it would be useless to you because of the means you used to obtain it. Our system of law forbids confessions obtained under duress."

"I'm impressed. You're dredging up the law? After what you did?"

"The law is to keep the accused from the hands of the mob. I'll use it to the limit, use whatever means necessary to save myself."

"Ain't no saving for you here, bo. Consider this room to be an independent country that never heard of the Constitution."

"You're bluffing. That sense of honor you have won't allow you to carry this charade too far, else you'd have killed me instead."

"*That* could still happen. The others in this place will sooner or later get tired of bringing you food and carrying away your crap. Wouldn't take much to just forget to come down here. After a couple of days with no water, you won't have enough spit to shout for help. No one's around to hear you, anyway." I could see I was hammering home a few dark thoughts that had already occurred to him. "Maybe the whole point of this is literally an eye-for-eye. We keep you on ice here for two weeks, same as you did for Sarah. Then at the end of it we drop you into a cesspit. There's a prospect to keep you warm. You better hope you are thoroughly dead before we do it."

He shook his head, smiling like he was back in charge again. "No, you won't go that far."

Good. He was starting to repeat himself. That meant he was short on thinking and long on fear.

"You want my confession because you still have respect for the justice system. If you were as bloody-minded as you're pretending to be, it wouldn't matter. You'd kill me."

"Don't think I won't. But if I don't have to, if the state can do it for me, then I'm glad to step aside and let them through."

"What do you mean? Kidnapping isn't a capital offense."

I paused work on the phonograph, straightened, and paced over to him. He sat up a bit more, unsuccessfully hiding his alarm. "Up."

He cautiously stood, bracing, maybe thinking I'd slug him one. That would have felt good to me, but I abstained this time. He flinched when I picked up his cot and carried it out of reach.

"What are—" He almost visibly bit his tongue trying to shut down his curiosity.

Next I removed his roll of toilet paper and the chamber pot, which was fastidiously covered with a towel. I carried them, carefully leaving them on the floor well outside the room. Except for his clothes, they were the last throwable things Dugan might have used to damage the phonograph and records. Escott and Vivian shot me interested looks, but I didn't break stride, just winked in passing.

When I returned, Dugan had his back to the wall, very vulnerable. He didn't know why I had removed his few comforts, but there must have been some bad throughts going through his head about now. I could smell fear flowing off him like sweat. It was about damn time.

From my pocket I pulled out the news clipping about the bodies found at his former hideout. Giving it over, I waited until he'd read enough. "I can't remember. . . . Does Indiana have a death penalty or not?"

He let the clipping drop, shaking his head, seeming to relax. "There's no proof who did this. Certainly none that could ever involve me. They might have been killed by the other men."

"I'm sure I can ask Vinzer and the rest what they remember about it. And you know I *will* get the truth out of them. My guess is they'll be more than happy to sell you out to save their own hides—and for that I won't have to talk to them at all. The cops can get it from them."

"Then what—?"

"Concentrate, Gurley, you're showing sloppy in the brain department. The confession. We want your confession just to keep things tidy. I don't like loose ends. You disappearing and leaving behind a statement of guilt is better than you just disappearing."

"Oh, *that* threat should make me eager to do as you want. The longer I resist, the longer I live."

"That's right. You get to live right here. Just as you are." I waited a moment. "For as long as it takes."

He went still. It was hard to tell with the obscuring beard and low lighting, but he seemed to go very pale. I could hear his heart suddenly hammer loud from the shock, then subside. "That's a bluff. You wouldn't."

"How do your clothes smell today, Gurley? Ripe enough for you yet? What you're wearing is all you'll get until it rots off your body. No fresh underwear. No clean socks. No warm blanket. No toilet. A concrete floor, bread and water. Only way you'll ever shed that shirt is to tear it off, and you won't get another. Ever been to a zoo when they haven't hosed out the monkey house in a while? That's nothing to the kind of stink that's going to build up in here. Maybe you'll get used to it since it's your own, but I'll feel sorry for the guys bringing your food. Of course out of pure self-defense they might rig a garden hose down here to spray your crap down the drain. If you're lucky."

"Other prisoners have been through worse. I can survive."

"After a few *days* of this a regular prison will be paradise. There you can have a real shower and books to read. You like to write so much, you'll have that as well. You can even look at the sky . . ."

He laughed. "You're bribing me with *prison*?"

"Compare what you have here and now to what you could have if you cooperate. Take as long as you like to think it over. I have the time."

"It won't happen, Fleming. I won't give you the satisfaction."

"Suit yourself."

"My confession will be worthless. I know you think it will damn me in court, but I'll deny it. I'll make them believe me. The system is set up with the assumption that a man is innocent until he's proven guilty. I don't have to say anything to get free. *You* have to prove it. A forced confession will not hold."

I shrugged. "But you and I both know you're guilty. I was

there, remember? 'Clean like your grandmama used to' you told your boys; then you sent the other guys outside to prepare a grave for Sarah."

"We didn't put her in it."

"A fine point that won't wash with me. You're guilty, and I want you to tell everyone all about it. You like to write so much, here's a chance to express yourself. Why don't you tell the world how unfair it is that a genius like you has to resort to kidnapping to make ends meet? Or would you rather talk about the best method for conning your girlfriend out of ten grand?"

"How did you—of course, you managed to follow me out. You listened and made assumptions about my relationship with Miss Kennard."

"Yeah, all that and more. Her, me, and your cousin Brockhurst had a sweet little powwow earlier tonight. It'll do your heart good to know you were the focus of our talk. Did your ears do any burning? That would have been us."

"What did you tell them? They'd never believe you."

"I didn't have to say much. It was you doing the convincing. And reading some of your boats. The cranes didn't interest them, but the boats had quite an impact. I can't wait to send this stuff in to the papers. Should make quite a story—once they make up their minds what to print first. If you're hoping for their help in the future—"

"I can talk around that," he waved the origami pieces to unimportance. "I can explain all of it away. They're only notes for a novel I'm planning to write or a collection of essays and philosophical arguments. You only showed them the negative side, you see. I've not yet written the counterviewpoint yet."

"It'd be more believable to say you were just practicing your penmanship. Forget it. No editor will help you. You're nothing to your friends now, either. You see, I was very thorough. Have a listen, Gurley."

I got the phonograph turntable spinning. Put on the first record. Put the needle in the record's groove. Turned up the volume knob. At first the indistinct sounds confused him, then as the talk clarified and progressed, nudging his memory, the dawning came.

And for him it was one *ugly* morning.

After about five minutes, I got tired of looking at his blanched face while he listened and let myself out, leaving the record to drone on and on and on.

Escott and Vivian had removed themselves from the immediate area. That may have been Escott's idea, to keep her from hearing anything about me not easily explained. He also might have wanted to spare her hearing Dugan's unvarnished opinions about Sarah.

We walked out of distant earshot. I checked my watch so I'd know when to go in and change records.

"Well done," whispered Escott, as pleased as I'd ever seen him. "Very well done. That mention of the monkey house at a zoo conjured an especially vivid picture."

Not to mention odor. "You should have seen his mug when he recognized the conversation on the record. Thought he was going to choke."

"I may go so far as to say that you actually shut him up."

"That'll be the day," I said. I was feeling good about what I'd accomplished but realistic about the kind of payoff we could expect.

Vivian noticed my lack of smile. "You are not optimistic, Mr. Fleming?"

"The guy's crazy. He's had the wind knocked out of him, and he's scared, but he'll recover and get back up again. He won't trade his freedom—such as it is down there—for a pair of fresh socks. He'll convince himself that he can still get away with it. Even if he writes a confession like we want, he'll deny it, say that it's a forgery, say whatever it takes to wriggle free."

"Will that happen?"

"No, ma'am. I was serious about sending samples of his observations on life in to the papers. It won't convict him, but it won't make him any friends, either. The editors will stop with the sob-sister cra—er—stuff. He'll eventually go to jail. Those three mugs in his gang will tell the truth about him and be believed. I'm just sorry we can't keep this out of court."

Between Dugan's refusal to cooperate and his immunity to my hypnotic influence, he would get a trial; there was no way of sparing Sarah from the ordeal. Escott and I planned out how to make her testimony less important in the evidence, though, and this was the best we could come up with for the time being. Turning the gang and public opinion against Dugan was part of it, along with his friends withdrawing their support of him. If I had to, I'd find a way to make a night visit to the judge, lawyers, and every man and woman on the jury. It's a hell of a thing to have to fix a trial to make sure a guilty man was indeed found guilty.

"How much longer do you think this will take? If he's so stubborn . . ."

"I can't say, but I think he'll come around soon. He thinks almost like a kid. If he talks with enough sincerity, then of course people *have* to believe him. He can't imagine they would do otherwise. Once he's convinced himself he can beat the charge, he'll cooperate with us. I figure for him to hold out a little while longer so it looks good, then have a change of mind. He'll want us believing he's been broken. Maybe he will be; I don't care. With his confession, used or not, and the witnesses against him, he's got a snowball's chance in Miami of squirming away from this mess."

"But we can't keep him from telling others about his imprisonment here."

"No, but we will put enough sleeping pills in him to knock him out, clean him up, then Charles here can deliver him to the DA's office before Dugan's fully awake. He won't know what hit him."

Escott would be heavily disguised. I suggested he play a cop and claim that Dugan turned himself in. If a hubbub didn't happen, Escott was to make plenty of noise to create one, then slip away unnoticed.

"In the meantime, everyone in this house gets rid of all trace of Dugan's presence. Put back the old junk that used to be in his room in the first place, and everyone just go on with their work like normal. Even if he gets someone to come by for a look, they'll take him for a crank, be annoyed for wasting their time. Providing your people can lie through their teeth."

She smiled and nodded confidently, seemed reassured.

"Dust," said Escott glancing at our dim surroundings. "There won't be much dust on the items or the room's floor. Someone could notice that detail."

Vivian agreed. "Suppose I have the whole basement cleaned up to look the same?"

He shook his head. "That would have a reverse effect. Why of all times would you do that now? Dugan would pounce on it. However, I'm not without some experience at dressing a stage scene. There's a device that *puts* dust onto things. I'm sure I can find one and employ it to good effect."

"So all we need do is wait him out?"

"Pretty much," I said.

"I've an awful thought: we know he's unbalanced. My goodness, all the ravings he made about vampires and disappearing people and who knows what convinced me of that. Suppose he convinces others?"

It was a good point. Crazy people went to nuthouses, not prison. "Let's worry about that only if it happens."

Escott gave me a questioning look, and I nodded. Yeah, I could get to the examining doctors, too. The ripples were getting wider and wider on this case. Maybe I should have just clobbered Dugan and the others a little too hard at that Indiana house and dumped them all in the cesspit. Life would be a lot simpler.

In the distance I heard something like music. "Is that your doorbell?"

She listened. "I didn't hear anything."

"I'll see to it," said Escott, trusting my ears.

"And I." They went upstairs.

I checked my watch. Still some while before I had to change records. Might as well see who was calling at this hour. An enterprising reporter who'd snuck over the front gate. Or noticed the back was still open.

Or—as it turned out—Anthony Brockhust and Marie Kennard.

Oh, brother.

I hung far back in shadows as Escott peered through a side window, then opened the big front door. The unlikely couple crowded close to each other on the entry, shivering in the wind. Anthony darling looked embarrassed; Marie looked angry.

It was my fault. I'd mentioned Vivian's name in front of them when telling Escott where he should go to ground. They knew he'd been working for her. No need to follow him, just drive over later. Marie must have gotten herself worked up and talked Anthony into a showdown. He didn't seem too enthused, though.

"You. Escott is it?" said Brockhurst.

My partner was surprised. A rare event in itself. "What on earth are you doing here?"

Vivian bustled forward into their view. "Mr. Brockhurst? Miss Kennard?"

Marie pushed across the threshold, glaring around. I ducked back behind a marble pillar. "He's here. You've got him here, haven't you?"

"Got who?"

"Gilbert Dugan. That Fleming beast has him locked away someplace, I just know it. You tell me where he is!"

Vivian held her ground rather well. "Young woman, I will ask you to leave my home this instant."

"Tell me where to find Fleming or where he's hiding Gilbert, and I will."

Brockhurst did a little wavering. "Please, Mrs. Gladwell. Just tell her what she wants, and we'll leave."

I will never understand how you can present absolute, unshakable proof that a man is no good, only to find the woman that loves him will completely ignore it.

"We just want to help our friend. . . . Marie is convinced that—"

Vivian seemed to get taller. "How *dare* you come into this house and ask for help for that monster after what he did to my little girl?"

"Lies!" Marie blazed. "He's innocent, and you know it!"

Brockhurst made an unhappy placating gesture. "Please, Marie, you must remain calm or—"

"Mr. Brockhurst," said Escott tiredly. "Take Miss Kennard and remove yourselves immediately. I've had a long and painful night, and though it would grieve me to put bloodstains all over the superb rug you're standing on, I am not adverse to doing so in a good cause."

By God, he had his Webley out. His voice was conversational, but he was as pissed as I'd ever seen him. You could see it in his eyes.

"Charles . . . ?" Vivian was shocked. The others stood frozen.

"Brockhurst, I am an excellent shot, but a gun of this caliber makes a very large and messy hole even in a noncritical area of the anatomy. I cannot guarantee that I would entirely miss an artery, in which case you would bleed to death in a very short time. Now, get out and do not come back."

"M-Marie. Come on." He'd gone death pale.

"Damn it, Anthony, he's not going to shoot you!"

"I-I rather think he would." Brockhurst grabbed her arm and dragged her out. She protested, voice rising like a siren. Vivian slammed the door shut before the peak came, bolting it, then stared at Escott.

He coolly put the gun back in his shoulder holster. "I apologize for that display, but there are certain occasions when civility is wasted. That was one of them."

"Would you have shot him?"

He considered. "Yes, I believe I would. Not to kill, but he'd have been limping for some months and be reminded of the encounter every time it rained."

"You'd have . . . oh, Charles." She seemed disappointed.

I started to step forward, intending to explain some of what the real world was like outside of her high-hat society, then realized I'd badly miscalculated her reaction. She abruptly threw her arms around him and landed one whopper of a kiss square on his lips. First my jaw sagged, then dropped straight to the floor, for Escott's arms went around her fierce and hard, and he kissed her right back. He kissed her back and kept *on* kissing her.

Ye gods.

I started for the longest time, not quite believing it. After a bit, I blinked, looked away, and looked back, but they were still at it and didn't seem to be slowing.

Ye gods. Again.

Jeeze, I never suspected he had *that* kind of osculation going for him. Good night and little fishes, but much more and there'd be a new event for the next Olympics.

Now wasn't the time to make my presence known or to even say I'd been in the same county. I slipped off as quietly as I could down to the basement and left them to it.

"Wow," I puffed at the foot of the wooden stairs. There was a lot to think over, only my brain wasn't doing much, still being in shock. When a thought did surface, it was to wonder what Bobbi was doing about now. I'd have to get the number of that hotel from Coldfield. Late as it was, she might be awake.

But . . . I still had business to finish here. And in other parts of Chicago.

Damnation. I had to give myself a shake to shift gears. It was hard going, but eventually I got focused on the task at hand.

The makeshift cell was silent. The record had run itself out by now, the needle clicking away on blank surface. I went in.

Dugan was on the floor, back against the wall, his long legs drawn up, manacled arms resting awkwardly on his knees. He had a sour expression, which was good. Anything to shatter his ingrained confidence in the stupidity of his fellow man and how to take advantage of it. He had been banking on that quality to get him out of trouble. Not anymore. He watched, wordless, while I changed records, stowing the first one away in the flat box.

"Why don't you just kill me?" he asked, just as I steadied the needle over the outer grove.

"You want me to?"

"It's preferable to dying like this. Shoot me. Snap my neck. Or maybe you would rather drink my blood."

"Thanks, but I'm not that desperate. Want to save yourself some suffering? Pen and paper's right there." I pointed to where they lay on the floor just within reach of his chain leash. "Tomorrow night you can be in a nice warm cell, have a hot shower—"

"You seem fixed on bodily discomfort as a method of persuasion."

"Because it works. I heard it worked great in the Tower of London once upon a time."

"You heard? Or you saw firsthand?" He was giving me a good, hard stare.

How old did he think I was? Well, it wouldn't hurt to play along. "I'll leave it for you to decide. Lemme tell you about something. There used to be this thing in the castles back in the old countries, a hole, more of a pit, really. No way to tell how deep, and I'll tell you why in a minute. They used to throw prisoners in and leave 'em there. If they were lucky, the initial fall killed them straight off. If not, then they starved to death on a pile of their own shit. The king, or whoever dropped them in, shoved a big metal grate over the hole, and walked away and didn't come back until the next time he had someone he wanted out of the way. The reason you couldn't say how deep that pit ran was because of the layers and layers of bones that piled up over the centuries. Maybe it'd started out a hundred feet to the bottom, but there were so many bodies that the latecomers only had a twenty- or thirty-foot drop."

He remained silent.

"I tell you that because you're damn close to experiencing that yourself. It wouldn't take too much for me to find a really deep cesspit . . ."

"I get the idea, Fleming. From what you've said already, I'm expected to sit here and suffer in this more modern version of such a place until I give in. I will not be intimidated."

I shrugged. "Fine by me."

"You are such a fool!" He was finally showing what was behind his usual cool face. Anger. Frustration. Oh, yeah, this was getting better and better.

"Really? I'm not the one chained to the wall for being a bad boy. From what I heard, you should have been here years ago."

"Look at yourself!"

I spread my arms. "What?"

"You're *wasting* what you are!"

What was this about? "*I* am?"

"The abilities, you have, the powers, if I had even a tenth of them—"

"Whoa, there, Raffles. Then I would have to kill you."

"You've got so much, and you squander it playing saloon-keeper, helping out that would-be knight errant on your tiny little crusades in defense of what? Worthless creatures like that idiot female. She drools, Fleming. *Most* attractive!"

"Well, let's see how you look after a week down here and then I'll decide who I want to take out for ice cream."

"If you're afraid to use your talents yourself, then let me guide you. You're wasting them. You can go anywhere, do anything if you just——"

"Dugan, tell it to the Marines, I'm not interested." I dropped the needle, and Dugan's voice, sounding condescending and in charge, came out of the speaker. "I'll be back when this plays out. I suggest you stop worrying about how I live my life and think how you want to spend the rest of yours."

"Fleming——!"

I backed toward the door. "Your choice. A confession now before things get really bad will save you a lot of future grief. You have to decide how much suffering you want to go through, how much your pride's worth to stick it out. I don't care one way or another. You won't impress me with how long it takes for you to change your mind."

I heard a step behind me. Escott, I thought. Talk about bad timing. I did not need him crashing my big exit. I'd finally gotten Dugan upset enough to shout about something, even if it wasn't concerned with what I had in mind. He must have been doing plenty of thinking, just not on the right subject. This wanting to make use of my abilities must have been what Dugan had in mind all along. Another experiment. Well, to hell with that——

Escott punched me hard in the back. Too hard. As though he'd used a sledgehammer. Otherwise, I wouldn't have felt it this badly, wouldn't have grunted as my knees gave way; wouldn't have pitched forward onto the cold floor. What the——

A broad face leaned within my suddenly blurred view. Not Escott. Not . . .

Hog Bristow grinned down. "Hello, punk. It's buckwheats time."

15

I WORKED out I was hurt, and whatever it was continued to hurt, growing worse. I tried to vanish. Never mind if Bristow saw. Nothing happened. No pleasant escape, no weightless gray limbo, no healing. Something terribly wrong in my back. I flopped one arm around, fingers encountering, then grasping what felt like a screwdriver handle. Quick before anyone could stop me I pulled hard, and heard a man's hoarse cry a full second before the blinding pain shot up through my skull.

Bristow laughed. I'd smash his face to jelly once I got this damned thing—it snapped away . . .

But the pain continued.

In my hand was the top part of a rusty ice pick. The rest of it, at least half a foot of disruptive metal, remained in my back, screwing things up inside, preventing me from vanishing. To hell with that, I could still fight. I surged toward Bristow, but he danced out of my way, leaving it clear for his men to step in. Three of them. The one I'd decked earlier was recovered, now armed with brass knuckles.

They went to work on me, or tried to. I landed enough punches to get some respect, but that also made them mad. Fists and feet, clouts and kicks rained on me. One bright boy hammered on my lower back where the ice pick point was imbedded. That was the worst. I roared and swung, sending him hurtling across the room into Dugan.

Things blurred again. I was on the floor again. Didn't know how I'd gotten there. Head felt like a drum. Could barely hear. Could *not* move.

". . . killed him, you idiot," growled Bristow.

"He can't be dead." Sounded like Dugan. But his voice also droned tinnily from another direction.

"Shuddup, you. Turn that crap off, I can't think. What is that?"

They shut off the phonograph. "Donno, Boss. Looks like a homemade record."

"Break it," cried Dugan. "Break them both!"

"I said shuddup. Who the hell are you?"

"I'm being held prisoner here. Please, help me. I'll pay you anything. Get me out of here."

"Why you chained up like that? What the hell kinda place is this?"

"There might be a key to these manacles outside, send one of your men to look."

"Screw that; you answer me."

"Sir, there's no time. The other people in the house may have heard, they could be calling the police. Take me with you, and I'll tell you everything."

"Nobody knows that much. Reef, why'd you hit him so damn hard? I oughta buckwheats you to learn you better."

"He can't be dead," Dugan insisted. "Not Fleming."

"Why, he your boyfriend? Well, too bad for you, gunsel."

"You don't understand, there's something different about him. He's—he's playing possum."

Bristow snorted.

"Boss," said one of the others. "We should get outta here. Let's leave 'em and go."

"Take me with you. I can help!" Dugan's voice was high, desperate.

"We don't need no help," said Bristow.

"I tell you he's not dead. Let me loose, and I'll prove it!"

"You're nuts. Why else would they chain you up?"

"Because they're monsters! I'll gladly explain everything, but not here."

"Hey, Boss. I think nutzo there has somethin'. Lookit this."

Fire in my back as Reef thumped on the ice pick; I flinched, gasped involuntarily. He turned me over, pried open one of my eyelids. Saw me looking back.

"He's still kicking. Not a lot."

"It's enough. You guys get him in the car. You, where you know him from? Why you on the wall like that? You doing some kind of sick games down here?"

"No-no-no! He's been holding me prisoner for something I didn't do. We're mortal enemies. I can help you with him."

"You're the one needs help."

"I can be useful, and I can pay."

"You don't look like you got a plug nickel."

"I assure you I can! Five thousand dollars! I can get it!"

Another snort. "What the hell, why not. You got the money, I'm ahead. You ain't got the money, you don't have a head." He laughed heartily at this. "Reef, find that key he talked about."

"Don't need one, Boss."

An almighty bang filled the room, followed by swearing.

"You trying to kill us? That bullet bounced! You stop!"

"But he's loose. In one shot. Pretty good, huh?"

Bristow swore and rumbled orders. Reef and another man hoisted me up. They complained about the weight. I twitched to life and kicked, trying to get clear. They came after me; one of them threw too slow a punch. I froze onto his arm and twisted, trying to tear it off. He screamed and just managed to break free with some help. The help was Reef putting one of his heavy shoes into my side. I grabbed and hauled on his leg. Felt like I was moving in syrup, but I still had strength in me. Reef crashed over, yelling. I rolled, taking his foot along. Felt something snap. Heard another scream. Hands on me, tearing, punching.

Face into the floor. How'd I get here?

"He broke it, goddammit! He goddamn broke it!"

I lurched up, spotted Bristow, and lunged at him. He dodged, but I grabbed a meaty shoulder and hung on, pulling myself up, trying to get a choke hold. Yelling, men hitting me . . . the sharp, confined crack of a gun, my legs going out again. Cold concrete, fire in my left side, bloodsmell.

"You kill him, Boss?"

A pause as they investigated. Someone turned me over.

Dugan. Free now. Chains still dangling from his wrists. Leering in my face. He tugged at my clothes, digging for the wound.

"What're you doing?"

"Just look!" Dugan had my shirt yanked out of the way.

"So?"

"Watch! Watch what happens to him!"

"What the hell . . . ?"

Knew what they'd see, tried to move, but there was a flash of light that left me stunned. Someone had hit me again. Must have used wood. As they watched and waited, I had the time to realize they were going to kill me. They would succeed. Of all of them, Dugan was the one who would know how to do it.

Couldn't let him . . .

"See! It's healing right up!" he cried.

I lashed at him, hands on his throat, my lips peeled back in a breathless snarl. He struggled, tried to get away—

Shot.

My right side, down in the belly. God, I couldn't stand it. Blood rushing out, the terrible burning as outraged flesh forced itself to knit together. Wanted to vanish, anything to stop the pain.

"You see?" Dugan panted hoarsely. "You can't kill him."

"Oh, yeah?" Bristow sounded interested.

"Boss, we gotta get outta here. Someone upstairs will have heard."

"Yeah-yeah. Get 'em. You, there, you wanna help, you get Reef walking. Tib, Lissky, pick that skinny bastard up, and get to the car."

"But, Boss . . ."

"I said he was buckwheats, and I keep my promises. Hey— I told ya to help Reef."

Noise across the room. The rattle of chains, then a cracking as Dugan broke the two phonograph records to shards. "Yes, of course, right away. Where are we going?"

"Never you mind."

Long climb up the stairs. I was too hurt to hinder them. They'd just drop me, and I could break something in the fall and make it worse. Had to wait, marshal my waning strength.

If I could just get that metal pick out of me . . . my back . . .

Escott. Where was he? He must have heard something. Maybe waiting for the right moment, too. He'd want to keep Vivian out of the line of fire. Get her safe, keep everyone in the house quiet, then move in.

But he stayed clear. No sign of him as they hauled me through the kitchen. Had they taken him earlier? I'd left him in the front; these guys had come in by the back. He could have completely missed them. There were a lot of walls in between.

Their car with the missing door was parked next to my Buick. They couldn't have followed me here or they'd have crashed the party sooner. Must have trailed Brockhurst instead. They'd have remembered him and Marie, maybe stopped them, asked questions, thinking it would lead to me. Had those two been in on it? Ring the front bell, draw attention in that direction?

Bristow opened the car; Tib and Lissky dropped me in the trunk. I landed bad, bit off the cry as the pick point seemed to drive in deeper. Tib slammed the trunk lid down. Felt jouncing as they loaded into the car. Dugan, too. Could hear his voice against Bristow's rumble, then the engine gunned, and we rolled forward, bumping over uneven ground before finding the pavement. Swoop and bump as we made the road.

My guts wanted to turn inside out. Sick and sweating, I was able to move, but each time cost me. Pretzeled around with one arm, searching for the pick point. My fingers were numb and slick. They brushed against bloodied skin.

Smooth bloodied skin. No sign of the broken-off point. None. Oh, dear God, I'd healed up with the damn thing *inside* me.

* * *

Wanted to pass out. My body didn't cooperate. Was conscious
of every awful moment of an endless drive full of turns and
pauses. The thrum of the motor, the stink of exhaust when I
once chanced to draw breath. Cold seeped into my bones,
made me shiver. If I could stop it, make myself hold still, not
respond to them, look dead, they'd leave me alone. Dugan
might see past the ruse, though. He knew a little about me,
what I was, but how much?

They finally stopped and got out. The stillness and silence
pressed hard, made me think they'd left for good. In a couple
days some curious cop might have the car towed, in a couple
more days someone might open the trunk and find me. What
was left of me. Would I live that long? I didn't know. Didn't
want to know.

The lid shot up. Tib and Lissky again, grunting and heav-
ing me around like a sack of rocks. I tried to be completely
limp, eyes slitted. Glimpse of a dim, empty street, tall, flat-
sided buildings. A single light glowing harsh blue on a pole
far, far away at the end. Familiar smell in the air: farmyard
stench mixed with death. If my heart had been beating, it
would have leaped. We were near the Stockyards.

"What place is this?" Dugan again. He was supporting
Reef, who hopped along on his left foot.

"Get in or I'll plug ya!" Bristow. Sounded drunk.

Tib had my shoulders, Lissky my legs. They walked
clumsy, lugging my weight with small steps. A doorway.
High, looming walls. A second door. Metallic clunk and
snick, wash of cold air. Colder than the January air outside.
Bloodsmell everywhere. My corner teeth emerged, lengthened.
Instinctive hunger. Needed to restore what I'd lost.

"Down over there," said Bristow.

They dropped me sprawling. More concrete. Like ice. Bloodsmell permeated it, but there was no blood. High above were metal rafters, a system of pulleys and rails like at a laundry, but bigger, bulkier. Hooks, chains, massive things hanging from some of them like misshapen Christmas ornaments. A meat locker of some sort. Those were sides of beef.

"Legs," said Bristow, the word visible in the clammy cold.

One of them put my ankles together. Instinct told me what might be coming. Memories of stories Gordy passed on told me what *would* be coming. I fought, kicking; wordless, panicked, desperation gave me a burst of strength. I broke Lissky's arm. He fell away, cursing. Tib slammed into my temples with the brass knucks until I didn't have anything left but the pain. He tied my feet. Heard a rattling. Too heavy be Dugan's chains. What . . . ?

Tib dragged a meat hook down and slipped it under the knots between my ankles. The hook was attached to thick chain that looped into a pulley system. It was how they hung the beef up. My turn, now. He hauled sharp on more chain, like drawing a curtain.

I was yanked fast across the rough floor, then my legs bobbed straight up, carrying the rest of me helplessly along. My lungs rushed into my throat, trying to come out. Lifted clear from the floor, I swung dizzily, twisting, arms dangling. He pummeled my gut a few times like a boxer testing a new bag, then grabbed my hands, tying them behind me. With a knife he cut my coat and shirt off. My pale skin puckered against the freezing air.

Bristow's upside down face came into view. Bleak eyes, small teeth, the lower ones yellowed and so level they looked

filed. "Still with us? That's good. Jeeze, what with his mouth?
You ever see anything like that?"

Dugan, still manacled, stood off to the side. "What are you
going to do to him?"

"The same thing I'll do to you if you don't make good on
that five grand you promised."

"Let me go, and I'll fetch it. Send one of your men along
with me." He gestured at Lissky, who hobbled away, clutching his arm. He made it through the metal refrigeration door
to join Reef sitting in the outer room.

"It can wait 'til I'm done. You watch an' learn something."

"You won't be able to kill him. Not the way you think."

Bristow grinned. "Good." He took off his topcoat and
tight-fitting jacket, giving them to Tib.

"You're wasting him! He's more useful alive!"

"Not to me." He rolled up his shirtsleeves and held his
hand out. Tib put the knife into it.

"You can't do that! I have to—"

Tib backhanded Dugan, who emitted a yelp and staggered
away, fingers to his suddenly bruised face. He looked dumbfounded.

"Bristow."

He turned. "Huh?"

I struggled to take in a breath. "Bristow . . ." It came out
uneven, barely audible, but brought him over.

"What d'ya want, fancy boy?"

"Nuh . . . you. You want. Gordy?"

Bristow chuckled. "Now ain't that how it always works.
Show 'em a little tough and they'll sell their gran'ma the first
chance. What about Gordy?"

"I can. Give him . . . to you."

"Oh, yeah? Where is he?"

"Cut me down. Just leave. I'll tell you."

"That's no kind of deal."

"You get Chicago. I want nothing. Just walk away."

"An' leave you alive?"

"I won't live through this."

Another laugh. "Bet your ass you won't."

"You want Gordy?"

His eyes glinted. "I *already* got him, fancy boy. Don't need your help at all."

The knife blade flashed bright under the high, dim lights. *Oh, God, no* . . .

He started in.

I'm not brave. Screams ruptured out of me same as for any tortured animal. They didn't sound remotely human. I shrieked and bucked until empty of air, then continued to jerk and twitch with each new slice. Blood ran down my flanks, my face, into my eyes, my mouth. I tried to swallow it back again. I prayed for Escott to find me. I prayed for death to end it. What blood was left in me billowed into my skull, keeping me conscious. The only respite was when Bristow paused to drink from a flask. His shirt got splattered with gore. He didn't seem to notice. His eyes were vacant. No way to tell if he could see anything, but he had to as he carved me like a turkey.

Off in a corner, Dugan reached his limit and vomited his guts out.

Bristow noticed that much and laughed at him.

Tib took advantage of the pause. "Boss, we gotta look after Reef and Lissky pretty soon."

"We will."

"But that shit smashed 'em hard."

"An' I'm givin' him payback for it. So they gotta little hurt, have 'em call their mamas if it's so bad. We can't leave yet, and they know it."

"When will he get here?" This from Lissky, calling from the next room, his voice tight.

"When you see him. What's your hurry? You got a show to watch."

He started on me again.

I couldn't stand it, thrashed like a fish. Screamed without breath, begged for it to stop. Begged in silence, mouth working, nothing coming out.

Then by chance Bristow got too close to my face. He may have been trying to cut off one of my ears. I was crazy by then, reacting, not thinking, unable to think. I bit into the thick flesh of his bared forearm and held on, teeth grinding into the tough meat.

His turn to bellow, to try breaking free. I clamped hard, mindless with pain and hunger, sucking greedily at his blood while it was there to be had. He'd reduced me to this.

He went crazy, too, yelling and beating at me, finally stabbing with his knife. I felt the blade like vague body blows. Any one of them fatal to a normal man, just more agony for me. No ending to it.

Bristow finally wrenched away, his deep voice gone hysterically high as he clutched his wounded arm. He'd stripped off some of my skin, I ripped out a piece of his in turn. It tasted strangely sweet as I sucked the last of his blood from it like an orange slice. When nothing more remained, I spat out the meat. It hit the wet floor, making a little splattering plop in the blood already there.

Someone was using me, giving me a soft voice, making me laugh, a long thin, insane sound. It didn't last. I held still, trying to ease the sickening to-and-fro swing of my body.

Dugan cautiously came up, eyes wide, and steadied me. Green-faced, he glanced at Bristow and Tib. Bristow streamed curses while a grimly silent Tib wrapped my shredded shirt around his boss's arm.

"Why don't you vanish?" Dugan asked, sounding desperate.

Felt that laughter again. It didn't make it out. Too weak. Too hungry.

"*Why?*"

I sucked blood-tainted air and breathed a soft word. "Pick."

He was confused. "Pick what?"

"Getitout. Back."

"You mean that ice pick?"

"Ssssh. Yesss . . ."

He couldn't find it, though. Not under all that damage, not now. He blanched and looked helpless.

Bristow shook away from Tib. "That sick bastard! I'll kill him!"

Seeing what was coming, Dugan ducked clear and ran.

I didn't see, but felt it, the streams of fire like comets plowing through me, my body twitching for each bullet that struck. The gun thundered in the cavernous building four times, then clicked on empty chambers as Bristow kept pulling the trigger.

"You got him, Boss," said Tib when the echoes died.

Bristow didn't want to believe. He approached, prodded me with the gun muzzle. It was hot. I didn't notice. I was past that; my red life poured out front and back, leaving a drained husk. Couldn't even blink.

He struck again, using the knife, digging viciously into my shoulder.

Nothing. Some part of my brain cried anguish, but the message never got out.

"Too quick," Bristow muttered.

"Yeah, Boss," agreed Tib. "You wanna let's go take care of that arm?"

"You see me whining? We wait 'til he gets here."

"Yeah, Boss."

"Where'd that gunsel go? Did he leave?"

"No, Boss." This from Reef. "He went off into the building. Ain't no exits there."

"You sure?"

"All the doors is locked inside 'n out. Keeps the workers from lifting the beef after hours. C'mon, Boss, let's leave 'em. We can meet this other guy tomorrow."

"And have Gordy up and looking for me by then? No."

"Kroun said he croaked."

"I don't believe that. Not 'til I see him hanging in here I don't. We meet up and go finish things for sure."

"What if he don't show?"

Before Bristow could reply, someone banged on the outer entry door. "Open that," he ordered Tib, the only man still undamaged.

Tib pushed on the horizontal opening bar. "It's about damn time."

Strome walked in, ungloved hands hanging loose, his overcoat open, same as the jacket beneath so he could easily get to his gun. He took two steps in, giving Reef and Lissky a critical eye. "What happened to you?"

"In here," said Bristow.

With a nod to Tib, Strome came into the locker, squinting in the low light, stopping when he saw me.

"Jesus, Mary, and Joseph," he said. "What the hell you been doing here?"

"Little party. You're late."

"Had to take care of stuff at the club. Derner wanted to keep me there."

"You're not welching on us." A warning tone.

"No, I'm not w—"

"You were falling down drunk tonight—"

"I wasn't drunk! Just got tired is all. I was sleeping. What is this? Who's that guy?" He came close. Drew a sharp breath. "Shit! You know who that *is*?"

"Dead meat." Bristow sounded satisfied.

"But it's *Fleming*. He and Gordy are that tight."

"Then they can play pinochle in hell together for all I care. He's dead now, and Gordy's on his way out—if you hold to what you said."

"I'll hold if you do, but jeeze . . . Fleming. What'd you do to him? I heard the guy was indestructible."

"Only 'cause he never met me."

"Never saw it hit anyone that way before. Jeeze. He looks a week gone already." Strome stared a moment more, then shrugged. "Let's get going."

Bristow needed help with his suit coat. Tib assisted. They got Bristow's good arm in its sleeve, draping the rest over his shoulder. Strome, ignoring me now, watched their struggles, his hand slipping inside his own coat.

In the outer room I heard the street door softly open.

Lissky said, "Hey . . . !"

The rest was drowned by sudden gunfire.

Bristow and Tib came alert, but too late. Strome had his .45 out and caught them both from behind. Almost in unison they dropped to their knees and heeled over, strings cut. I gently swung and sensed blood that was not my own flooding the air, longing for it.

"You got 'em?" Strome called out in the silence.

"Yeah. You?"

He experimentally kicked each body. "They're gone."

Derner stepped in, frowning, eyes first for Bristow and Tib on the floor, then wide on me. "Jeeze, who's . . . ?"

"Fleming. Can you believe it? Lookit how they did him."

"Gordy ain't gonna like that."

"He can throw him a big funeral to make up for it."

Derner shook his head. "That kid had something, but he was too cocky."

"Hurry an' let's get these bums inside. You put the fix in with the manager?"

"Yeah, everyone has the weekend off. We got plenty of time to clean up later. No one's coming here."

They holstered their guns and proceeded to drag Lissky and Reef into the meat locker, lining them up next to their boss on the floor.

I gently swung, helpless, struggling to make a noise, to move, anything to attract their attention. With all my effort behind it I managed to blink. They missed it. I had no strength left for another try.

They shut the light, slammed the door, locked it.

Pitch black. Not the vaguest glimmer of outside glow.

They shut and locked the outside door. Distant noise of a car starting, driving off.

Silence.

I gently swung, suspended in the darkness, and prayed for death.

* * *

Hours seemed to go by before I heard a sound. A stealthy sigh of working lungs. A chain clinking. The soft pad of a footfall.

Then Dugan blundered into one of the sides of beef and made a lot more noise disentangling himself.

His teeth were chattering. Heart racing as he fought to control his breath, keep it quiet. He made his way slowly toward the front. Not an easy task in the dark. Must have used the straight rows of hanging meat as a guide.

He reached their end, though, and had to strike out over the open floor. I could imagine him, arms extended, frozen feet cautiously questing, in a panic that the gangsters would return or that cold would get to him before he could escape.

A gasp as he encountered a wall. His hands lightly scrabbled, searching for the door, the light switch. He found the door first, pushed on the latch bar. It clunked uncooperatively. Locked. He fought with it, rattling hard, not caring about noise, now. It remained stubbornly in place.

More scrabbling, then the lights sprang suddenly on.

Dim as they were, he winced against them. Still in stocking feet, coatless, he'd wrapped his chains up around each arm to keep them out of the way and quiet. They came unwrapped when he saw the bodies and staggered back from them. He stared down, as though not believing them, stared for a long minute, before pouncing on Tib. He took the dead man's shoes off, hopping as he fitted them on his own feet. He began struggling for the topcoat, then spotted Bristow's where it lay discarded on a bench. Dugan wrapped his chains around again and hauled it on over them, buttoning every button. He searched the pockets, didn't seem to find what he wanted, and went on to the other men. He turned out wallets and guns and keys—which were useless, since the door locked on the outside.

He studied one of the guns carefully before picking it up as though it were a rattlesnake. A semiauto, he didn't seem to like the look of it. One of the others in his little kidnap gang must have been the trigger man for that old couple killed in Indiana.

Dugan rose, turned, and aimed shakily at the metal door. He worked up to it, eventually pulling the trigger. Nothing happened. He didn't understand the safety was on. When he looked for it, pulling and pushing at things, he managed to eject the magazine. He put the weapon down in disgust and tried the door again, this time throwing himself against it.

That didn't work either. He lifted another gun, Bristow's. A more simple revolver, but all the chambers were empty. He found that out when he tried to use it. He got two more off Tib and Lissky, and finally figured out how to shoot. He used up all his bullets on the door, missing at point blank range because he kept turning his face away each time he fired.

All that effort and he was still trapped. There were lots of holes in the metal framework, some of them even close to the latch, but none had broken the lock. He lay partly on his back, braced, and started methodically hammering the door with his feet until he got too tired.

Panting, he rested, and looked around. What he needed was a crowbar. He could use it to pry apart the wooden walls that faced outside, which is what I'd have done instead of attacking the reinforced entry.

He scavenged noisily out of my view. I could follow his progress by his rattling chains. They'd slipped down his wide sleeves and now dragged musically on the concrete.

When he returned, he had other chains and hooks.

And very unexpectedly, he lowered me to the floor.

My head was cocked at an awkward angle. I couldn't see what he was up to, but vaguely felt him working on my ankle bindings.

He wasn't trying to help me. It was the hook from which I'd been dangling. He'd wanted *that* hook, which was closest.

The cold made him clumsy. It took him a while to link everything together, and he was hampered by his manacles. Eventually he ran a length of chain to the door, along with another hook, looping it around the horizontal push bar.

That didn't work either. When he hauled on the chain and pulley that had dragged me up, all it did was snap the bar from the door. The broken pieces cracked in half, the chain whipping dangerously around in recoil.

Dugan sagged. Apparently that was his last brilliant idea. I had a couple but couldn't express them. However, I was lying flat, which was much better, even if my arms were pinned and numb under my back. I could sense the remaining blood in me slowly settling, spreading out to where it was supposed to be.

Without having to struggle against gravity, I managed to bring in a small trickle of air . . . and blow it out again, whistling against my teeth.

In the heavy silence, the sound galvanized Dugan. He turned like he'd been struck and glared down at me.

Glaring back, I blinked. Twice.

He didn't want to come closer, wary after what I'd done to Bristow, but he had to in order to hear.

"You're alive?" he whispered.

I was dead. The rest of me just hadn't caught up yet. I drew air, timing my words, choosing them. "Willhelpyou."

It took him a bit to digest this. "Help me? Why?"

"Wannalive."

He couldn't seem to work out whether that was a reply or a question. "How can you help me?"

"Bloodfirst."

"What? I'm not feeding you." He looked disgusted.

"*Theirs.*"

He gaped. "I can't!"

Breath. "Thenweboth." Breath. "Freezetodeath."

Dugan thought it over. Not for long. "What do I do?"

"Cutone. Getblood. Pan. There."

He cast around, spotting a stack of wide flat pans against the wall. They were shallow, only inches deep but a couple of feet across. I didn't know their precise use, but with Dugan's help I could improvise a horrifying new one.

Fear made him a quick study. He fetched a pan. A few words at a time, I told him what to do. He got the ropes off my ankles and used them on one of the dead men, similarly trussing his feet. Tib. Dugan used the hook and pulley again, and lifted the body up until it hung upside down over the pan.

Then Dugan found the knife and, hands shaking, cut deeply across Tib's throat.

Only he wasn't quite dead, either.

Tib choked and gagged himself conscious. His flailing arms set him swinging, and he made a hell of a mess as his arterial blood shot across the floor. Some of it splattered me, but not near my mouth. Dugan actually screeched, completely unnerved, darting out of range of Tib's clutching hands.

It seemed to take forever for him to die, swaying like a clock pendulum, but eventually his fighting weakened and slowed and stopped. The last of his blood trickled into the catch pan below. It steamed in the cold air.

I was still tied at the wrists. That didn't stop me. The bloodsmell was crazy-making. I wriggled toward it, too weak to crawl, too desperate to wait.

Dugan, visibly fighting revulsion, came over and cut the last of the ropes. I couldn't feel my arms but used them, dragging myself up and over the edge of the pan.

Human blood, more than I'd ever dared take from a living person before. No problem about the living this time. It had pooled at my end, and I pressed my face into it, drinking deep. Cooling already, it was still sweet . . . and terrifying. I ignored the latter and fed, and I felt my body trying to heal itself, using every ounce I took in, flushing me with warmth, then fiery heat. My back and sides burned steadily, then suddenly were much too hot. Had to stop, gasping. It was almost like being skinned all over again, but in reverse. Couldn't hold back these cries, either. I fell away, shuddering, convulsing out of control.

If I could just vanish, the awful healing process would be done in an instant, then I'd materialize again, tired, but whole.

Impossible with that metal point in me. The idea of asking Dugan to cut it out . . . no. Couldn't trust him, didn't dare. He hovered just out of reach, his face a mask of hope and horror as the shakes tore through me.

The spasms gradually eased in force, then stopped. I felt drowsy, but the pain of hunger kept sleep at bay. The bloodsmell tormented me to get up again and take more. The longer I lay the worse it became. When the craving overcame my lethargy, I drank again until all the blood was gone. Then I slumped and rested, waiting, relishing the slow restoration. Everything hurt, though not as badly; I was still impossibly fragile. My hands, arms, were skeletal, the skin shrunken. My face must have looked like a skull with eyes and hair.

"More," I said to Dugan. My voice was odd, hoarse. All that screaming had taken its toll. "Get me another one."

"I can't. I can't touch them." He'd pressed against the door.

I gave him a look. "You will. If not them, it'll be you. Sooner or later, you'll fall asleep in this cold. What you wanna bet that I last longer?"

He made a small noise in his throat, and he stooped to lug another man over. Bristow. He'd been shot once, seemed to have caught it in the heart and hadn't bled too badly. It took ten long minutes for Dugan to swap the bodies around. He hesitated over cutting this new throat.

Impatient, I saved him the trouble and moved in. Kneeling put me on a level with Bristow's neck. He dangled, meaty arms hanging out from his thick body, looking like his namesake, a slaughtered hog.

As I drew near and stretched his neck just that much more, I realized he was also still alive. His eyes were open. And aware.

Oh, but this was *good*.

"Hello, Ignance," I whispered, grinning.

He gave a little moan. He wasn't too far gone. He could still be afraid. Maybe in his tiny little brain he'd finally worked out that there really was something different about me, something he should have been afraid of all along.

I drew in his fear-scent, tasting it like wine with nose and tongue. Heady stuff. Unforgettable. Unique. Delightful.

It stirred things in me, long-buried things. Stuff I never looked at if I could help it. Dark, bloody insanity was the least of that dreadful hoard of sickness. It surged up and caught me hard, and this time I saw no reason to resist its pull. It was right, had always been right. Why hadn't I *seen* that?

I bit, hard and careless, tearing Bristow's flesh as he'd torn mine. He wailed and fought, not as strongly as Tib, just enough to make his blood pump out that much faster. I didn't get it all at first, but God, what was there . . . satisfying and potent. Who'd have thought the bastard would taste so wonderful?

My strength growing, I held him fast and fed and fed and fed. I could *feel* my limbs filling out. It had never hit me this strongly before. I'd enjoyed human blood, from the smallest sips taken in the ecstasy of love to vast gulps while trying to save my life, but it had never been this intense in its effect. Those other times I had not been trying to kill. Not on purpose. I'd come close to it, once, seduced by curiosity and lust. In the end, and, just in time for my victim, I'd snapped out of the spell. Not so now. No need for it. I wanted this man dead, and I would be his willing and joyful executioner.

His struggles diminished, eventually ceased. His heart fluttered frantically a little longer, trying to push blood that wasn't there, before giving up. He slipped quietly into that last silence with me still strongly holding him, feeding from him.

Cooling, but yet sweet. I drank long. Gravity, not a pumping muscle made that red fountain flow. The taste changed now that he was dead. The headlong rush of vitality too quickly faded, making the blood no different from that which had been stored in a bottle. Regardless, I drank like a bum on a binge, past the point where need ended and greed began.

Then past that point as well.

"Fleming! *Stop!*"

Continuing to drink, I sluggishly looked over. Apparently

the sucking noises had been too much for Dugan's sensibilities.

He seemed aghast, was on the verge of tears. "You weren't like this in the cattle pen."

No, but I'd not been this close to death then. I could look back on that moment with fond affection for my complaisant innocence. How neatly I'd accomplished that feeding, taking care not to spill, being so tidy with my handkerchief. Now it was as though I'd bathed in the stuff.

And I *liked* it.

Slowly, I pulled away. There was nothing left. I'd taken it all.

"You were curious about me, my *kind*," I said, fighting off the threat of more thin laughter. "Well, here it is with the gloves off. Whatd'ya think?"

He had no words, though his expression was eloquent. He wanted no part of it.

I was oddly lightheaded. Had the impression I was standing outside of myself, hands clasped, watching a play starring me. It had been a very long time since my last experience with this feeling, but I remembered it. I was drunk. Very drunk. The alcohol in Bristow's blood had me all but reeling. It felt *good*.

I levered to my feet, off balance a moment. It was reassuring to see everything solidly back on the floor again and no longer clinging to the ceiling. "And you didn't care for Sarah 'cause of a little drool? How about the unvarnished undead? You should give it a try!"

"You promised to get us out of here," he said, easing along the wall away from me.

"I guess I did, and I'm a man of my word."

What a amazing song the blood made, playing light

through my brain. No beating heart within to keep time, but you couldn't have everything. I was still able to dance, though, and cut a turn on my way to the door. Nearly slipped. The floor was slick. What a mess. Not mine to clean up. I'd have one of the waiters see to it. I'd bring the whole damn crew down here, band and all. In a space like this, the music would boom through the huge building. Lots of room for dancing.

Fell against the door. It rattled. I threw a disgusted look at Dugan. A grown guy like him, and he couldn't take care of a little thing like this? It was cardboard, nothing but cardboard. Pressed against it, tried to vanish. Oh, that wasn't working right now. No matter. One good shove.

Ow. Bare wet shoulder on freezing cold metal. All right, another shove, hit it hard and fast.

Crack, crash, thump, as its hinges came out and the slab of metal-sheathed wood slammed open and fell with a boom. Dark office. Didn't hold my interest. Stagger across to the other door. Huh. Even that sissy in the back could take care of this one. Well, maybe not. I went against it before noticing it opened inward. No problem. Grasped the knob and pulled it like a bad tooth. Let it fall with a clunk. No lock, no prison. Very simple. I greeted the fresh night air.

Damn, that tasted fine. *Much* better than the stale stuff trapped in the meat locker.

Dugan hurtled past me. There was a car in the street, missing its driver's door. He got into it, jangled some keys. He was shaking, stealing quick looks at me while trying to find the starter. The motor turned over, and he gunned out, nearly stripping the gears in his haste.

I wanted to chase after him, but it was just too much trouble. He'd go to his friends. I'd look them up later. We'd have a big party. I'd find out just how much Four Roses Anthony dear could pack away in one sitting. Maybe Bobbi would oblige me and sock back a bottle, then I'd take it out of her again so I could keep on feeling like this. We'd make a contest of it. . . .

Missed my footing and fell. Landed painfully in a wet gutter. Rolled on my back in the cold street. This wasn't nice at all.

Took stock. Pants and shoes, but no shirt and coat. Can't get into any class places without those. No money. Wallet was in my missing coat.

Not promising, said the spectator outside of myself. He looked just like me but was dressed and cleaned up. Indulgently bemused expression on his mug. Held my wrist toward him. I still had my watch. So what if it was so thick with dried blood I couldn't tell the time. I could pawn it for some booze. . . .

The spectator wasn't applauding this performance. He shook his head and pointed toward the wings. I didn't like being onstage anyway. MC work was as far as it went; leave the entertainment to the talents.

Crept to my feet again, left the gutter, began walking. No shirt, no shelter, and it was getting damned cold all of a sudden. I should go back and find my clothes . . .

They've been cut off, the spectator told me.

Shied away from thinking about what happened after that.

I plodded on, vaguely recognizing the streets. Of course. Escott's office was around here. Rent was cheap this close to the Yards. The stink was hell in the summer when the wind was wrong, but you got used to it. One more corner, halfway down the block, up the stairs . . . only to find the pebble-glassed door with his name painted on it was locked. Couldn't remember where the key might be. Too bad. I pulled the knob off this one, too, and pushed inside.

This place was too plain. Just the same old desk and chair and empty white walls. I'd go nuts in here. Maybe that was his problem. He was nuts and didn't know it. But then I heard all English guys were crazy.

I dropped behind the desk and grabbed the phone, dialing the number and waiting a while before realizing I'd not taken the earpiece off its cradle. That was damn funny.

But the spectator visibly sighed, rolling his eyes. *Try again*.

I did so, calling home. Let it ring a dozen times. Gave up. Who should I call next?

The spectator pointed at me.

Well, that made sense. I dialed. Ring-ring-ring a lot of times, then a man said hello.

"Hello?" I echoed back.

"Is that you, Mr. Fleming?"

"Hello, I'm calling Mr. Fleming. He's got to be there or I wouldn't have called."

"This is Wilton, Mr. Fleming. You okay? You sound funny."

So there I said to the spectator. I *can* be amusing. "I am great! Strome and Derner are okay like me. Maybe. You tell that to Gordy. They didn't stick around an' they shoulda—"

"Is Mr. Escott there?"

"Strangely, he is not, and this was his office the last I heard, but Bristow is bust-o, only you can't tell anyone. Wasn't me that did it. Wish it had been, but the tooth fairy ain't taking orders."

"You want I should find Mr. Escott?"

"Why? Does he owe you money?". I began to snicker, couldn't stop.

"Where are you, Mr. Fleming?"

"On the damn phone, where do you think?" Another burst of laughter. I couldn't stop at all.

"You need some help?"

"Yes, I think I do. We'll put in to the NRA tomorrow. Work for everyone. Bulldozers and picks and shovels, and we'll make a new parking lot. Picks . . . pick, ice pick. Those things hurt like hell. Did you know that? They still do. Ow." I hung up, satisfied I'd done a good job.

Crick in my back from all the work. A really *bad* crick. It had no business hurting that much. Maybe if I had a nap, it would go away. Escott kept a cot in the next room. He wouldn't mind me using it.

This half of the joint was plain, too. He should do it up like my nightclub. Put in some pictures or something. I swiped sullenly at an unrelieved white wall, leaving behind a smear of red. Uh-oh. Tried to wipe it off. Made it worse. Washroom, towels there. Clean it before it dries.

Stared with shock at the empty mirror over the sink. Now that was taking the plain-jane stuff just too damned far. Where had I gone? The spectator reflection peered over where my shoulder should be, shrugging.

Well, a lot you know. He looked way too much like me. Maybe I could look at him instead of the mirror.

As long as I was there, I washed my hands. God, that water was cold. Sluiced it over my arms, face, and torso. The sink filled up with red; the floor and walls got splattered. A new job for the waiters. They'd want a raise for this.

A very insistent alarm clock went off. I shut the water and, dripping, searched for the annoyance. It was still dark out. I didn't have to get up for work until eight. My editor didn't come in until nine, and what he didn't see wouldn't hurt me . . .

Ringing, ringing. Oh. It was the damn phone.

"Hello?"

"Jack? Are you all right?"

"I'm great! Who's this?"

He sounded surprised. "It's Charles. What's happened to you? Where's Dugan?"

"Driving around—"

"*What?*"

"He didn't look so good, but I'm just great!"

Pause at the other end. I cheerfully waited him out. "Jack, I want you to stay right there in the office. Promise me you won't leave."

"Sure. Bring up a bottle. There's a legger lives just around the corner from me. His stuff won't blind you. You know the one?"

"Erm—yes, of course. You'll stay there?"

"We need ice."

"I'll get some. You sit and wait for me, all right?"

"Sure!"

There was a hard clunk as he hung up. Guess he was in a hurry. Poor duck should get out more. *Where* had I met him . . . ?

Gosh, I was cold. Still hadn't quite cleaned up all the way, either. Won't get a girl at the party looking like this. Where was my shirt? Maybe I should stay home for once. Funny kind of house. You call that a bed? Was I back in the army again? Naw, couldn't be, this place didn't have any roaches. France was full of 'em. Rats, too. They liked the trenches.

Uh-oh, something ugly down *that* road I didn't want to see again, either. Pull back, look for a flop instead. There, easy does it so the cot doesn't break under me. Wrestle the blanket around. Warmer, now. Hey, a radio. I must be rich. Nice one, too. Didn't have to wear a headset to listen.

Dance music. Funny stuff. Didn't like it. Twirled the dial. Lots of static. Everyone's gone to bed already, dammit. There, couple of guys talking. Sounded like Shakespeare. Yeah, that'll put me out.

Their recording must have gotten scratched, the needle stuck in the same groove. One of them kept saying wake up, wake up. Then he started shaking me. Ow. That hurt something in my back.

"Lay off, f'cryin' out loud! You'll wake Mom 'n' Dad!" I waved away one of my older brothers, trying to bury myself under the quilts. Those guys were always picking on me.

"Jack, are you all right?"

"I'm *great!*"

16

STAMPED tin ceiling above me, painted white. Escott's worried face eclipsed my view of it.

"Charles, let me see." Now Bobbi's face. Also worried. "Jack?"

I smiled. She could always make me smile.

Escott murmured. "For God's sake *don't* ask him if he's all right."

She nodded. "Jack, what happened to you?"

I went on smiling, but felt it die. It seemed to make them more worried. Worked my lips. Had to remember to breathe in to speak. Couldn't speak even then.

"Jack." She took my hand. "Look at me. What happened to you?"

Shook my head. Smile twitching on and off. "Bad things. You don't wanna know. Wish I didn't."

She bent to kiss my forehead, which was nice. She smoothed my hair with one cool hand.

I felt tears spring up in my eyes. Blinked futilely against them.

"You're all right now. Whatever it is, you're safe."

Wanted to believe her. Couldn't. A tear leaked out, trailed past my temple and into the pillow. Damn. She shouldn't see me like this. I had to stop. Sat up fast, found my legs, stumbled to the washroom, shut the door.

"Jack?" Escott just outside.

I ran water into my cupped hands. Rinsed my face. Checked the mirror for results.

Oh.

Looked around for the spectator guy, but he was gone. Very lonely without him. *He* understood.

Bobbi called through the door. "Jack, we'll wait in the office. Take your time, sweetheart. Okay?"

Thought too long over what answer to mumble. They shuffled out.

Stopped the water, dried, noticed I was cleaner than when I'd gone to bed. Pants and socks gone. Fresh underwear on. I was even shaved. How had that happened? When? And those scars . . . long uneven white ridges threaded along my chest and arms. Lots of them. Too many. They felt tender and pulled uncomfortably when I ran my hand over them. But they were faded, might fade some more. Good. I didn't like them at all.

Through the wall Bobbi whispered, "Charles, what's wrong with him?"

A pause. "Something truly awful." He sounded helpless.

"This is me. Don't pull punches. If you know anything . . ."

"Bristow made some threats toward him. From the evidence

I saw at that . . . that place, I believe he carried them out."

"What kind of threats?"

I turned the water on full so I wouldn't have to hear. Left it running as I softly opened the door. Crossed the small room to check the window. Dark out. Of course. Always dark for me. Always and ever.

Clean clothes on a chair. Mine. All the necessities, even a bag of my home earth. Where were my old clothes? No sign of them. Wallet was there. Keys. How did they . . . ?

Oh. He's seen. Had been there. Knew. Knew everything.

I dressed. Noticed a tang in the air. Bloodsmell. Human. On that wall. Nothing showed against the white paint, but it looked a little different from the rest, cleaner. The smell lingered, though. Had a memory of making a mess on it. A mess all over the place. The washroom had been scoured with soap and bleach. Escott was a fanatic about neatness, but he'd not gotten everything. Wish he could scrub my brain out.

Awkward bending as I put on socks and shoes. There was a sharp, ugly twinge in my back every time I moved. Hurt like . . . well, not like hell. I'd learned what that was now.

How did Escott know about the meat locker? Who told him? Things had been going on without me today.

Shut off the water. They were quiet in the other room. They got even more quiet when I emerged. Bobbi was in one of the client chairs opposite Escott, who was behind the desk. She half rose, but I lifted a hand, halting her. She sank into place again. Escott had me under close, concerned watch. I couldn't quite meet their eyes.

Made a circuit of the room, peered through the blinds. Same old street. Looking the same as it had through the other window. Dark out. I really didn't like that. Not a damned thing I could ever do about it, either.

Bobbi was next to me. Hadn't heard her move. She cautiously took my hand. "Come and sit down," she said.

All right. She led me to the chair next to hers, still holding on. I didn't like that. Gently disengaged and sat, arms draped loose on my knees.

"Are we all sufficiently ill at ease yet?" Escott asked.

I breathed out an odd laugh. It hurt.

"Good. Jack. Tell us what happened." He clasped his hands on the desktop, leaning forward to listen as though I was one of his customers.

Oh, God. "Y-you first."

The eyebrow bounce. The left one. I wondered if he knew he did that. "Very well. Vivian and I went up to answer the door. Brockhurst and Marie Kennard were there—"

"Yeah, I know. After."

"I heard a commotion coming from the basement and soon ascertained that Bristow and his men were an unwelcome presence on the premises. Vivian wanted to call the police, even if it gave away that she'd kidnapped a kidnapper. I persuaded her to do nothing, thinking that you would take care of the situation in your own way. I kept waiting for you to make a move, and for some reason, you did not."

"I . . . couldn't. They hit me. Pretty bad."

"I saw you being carried out and that they'd freed Dugan."

"He offered Bristow five Gs. So off he went."

"Not wanting to shoot them in the house, I tried to follow. I got as far as the street. One of them had put holes in my tires. Yours, too. By the time I got Vivian's car from the garage, you were all long gone. If I could have—"

" 'S okay. You wouldn't have liked that party."

"They took you to that meat locker . . . ?"

"Bristow promised buckwheats. He delivered."

Escott waited for me to go on, but I didn't. Bobbi reached for me again, but I leaned away from her, getting up to look out the window. Same street. This time with a car driving past. I watched it narrowly until it was gone from sight. Relaxed a little. Until the next car drove by.

"Jack. What happened?"

"I got away. Came here. Your turn."

A pause. I could hear their hearts, their lungs, sighing. All that life rushing through them, and they couldn't have been aware of it. Not like me. I paced the room twice, going back to the window. No cars. Good.

Escott continued. "I phoned Shoe and asked him to put people out to search likely places for Bristow's damaged vehicle. Then I went to the Nightcrawler and talked to some very unpleasant sorts who were not very helpful. They said Strome and Derner were gone and could not say where. Like you, I suspected those two might have thrown their lot in with Bristow. Next I tried to find Brockhurst to see what his involvement might be. It could not have been a coincidence that he and Miss Kennard turned up at the same time as those brutes."

"You find him?"

"Yes, at his flat. He was drunk. Seems to have a fatal, unrequited affection for Miss Kennard that keeps him in his cups. I learned that after they left Crymsyn, they were pounced upon and questioned by Bristow. He put the wind up them, right in your own parking lot, apparently gleaning that they all had common umbrage against us. This also reawakened Miss Kennard's resentment for you and her self-delusion toward Dugan. Bristow then let them go to find me. They knew I'd be at the Gladwell house that night. He may have been thinking to get to you through me, but he found you first, instead."

I rubbed a hand over my face. Sighed. And looked out the window. The night was still there. Hours of it lay ahead until I could be unconscious once more.

Bobbi next to me again. She was so serious. "Jack, talk to me."

Shook my head. Couldn't speak. Couldn't meet her gaze. If I did, the tears might start up again.

She backed away, went to stand behind Escott. He put a hand on her arm as though to steady her. Or maybe himself. He mouthed a word at her I didn't catch.

Two cars in the street. They passed each other right under the window. Were they the two I saw earlier or different ones?

"Gordy woke up today, Jack," she announced.

I'd nearly forgotten him. That crisis seemed a hundred years ago. "Oh, yeah?"

"This morning. The doctor took that as a good sign."

"That's good, real good." Not much point in saying more.

Escott cleared his throat. "Strome and Derner have nearly taken themselves from the suspect list. They went to Dr. Clarson's last night to see Gordy but were of course denied admittance and detained. Shoe held them incommunicado until he was able to get me there. They weren't inclined to speak about you but loudly denounced Bristow as the shooter and played up their part in removing his threat. Just to be certain, I think you would be wise to interview them. They're at one of Shoe's garages."

I might. They'd had a hand in saving me, albeit unknowingly. "Did you . . . did you call here last night?"

"Yes, I did. Your man Wilton tried to phone me at Vivian's about hearing from you. She had Shoe's number and passed on the message. It was a great relief, but you were rather odd. Do you remember?"

A breathless chuckle. I grinned out the window. "I was *so* drunk."

"Drunk?" Bobbi whispered. "But I thought he couldn't—"

Escott held up a warning hand. "How did you get drunk?"

"Oh . . . had some help from Bristow." Wanted to change the subject. "Gordy's better, you said?"

She grabbed the question like a life preserver. "He woke up, talked clear, and took some food. Dr. Clarson said if there's no infection, he should be just fine, but he has to stay in bed for now. Gordy wants to see you."

"Later. When he's stronger. Okay?"

"Sure. No hurry."

"Jack?" Escott. He looked real tired. "What happened to Dugan? Do you remember?"

"Oh . . . he ran away. He cut me free, and I got him out, and he ran away and didn't even say thanks. I really hate that guy. He did me a favor, but God, I really hate him."

Dugan had seen me with the mask off. Seen what was really inside me. Had carried that off with him. I couldn't have that.

"We all hate him, Jack. Are you still interested in hunting him down?"

"My God, Charles, he's not ready for—"

"Yeah," I said, coming away from the window. "Let's go hunt him down. Where?"

"I've a spare overcoat in the closet in back. You go put it on, and we'll leave."

"Okay." I moved past them. Went to the closet and rummaged. He kept a lot of spare clothes here, some of them disguises he found useful in his work. It took me a minute to find the right coat.

"You can't take him out while he's in that state," Bobbi said, speaking low.

"He needs to do something else besides stare out that damned window."

"Yes, but is he safe? With you? With others?"

A pause. "I don't know. But I suppose we'll learn soon enough."

I returned, coat in hand. "I need help with this. Putting it on."

They both looked puzzled. "Why is that?" Escott asked.

"Bristow. He nailed me with an ice pick. Part of it's still inside. That's why I couldn't vanish when he had me. I'm sorry."

Bobbi went white. "Where is it, Jack?"

I gestured vaguely at my back. "Just under the skin. You can feel it there. Knew guys who had shrapnel the same way. Too deep or too much trouble to dig out. But I think I want to get rid of it."

"Oh, dear God." Escott looked appalled.

"Yeah. . . . You think you could get Doc Clarson to dig it out sometime tomorrow? If he does it during the day I won't feel anything."

"We'll . . ." He swallowed hard. "We'll arrange something for you. I promise."

"That's good. Real good. Help me with the coat?"

"Yes. Of course."

The fit was pretty good, us having nearly the same build. Escott helped Bobbi on with her fur-trimmed coat, and she stayed busy pulling on her gloves while he locked up.

"Is that new?" I asked, pointing at the doorknob.

"Yes, it is," he answered evenly.

"I broke the other one, didn't I? I'm sorry."

"It's all right."

Down to his car. I opened the passenger side for Bobbi, carefully easing in next to her. Her leg happened to press against mine during the ride. Ordinary contact. Nothing to be worried about. Not too much. There was no room to shift away from her touch. Just had to endure it.

Escott drove around to Brockhurst's neck of the woods, and we went into his building and up. Escott knocked loudly, but no one answered, so he broke in using his lockpicks. Bobbi hung back while we made a quick search for Dugan. No cousin Gilbert, but Anthony darling was snoring away in bed, the stink of booze thick and sour in the air. He wouldn't wake up, so dealing with him had to be postponed. Just to be thorough, we went through his papers and wastebaskets but found nothing useful, not even origami cranes. If Marie didn't believe in Dugan's guilt, then Anthony apparently did. We left him to finish his nap.

I envied him that superb unconsciousness. In such a state you didn't have to struggle to keep memories at bay.

Marie Kennard lived in the same area but in a different apartment building. Respectable flats for the well-to-do. We walked unchallenged past the lobby's empty reception desk, into an elevator, and up to one of the near-the-top floors. Escott led us to a door, knocking three times, very loudly.

Muffled reply within. "Yes, who is it?"

He made his voice raspy and older, his accent pure Chicago.

"Maintenance. You had a plumbing problem?"

Marie Kennard opened the door. "What plumbing—oh God!" But she was a fraction too late trying to keep him out. She began a full-throated shriek, but he was quicker, clapping a hand over her mouth and grabbing her, half carrying her in. Bobbi and I shot through in their wake and shut the door. Walking fast, I searched each room and closet in the place, looking for Dugan, catching another sharp twinge when I bent to check under the bed. I emerged and shook my head.

Marie put up quite a fight, going red-faced and desperate. Escott needed help. Moving hurt, but I got her ankles. Between us, Escott and I lifted her bodily and carried her to a chaise lounge in front of a set of windows with a nice view of the lake. We put her down and with difficulty kept her in place until she finally got too tired to struggle.

Bobbi leaned in close during the pause. "Miss Kennard, we're only here to talk. Do you understand?"

Marie's eyes blazed with full, murderous comprehension.

Escott looked at me. "Jack, would you mind very much making her a tad more cooperative?"

"Uh . . ."

"I know it's a great favor, but it will shorten our time here."

"Yeah, okay." I sat gingerly next to her, still holding her legs. She was terrifically on guard, but under her fury was profound fear, and I knew how to use that. It took some concentration on my part, though. I felt strangely rusty.

After a few minutes and some gentle words, it was safe for Escott to take his hand away, shaking it and flexing his long fingers. "Thank heaven she didn't think to bite me."

"Is she all right?" asked Bobbi. She knew about my acquired talent, but rarely got a firsthand look.

"Perfectly fine," Escott answered for me.

Marie stared calmly at the lake. I got out of the way, going to stand by the window. I could see lots of cars from up here, but they were a long, comfortable distance away.

Escott asked the questions and got truthful replies; none of the news was good. Marie had no idea where Dugan might be or where he might go. The really bad flash was learning that he'd called her in the wee morning hours and arranged a meeting. She went to a place in a nearby park, bringing him a suitcase packed with ten thousand dollars in cash and a hacksaw.

Bobbi was livid. "How *could* you?"

"Because he's innocent," was Marie's perfectly reasonable reply. She was under my influence, so that meant she said what she honestly believed.

"After hearing those records?"

Marie sniffed. "Fakes."

And nonexistent now. Dugan had thoroughly smashed them.

"You *idiot!*"

I flinched at Bobbi's tone but didn't think either of them noticed.

"When will you see him again?" asked Escott.

"He'll let me know. He'll send for me."

"Don't hold your breath," Bobbi growled, *sotto voce.*

Escott pressed forward. "When that happens, you're going to let me know as well, day or night. Jack? A little more suggestion work, if you would." He explained what he wanted, and I planted the idea in her head. She wouldn't remember any of it.

"How long will that last?"

"A few weeks, maybe a month. I can come back and bolster it again."

"Then we are done here. Miss Kennard, would you be so kind as to let us out?"

She serenely obliged.

There was a little table by the entry, a place for her to park her keys and purse. Some other small object was with them as well. Escott noticed me staring, spied it, and picked it up.

"What's this?"

Marie, still under, said. "That's for Jack Fleming."

"What?"

I answered, taking it from him. "Dugan knew I'd be coming here. Knew I'd put the eye on Marie. That's why he didn't tell her anything. He'll probably never contact her again."

Marie made no response to this.

The object looked like an origami boat, but this one had no triangle sail, no folded superstructure like the others he'd made. It was a small, simple rectangle with a matching lid.

"What is that?" asked Bobbi.

"Message to me from Dugan. It's supposed to be a coffin."

"Dear God," Escott murmured. He took it back, carefully unfolding the pieces. "Nothing written on them—in green ink or any other color."

"The coffin's enough to make his point. He's not through with me yet."

"What more could he possibly want? The wise thing is to stay as far away from you as possible."

"He's plenty wise, just not sensible."

I told Marie to forget all about our visit. She agreed and let us out, and we rode the elevator down.

"Despite this little warning," Escott said, refolding the coffin pieces, "That went rather well. A pity Dugan wasn't there."

I privately thought it was a good thing. I didn't want Bobbi looking on while I killed him.

Derner and Strome were next.

Bobbi must have sensed something, for she twice asked if we couldn't wait until I'd rested more.

"It's okay," I said lightly, watching the street. It was narrow and deserted. Shoe Coldfield had had Gordy's men disarmed and taken to an anonymous car repair shop, where they were confined to an empty garage. Escott had gone in ahead of me. I waited on the sidewalk; Bobbi stayed in the car. She had the window rolled down to talk with me, and the accumulated warmth from the Nash's heater soon dispersed.

"But you're not okay, Jack. For God's sake, *look* at me."

It was difficult, but I managed a smile for her.

"Whatever happened, I'm right here. I'm here whenever you need me. You can talk to me. You can *touch* me."

Instinct told me just saying "thanks" to that would have hurt her, so I nodded.

"I said you can touch me."

So she had noticed. She held her hand out to me. I hesitated. The more I waited, the more upset she'd be. Finally took her hand. Couldn't feel it. Told myself it was her gloves being in the way. I didn't have any on; my fingers must be numb from the cold.

Comforting little lies.

Escott showed himself from the low brick building and said it was time. I broke away from Bobbi and went inside.

Dark. I froze in an entry that smelled of motor oil. Dark all around. Faint gleam of yellow at the end of a long hall. I hurried to catch up with Escott.

Light. Had to stifle showing my relief. On the right, an opening led to the garage. Coldfield wasn't there, busy with his own nightclub and watching over Gordy, but a few of his well-armed men stood guard on Derner and Strome. They were down in the grease pit and looked dirty and pretty pissed. Until they saw me; then they looked thunderstruck.

"Jesus H. Christ," said Strome, eyes popping.

"Wait a second, he was—" Derner lost the thread of whatever he wanted to say as I crouched on the edge of the pit.

"'Lo, boys," I said evenly. My voice sounded lower than usual, more hoarse. Maybe my vocal chords had been scarred from all the screaming. They should have healed.

Strome finally spoke. "Fleming. You okay?"

I thought that one over. "What do you think?"

"That was you I saw. You was . . . was . . . I mean—"

"Yeah. Bristow gave me a bad night. I owe you one for taking care of him and his goons. You might have stuck around a little longer and cut me down, though."

"Christ, but we thought you was dead!"

Derner nodded agreement. "If we'd known, we'd have—"

"Yeah-yeah. Never mind. I got other things for you to do, now."

"You mean, you're—"

"I'm still in charge until Gordy's on his feet. We straight on that?"

Both nodded in fearful agreement.

"Good. You can come outta there." I glanced at the guards, jerked my chin toward the door. They slowly moved off. Escott remained in place off to the side, watchful. Whether for me or these two birds, I couldn't tell. Derner and Strome took the steep steps up out of the pit, futilely dusting themselves. The grease stuck with them.

"You guys are gonna talk and then you're gonna listen," I said.

"Yes, Mr. Fleming," said Derner.

I asked the questions that needed asking. Hypnosis was not necessary. They were too spooked to lie. Each searched my face for some sign of what I'd been through. I let them keep whatever they found. I'd earned it.

When they were done answering me, I said, "I'll fix things with New York later. For now, you're gonna do me a favor. There's a man I want you to find. You know that society kidnap guy? Dugan? Picture's in all the papers?"

"We saw," said Strome, guardedly.

"I want him. Alive. He's got ten grand in cash and a head start, but you are gonna track him down and bring him back to me. Whatever it takes. Whoever finds him keeps the ten Gs. The faster he's found the more money he'll have left."

I had their full attention.

"You use the organization any way you have to to find Dugan. He has to be alive or the deal's off. I'll give you a grand each to get you started. Use it for bribe money, whatever it takes. You two are gonna be stand-up with me on this or I will skin you alive. And I know how to do that, now."

Their color drained away under their face dirt.

"Learn anything?" Bobbi asked when Escott and I got back in the car.

"Just the refining of a few points," said Escott.

She took my hand again as I eased into the seat. I didn't pull away because she told me I could touch her. I could touch, just not feel. Not like before. "What points?"

He started the car and fed it gas. "That Derner and Strome made a decision last night to stick by Gordy and brave the consequences, if any, from the New York bosses. Bristow committed a breach of protocol by shooting Gordy, thus showing himself to be untrustworthy."

"Took them long enough," she grumbled.

"Gang politics are often a complicated matter. Those two men had a good deal of thinking to do, and they're not too terribly good at it. Jack had a positive influence on Derner, though. Seems he posed the obvious question: Who would you rather have in charge? That simplified things."

"It seems pretty simple to me."

"But not to Mr. Derner. He had to take into account the dynamic of Gordy not surviving to return. In which case he decided the next logical man in line for the post should be Jack, not Bristow."

"Jack? Running Gordy's operation? He'd hate it."

"But Derner knew he'd be good at the job. Bristow would not."

A memory from last night—not one of the bad ones—dredged up. I said, "Derner argued with me all the way, though. I'd give an order, he'd argue."

"Exactly," said Escott. "Which is why he'd want you over Bristow. You let him have his say. Bristow would have killed him for it. Derner eventually figured that out."

"What about Strome?" she asked.

"Well, apparently last night Jack sent him packing home for a long nap to keep him out of trouble, which was interrupted by Bristow. He had approached Strome days earlier about betraying Gordy and was now in a perfect position to obtain information crucial to completing the assassination. By this time, Strome had done some thinking of his own. He agreed to Bristow's terms, promised to first set things up, then to rendezvous with them at the meat locker. Once on his own, he went to Derner to plan out how to eliminate Bristow. Neither of them knew Jack was going to be there."

If they had, would they have arrived sooner? Tried to help me?

"But when they found out?"

"By then they thought he was dead. I'm not clear about the exact circumstances, but they must have been fairly grim."

"Dugan was there, too. How could they have missed him?"

"They didn't know about him at all. He might have been tied up out of sight or hiding. I'm sure when Jack's ready, he'll fill in the picture."

She squeezed my hand again. I tried not to wince. Her touch didn't hurt; it was all the feelings behind the touch. Though warm and soft, they hit like spear points. I couldn't respond to them, didn't dare. Inside I was scraped out and hollow, as though Bristow had stripped my guts and heart away along with my skin.

Escott settled a few more details for her, winding us back toward his office. But he passed it by, heading toward the Stockyards, turning onto a particular street. One I never wanted to see again.

"*No,*" I whispered. I'd forgotten to breathe in, so they didn't hear.

He stopped before a high, flat, windowless building full of darkness and unthinkable agony. I felt clammy sweat popping out along my newly healed flanks.

Bobbi saw the look in my eyes. "Charles, what are you doing?"

"That which is necessary."

"This can wait."

"No, it can't. Strome and Derner are even now making arrangements to clean everything up before the mess is discovered. And I think it will be better for Jack to get this over with as soon as may be." Escott cut the motor. He came around, opened my side. "It will be all right, Jack. I promise."

No it won't. Nothing's all right.

The place was nearly the same. The front door had been shoved back into place, held there by new hinges and a large, shiny padlock. He went up to it, unlocked, then returned for me. Held the car door expectantly, waiting for me to move.

"You can do this," he told me. "If you survived what happened here, you can survive this."

Dear God, I don't want to go in. I knew why he was doing this to me. I understood that it was necessary. All that awaited in there was harmless to me now. I just had to see it for myself. He wouldn't force me. No way he could. He'd wait for me to do it myself.

Standing firm in the cold he waited long enough. I inched out. Bobbi slid across the seat, taking my arm like I was an invalid. I let them lead me up and in.

Balked in the office. "It's dark," I whispered, staring straight ahead. There was a ball of ice in my belly, heavy, weighing me down too much to move.

Escott hastily found the lights.

It was colder than it should have been. The door to the freezer was only propped in place, held there by a length of two-by-four angled against it. Escott removed that and with difficulty shifted the warped slab of a door over enough to allow entry.

Bloodsmell swelled at me like a tide. The stuff was old, stale, decaying, yet I felt the strong tug of my corner teeth trying to emerge. Maybe I wanted to forget what was in there, what I'd done, but my body remembered, and anticipated a return to the revel.

Escott put the lights on in there, too. From where I stood I could see the bodies, with Bristow hanging exactly as I'd left him. There was some irony in that, him ending up dead the way he'd planned for me, but I couldn't appreciate it. His face was bone white where it should have been purple with discoloration. I'd drained him dry, preventing that. His eyes were open and dulled, yet strangely less empty than when he'd been working on me.

"Jack." Escott held his hand through the opening.

I was expected to follow him in.

Bobbi looked anxiously at us. She couldn't see what lay beyond. I dredged up a memory of kindness and said, "You need to stay out here."

She shook her head, going stubborn. Couldn't remember her ever giving me a look like that. "You and me both, brother," she said.

I hesitated. Part of me understood the why of this; all of me didn't want to go through with it.

Escott's voice was soothing, persuasive, almost like mine when I hypnotized people. "Jack, whatever happened in there, whatever you did, it was to survive. There's nothing shameful in that."

"But I . . ." He didn't know, could *not* know what I had done, how I'd gloried in it. If he did, then neither of them would be here trying to help me.

A ghost of a smile. It was sad with knowledge. "Jack, believe me when I say I also know what it's like in hell. We go mad for while . . . and then we get better. Don't we?"

Faces tight, they waited for my answer.

I felt it choking my throat. Shook my head. "There's more to it. What they did to me . . . what I did. I don't know if I can . . . if I can get well from that."

"Do you want to?" Bobbi asked.

"Yes . . . but . . ." God, it hurt to say it. "I don't know how."

She touched my face. "We'll help you find out how."

I didn't flinch away. Caught her hand. She wore black gloves; her rose scent was all over them. They were made of suede, very soft. Could feel their texture.

I could *feel*.

Closed my eyes and held her fingers against my face. They were warm, felt that even through the leather.

"Jack, what is it?" Escott asked.

I gave one involuntary shudder, like a sleeper reluctantly waking, then looked him in the eye. Looked at her. Straightened my spine. That made my back twinge, of course, but the pain would go away soon enough. It would take longer for other agonies to depart, and I accepted that still others might always remain.

If I let them.

"We can leave now," I finally said. "I don't have to go in there anymore."

"You're sure?" He seemed dubious about my sudden recovery.

I sketched a very brief smile. Didn't know if I meant it, but it was something they needed to see. "Yeah. I still have a saloon to run, don't I?"

"Yes, you do," said Bobbi, barely above a whisper. Couldn't tell if she was buying this or not. "But—"

"I'll be all right. I promise. Let's go take care of business. Okay?"

They exchanged quick glances. I didn't give them time to voice additional worries or think up objections as I led the way out, not looking back.

Once on the open street, I breathed out the last of the slaughterhouse stink, emptying my dormant lungs. The thin vapor plumed up and vanished in the icy night sky.